TOGETHER AGAIN AT THE CORNISH COUNTRY HOSPITAL

JO BARTLETT

First published in Great Britain in 2025 by Boldwood Books Ltd.

Cover Design by Alexandra Allden

Cover Illustration: Shutterstock

A CIP catalogue record for this book is available from the British Library.

Paperback ISBN 978-1-80483-980-5

Large Print ISBN 978-1-80483-982-9

Hardback ISBN 978-1-80483-987-4

Ebook ISBN 978-1-80483-981-2

Kindle ISBN 978-1-80483-979-9

Audio CD ISBN 978-1-80483-984-3

MP3 CD ISBN 978-1-80483-986-7

Digital audio download ISBN 978-1-80483-983-6

This book is printed on certified sustainable paper. Boldwood Books is dedicated to putting sustainability at the heart of our business. For more information please visit https://www.boldwoodbooks.com/about-us/sustainability/

Boldwood Books Ltd, 23 Bowerdean Street, London, SW6 3TN

www.boldwoodbooks.com

This book is dedicated to my good friend Beverley Hills' mother.
For our beloved Pamela/Mum, who is missed every day.
With all our love Jeremy and Beverley xx

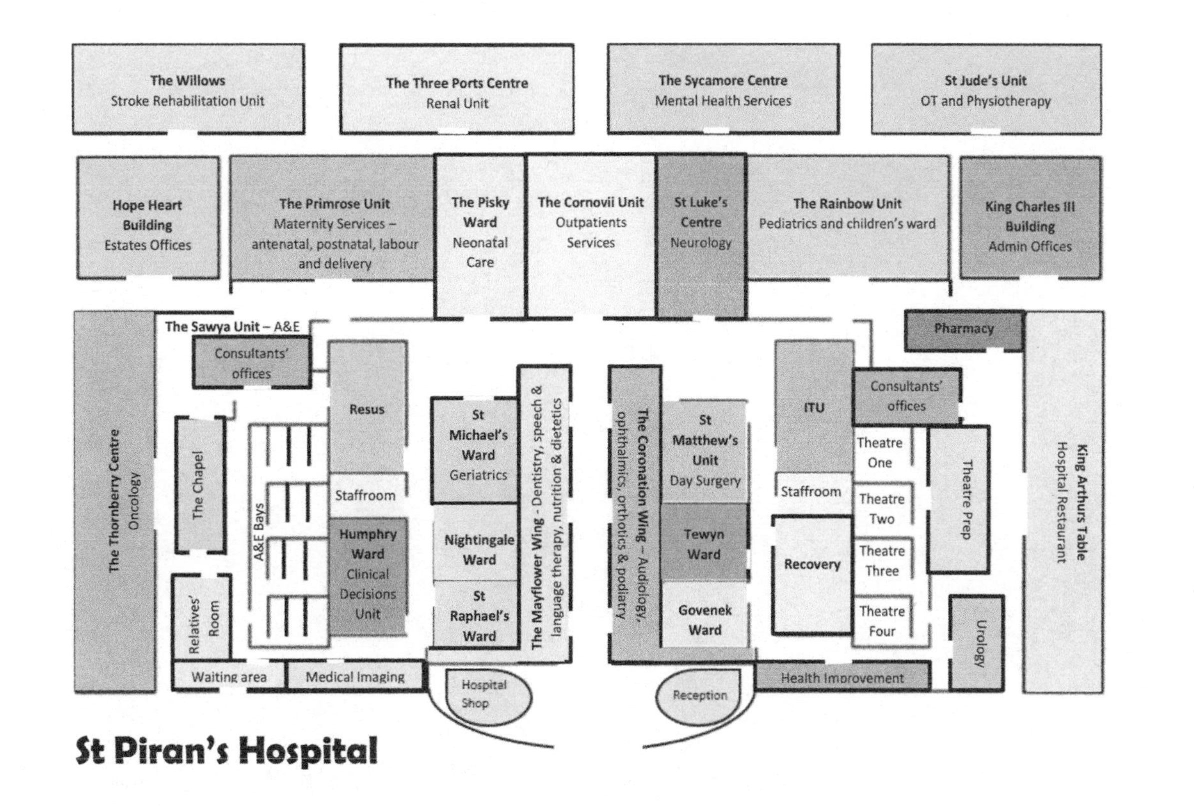
The Willows
Stroke Rehabilitation Unit
The Three Ports Centre
Renal Unit
The Sycamore Centre
Mental Health Services
St Jude's Unit
OT and Physiotherapy
Hope Heart Building
Estates Offices
The Primrose Unit
Maternity Services – antenatal, postnatal, labour and delivery
The Pisky Ward
Neonatal Care
The Cornovii Unit
Outpatients Services
St Luke's Centre
Neurology
The Rainbow Unit
Pediatrics and children's ward
King Charles III Building
Admin Offices
The Sawya Unit – A&E
Consultants' offices
Resus
The Thornberry Centre
Oncology
The Chapel
A&E Bays
Staffroom
Humphry Ward
Clinical Decisions Unit
Relatives' Room
Waiting area
Medical Imaging
St Michael's Ward
Geriatrics
Nightingale Ward
St Raphael's Ward
The Mayflower Wing - Dentistry, speech & language therapy, nutrition & dietetics
Hospital Shop
The Coronation Wing – Audiology, ophthalmics, orthotics & podiatry
St Matthew's Unit
Day Surgery
Tewyn Ward
Govenek Ward
Reception
ITU
Staffroom
Recovery
Consultants' offices
Theatre One
Theatre Two
Theatre Three
Theatre Four
Theatre Prep
Pharmacy
Urology
Health Improvement
King Arthurs Table
Hospital Restaurant
St Piran's Hospital

1

Lijah could still hear the screaming when he slammed the door behind him with a resounding bang. All the voices clamouring for his attention and shouting his name, made it feel as though the walls were closing in around him. He had to get out, but he had no idea where to go. There was only one place that had ever given him the kind of peace he was craving, but he wasn't even sure it existed any more, at least not in the way he'd known it.

'Great show, Lij.' Nick followed him into the room and clapped him on the shoulder. 'They can't get enough. Must be great to be you and have thousands of women fall in love with you every time you step on stage.'

'You don't do too badly off the back of it.' He couldn't keep the bitterness out of his voice, but the comment wasn't really directed at Nick. He was a good guy, and someone who'd been loyal to Lijah from the start, acting as his roadie when the gigs had been far from glamorous, and the pay had usually been the price of a couple of pints if he was lucky. Lijah would never forget one particularly seedy pub he'd performed at, where their feet had stuck to the floor, and the windows had been so thick with grime that it was dark inside even when they'd arrived to set up, at 6 p.m. on a June evening. The fee for appearing, if you could call it that, was supposed to be the princely sum of forty pounds. Lijah had promised half to Nick, because he'd missed a shift at the restaurant where he worked waiting tables, in order to help Lijah out. They were both supposed to be studying hard for their A levels, the exams just days away, but neither of them were focused on that. Lijah had all his hopes pinned on being the next big thing and escaping what felt like the suffocating tweeness of life in Port Kara, a picture-postcard village that clung to the edge of the Cornish Atlantic coast above turquoise blue waters, when the weather was good. It was idyllic, if you wanted the beach life, or if cream teas in quaint little tearooms were your idea of a good time, but Lijah had wanted so much more than that, and against all the odds he'd got it too. It had meant leaving some people behind, who he hadn't wanted to say goodbye to, but no one got success without sacrifice and the drive he'd felt to follow his dreams had made it feel worth it at the time. He wasn't sure he'd have done it without Nick. Having his friend by his side had been like taking a piece of home with him, when he'd moved to London at nineteen.

It seemed almost impossible now that they'd had nights like they'd had at the Lord Nelson pub, when the burly landlord had reneged on paying the paltry fee he'd offered Lijah, because the small crowd had been too into the music and hadn't bought enough drinks as a result. The landlord, six foot four of muscle and beer gut, had claimed that it had lost him money to have Lijah there, and that he wasn't paying. Backed up by a barman who could have been his twin, it hadn't been something Lijah and Nick could compete with. Instead, Lijah had tried to argue the point that he'd brought brand-new customers in, who were still there after the performance, finally buying more drinks, but the landlord wouldn't budge. Nick had disappeared during the confrontation, while the landlord and the barman had hemmed Lijah into a corner until he had no choice but to pretend to agree that they'd done him a favour and given him exposure he 'should be grateful for'. That last bit had been laughable. The Lord Nelson was a dive, not somewhere he was ever going to get spotted, or even build up a new following he hadn't brought with him. But he'd known that kind of experience was part of it, the rough road he was going to have to travel to get to where he wanted to go, and he told himself that one day he'd look back on all of this and laugh. He did too, although much sooner than he expected. Nick had suddenly reappeared to help Lijah out with his equipment, but when they got around the corner from the pub, he set his backpack on the floor and instructed Lijah to try and pick it up. It weighed a tonne.

'What the hell have you got in there?'

'Have a look.' Nick was grinning, not looking one bit like a man who'd just been scammed out of twenty quid and lost a night's wages for nothing.

Lijah opened the bag, and a slow smile had spread across his face too. 'Jesus. How did you manage that?'

'Nick by name and nick by nature.' He'd laughed then, before hauling the backpack containing four litre bottles of Jack Daniels on to his shoulder. 'That'll teach the tight-fisted bastard. I whipped their whole supply from the grotty stock room out the back while they were pinning you up against the wall. So I'd call this evens. We should be able to get our money back and even a bit more if we sell it on. Or we could just enjoy it...'

'What if there's CCTV?' For a musician, Lijah had never been much of a rebel when it came to breaking the law, and he also had a big fear of getting a police record. He'd read about other singers whose careers had been stalled when'd they'd been refused admission to the US as a result of a criminal record. A bit of shoplifting in his teens had completely derailed the career of one guy who'd won a place in the final of a big reality TV show, but who couldn't go to US for the next stage of the competition. He'd known that if he ever got his big break, the US market could be a complete game changer, the route to getting his music heard by millions. Lijah had never been fixated on the fame, although he would have been lying if he hadn't thought about owning a massive house with a pool, or swapping his bike for a Range Rover, but all eighteen-year-olds had those kinds of dreams in one form or another. What Lijah had really wanted was to be able to make his mum proud. She'd been through a lot and had sacrificed so much for him, and she was thrilled by every little thing he achieved. He'd wanted to make sure she stayed that way, and that if he ever made it, she'd never have to worry about money again. He couldn't let his mother down by getting arrested. She'd be heartbroken that after all her sacrifices he'd turned into a wrong'un anyway, just like his absent father. But when he'd looked at Nick, unable to keep the tremor out of his voice as he'd asked about the CCTV, his friend had just grinned again.

'CCTV, you're joking, aren't you? I don't think that tight old bastard even owns a dishcloth never mind anything as high tech as CCTV. Don't worry Lij, I'd never let you get ripped off or do anything to get you in trouble. You can trust me with your life if it comes to it.' It was the moment Lijah realised his best friend was right, and he'd decided then and there that if he ever fulfilled his dream, he'd be taking Nick with him. It was a promise he'd kept, just as Nick had always kept his promise to keep Lijah safe. Except there'd been one person Nick couldn't keep Lijah safe from, and that was himself.

It was hard now to remember when the unravelling had

started, but he would never forget the first panic attack and the certainty he'd felt that he was going to die. He'd been about to go on stage in Paris, one of a series of amazing places he'd always dreamed of appearing, a wish that was being fulfilled on his first world tour. Three UK number ones, two of them matching that success in the US, and a multi-platinum album, and all his dreams were coming true. But even as he was stepping out in amazing venues to perform, there was a voice inside his head telling him this wouldn't last, and that the second album he was in the process of writing would be a massive flop. Imposter syndrome and anxiety collided. Thank God his mum, Maria, had been there.

She'd been the one who'd got him through that first panic attack and ensured he made it to the stage to perform in front of 20,000 fans. It was her who'd encouraged him to get medical help and he'd been diagnosed with anxiety and burnout. He'd managed it by stopping drinking, which had definitely helped reduce the anxiety, and by following the treatment plan his doctors had come up with. He'd released an even more successful second album and he'd been in LA, about to embark on second world tour, when disaster struck. Maria had suffered a massive heart attack during a holiday to Scotland with his Aunt Claire and had been admitted to intensive care. He'd got on the next plane there, but he didn't make it in time. His mother, the woman who'd given him everything, had gone before he'd been able to tell her how much she meant to him. The grief had been so overwhelming he couldn't face it. He'd started drinking again, much more heavily than before, and taking whatever else he could to try and numb the unbearable pain. Lijah threw himself into work, going ahead with his world tour and pushing himself as hard as he could, so he wouldn't have to think about the fact she was gone, and that she'd never be coming back. But the grief had found him anyway, the panic attacks were back and this time his mum wasn't there to comfort him. Instead, he was taking more and more prescription medication, handed over by doctors who didn't seem worried as long as they were getting paid. Lijah knew it was dangerous, and that he was playing with fire, but he didn't care, he just had to get through this tour. Except tonight, as he'd come off stage, something inside him had snapped and he knew he couldn't go back out there again. Performing had been like oxygen to him for as long as he could remember, but he couldn't do it any more. The moment he'd turned to walk off stage, he'd known it was over.

'What's going on, mate? I'm worried about you.' Nick was standing in front of him now, putting his hands on Lijah's shoulders, until he was forced to look into the eyes of his old friend.

'Are you worried about me, or are you worried about the money?' Lijah knew how unfair he was being, but he couldn't seem to stop himself. Nick had been the most loyal friend he could have asked for, but he was surrounded by far too many people who saw him as a meal ticket, and it was easy to become cynical about everyone's motivations. But Nick didn't deserve any of the bitterness he felt, that should have been directed elsewhere. It was far too easy to lash out at the people he loved and there weren't many people who fitted that bill now that his mother was gone.

'That's bullshit and you know it.' Nick knew him far too well and he wasn't going to be fobbed off. Lijah owed it to him to be honest and, if he was really doing this, Nick should be the first to know.

'I'm done.' Lijah shrugged. 'I can't do this any more. I don't want to. I want to go home.'

'To London?'

'No, to Cornwall.'

The look on Nick's face said it all. Even he thought Lijah had lost it this time. Cornwall hadn't been his home in over a decade, and the person who'd made it feel like home was gone. His Aunt Claire now lived alone in the house he'd bought for her and his mother. Claire was the only person who understood the bond between Lijah and his mum, and what losing her had done to him. His aunt had begged him to come back to Cornwall and take some time out, but he hadn't been able to face being there without Maria. He'd been certain that burying himself in work was what would get him through, but he knew now how wrong he'd been. Lijah needed to spend time with his aunt, and to confront the memories of his mum, even if the idea still terrified him. It was going to be torture, but if he didn't finally face up to his grief it was going to kill him eventually, because it was already eating him from the inside out.

Lijah looked at his oldest friend again. 'I need to be near Mum, but I can't stay at the house with Claire. It'll be too much.'

'I'll organise it.' Nick nodded, suddenly seeming to understand and he wrapped his arms around Lijah. 'It'll be all right mate. You'll get through this.'

Lijah nodded, but he wasn't so sure. And if getting through it meant coming back to all of this, he wasn't sure he wanted to. Right now, he was a thousand times more desperate to return to Port Kara than he'd ever been to escape.

2

Amy's alarm was going off and she couldn't open her eyes; she knew she had to, but they just wouldn't comply. It was the last shift in a block of nights, and her body had refused to adjust this time and buy into the falsehood that sleeping in the daytime was an easy transition.

'I can't face the thought of getting up and you're not helping.' Finally peeling her eyes open, Amy gave Monty, her little Jack Russell, a gentle nudge. She'd inherited him, when his elderly owner, a lady called Joan who'd been a patient at the hospital, had died. She'd first been admitted to A&E after a fall, and her main concern had been getting home to her little dog. Thankfully, they'd soon been reunited, but six months later Joan's heart had begun to fail, and she'd been re-admitted to A&E on a number of occasions, each time Monty had remained her major concern. Amy had been her nurse on three of those occasions, before Joan had finally been admitted to the cardiac unit, and every time Amy had agreed to make sure Monty was taken care of until Joan got home. The first couple of times, she'd arranged for the little dog to be fostered by Caroline, whose daughter, Esther, worked with Amy at the hospital.

It would have been impractical for Amy to care for him, despite how gorgeous Monty was, with the jet-black patch over his eye a marked contrast to his otherwise snow-white body. But on the third and final occasion, Caroline had been on holiday, and Amy had been about to start a week's leave. Given that she was only planning to potter around at home, there'd been no reason why she couldn't care for the dog. What she hadn't known was that Joan would never go home again. After she'd died, none of her family had been interested in taking on the dog. Monty had already been pining for Joan and the only way he could sleep was when he was curled up on Amy's lap or pressed into the small of her back. So when Joan's son said she was welcome to keep him, she found she couldn't let him go. It meant spending a small fortune on doggy day care and dog walking services when she was on long shifts, but he was worth every penny, and she loved him to bits.

Having Monty had its drawbacks, though. It was even harder to get out of bed, after a grand total of four hours' sleep, when she was so cosy underneath her duvet, with Monty perched on top. It was probably a bit tragic for a just-past-thirty-year-old to admit her bed was her happy place, but with a job like Amy's, it probably wasn't surprising. To say that being a nurse in A&E was full-on was an understatement, but just lately it seemed even busier. One of the clinical leads was on maternity leave, Amy's best friend and fellow nurse, Isla, was currently on a career break, touring Australia and New Zealand, and another close friend, Aidan, would be going on parental leave soon too. All of that, along with some other recent staffing changes, meant Amy seemed to be working with agency nurses a lot more often lately and it just wasn't the same. Working in A&E often bound staff together like family, because they were so reliant on one another, and they could anticipate each other's needs and actions in a way that wasn't possible with temporary staff. She just hoped Isla would be back before Aidan left. There would be nowhere near as many laughs if they were both off at the same time, and Aidan would be away from work for at least six months.

'Monty, come on, we can't lie here all night, I've got to go to work.' Amy gave the dog a gentle shove and he opened his eyes indignantly, as if he'd been rudely awoken from a rare snippet of sleep, when the truth was he slept about twenty hours a day when she was on nights. She had a nanny cam on her phone when she was at work, and could watch him coming in and out of the dog flap she'd had installed in the door to the garden, but he slept almost all the time when she wasn't there, except when Dolly, the dog walker, came over to take him out. It was quite impressive, and tonight she was more than a little jealous that Monty would be going back to bed while she was starting her night shift. Although he still wasn't making any effort to move.

'How about some breakfast? Or dinner? Or whatever the hell we're supposed to call what we eat before I start my night shift.' At the mention of the word dinner, Monty's ears pricked up and he immediately started nudging her hand, suddenly wide awake.

'Come on then sweetheart, let's get you fed.' Finally hauling herself out of bed, Amy sighed as she caught sight of herself in the mirror. She looked every bit as tired as she felt, and she felt exhausted. Thank God for coffee, because she was going to need a hell of a lot of it.

* * *

An hour later, Amy was ready to leave for work, and the sight that greeted her in the hallway mirror was a lot less scary than her reflection in the bedroom had been. She didn't wear a lot of make-up these days and she could look at herself in the mirror and recognise her good points, but it had taken a long time to get there. She'd been foolish enough to let some of the men in her life affect the way she saw herself, but not any more.

'You're like the ugly duckling in reverse.' It was an insult her brother had levelled at her regularly in the past and it was something that had impacted her far more than she'd realised at the time. 'You started out as a really cute kid and ended up like...'

He never finished the sentence, but he didn't have to, the implication was loud and clear, and she knew what she was. If not ugly, at least nothing special. Since splitting up with her first ever boyfriend, who for some reason had genuinely seemed to think she was beautiful, she could probably count on the fingers of one hand the amount of times she'd been told she was. When it happened, it was usually a drunk guy in a club, taking his last chance at pulling by trotting out a line he didn't mean. Her ex, Zach, who'd been on again and off again for much of the past five years had never once said it to her. Occasionally he'd grudgingly said she looked 'nice', if she'd pushed him for a verdict on her appearance, but he hadn't been effusive to say the least, and his wandering eye – not to mention other wandering parts of his anatomy – had told her all she needed to know about how much she'd mattered to him in the end.

Zach had been far freer with advice about what she could do to improve the way she looked. She couldn't believe how willing she'd been to try some of his suggestions, or how long she'd put up with his behaviour, but men like Zach were very good at spotting vulnerability and that was something she'd had bucket loads of when they'd met. She had still been nursing a broken heart from the end of her first ever serious relationship, even though it had been over for years. She'd been the one to end things, because she'd never felt good enough. And she'd rather finish it on her own terms, when it was eventually going to happen anyway. She hated feeling that way about herself, so when Zach had started to suggest 'little changes', it was the desire to improve her self-esteem that had persuaded her to give those things a go, until in the end the girl looking back at her in the mirror didn't even feel like Amy any more. Suddenly she had long, sleek hair that fell down past her shoulder blades, the result of scarily expensive extensions, and that was just the start. Zach had bought her a makeover treatment at a local salon one Christmas, which had involved permanent make-up and Russian eyelash extensions, amongst other things. Amy had to admit the result was transformative, but she felt uncomfortable in this strange new skin and, even if she'd wanted to maintain it, she just didn't have the time. Long fake nails hadn't been practical for work either, and bit by bit she'd realised that rather than building her confidence, feeling as if she had to look completely different had eroded her self-esteem even further instead.

Zach hadn't been impressed when she'd ditched his suggestions and gone back to looking like the girl he'd first met, but the most surprising part was that Amy wasn't that girl any more. She'd changed in ways she'd never imagined, ways that lasted far longer than any beauty treatment ever could. She finally knew who she was and what it was she wanted. It didn't mean she didn't make any effort with her appearance, but the choices she made now were for her and what made her feel good.

The relationship with Zach been a huge learning curve, it had taught her she was worth so much more than he had to offer. Amy had built a life for herself she could be proud of, and that realisation had finally given her the confidence she'd been searching for in all the wrong places. She loved her job and, in her most recent performance review, Esther had said she had what it took to go 'all the way' with her nursing career. Even better than that, she had a great group of friends who didn't want to change anything about her. Amy's parents told her all the time how proud they were, and even if her brother was difficult, every family had someone like that, didn't they?

Finally breaking up with Zach for good had been the biggest confidence booster of all, and she was determined never to settle again. She might still believe in love, but if someone came into her life, there'd only be space for them if their presence made it better than it already was. She was never going to let a relationship take things away from her again. Amy would much rather it was just her and Monty forever, because life was pretty damn good as it was, even if the night shifts sometimes felt a tiny bit like torture.

'Be a good boy, Monty. I'll put some music on, so you don't get lonely.' Amy switched on the radio, as she always did when she had to leave the dog on his own.

She smiled for a moment as the strains of 'I'm Your Man' by Wham! suddenly filled the air, instantly transporting her back to another time and place. She could picture Lijah as if he was standing next to her, the first boy she'd ever loved, the one she'd pushed away despite desperately wanting him to stay. But nostalgia was every bit as dangerous as pretending to be someone she wasn't, and Amy didn't have time for either of those things any more.

'Right sweetheart, I've really got to go to work.' Amy bent down and stroked the little dog's head one last time.

Her life might be a million miles away from the one Lijah led now, but that was fine with her. Who needed a rock-star lifestyle when you had an amazing job, a great group of friends and the cutest dog in Port Kara to come home to? That was more than enough for Amy and the past was exactly where it needed to be, firmly behind her.

3

It was 8 a.m. and Gwen had already been up for three hours. Putting the coffee on her husband's bedside table, she sat down with a thud, hoping that might be enough to wake him up. Barry groaned a bit, but didn't open his eyes. Slipping an ice-cold hand under the cover, she heard him gasp when it made contact with his thigh. March had lived up to its promise to come in like a lion and it showed no sign of letting up even though there were only a few days left of the month. The wind outside was threatening to whip the heads off the daffodils that had turned the garden into a sea of yellow. It was the only part of the garden Gwen could stake a claim to. She had planted the bulbs years before and had then left them to their own devices. It was up to them whether they decided to grow or not. She loved having a pretty garden, but she hated gardening itself. It was too slow for her and required far too much patience. Thankfully Barry loved it.

'Keep your hands to yourself woman, I'm not in the mood.' Barry finally opened one eye.

'If I move my hand a few inches upwards, I guarantee you'll change your tune.' She raised her eyebrows, and he smiled.

'Why don't you give it a go?'

'I've got to get to work, sorry.' She shrugged, but she was glad to see disappointment flit across her husband's eyes. Even after more than forty-five years together, that side of their relationship had always been strong, and she knew from some of her much younger friends that lots of couples slid into companionship far earlier in their relationships. That was fine, if you were both happy with it, but she was convinced it was one of the things that kept her and Barry young. She got a kick out of giving near-the-knuckle advice to others, and forcing them to revise their opinion of people in their seventies. Except the truth was, just lately, it felt as if she was merely going through the motions. She was hoping the feeling would pass, just as it had during the menopause, but she was secretly relieved to have a reason to turn Barry down, rather than having to admit she didn't have the desire at all just lately.

'You do know you're retired, don't you? I thought this stage of our lives was going to be all about long, lazy lie-ins and breakfast with the papers.'

'Have you forgotten who you're married to?' Gwen pulled a face. She couldn't think of anything worse than slowing down; she'd always been a whirlwind and Barry had seemed to enjoy being caught up in the vortex. She'd been a midwife for five decades, had raised a family, and got involved in every community project she could find, as well as enough hobbies to mean that down time wasn't an option. All the activity had helped her stay as slim as she'd been in her twenties, and she made an effort with her appearance, her ash-blonde hair cut into a sleek bob, subtle make-up, and a carefully chosen range of outfits that brought out the blue of her eyes. She and Barry squeezed in grandparenting duties when they could, but they didn't offer regular childcare cover while their children worked, because they were just too busy. Running the hospital shop at St Piran's Hospital and coordinating the volunteers was just the latest in a long line of responsibilities she'd taken on. Lately she had to admit it was taking its toll, but if the alternative for her was knitting, and a pipe and slippers for Barry, she'd grit her teeth and keep going.

'How could I ever forget who I'm married to Gee, when it's the best thing I ever did?' He squeezed her hand. He was the only person who'd ever called her Gee, a nickname he'd given her years ago. Despite their busy lives, Barry had been the one constant. He was her best friend, co-adventurer and partner in crime, but just lately he'd begun to change, saying that maybe they shouldn't be out of the house quite as much, or have so many hobbies. He'd recently suggested swapping dancing for golf, the idea of which had horrified Gwen, because it would have meant she had to admit to losing some of her get up and go too, and she was still hoping that would pass. Instead, her reaction had been to double down and volunteer for more shifts at the hospital, even though some days it felt like she was wading through treacle.

Barry's eyes were still fixed on hers when he spoke again. 'I just wish we could spend a bit more time together.'

'We spend loads of time together, we've got the dance show coming up and—'

'I meant here, at home. Just the two of us.'

'I thought we'd talked all this through. Did you make an appointment to see the doctor?' Gwen's tone was tight, but she couldn't help herself. She was worried. Her friend Caroline's husband had started wanting to do less and less, and it turned out he had prostate cancer. Deep down, she knew the situation wasn't comparable and that the anxiety she was feeling was misplaced. Barry was still active and kept far busier than many men twenty years younger, but there was a deeply entrenched reason for her not wanting to slow down. It was something that terrified her and she wasn't ready to admit, even to herself, that there'd been one or two warning signs just lately.

'I'll make an appointment to see the doctor if you do too.' Barry's eyes still hadn't left her face. He could read her far too easily, but she shook her head so hard it hurt.

'I don't need to see a doctor.'

'Gwen.' His tone was forceful and his use of her full name added emphasis, but he wasn't finished yet. 'You're exhausted, but you're not sleeping, you're losing weight and you're pushing yourself to do stuff it's obvious you don't have the energy to do.'

'No, I'm not,' she snapped, unable now to silence the voice inside her head that was telling her Barry was right. Some of the symptoms he'd listed were so similar to the ones her mum had suffered. No. She couldn't go there. She wouldn't. 'Maybe you're right, maybe we both just need a little break and some time on our own together. They're doing a pre-season deal at the hotel on the Sisters of Agnes Island. Could I persuade you to join me?'

Gwen slipped her hands under the covers again, her hand reconnecting with his thigh, but she felt him tense.

'You're not getting out of this conversation by changing the subject.'

'I can't win, can I!' Gwen snatched her hand away. 'One minute you're asking me to spend more time with you and the next you're turning down a night away. If you want to slow down to a stop, Barry, that's up to you, but I refuse to get old before my time.'

'Not even you can stop the ageing progress, Gee, and I know why you're scared.' Suddenly his tone was far softer, but all it did was fan the flames of her anger.

'I'm not scared. I'm just sick to death of you trying to make me take things easy when you know how much I hate that.' Getting to her feet, Gwen ignored his outstretched hand and his plea that all he was trying to do was help. Stalking out of the bedroom she slammed the door behind her. She hated rowing with Barry, and it felt so unfamiliar, because they'd always been able to talk about anything. But recently things had been tense, and his determination to make her revisit a place she didn't want to go to was probably why she felt so unlike her normal self just lately. It had to be that, because the alternative was far too awful to contemplate.

Gwen knew some of her friends were scared of getting older, but that had never bothered her because the opportunity was a privilege denied to so many. She'd spent years convincing herself that it was her attitude to ageing that mattered, not the number of candles on her next birthday cake. Except now things were happening that were forcing her to confront what she already knew to be true: sometimes it didn't matter how positive or young at heart people were, ill health could still seek them out. The thing that scared Gwen far more than ageing itself, was the possibility that the disease which had taken her mother from her, had finally caught up with her too. She'd spent decades desperately trying to outrun it, and so much of who she was had been shaped by her determination to seize the day because of what she'd witnessed during her mother's illness. But if Gwen was going to suffer the same fate, no amount of twirling around the dance floor or jumping out of aeroplanes would change the outcome. She was so terrified she couldn't bring herself to voice her fears out loud, even to Barry, and she'd never felt more alone in her life.

4

'I swear to God I am going to have to unfollow Isla if she posts one more of these videos.' Aidan leaned towards Amy and showed her what he'd been looking at on his phone. It was taken from the window of a campervan travelling along Lindis Pass in New Zealand, which cut through a stunning mountain range.

'Me too.' Amy grinned, knowing neither of them meant it. They were both just so glad Isla was enjoying herself, following a diagnosis of chronic myeloid leukaemia which had spun her world on its axis. Despite being an incurable condition, it was manageable in the same kind of way as diabetes, and as long as it didn't progress to acute myeloid leukaemia it wasn't life threatening. It had been a black cloud hanging over Isla's head, nonetheless, until she'd come to terms with it, and it had been Reuben, Aidan's nephew, who'd helped her to do that. He was now Isla's boyfriend, as well as her travelling companion out in New Zealand, and Amy strongly suspected he would be a permanent fixture in her friend's life on their return. She really liked Reuben, not least because he treated Isla so well, and it gave her hope that the best relationships could happen when you least expected it.

Amy had seen so many of her friends find love over the last few years and despite her determination to be alone rather than settle for second best, she still wanted that for herself. She didn't *need* to be with someone, but that didn't mean she didn't still *want* to have a family of her own one day. Her career was progressing well and she'd recently applied for a master's degree in order to become a clinical nurse specialist, but, deep down, she knew her job would never tick every box.

During some of the off-again phases in her relationship with Zach, Amy had tried online dating and that was one thing she'd never do again. Some of her friends had met wonderful partners on the apps, but she seemed to attract every bottom feeder with access to a smartphone. She'd been sent enough pictures of male anatomy to re-train as a urologist, and to know that penises came in more shapes and sizes than she'd ever imagined possible. It had been Aidan who'd told her to save one of the pictures, so she could send it back to anyone who sent her one in the future. He'd suggested she accompany it with a simple message, before swiftly blocking them.

'This one's mine.'

She hoped it would make some of them think twice before doing it again, but even armed with advice from Aidan, she'd decided online dating wasn't for her and not just because she'd received so many stomach-churning pictures. She'd had requests from guys to wear her nurse's uniform out on dates and a couple of men who hadn't shown up at all. But the top prize probably had to go to the man who'd called her by his ex-girlfriend's name all night and, who instead of apologising, had said it was okay because Amy reminded him of his ex, so it was probably just as easy to call her Milly. It had been enough for her to delete all the dating apps. She might still want the traditional white picket fence life one day, but she wasn't prepared to settle for someone she couldn't trust completely. She'd been there before, and she was never going back.

'What's it going to be today, a mocha or a caramel latte?' Amy looked at Aidan as they reached the Friends of St Piran's shop. It was positioned at the entrance to the hospital, and there were several bistro tables outside, which had made it into a regular hangout for some of the staff. It had decent coffee too, which wasn't something readily available elsewhere in the hospital, and Amy hadn't needed any convincing to accompany Aidan there at the end of their shift. It had been a long night, and they hadn't had the chance to catch up properly, so it would be good to have a chat before they headed off on their separate ways for a few days. The hospital was just starting to come to life, and the shop only opened this early because one of the volunteers always came in to take delivery of the daily newspapers.

'It might have to be an Americano.' Aidan pulled a face. 'I know, I know, unheard of, but Jase is picking me up in half an hour, and we're going to the IKEA in Exeter. He's insisting there are some things we've got to buy from there for the baby. So I'm going to need some far less diluted caffeine to get me through. We're staying down there for a night in a hotel he got a last-minute deal on, and we're going to the cinema and having a meal out in a restaurant that isn't remotely child-friendly. Jase reckons we need to get all these things in while we can.'

The smile on Aidan's face made Amy smile too. Her plans for the next three days, following the end of a block of nights, were very different to her friend's, but she couldn't wait. She was going to buy some trashy magazines and all her favourite foods. There'd be long walks on the beach with Monty, and then Sunday lunch over at her parents' place, while her brother was out fishing, where the little dog would chase around the garden with her parents' English Mastiff, Bernie. They were like little and large, and the sight always made her smile. She might catch up with a friend for a drink too, but she deliberately hadn't made any set plans. Amy was a sociable person, but after ten years in nursing she knew she needed a bit of down time to adjust from nights to days.

'Okay, I'll grab the coffees. Chocolate?' She looked at Aidan again and he pulled a face.

'Well obviously. I'm switching to an americano, I'm not dead.'

'Of course, sorry.' Amy laughed at the look of mock indignation on her friend's face. She grabbed two bars of chocolate and headed towards the counter, where Gwen was standing, staring down at a newspaper. It wasn't like her not to be giving her full attention to the job or busying herself restocking the shelves with the newly delivered magazines. A retired midwife, Gwen was a force of nature, who seemed to know everyone in the Three Ports area, never mind St Piran's. There was no subject off limits, and nothing on which she wasn't willing to share her advice. She'd also do anything to help someone out if she could, and she was the antithesis of a slacker. So it was a shock to see Gwen standing there reading, as Amy approached the counter. The older women's head snapped back the moment she realised Amy was there and she jabbed at the open pages of the newspaper in front of her.

'Amy, of all the people! I was just going to text you about this, have you seen it? Has he been in touch?' Her words were coming out in a rush, but Amy had no idea what she was talking about.

Gwen thrust the newspaper towards her and she immediately spotted the photograph of Lijah Byrne, hurrying through an airport, dressed more like someone about to go for a jog than a pop star. He was wearing a dark coloured tracksuit, with a beanie pulled low down almost covering his eyes. Even in the photograph she could see he looked tired, a generous covering of stubble grazing his chin. He wasn't the sort of musician who looked polished and airbrushed, there was an edge to him, his dark curly hair always what her grandmother had described as being 'a little bit too long for its own good'. But Amy had always loved Lijah's hair. It still shocked her just how many young men had tried to adopt his style, but he wasn't easily imitated. In meant there was no mistaking who the photo was of, even if the headline hadn't screamed: 'Lijah lies low!' And the byline: 'Back in the place that inspired so many of his songs.'

'Did he tell you he was coming back?' Gwen's eyes were shining; she was clearly excited about the possibility of someone as famous at Lijah suddenly popping into the hospital shop. Port Kara and the surrounding area had its share of celebrities living in fancy holiday homes, and far more than its fair share of celebrity chefs, but St Piran's was hardly a hot spot for the rich and famous to hang out.

'We're not in contact. I keep telling everyone that.' Almost as soon as Amy had told her friends that she'd once dated Lijah, she'd wished she could take the words back. She'd expected a lot of incredulity and plenty of mickey taking – it was the love language of her friends at the hospital and what got them through some very tough days – but what she hadn't expected was for them to be convinced Lijah still had feelings for her. Admittedly the lyrics of his songs did often refer to what could be construed as a teenage romance and there'd been some lines, on his first album, that even she'd wondered about:

Still miss the girl in my teenage dream, like an eighties
pin-up, you're my retro queen.

Lijah had been good at telling Amy what he liked about her, and her insecurities had made her ask the question far too often. It must have driven him mad, because it drove her mad too, but back then she couldn't help it. There'd been a long list of things he'd said he loved about her, when she'd sought reassurance. It had amazed her because if she'd been asked to name one thing she liked about her appearance, she'd probably have struggled. There were things she liked about who she was, and her ability to laugh at most things – including herself – meant she'd always made friends easily. But she hadn't looked the way girls her age were supposed to look in her teens, when all her friends were slim, in cropped tops showing off belly button piercings, and with legs so thin they reminded Amy of newborn foals. It had taken years for her to get to where she was now, and sometimes she wondered if Lijah would even recognise her as the girl she used to be.

No one had expected them to get together, least of all her, and for a long time they'd only been friends. Lijah had been the subject of her unrequited affection since she'd first spotted him in Year 7, but it wasn't until Year 9 that a chance conversation had sparked the connection between them. They'd discovered a shared passion for music from the eighties, which had been the soundtrack to the youth of their parents' generation. It had led to a friendship that had become really close by the time they were fifteen. Lijah was an only child, who'd lived with his mum and his aunt, both of whom Amy had grown close to. The four of them would sit listening to music together, talking and laughing. It had been a home from home for Amy, but she'd never allowed herself to believe that it might go beyond friendship for Lijah. Everything in his life was about music and she'd been convinced that their friendship was just an extension of that. Then she'd helped his mum, Maria, organise his sixteenth birthday party.

That night Amy and Lijah had shared a moment that had changed everything and for three years they'd been each other's whole worlds.

When Lijah had first told her she reminded him of Kate Bush, she'd laughed. Admittedly she had the same hazel eyes, edged with dark lashes. She'd worn her dark hair long back then too and it wouldn't have needed a lot of back combing to give her the unruly look that had been de rigeur for much of the eighties, but that's where the similarity ended. Kate Bush was the epitome of cool, Amy was just Amy. The few times she'd gone clubbing with friends in the sixth form, she'd been the girl who kept an eye on other girls' drinks to make sure the boys chatting them up didn't try to slip anything into their glasses. But Lijah had like her – loved her, so he'd said. They'd shared such a lot of interests, and told each other their biggest secrets and darkest fears, laughing so hard so often, that in the end she'd believed his feelings for her were real, and she'd known without doubt that hers were. People often said that teenagers didn't know what love was, but that wasn't true. She'd loved Lijah and a part of her probably always would, but she doubted he gave her a second thought these days, except when he needed a line for a song about the boy he used to be. 'When I was me' seemed to be playing everywhere and, if she'd let herself, Amy might even have been able to buy into her friends' fantasy that Lijah Byrne was still writing songs about her after all these years. Two lines in particular made it feel as if he was singing to her.

You were gonna be my everything, but you never left that place,
On that corner where I kissed you, where I still picture your face.

She could still see him standing on the spot where they'd said their final goodbyes, at the end of the gap year they'd spent together after leaving school. It was Amy who'd broken things off when Lijah had announced his intention to go to London to try and make something happen with his music. He'd wanted her to transfer her university place from Plymouth to somewhere in London, coming up with plans for them to live together, and joking that he'd happily sneak into her halls of residence every night if that meant they wouldn't have to be apart. She'd wanted to say yes, so desperately, but if Lijah had any chance of making it, he needed to be able to completely focus, and if they were meant to be together, they'd find a way to do it. That's what she'd told him, and she'd refused to back down even when he'd begged her to reconsider. Even now she wasn't 100 per cent sure why she hadn't gone with him, but she knew it hadn't been entirely selfless.

It had almost killed her to turn him down, but she suspected it had been an attempt to protect herself from getting even more hurt eventually. He talked about trying to keep things going long distance, but Amy had known it couldn't last.

The bubble she and Lijah had existed within for more than three years belonged in Port Kara, where they had spent most of their time together in his room, listening to the music they loved and painting a picture of a future that seamlessly blended two such different worlds, which could never have worked in reality. Her friends had warned her that Lijah would outgrow her if he achieved the success he was craving, and it was all too easy to believe. She'd witnessed it first hand, after all, other girls hanging around wanting to spend time with him, even at the small gigs he performed in pubs, or when he was busking down by the harbour. Whether Lijah made it or not, there'd be someone to turn his head as soon as they stepped outside that bubble, she'd been sure of it. And as soon as he had made it, she hadn't been able to avoid the evidence that she'd been right. There'd been other musicians, actresses and more than one model in his life. All of them had been Kate Bush cool, so any idea her friends at the hospital had that Lijah might still think about Amy was laughable. She didn't even think about him that way any more. It would have been sad if she still fantasised about him coming back into her life, the way she had in those first few years after they'd split. The trouble was, she hadn't been able to stop using her relationship with Lijah as the benchmark against which she'd measured all other relationships, and she could admit now that it probably hadn't been all Zach's fault that theirs had failed. He must have felt the comparison, because she did, and sometimes it worried her that she might never find someone who measured up. First loves were like that for everyone though, and the memories existed in a rosy glow of nostalgia. They'd been so young back then and they'd have both changed so much. There was no way Lijah would be the boy she remembered any more than she was the girl he used to know.

'Things can change.' Gwen's voice broke into her thoughts. 'You might not have been in contact up until now, but he's coming home. So you never know.'

'I don't think he dates mere mortals like me any more.' Amy might still believe in love, but she didn't believe in fairy tales. They'd kept in touch for a little while, but it had almost been more painful than not talking at all and in the end it had petered out altogether. If Lijah had wanted to reach out to her, he could have done it any time over the past decade, but he'd never sought her out when he came home, not even after his mother died. What she and Lijah had shared was just a happy memory, the same memory he probably drew upon when he was looking for inspiration for his songs.

'You're not a mere mortal, you're an A&E nurse.' Gwen gave her a level look. 'Not to mention the fact that you're a ray of sunshine wherever you go, you rescue dogs that need rehoming, get every party started and, if all that wasn't enough, you're beautiful too.'

'You have to say that, you brought me into the world.' Amy grinned; it always felt good to be on the receiving end of one of Gwen's pep talks. If anyone was a ray of sunshine, it was her and, if you'd been born in the Three Ports area, as Amy had, there was a good chance she'd have been the midwife to deliver you. That was the sort of experience most mothers never forgot, although it would have been impossible to forget Gwen in almost any circumstances. She had an incredible memory for names, and she'd recognised Amy's mother immediately when she'd visited the hospital to see her daughter, not needing any prompting that her name was Kerry. That was the day Amy had discovered that the very first person to hold her had been Gwen, and it was something they still enjoyed ribbing each other about.

'I've seen you naked, don't forget.' Gwen winked. 'So if Lijah Byrne does come back on the scene, don't think there's any chance of you keeping it a secret from me.'

'Don't worry, you'll be the first to know.' Laughing, Amy was about to order the drinks, when a sudden commotion outside the shop made her turn and look behind her. Then she heard Aidan shout.

'Ames quick, I need your help!'

Amy broke into a run in response, rushing back through the entrance to the shop to see him cradling a child in his arms, the woman standing next to him crying hysterically and shouting at them to help her little boy.

'What's happened?' Amy had enough experience of emergency medicine to be able to keep her voice level, even if the circumstances were about as scary as they came. An unconscious child would always fall within that category.

Aidan looked at Amy. 'He's unresponsive, but he's got a good pulse and steady breathing, so I don't think there's any immediate danger.'

'We need to get him to resus. Shall I go and grab a trolley?' There were wheelchairs in the reception area opposite the shop, but they couldn't put an unconscious child in a wheelchair without the risk of him falling out, or possibly compromising his airway if they couldn't maintain a stable position.

'I could just carry him.' Aidan looked uncertain, even as he made the suggestion. The child appeared to be about six or seven, but that was a lot of dead weight to carry. The boy's mother was crying so hard Amy didn't rate her chances of persuading the woman to do anything, and she still wasn't sure whether to just run and get a trolley, but she decided to make another suggestion, as much to help the boy's mother calm down as anything.

'It's going to be okay, but we need to get your son to an area where we can get him properly checked over. The quickest way is for you to sit in the wheelchair and hold him, can you do that?'

The woman nodded, for a moment seeming to regain some level of control, but when she tried to speak it came out as a strangled plea. 'I can't lose him, he's all I've got.'

'You're not going to lose him.' Amy couldn't know that for certain, but she was as confident as she could be that he wasn't going to die. There were lots of reasons a child could lose consciousness, all of them worrying in their own way, but the fact that his vital signs were so strong offered a lot of reassurance. As Amy took hold of the other woman's arm, and guided her to sit in one of the wheelchairs, she could feel how much the boy's mother was shaking. 'What's your name?'

'Demi, and my son's name is Fletcher. We were visiting my mum, they said she won't make it through another day, and I wanted him to have the chance to say goodbye. But as we were coming back down in the lift, he just seemed to collapse.' She started crying again then and Amy briefly put a hand on her shoulder, before Aidan lowered the little boy on to his mother's lap.

'That must have been terrifying, but you're in the best place possible to find out what's going on, and we'll be able to get Fletcher whatever help he might need.' Amy squeezed Demi's shoulder again and gave Aidan a brief nod, the two of them not needing to exchange words. Like her, he'd be hoping that Fletcher's loss of consciousness was down to something relatively easy to fix, like a temporary drop in blood sugar, or emotional distress in response to what sounded like a very difficult situation. But there was a chance it could be caused by something far more serious and Amy just hoped her assurances to Demi that everything would be okay, wouldn't turn out to be a lie.

5

The day staff had taken over Fletcher's care as soon as Aidan and Amy had reached the emergency department. The paediatrician on call had suspected hypoglycaemia, and Fletcher had regained consciousness almost immediately after they began to administer IV fluids. The doctor had started firing questions at Demi related to the possibility that Fletcher might have type 1 diabetes, but the forcefulness of his approach had made her burst into tears again.

'See if you can get some sense out of her, while we get started with some tests, can you? She seems to trust you and if there's something else going on, you've probably got the best chance of getting to the bottom of it,' the paediatrician whispered in Amy's ear as Demi clung to her son's hand.

'They think this is my fault, don't they?' Demi looked straight at Amy after the paediatrician left the cubicle. 'They think I've been neglecting Fletcher.'

'No, of course not.' Amy was aware that the doctor might consider it a possibility, but she didn't believe it. Over the years she'd seen things she wished she hadn't, parents who'd deliberately hurt their own children, or endangered them as a result of neglect, stopping at nothing to try and cover their tracks, but that's not what she saw in Demi. 'We're just trying to find out a bit more about what happened before Fletcher collapsed, that's all. We need to ensure he gets the right treatment as soon as possible.'

Demi shot a look at her son, who by now was watching something on her phone, his face illuminated by the screen, and wearing a pair of green wireless headphones, topped with a row of dinosaur scales. He looked blissfully unaware of all the drama he'd caused; only Demi's puffy, red eyes gave the game away. 'He said he was hungry before he collapsed, and he'd gone a bit pale. I should have fed him before we went in to see Mum, but we were in a rush and anyway, I didn't have any...' She hesitated for a moment, seeming to catch herself. 'We just didn't have time.'

'It sounds like it might be his blood sugar levels, and there's a chance it might be diabetes, but it could just be down to the fact Fletcher hadn't eaten for a while.' Amy couldn't help noticing how fragile Demi looked; her arms were so thin they were barely any bigger than her son's. There was always a fine line to tread between nursing and social care, but she had to ask.

'Are there ever times when you struggle to have enough to eat?' Amy kept her voice as light as she could for such as heavy question. The last thing she wanted was for Demi to feel judged in any way, because that absolutely wasn't her intention. It was clear how much Demi loved her son, and Amy didn't doubt that she was doing her best, but she needed to be certain there wasn't more to the family's situation.

'We get by.' Demi had straightened her shoulders, defensiveness prickling her tone. 'Money's been tighter since I gave up work to look after Mum, before she came into hospital. Even his headphones are hand-me-downs from a friend.'

'There might be support you can access that will help you to do more than get by. You shouldn't have to go without because you've been caring for your mum.' She didn't add that Fletcher shouldn't have to miss out either, but Demi had clearly picked up the implication.

'I make sure Fletcher doesn't go without.' Demi's defensiveness gave way to a shuddering sigh. 'Although that's more down to the kindness of others, like your friend, Aidan.'

'I didn't realise you knew him.' Aidan had needed to leave to meet Jase not long after they'd brought Fletcher into A&E. He'd asked Amy to text him later to let him know that the little boy was okay, but he hadn't given any indication of having known the family.

'I don't, as such, but his husband, Mr Kennedy-Taylor, is the headteacher of Fletcher's school. And I've seen Aidan at some of the events, raising funds for the school, including the Humpty Dumpty club. They managed to raise enough to fund places for the whole school year.' Demi must have picked up on Amy's confusion. 'It's a club for children who benefit from having a free breakfast at school. With that and the free school lunches he's entitled to, I only have to worry about a snack in the evening for Fletcher, and feeding him at the weekends. I only eat at home when he does, and I can get by on just an evening meal. But it's half term this week, and this morning there was nothing left. I was going to go to the supermarket last night, to see if they had any bits reduced, but with Mum being so poorly I didn't leave here until late, and I couldn't leave Fletcher at his play date for any longer. He had pizza there, and ice cream, so I thought he'd be okay until later. The doctor is right, it's all my fault he's ill.'

Tears had sprung into Demi's eyes again and she wasn't the only one. It shouldn't have to be that way. All Demi wanted to do was take care of her little boy, and it had been her desire to care for her own mother, during her final days, that had made that near on impossible. There was something wrong in the world and it made Amy's heart hurt. Walking over, she wrapped her arms around Demi.

'It's not your fault and I promise you won't have to worry about not being able to feed Fletcher or yourself again.'

'Thank you, thank you so much.' Demi rested her head against her shoulder, and even though Amy had no idea how she was going to fulfil her promise, she knew for certain that she would. Whatever it took.

6

One of the things Gwen loved most about her volunteering role at St Piran's was doing the rounds with the hospital trolley. It meant she got to visit lots of different wards and had the chance to chat with all kinds of people. Barry had always teased her about being incurably nosey, but she preferred to think of it as inquisitive. She was just interested in other people's lives and in hearing their stories, and over the years she'd made some good friends as a result of chance encounters that had sparked the start of a conversation. She'd never had as much time for reading as she would have liked, mainly because her determination to be on the go all the time meant she didn't have the concentration it took to focus on much more than a magazine when she finally sat down. Instead she got her fix for stories from the lives of the people she met.

As a midwife she'd been trusted with patients' secrets, and aspects of their lives they hadn't even told their loved ones. More than once she'd supported women whose partners thought they were pregnant with their first child, when in truth it was only the man's first child. Gwen had always thought it was sad that these women, who were about to share the most intimate experience possible with the person they professed to love, hadn't felt able to tell their partners about their past. She'd always been an open book when it came to Barry; there'd never been anything she hadn't felt able to tell him about her past, and no subject affecting their present that had felt taboo to broach. But just recently he'd been pushing her to revisit one of the most difficult parts of her past, and suddenly it felt like every conversation with him was loaded. She didn't want to confront all the feelings it would rake up and she was nowhere near ready to face the 'what ifs' about their future if she ended up sharing her mother's fate. One thing Gwen hated more than anything was the idea of losing control of her own life, and a progressive and debilitating illness was her worst nightmare, not least because she'd witnessed it first hand. It was far easier to bury herself in work, listening to the patchwork of stories and problems that made up other people's lives. There were other volunteers running the shop today, but she was in no hurry to finish her round and head home, where Barry would be waiting. Her casual chats with the patients could draw out all day long as far as she was concerned.

St Michael's had always been one of Gwen's favourite wards. The patients were all under the care of the specialist geriatric team, and had a range of medical conditions, including both physical and cognitive illnesses.

Camilla Armstrong had been in St Michael's Ward for several days, after a chest infection had turned into pneumonia. She was out of danger by the time Gwen first met her, having spent the first two days in intensive care, but she'd still been tearful and stressed. Camilla's concerns weren't about her illness. She'd been panicking about when she could get home to her dogs and, perhaps more surprisingly, to her horse. When Camilla had told Gwen about the horse, whose name was Bojangles, all of the assumptions she'd had about the frail, older woman sitting in the bed in front of her had to be questioned. She'd spoken about riding Bojangles through the fields near her cottage, and Gwen had found herself wondering for a moment whether Camilla was living in a different place and time inside her mind. She'd seen it often enough before: elderly patients talking about needing to buy school shoes for their children, or even calling out for their own mum and dad. Sometimes it was nothing less than tragic, but at other times she tried to hold on to the idea that it gave those patients comfort. One thing Gwen tried never to do was picture herself in those same circumstances, it was too close to home. She didn't know if her mother had ever reached the stage where she'd forgotten who she was, but she'd lost the ability to express her thoughts, even the sort of jumbled memories some patients shared with Gwen, and in many ways that seemed even worse.

'Camilla keeps talking about having a horse.' Gwen had looked at one of the nurses quizzically, gesturing towards Camilla, but the nurse had nodded in response.

'Oh yes, Bojangles.' The young nurse smiled. 'We thought Cami might be a bit confused at first, but she asked me to call Kirsty, the woman who keeps her horse in one of the stables at Cami's place, in return for helping with Bojangles, and he definitely isn't a figment of her imagination! She's horse mad. It's been her whole life apparently.'

Afterwards Gwen had gone back to chat to Camilla, who'd insisted that Gwen call her Cami, as all the people she liked apparently did.

'Only my father ever called me Camilla, and a lot of the time he was terribly cross with me for something or other. So now it feels like I'm being told off whenever I hear someone say it.'

Gwen had happily ignored the end of her shift so that Cami

could tell her more about her beloved animals, and the others she'd owned right back to when she was growing up at Portharren Manor, a sprawling country estate to the west of Port Kara. It was like someone had turned a light on inside of Cami, and Gwen had felt terrible for doing the thing she'd sworn she'd never do, making sweeping assumptions on the basis of the person's age alone. Today she wanted to try and make amends. She'd bought a copy of *Horse and Hound* magazine, and had placed it casually on top of the other magazines on the trolley, just before she got to the ward. They didn't stock it in the shop, and she wasn't sure if it was something Cami enjoyed reading, but she decided it was worth a gamble.

'Hello again Cami, how are you doing now?' Gwen stopped by her bed and the other woman wrinkled her nose.

'It's a frightful bore being trapped in here.' Cami announced her status in a cut-glass accent, so refined she made the Duchess of Cambridge sound as though she could audition for a role in *EastEnders*. 'I know I'm horribly ungrateful, when all the nurses work so hard, but it's terribly dull and I loathe being stuck indoors.'

Gwen had to press her lips together for a moment to stop herself from laughing. There was a flamboyance about Cami that verged on the theatrical. It reminded Gwen of when her daughter had made very over-the-top pronouncements as a child about just how unbearable life could be when it wasn't going her way. Gwen's daughter had ended up being a big fan of amateur dramatics and it seemed Cami might have some untapped talent too.

'At least you're not missing any good weather. It's blowing a gale out there today.' Gwen smiled and lifted a couple of the magazines up from the trolley. 'Maybe you could think of this as an opportunity to catch up on some reading, I bet you never get the chance to do that when you're at home.'

'That's true.' Cami's response didn't sound particularly enthusiastic, but then her eyes rested on the copy of the magazine that Gwen had bought especially for her. 'Oh gosh, I didn't dream you'd stock the *Horse and Hound.* How marvellous, and it's got just the article I need.'

As Gwen passed her the magazine, Cami jabbed a finger against the front cover which detailed various articles, included one entitled 'joint care made easy'.

'Is that for you or the horse?' The joke had come out of Gwen's mouth before she'd had the chance to stop it. That sort of thing happened a lot, and she knew she had a reputation for having a cheeky sense of humour. She might not want to write people off on the basis of their age, but there was nothing Gwen wouldn't make a joke out of if the situation and the timing were right. It was the only way to get through the tough times. The trouble was, she barely knew Cami, and she had no idea whether the other woman would find it funny or offensive. For just a moment there was silence, and then Cami started to laugh.

'I should probably get the vet to put us both out of our misery! Perhaps she'll give me a good deal, one of those where you buy one and then you get another one free.' She laughed again and Gwen couldn't help joining in, partly because of the way she'd worded it, but then Cami started coughing.

'Are you okay? Sorry, I shouldn't have made you laugh when you're not feeling well.' Gwen looked to see if she could spot one of the nurses, but none of them seemed to be around. She handed Cami a drink from the table in front of her, but the coughing had already eased and she shook her head.

'Nonsense, whoever said laughter's the best medicine was absolutely right.' Cami leaned towards the locker at the side of her bed. 'How much do I owe for the magazine? It's going to be a life saver having something decent to read, I just know it.'

'It's my treat, you made me laugh too.' A twinge of regret twisted in Gwen's gut. She didn't usually need a reason to laugh, it came easily to her, but lately it was just one more thing that seemed to be drifting further and further out of reach.

'I couldn't possibly let you pay for it.'

'It's fine, honestly, it was a free sample for the shop, to see whether it might be something we'd consider stocking in future.' Even as she told the lie, Gwen wasn't sure why she was doing it. There was something about Cami, though, an echo in her faded blue eyes of Gwen's mother, who'd been just as tearful and panicked during her early admissions to hospital as Cami had been the first time they'd met.

Gwen went above and beyond for lots of people, but the pull she felt towards Cami was even stronger than her usual desire to make patients' lives a little bit better. She wanted the outcome to be different this time around. She didn't want her new friend to fade away until she was barely more than a shadow of the woman she used to be, just like her mother had done. It was stupid, the situations were so different, but she knew that wouldn't stop her coming back tomorrow with something else she thought might perk Cami up. If there could just be a happy outcome this time around for the woman with the pale blue eyes, then perhaps there'd be a happy ever after for Gwen too.

* * *

Gwen was bone tired and all she wanted to do was flop on to the sofa and watch TV, but she couldn't. She was hosting a get together for the Mrs Adventures club after work. It was one of the groups she'd started since retiring and she usually loved getting together with the other women. Sometimes they'd catch up just to chat and talk about their lives, the good bits, the bad bits, and everything in between. At other times they'd get together for a specific event, or to plan their next adventure, hence the name of the group. So far there'd been zorbing, clay pigeon shooting, quad biking and even a tandem handglide with qualified instructors. It was a rebellion of sorts, and proof that just because you were a woman of a certain age the adventures didn't have to stop.

Tonight there was no specific agenda for the meeting, but they were overdue another adventure. Normally by now she would have planned one; she often had the next idea brewing even before they'd completed the latest one. Right now, she couldn't muster up any enthusiasm and it had crossed her mind to cancel the get together, but she couldn't do that. It wasn't because her friends would have held it against her. They'd probably have been happy to meet elsewhere, or just to give the meeting a miss this time. The reason she couldn't cancel had nothing to do with letting them down, it was because she was scared. If she started pulling out of things it would become a slippery slope. She already felt as though she'd lost her zest for life and it terrified her.

That sort of apathy had plagued her once before, and it had terrified her then too. She'd been convinced it was a sign of the illness she dreaded, the illness that had robbed her mother of who she was, before eventually robbing her of her life too. Alys Evans had been a power house, who'd had six children including Gwen, and had run a sheep farm with her husband, Ivor, a few miles outside Porthmadog. Growing up in Wales had been idyllic for Gwen, but when Barry's job had taken him and Gwen to Cornwall, it had become their adopted home and these days she considered herself a proud Cornishwoman, not even her accent gave her away.

Despite her love for her adopted home, Gwen had missed Wales, and her siblings, but most of all her mum and dad. There'd been a couple of times she'd even considered moving back. The first had been when Gwen had become a mother herself, and had felt the draw to be back near her own mum, leaning on her for support, particularly in the early months when she'd felt lonely and isolated. But Gwen had done what she always did, taking matters into her own hands and starting up a mother and toddler group, long before every village had one of its own. The second time she'd felt the pull to go home, had been when her father had died, but her mother wouldn't hear of it. Alys had been fifty-five years old when she'd lost her husband, who'd been ten years older than she was. She'd stated her intention to continue running the farm, and had brushed away the concerns of her children. Gwen's eldest brother, Rhodri, had offered to join their mother on the farm full time and Gwen's misgivings had begun to fade. There were three hundred miles between Porthmadog and Port Kara, and, with a young family, Gwen didn't manage to get back to the farm nearly as often as she would have liked. By the time her mother's fifty-seventh birthday came around, it had been almost six months since they'd seen one another.

'Mam seems to be ageing fast these days.' Rhodri's warning on the phone before Gwen arrived for her visit should have prepared her for what she saw on her return to Wales, but it didn't. Alys was barely recognisable as the feisty force of nature she had always been and, when she'd turned to look at Gwen and the grandchildren, for one terrifying moment Gwen had thought her own mother didn't recognise her. Then Alys had suddenly given a physical jolt of recognition. Despite Gwen's initial relief, the changes in her mother were evident; she seemed to be struggling with how to phrase things, and had developed repetitive patterns of behaviour, which included folding and refolding the stack of tea towels she kept under the sink hundreds of times during Gwen's visit.

Gwen's youngest sister, Elena, had moved in by then to help Rhodri out. She'd told Gwen that Alys's GP had dismissed her behaviours as symptoms of 'the change', but had confided her fear that things seemed to be getting worse, even though she should have gone through the menopause by now. Much to Alys's displeasure, Gwen and her sister had insisted on taking their mother to the doctors again. There'd been a series of tests and some dead ends, before Alys had finally been diagnosed with primary progress aphasia, a form of dementia that eventually left her a shell of the woman she'd once been.

Barry had supported Gwen's decision to return to Porthmadog to help care for her mother, but Elena and Rhodri wouldn't hear of it, telling Gwen that nothing had made Alys prouder than the success of her daughter's career as a midwife. Instead, she'd visited as often as she could, and had used all her holiday allowance to stay at the farm and provide respite so that her sister and Rhodri could take a break. It was almost five years to the day of diagnosis that Alys had succumbed to her illness. She'd been sixty-two when she'd died and Gwen hadn't been sure whether she'd feel anything at all when she finally lost her mum, because she'd already been grieving her for years. To her surprise, a wave of devastation had hit her harder than she'd ever have imagined possible and for a while her grief seemed to swallow her whole. She wasn't just grieving for the loss of her mother, she was grieving for the loss of those final years, when Alys had no longer been Alys, and for everything the family had been robbed of as a result.

When Gwen had started to struggle with her memory in her early fifties, and had found herself trying to grasp words that felt fully formed in her brain, but which for some reason wouldn't come out of her mouth, she'd been devastated all over again, convinced she was about to receive the same diagnosis as her mother. When tests had revealed that in her case the symptoms really had been down to the menopause, Gwen's whole body had flooded with relief. She'd had a horrible couple of years, but it had been manageable, knowing that it would pass, and she'd been convinced that she'd escaped the possibility of inheriting her mother's condition. Except in the last few weeks, the words of the consultant she'd seen back then seemed to be ringing in her ears.

'Having a parent with primary progressive aphasia does make it more likely that you'll inherit the disease.'

Gwen couldn't blame the symptoms she'd been experiencing lately on menopause, and she'd been too afraid to even google them. A voice inside her head had kept up a running commentary instead, telling her that she didn't need tests, she knew what this was, and that no one could expect a lucky escape twice over. There was no denying the symptoms either. She seemed to lose her train of thought at times, her motivation and energy levels had fallen through the floor and sometimes she struggled to focus on what other people were saying. She just didn't feel like herself any more, but she couldn't bear the thought of anyone else realising, so she put on an act of being the same old Gwen. She might be laughing and joking the way she always had, but on the inside it was as though something had already died, her joie de vivre snuffed out like the flame on a candle.

Thankfully no one at the Mrs Adventures club seemed to have realised that Gwen was there in body alone. There'd been animated chat between the rest of the group, and Gwen had thrown in a few of her usual one liners. She'd laughed when everyone else did, and made sure she kept the drinks flowing. She just wasn't feeling any of the things she usually felt during a night in with the girls, and it was almost as if she was watching herself from above, rather than actually being there.

'My cousin who lives in Kent is doing a wing walk to raise money for her local hospital and I was wondering if that could be our next adventure?' Caroline was the mother of one of the A&E nurses at St Piran's, Esther, and she and Gwen had become good friends over the past couple of years, especially since she'd started volunteering in the hospital shop.

'Exactly how sturdy are these wings?' Frankie, Gwen's best friend, who was also a midwife, raised her eyebrows. 'When I went into the village shop last night, all of the drinks in the refrigerator cabinet started rattling when I stomped past. It was like I was creating my own reading on the Richter scale.'

'Oh shut up.' Wendy laughed as she gave Frankie a gentle nudge in the ribs. 'As a member of staff, I know I should support the idea of raising money for the hospital, but I'm about to marry the love of my life after more than two decades of living with a total knob. So can we at least wait until after the wedding?'

'Good idea.' Connie nodded. She'd been a patient at the hospital when Gwen had first met her, and she'd made a remarkable recovery after a serious accident, but it turned out she was still willing to play up her injuries when it suited her. 'I'm just not quite sure I've got the strength for something like that any more. Not after the accident.'

'I'm not sure I've got the right pants for it.' Frankie wrinkled her nose. 'I have problems holding on to the contents of my bladder if I drive round a corner too fast.'

For the first time that evening, Gwen's laughter was genuine and the conversation quickly derailed into an exchange of experiences about just how much of challenge it was to be a woman of a certain age.

'I should probably have done more pelvic floor exercises after I had Esther.' Caroline lowered her voice as she shared the hushed confession. 'But I remember trying to do them one day when I was sitting on the bus, just like my midwife had advised. Ten minutes into the journey, the bus suddenly pulled over and the driver shot upstairs. He'd seen me in the mirror up there, you know the one they use to keep an eye on the passengers, and he thought I was having a funny turn because of the pained expression on my face. Turns out I can't clench anything *down there*, without clenching the muscles in my face too!'

'I bet Gwen knows some techniques.' Wendy looked in her direction.

'I think I might have left it a bit too late.' Caroline frowned, but Gwen shook her head.

'It's never too late. I helped a patient once whose pelvic floor was so far gone, she almost turned her daughter's birthday trip to a trampoline park into a pool party.' Everyone was laughing so much by then, that they wouldn't have heard the technique Gwen recommended, even if she'd tried to share it with them. It felt so good to just laugh with her friends, and forget about the nagging voice in her head for a little while.

'Did you have a good night?' Barry came up behind her as she stood in the kitchen once the others had left, and slid his arms around her waist. 'I could hear you all laughing from upstairs.'

'Probably best not to ask what about.' She smiled, leaning back into him and feeling better than she had in weeks. Maybe she really had just been tired, and all she'd needed was a night in with the girls to pep her up.

'Any gossip you can pass on?' Barry's tone was teasing and she turned around in the circle of his arms so they were face to face.

'Not gossip exactly, but Wendy has worked out where she wants to go on...' The next word had been on the tip of Gwen's tongue, ready to spill out of her mouth, but now it felt like a rock wedged in her throat. She could picture the image of what she wanted to say, see it so clearly, a red bridge and an island in the distance, but it was like the connection between her brain and her voice had suddenly snapped.

'On your next adventure?' There was concern on Barry's face as he watched Gwen, her mouth opening and closing like a fish out of water, but she was shaking her head.

'It's where you go on an aeroplane. You know, after there's a wedding.' Panic was washing over Gwen now and her eyes filled with tears as she looked at Barry again.

'A honeymoon?' She tried to nod in response, but the tears were rolling down her cheeks. How could she have forgotten the words to tell Barry that Wendy wanted to go to San Franciso on her honeymoon?

'It's okay darling, it's okay.' As he pulled her closer, her heartbeat thudded in her ears, but it still didn't drown out the voice that was back, telling her she could no longer deny it. If she couldn't even conjure up a simple word like honeymoon, there had to be something seriously wrong, and she was terrified the aphasia that had so cruelly taken her mother wasn't going to let her get away a second time.

7

Lijah had decided not to head straight to his mother's house to visit his Aunt Claire when he got back to Port Kara. He'd known he wasn't ready to stay in the house, but he'd been planning to see her as soon as he could, until Claire had told him that journalists were watching the place night and day. And they'd been following her when she went out too.

'I feel like Julia Roberts in *Notting Hill*, except I look more like Jimmy Krankie.' She'd laughed at her own comparison, and the warmth in her tone made Lijah smile for the first time in what felt like months. He had no idea who Jimmy Krankie was, but just hearing his aunt's voice made the aching homesickness that had threatened to overwhelm him recede a little bit.

Nick had managed to find them a house to rent, with the sort of security Lijah needed. He would have loved something more low-key than the sprawling clifftop property owned by tech billionaire, Luke Stanford, and his actress wife, Becks. It was exactly the sort of place you'd expect to find a celebrity living, but Nick had reassured Lijah that as far as the press knew, Luke and Becks were still living there and no one would bother him. It wasn't his sort of place at all. It was beautiful in its own way and the sweeping wall of glass on the side of the house that overlooked the sea gave way to breath-taking views, but somehow there was no heart in it. Port Kara had become popular with the rich and famous in the decade or so since Lijah had moved away, and he sometimes wondered if he'd have left at all if there'd been a chance to connect with people from the music industry back then. All he wanted was for people to listen to his music, and to be able to perform for an audience who'd chosen to be there to watch him, rather than one who'd quite frankly rather be left to their pints and scampi in a basket.

It would have been a lie to say he'd never dreamed of having a number one album, but he didn't believe there were many musicians who hadn't. What he had never really thought about was the downside that came with that sort of exposure, until it happened. Over the past few years it had become harder and harder for him to just be Lijah, the boy who wrote songs to heal the pain he'd been through growing up, and who spent every summer busking down by the harbour in Port Kara. That had been his first real stage, when a handful of people would show up on a regular basis just to listen to his music, singing and dancing along to some of the songs when they got to know them, and the passersby who'd stop for much longer than they'd planned, sometimes putting money into his open guitar case. Lately he'd found himself wondering if that was when he'd been happiest, but maybe he was looking back on it all through rose-coloured glasses. In his mind, every day back then had been sunny and the ones where he'd had to abandon his spot by the harbour, due to a relentless downpour, had somehow been forgotten. He didn't think about the times when he'd found bottle tops, foreign coins, half-sucked lollipops and a whole lot worse in his guitar case. Or the occasional rowdy person who'd heckle him or try to grab the microphone for their own rendition. Instead, he pictured Nick, always there to help out whenever he was needed, just like he was now, and Amy, the girl he'd written every song for back then, and whose face had been the only one he wanted to see when he looked out into the small crowd. They'd kept in touch for a little while, but she'd insisted they needed a clean break while he tried to make it big.

By the time he got his first record deal, she'd long since stopped responding to the messages he'd sent her. He'd kept trying at first, but then life had got busier and busier, meeting new people every day, whose names he'd never remember. He'd never forgotten about Amy though, and he'd often thought about getting back in touch, especially lately. But she was a part of that perfectly curated past that he'd conjured up in his head. And just like busking down by the harbour would feel completely different now, so would seeing Amy again. Still, that fantasy of what his life had been like had been one of the things that kept him going through his darkest days in the past year, and he didn't want to shatter that illusion.

Amy had written Lijah a lovely letter when his mother had died, which his aunt had passed on to him. According to Claire, Amy had been at the funeral, but he hadn't seen her. The press intrusion had made a terrible day even harder, and he'd barely had the chance to speak to anyone. There'd been over two hundred people at the funeral and even more who'd sent messages of sympathy; of all the messages he'd received, Amy's had meant the most. She'd written about Maria in a way that showed just how well she'd known his mother and she'd sent photographs too, of the four of them at an eighties revival music festival, in the summer before he left Port Kara, and his longing to go back to those days had been a physical ache. No one would have believed him if he'd told them he'd swap everything he had just to be back there, with his mum, Claire and Amy, but he truly would have done. In a heartbeat. He'd considered writing back, but once again the thought of shattering some of his happiest memories had stopped him.

'You look terrible.' Nick pushed his sunglasses down his nose and stared at Lijah over the top of them.

'Thanks, you're too kind.'

'You're welcome and I mean every word.' Nick grinned. 'Although seriously, mate, I think you need to get some fresh air. If someone leaked a photo of you right now, it would be all over the papers that you've sunk into a pit of drug addiction. You look like a poster boy for it.'

'Unless you count popping these every five minutes, I think I'm in the clear.' Lijah held up a packet of indigestion tablets that some might argue he was getting an addiction to. But he'd had two weeks of rehab and he hadn't gone back to any of the prescription medications after that. So if swallowing Rennies like they were Smarties was his biggest vice, he figured he was doing okay. He had to do it, to try and counter the constant feeling of nausea in the pit of his stomach, and he'd have eaten them by the shovel load if he'd thought it might help. It was like that feeling of dread right before an exam, or root canal surgery, except it never eased off. He'd seen several doctors, who all said it was down to the same thing: anxiety. The trouble was they all had the same solution for it, and he didn't want to go down the route of medicating for something like that, not after what had happened before. The only trouble was, he wasn't prepared to do the other thing all the doctors had suggested either, and try to get to the root cause of the problem. He'd decided a long time ago that talking therapy wasn't for him.

Music was usually the only kind of therapy Lijah needed, but even that didn't seem to be working now. He couldn't open all those old wounds, not without knowing for certain that he could close them again and all the attempts he'd made to start work on his third album had come to nothing. He just wanted to ride it out here, back home in Port Kara, until writing music started to work for him again. Cornwall had always inspired him, right from the start, and he was counting on it to do that again.

'You can bring your antacids with you. I just think we should get out for a decent walk.' Nick had always been like a pent-up animal if he wasn't doing something. Lijah had lost count of the number of times teachers had kicked Nick out of the classroom for fidgeting, moving about, or talking when he was supposed to be listening. He had an impulsivity sometimes too, like hiding one of the teacher's handbags to get a laugh, which had resulted in his suspension. He always needed to be doing something, his brain and his body so active that at one time he'd seemed scarily capable of self-destruction if he wasn't kept occupied. Lijah had insisted that Nick see someone, worrying that his friend might be heading for a breakdown, and Nick had been diagnosed with ADHD. The medication he now took helped, but for him the best medicine still seemed to be keeping active. Nick's energy levels made him perfect to be Lijah's roadie and latterly his head of security. He was naturally on high alert, but it meant that he was struggling with the current enforced confinement, and even though Lijah had been planning to try and do some writing, he could accept that his best friend's suggestion of a walk might be good for both of them.

'Okay, but when you say a *decent* walk, what are you talking about? I'm not sure I'm up for a hike to Lizard Point and back.' It would have been over a hundred miles, and Lijah didn't think for a minute that Nick would really want to go that far, but he had been running marathons for the past five years, and was currently in the process of training for an ultra-marathon that would cover a hundred kilometres. Lijah's training consisted of being fit enough to get through a two-hour show, but even then he was no Taylor Swift, and it mostly involved him standing with a guitar, or sitting at a piano. No one wanted to see his attempt at dancing.

'Just along the coastal path. If we turn right out of the gate that goes down to the private beach, we can carry on towards the harbour and on to Port Agnes, or fork right and head towards Port Tremellien. I promise it will be doable, even for someone of your delicate disposition.' Nick grinned again.

'All right, all right, give me five minutes, but if it's any longer than ten miles you'll have to carry me back.'

'It won't be the first time mate, and I doubt very much it'll be the last either.' Nick laughed, but Lijah's expression was serious as he turned to look at him.

'I've always been able to rely on you and I want you to know how grateful I am.'

'Jeez, we better go out before you start trying to hug me, or I start spilling my guts about how grateful I am to you for changing my life when no one else wanted to give me a chance. At that rate, we'll be having a good cry together before we've even had lunch.' Nick rolled his eyes. 'You've got ten minutes to get your arse outside, ready to walk, otherwise I'm ringing the press and telling them everything I know, and I know way too much.'

'That's true, but remember not all of that reflects well on you either.' It was Lijah's turn to laugh, and all Nick could do in response was shrug. They'd been through so much together over the years, and he was incredibly grateful to have always had his friend by his side. Never more so than in the months since he'd lost his mother.

* * *

'Who needs Malibu when you've got this?' Nick's question would have sounded sarcastic to anyone who couldn't see the view they could, but in Lijah's opinion the Cornish Atlantic coast was impossible to beat, especially on a beautiful spring day. Jagged cliffs rose up out of teal blue waters, their tops carpeted in what looked and felt like dark green velvet. He'd taken the beauty for granted when he was younger, and it was hard to believe now that he'd once thought of the place where he'd grown up as suffocating.

'I think I should get a dog.' Lijah could see a woman in the distance, walking with what he'd so far counted as at least four dogs. She was throwing a ball for them, with one of those launching devices which sent the dogs into a frenzy of excitement each time she threw her arm back. Their sheer joy was enough to lift anyone's spirits. His mother had got the first family dog, a corgi called Colin, the summer after Lijah turned six. He suspected now that it had been a way of distracting him when his father's promise to take him on holiday had come to nothing. Either way, Colin had been adored and when he'd died from cancer when Lijah was fourteen, the whole family had been devastated. It had taken them almost a year before they'd felt ready to get another dog. This time a cross-breed called Buster had been welcomed into their lives. He'd been the personification of joy, his whole body wagging when his tail did. He'd made it to thirteen and Maria had been even more devastated this time around, given that Buster had become her substitute child after Lijah had left home to pursue his career. She hadn't even wanted to talk about getting another dog for the first eighteen months, and Lijah had been about to broach the subject with her again when she'd died. He'd wished with all his heart that she had got a dog before her death, so that there'd have been something of her left to cling on to when she was no longer there. Since leaving home, it had never been the right time for him to get a dog of his own. He was on the road far too much, but now that he was home, it suddenly felt like something he might be able to think about.

'So you're planning to stay then?' Nick was doing a really good job of keeping his tone neutral. If he thought Lijah was crazy to consider staying in Cornwall long term, there was nothing in his expression that would have given his feelings away. As to whether he'd want to hang around if that turned out to be the case, Lijah wasn't sure. Nick still had a large extended family in the area, but he'd embraced a life where they'd spent much of their time in the States and up until recently he'd had a long-term girlfriend out there too. Lijah had never admitted he hadn't liked Aurelia, but she'd talked down to Nick and had seemed to spend most of her time trying to turn him into something he wasn't.

When Aurelia had met an actor who apparently ticked all her boxes without the need for a major overhaul, she'd left Nick for him. The one upside to Nick's heartbreak was that there was no reason now why he couldn't stay in Cornwall with Lijah, at least in the short term. But he had his own life to live and Lijah wouldn't hold his decision against him, whatever he chose to do.

'I'll be staying for now. At least until I'm writing again and the thought of performing doesn't make me want to lock myself into a dark room.'

'What if that never happens?' There was a flicker of something that looked at lot like concern on Nick's face.

'I'll find something else to do.' Lijah shrugged as if it was nothing, but the truth was it was impossible to imagine a life without music at the centre of it. He couldn't think that far ahead. 'Maybe I could ask her for a job.'

He gestured towards the woman who by now was only about fifty metres away. She was wearing a black T-shirt with the words 'Dolly's Dog Walking' in white letters on the front, with a mobile number he couldn't make out printed beneath it.

'Or you could start up in competition with her. Lijah's Leads has got a ring to it.' Nick grinned and Lijah had been about to respond, when a huge, black dog charged past him, barking furiously as it hurtled towards the dog walker. Seconds later, one of the other dogs cried out in pain as the larger dog – which Lijah could now see was a Rottweiler – grabbed it by the scruff of the neck and started throwing it around like a ragdoll.

'Get off, get off him.' The woman was screaming so loudly, it almost drowned out the sound of the little dog's cries, and the frenzied barking of the other three dogs she'd been looking after.

Lijah had already broken into a sprint, with Nick right behind him, and he reached the woman within seconds.

'He's going to kill him, help me, please.' Tears had streaked the woman's mascara and, even as she spoke, she tried lashing out at the Rottweiler, who didn't even seem to notice her.

'Shall we call the police?' Nick turned towards Lijah, who shook his head.

'It'll be too late by then.' He didn't even really have time to think about what he was doing and he knew it was probably a stupid mistake, but he couldn't bear the sight of the little dog getting hurt even more than it already was. He made a grab for the Rottweiler's snout, trying desperately to prize its jaws apart, even as a searing pain seemed to pass through his hand and up his arm. There were so many voices and so much commotion. He could make out Nick shouting at him to let go, but he couldn't, because the dog had a vice-like grip on him too.

'Deisel drop! Let go, let go now.' Another shout filled the air and for a moment nothing happened. Then, as the instruction to let go was repeated again, the Rottweiler suddenly released the little dog and Lijah from its grasp.

'Christ, Lij. What the hell did you do that for? It could have killed you, and... Oh my God, look at your hand.' All the colour had drained from Nick's face and, as Lijah looked down, he understood why. His right hand was covered with blood that dripped down towards his elbow, a small puddle of it already marring the carpet of green beneath their feet.

'Oh Monty, sweetheart, I'm sorry, I'm so sorry.' The dog walker was wrapping the little Jack Russell in the hoodie that had been tied around her waist. Looking up at the others, her eyes were filled with tears. 'I haven't got the car; we came straight from home and I've got to get him to the vet as soon as I can.'

'We'll drive you. It'll only take minutes for me to go back to the house.' Lijah made the offer, ignoring the throbbing pain in his hand. Nick could do the driving, it didn't matter as long as they got the little dog the help it needed.

'Lij, you need to get to the hospital.' Nick's tone was uncharacteristically firm, cutting off the dog walker before she could even respond.

'I'm fine.'

'No you're not.'

'We'll get the dog to the vets.' A middle-aged woman with a poodle under her arm walked over to them. 'Our car is on Beach Lane, about two minutes' walk from here.'

'Thank you, but I don't know what to do about the other dogs.' The woman cradling Monty in her arms still had tears running down her cheeks.

'We can take them back to our place, it's just off the coastal path.' Lijah shot his friend a look when Nick started to protest, hoping he understood the deal he was about to offer, without him spelling it out. '*After* that I'll get my hand looked at.'

'Oh my God!' The woman with the poodle looked at him for the first time. 'Aren't you—'

'I'm Eli and this is Nick.' It wasn't a lie. His birth name was Elijah, and he still used it when he didn't want to be instantly recognised by his name alone. He turned towards the dog walker, who looked to be in her late twenties. 'I take it you're Dolly?'

'Yes, but I'm not supposed to let anyone else look after the dogs. I promised their owners that I'd take care of them myself, it's why they trust me.' The tears started to come even faster, and Lijah wanted to give her a hug, but they needed to get Monty to the vets right away.

'I'm sure they'll understand. I promise we won't let anything happen to the other dogs, but right now I think your priority needs to be Monty.'

'Okay, thank you.' She mumbled the words and Lijah turned as the man behind him spoke.

'I tried to get the owner of the Rottweiler to stop, but he just ran up the hill with that bloody animal. I've seen them out here before and I had to scoop Susie up before that dog went for her.'

The woman holding the poodle shook her head. 'Disgusting. It wants putting down.'

'More like the owner does.' Dolly looked up. 'I'm just so glad you were all here, especially you.'

She turned towards Lijah and the woman with the poodle

nodded. 'You were a real hero. I hate to think what would have happened if you hadn't stepped in.'

Lijah didn't respond. The last thing he could be described as was a hero. He'd run away from a life most people could only dream of in order to come home, but he hadn't even had the courage to face his aunt yet, or truly face up to the fact that his mother no longer lived in the cottage he'd bought her. He wasn't a hero, he was a coward.

8

Lijah had tried to persuade Nick that all he needed was a couple of plasters and a bit of Savlon, but his old friend was having none of it.

'I know you don't think you want to perform again at the moment Lij, but do you really want to let your hand get into such a state that the option is taken away from you? And if it drops off altogether, I'm not volunteering to wipe your bum.'

'What if I put it in your job description?' Lijah couldn't help smiling despite the pain in his hand.

'Didn't know I still had a job.' Nick frowned and Lijah felt a stab of guilt. Walking out on the tour didn't just affect him, it had an impact on so many people. But Lijah had felt like he was drowning. He couldn't think too much about the ripple effect of his decision, otherwise he might never get back on track. Whatever happened, Nick would be okay, Lijah would make sure of that.

'Of course you have. If I do decide to quit, I'll think of something else we can do together. Maybe we could start a little landscaping business.' Lijah widened his eyes, anticipating Nick's response before it came, but the truth was he was only half joking. The thought of facing life without his best friend by his side seemed impossible, even if it would be incredibly selfish to ask Nick to stay.

'Lij, I love you, but you were not made for manual labour. You're far too delicate for that. I mean, Christ, we go for a walk and look at the state of you.'

'At least I know I've got one real friend who isn't paid to hang out with me because they'd sugarcoat the truth.'

'You don't have to pay anyone to hang out with you, buddy, they're queuing at the door.'

'It's not *me* they want to hang out with, it's...' He still cringed at using the word celebrity, or pop star. Somehow, despite all the fame and his undeniable success, he still felt like the same old Lijah deep down, the kid busking for bottle tops in the harbour. 'It's the lifestyle that appeals to them, the smoke and mirrors. None of them know the real me.'

It had become so hard to trust anyone over the past few years and to know whether the people who gravitated towards Lijah were genuine. Some of them just wanted to raise their own profile. When his second album had come out and the PR team at his record label had been determined it should exceed the success of his first, he'd been put in touch with the manager of another singer, Lucillia Rodriguez, who'd asked if he'd be interested in staging a faux romance over the summer. He'd been so gobsmacked, he hadn't been able to respond at first. Lucillia's manager had clearly taken that as the green light to outline the specifics. According to him, it was simple. They needed to be photographed together as much as possible over the summer, including some sufficiently intimate moments to fool the press and the public that their romance was real. An early denial of the romance would help add fuel to the fire. It would raise both their profiles, the manager said, perhaps even more so when they went their separate ways after a few months.

It was such a cynical idea and he didn't want to raise his profile, he wanted to be as anonymous as it was possible for a successful singer to be, so that he had the chance of making a genuine connection with someone again one day, because the truth was he did want a relationship. He wanted someone he couldn't wait to get back to. As it stood, the only person who fitted that bill was Nick and he couldn't keep expecting his old friend to put his own life on hold forever. Nick was great at what he did, and he'd had other performers approaching him over the years, but he'd never taken them on, so that he could be at Lijah's beck and call. This could be his opportunity to branch out, maybe meet someone new too, but Lijah knew Nick wouldn't even contemplate doing that until he was confident that Lijah would be okay without him. Part of him wanted to tell Nick that he didn't need to hang around for his benefit, except they'd both have known it wasn't true. He just needed a bit of time, that was all, but Nick needed to know it wouldn't be forever.

'I'm going to work out what I really want from life, that's the point of all of this.' Lijah gestured around him, indicating the reason why he'd rented the house that was three times the size of some of the venues he'd played in the early days. 'But you've got to work out what it is you really want, too.'

'I know exactly what I want to do.' Nick's expression was serious and nerves gripped Lijah. He desperately wanted his best friend to have the life he deserved, but the thought of not seeing him any more was already making his stomach churn. He forced himself to ask anyway.

'Really, what's that?'

'I want to get you to the hospital. After that we can work out the rest.'

'Okay.' Lijah nodded. His hand was still throbbing with pain, and he could tell how hot it was without even touching it. He could have called a private doctor, or gone to the nearest private hospital, but if he was going to try and build a new life for himself and learn to blend into the background the way he wanted to, he might as well start as he meant to go on.

* * *

Amy gave the woman who'd approached her to complain about waiting times a tight smile. Summer in Port Kara meant that the emergency department was busier than ever, but it had been a surprisingly quiet morning and the reason the woman had needed to wait slightly longer was because she'd been triaged as not needing urgent care. Amy was tempted to tell the patient, whose name was Chantelle, that she could make an appointment to see her GP to get some antibiotics for her problem if she didn't want to wait. Chantelle had an infected piercing in her ear, which she'd had done by a friend using a sewing needle and an ice cube when they'd had 'a few too many'. She was next to be seen, and Amy had been just about to call her name when Chantelle had come barrelling towards her, firing out her dissatisfaction so close to Amy's face that she could smell the stale booze on the other woman's breath.

'This place is a joke. You could drop dead before you got seen, what's the hold up for God's sake? It's like a morgue out here.'

'It is quiet today, but we still have to triage patients based on urgency and unfortunately there were other patients who needed to be seen in front of you, but I'm ready to see you now. If you'd like to come through, we can—'

As she spoke, Chantelle's phone began to ring, and she held up a finger to silence Amy.

'Hi hun!' There was a pause as the person on the other end of the line spoke, before Chantelle started again. 'Yeah it's a freaking nightmare, still waiting to be seen... I know, I know, what the hell do we pay our taxes for? I bet if I'd just turned up in the country I'd be seen straight away.'

Amy could feel the blood pulsing through her veins. It wasn't like this was the first time she'd heard a line like that, but it never made it any easier to hear. She was even more tempted now to tell Chantelle to go home and stop using an emergency department for something that could easily be dealt with in the community. There were other things she wanted to say too, like the fact that there would be no NHS without the many staff who came to the UK from other countries to work in an organisation that would grind to a halt without them. Sometimes it was really hard to treat all patients the same.

Amy had cared for an elderly widower just the day before, whose eyes had filled with tears when he'd talked about how lonely he was since the death of his wife. She'd wanted to take Albert home with her and look after him. He'd been so grateful to everyone and after one of the porters, Darius, had exchanged a joke with him, he'd told Amy it was the most fun he'd had in weeks. It had made her so sad that Albert felt that way and she'd spoken to Esther to see if there was anything they could do. Esther's mum, Caroline, volunteered for a befriending service in the community and by the time Albert left A&E, Amy and Esther had arranged for Caroline to go and see him, with a view to matching him up with a regular visitor from the service. There were various other activities Albert could get involved with too, all of which could help alleviate the loneliness he was clearly feeling. He'd still been on Amy's mind hours after she'd got home, but it had been the kind of day that made her feel as if she really could make a difference. Sadly, there were days when her job felt far more thankless and, courtesy of Chantelle, today felt like one of them.

'Yeah I'll be there, what time?' Chantelle paused again, listening to whatever was being said in response, and Amy's patience finally snapped.

'If you've got things you'd rather do than get your ear looked at, I suggest you go to see your GP at a more convenient time.' She couldn't keep the sarcasm out of her voice and in truth she didn't even try. Chantelle gave a heavy sigh and rolled her eyes in response.

'Better go, they're finally calling me in, and the nurse is giving me evils.' Chantelle laughed then at something the caller must have said in response. Digging her nails into the palm of her hand, Amy took a deep breath, really having to fight the urge now to tell Chantelle what she thought of her, especially when the conversation with the caller started up again. Amy had been just about to turn and walk away, when she spotted a commotion in the corner of the waiting area.

'Oh my God, I can't believe it's you!' The words of a teenage girl on the far side of the room were followed up by a high-pitched shriek, and then a question at almost as high a volume. 'Can I get a selfie?'

'Now's not really the time.' Amy was almost certain she recognised the voice, a split second before Nick turned slightly to the side, and any doubts she'd had about it being him vanished. If Nick was here, and people were asking for autographs, that could only mean one thing: Lijah was here too.

'It's fine, I can do a quick photo.' Lijah's voice was even more familiar, his gentle tone whisking her back to whispered exchanges as they lay in his bed, more than a decade before.

'Lij, your hand is still bleeding. I really don't think now is the time.' Nick's tone was insistent, but Lijah was already having his photograph taken alongside the excited young girl, who was pulling poses worthy of a professional model.

'Right that's it.' Nick caught hold of Lijah's left arm, and Amy could see the right one wrapped in a white towel that was stained with bright red blood. Ignoring the fact that Chantelle had now ended her call and was demanding to know where Amy was going, she moved towards them.

'My friend has been attacked by a dog and—' That was as far as Nick got before he registered that it was Amy standing in front of him, but Lijah was still half turned away, trying to placate the young girl who was begging him for just one more picture.

'Oh my God, Ames. Long time no see.' As Nick smiled broadly, Lijah spun around, his eyes meeting hers, and she desperately wanted to say something that sounded nonchalant and cool, but instead her mouth dropped open. It was much the same response she'd had the first time she'd ever seen him in the queue for the canteen in the first week of secondary school. Up until that point she'd still thought of boys as smelly and annoying, her older brother Nathan being the example by which she judged all males of the species, but Lijah had changed all that. It had been five long years before they'd become a couple, but that hadn't stopped her imagining, as an awkward eleven-year-old, in a too-big blazer, what it might be like to kiss him. She hadn't even reached the stage where she practised kissing on the back of her hand at that point, or by pressing her lips up against a poster of Justin Timberlake. All of that came later, but Lijah wasn't just her first ever boyfriend, he was her first ever crush. So the chances of her acting coolly around him, even after all this time, were almost nil.

'Your hand's bleeding.' Talk about stating the obvious. Lijah gave her one of his slow smiles, which still had the ability to make her lose the power of speech. Chantelle had followed her over and was now describing the oozing of her ear to her friend on the phone, completely unaware that Amy was having a conversation with Lijah Byrne.

'Yes, it's bleeding, but thankfully I'm in the right place, with just the right person to help me out.' Lijah locked eyes with Amy.

'You are.' As she spoke, a small crowd began to gather around them. Chantelle finally ended her phone call, having realised who Lijah was and clearly not wanting to miss out.

'It's my turn next and no special treatment here.' Chantelle nudged Lijah with her hip in a far too intimate gesture between strangers. 'But I'm more than happy to share my cubicle with you.'

'No need.' Aidan had suddenly appeared out of nowhere, his eyes widening as they met Amy's and he silently mouthed the words, 'Your hot ex.'

She knew he'd have plenty of questions for her later, but for now she was trying not to give away just how much Lijah's presence was affecting her. Amy forced herself to maintain a neutral expression, as Aidan turned towards Chantelle. 'You can come with me, we'll soon have that septic ear sorted out.'

'For Christ's sake!' Chantelle looked outraged that her very unattractive ailment had been shared within earshot of Lijah Byrne. 'Don't you have to take some kind of oath to keep things confidential? It's no wonder the NHS is in such a state with nurses like you two.'

'Don't worry we'd already spotted your ear from across the room.' Nick gave her a cool look.

'Not to mention overhearing your phone call about just how much oozing there was. I think we all forget how lucky we are that there are people selfless enough to deal with that kind of stuff, don't we?' Lijah shrugged, but there was a twinkle in his eye that Amy would have recognised anywhere. He was always the sort of person who stood up for others and it seemed that was one thing fame hadn't changed.

'Right, I think we ought to get that hand sorted out.' Amy desperately tried to suppress a smile, but she didn't quite manage it. Lijah and Nick had always made her laugh, and she had a feeling that would help them overcome any awkwardness there might be at seeing each other again after so long. She was always happy to find a reason to smile on a long shift, but she had no idea how hard that was about to become.

* * *

Nick had gone off in what he alleged was a search for a decent cup of coffee, but Amy couldn't help noticing it had coincided with her starting to clean Lijah's wound.

'How did you manage to get yourself into this?' She kept her attention on Lijah's hand as she spoke.

'Trying to do a good deed and separate fighting dogs. You know me, I always was one to act before I thought it through.' Lijah's tone was light, but she had to disagree. He'd always been thoughtful, the type of deep thinker who felt things so deeply they hurt. Lijah had known the pain of rejection from a very young age. Amy understood the pressure he felt not to let his mother see how much his father's behaviour had bothered him at times, lessening her pain by burying his own. He'd learnt to deal with it, but now he'd lost his beloved mother it was obvious there was a deep vein of sadness just below the happy-go-lucky exterior. He'd told Amy once that music was the only therapy he needed and his ability to translate that pain into something other people could connect with was almost certainly at the root of his success. Although the things she'd read lately worried her: rumours about him unravelling and planning to give up on music. It was like breathing in and out for him, and she couldn't imagine a version of Lijah without music in his life.

'I wouldn't say that, and whether you think things through or not, it's clearly paid off. I know how proud your mum was of everything you've achieved. She was such a lovely lady and I can only imagine how hard it's been for you since she died. I'm sorry I didn't get a chance to talk to you at her funeral and to tell you how much she meant to me.' Amy might have stepped out of Lijah's life, but she'd remained a part of his mother's right up until the end, and she knew Maria had valued that as much as she had.

'Sometimes I feel like I've lost my son, but I'm so glad I haven't lost you too.' Maria had made the admission to Amy once, her eyes filling with tears. Lijah had another life, a world away from Port Kara, one that didn't involve sitting on the sofa listening to hits from the eighties any more. She'd told Maria she felt the same and had made her and Claire promise not to tell Lijah they still met up on a regular basis. Amy had even driven Maria to appointments when she'd broken her wrist two summers before. She'd done it out of genuine affection, but she hadn't wanted it to make things awkward when Maria saw Lijah. On the day of her funeral, Amy had been desperate to talk to Lijah, to tell him just how much his mum had meant to her, but there had been journalists everywhere and he'd been surrounded by a wall of security all day, so she'd had to put it all in a letter instead.

'Thank you, your letter meant a lot to me. Mum was very fond of you too.' Lijah hesitated, forcing her to look up. 'I found quite a few photos of the two of you together.'

'That's nice, although all the photographs of that haircut I had in the second year of sixth form should probably be destroyed.' She laughed, but he shook his head.

'No, I mean much more recent photos than that.' He reached out briefly with his uninjured hand, her skin tingling where his fingers had touched the back of her hand, long after he'd removed them. 'Thank you for taking the time out to spend time with her, from what my aunt said it was always the highlight of her week when it happened.'

Of all the things she'd anticipated him saying, this wasn't one of them. She'd expected him to ask why they were still in touch, but he didn't. She wanted to explain anyway. 'It was the highlight of my week too. I missed your mum after you left and when I bumped into her in town a few months after, she told me she'd bought some more vinyl records she wanted me to listen to.'

'She probably bought them as an excuse to see you. I know she missed you too, because she told me.' He smiled and it took every ounce of self-restraint not to tell him how much she'd missed him after he'd left. She'd been determined not to be that person at nineteen, so she sure as hell wasn't going to be that person now she was thirty. Suddenly his face changed, the smile turning into something she couldn't quite define. It wasn't a frown, there was more torment to it than that. It was a kind of melancholy that was obvious even before his voice caught on his next words. 'I just wish I'd taken more time out to spend with her, now I'll never get the chance.'

'She knew how much you loved her, and she was so incredibly proud of you.' It was Amy's turn to reach out and, when she did, Lijah clasped her hand with his uninjured one, his fingers closing around hers. It was a gesture that felt so familiar and yet so alien, all at the same time.

'I found a whole photo album she put together from my sixteenth birthday party, do you remember that night?' His face was so open, but she wanted to ask him how he could even question it. That night had changed everything between them, it had changed her whole life, even the person she was now, but all she could do was nod.

'Of course I remember. It's still one of the best parties I've ever been to.'

'Me too.' She furrowed her brow. It was still *the* best party she'd ever been to, not one of them, but Lijah must have been to thousands of swanky parties. There was no way he felt the same about an eighties-themed disco in the village hall, but when she looked into his eyes she suddenly wasn't so sure.

'The album wasn't just photos either.' Lijah's eyes locked with hers as he spoke. 'She'd kept one of the invitations and even the card the DJ had used to advertise. It was such a great night, but it would never have happened without you.'

'I didn't do much.' She attempted a shrug, but he was already shaking his head.

'Yes, you did. You got me and Mum to be honest with each other for the first time in a long time.'

It had been a simple enough question when Amy had asked Lijah what he was doing for his birthday, as they'd sat side by side on the sofa about a month before he was due to turn sixteen.

'Not a lot, I never make a big fuss about it.' Lijah had attempted to sound nonchalant, but an expression had flitted across his face which Amy didn't miss.

'Why not? Sixteen is a big milestone, it's when you're...' She'd caught his eye then and her face had flushed red, because she'd been about to mention the fact that Lijah would have been legally allowed to have sex. But she didn't want him knowing that she thought about him in that way, when he only saw her as a friend. In her desperation to come up with an alternative ending to her sentence, she'd blurted out something that had made him laugh. 'You're allowed to buy cigarettes.'

'Not sure that's a traditional reason for throwing a party to celebrate.' He'd smiled in the way that seemed to transform his whole face, but the smile had slid away just as quickly. 'The reason I don't like to make a big thing of it is because the catalyst for my father walking out of our lives happened on my tenth birthday. He only came back once more after that and he caused a massive scene. So I prefer to play it down. I don't need any reminders of my father and neither does Mum.'

Amy's heart had ached for him. Lijah was her best friend and he'd been there for her when she'd been bullied by some of the other girls in her year. She really wanted to be able to do something nice for his birthday, to thank him for all he'd done for her, but she didn't want to bring back any painful memories. So, when Maria had confided in her that she wished Lijah would let her organise something to mark his sixteenth birthday, Amy had bitten her lip, not sure whether to tell Maria she had it wrong. But Maria had seen the expression that must have crossed Amy's face and had coaxed the truth out of her. When Maria discovered the real reason that Lijah had always insisted on not having a birthday celebration, she was determined to mark his sixteenth in the kind of style that would make up for years of low-key days, and she'd roped Amy in to make sure they got it right.

'I've always been the interfering sort, never afraid to stick my nose in someone else's business.' Amy smiled at him now, making a joke the way she so often did when emotions suddenly heightened. 'I think it's part of what makes me a good nurse.'

'I bet you're a great nurse, but then I knew you would be.' She didn't doubt his words; Lijah had supported her dreams every bit as much as she'd supported his, but then again, most people would argue that it was far easier to become a nurse than it was a successful musician. When she looked up at him, he was still holding her gaze. 'I always knew it was the right decision for you to choose nursing, but when we were together, I couldn't help wishing that you wouldn't.'

'We were so young, it would never have lasted either way.' She gave him a half smile, her words coming out with far more conviction than she felt, because there was a huge part of her that couldn't help wondering what might have happened if she'd taken a leap of faith when he'd left for London, just like she had on the night of the party. She'd had to take the risk of losing their friendship, so that they could become so much more and, despite how it ended, she wouldn't have traded their three years together for anything.

One of the things she'd loved most about Lijah was that he'd never been afraid to let people see just how much his mum and his aunt meant to him. He hadn't been remotely embarrassed at the fact that the two women had spent most of the night on the dancefloor at his sixteenth birthday party. Lijah had happily joined them and watching him up there Amy could no longer pretend she just *liked* Lijah, her feelings for him were much bigger than that. But she was realistic enough to know she didn't stand a chance with someone like him, or at least that's what she'd thought. Even when he'd come to her at the end of the party to thank her for helping his mother organise it, she had no idea what was about to happen. It was probably for the best, because if she'd thought he was going to kiss her she might have freaked out. When Lijah had suddenly leaned forward and tucked a stray strand of hair behind her ear, her heart had been thudding so hard she was sure he must be able to hear it.

'You're the best girl here, Ames. You know that, don't you?' His voice had been low. 'I just wanted to say how much I enjoyed tonight, and it was all because of you.'

'It was mostly your mum, I just helped with—'

'I didn't mean organising it.' Lijah had cut her off, putting a hand on her bare arm, his touch lighting her up from the inside and she hadn't trusted herself to speak. 'I like you Amy, and there's no one I enjoy spending time with more than you.'

She'd frozen to the spot then, not wanting to risk making a fool of herself by taking a step forward if she'd somehow misread the signs. Instead Lijah had closed the gap between them and, when he kissed her, it was everything she thought it might be and more. She knew they were risking their friendship, but it had been a chance she'd needed to take and, in that moment, she wasn't sure she could have stopped herself, because it was something she'd wanted for so long. There hadn't been a moment when she'd regretted that kiss, not even in the aftermath of their breakup when even saying his name had hurt more than she'd ever have believed. Torturing herself with what ifs would be a whole new form of torture, and it wasn't a path she was going to allow herself to go down, especially when Lijah would almost certainly disappear from her life again just as quickly as he had reappeared.

'We didn't give ourselves a chance to find out whether or not it would last.' There was something in his eyes she couldn't quite read, but the corners of his mouth were twitching, as if he might be trying not to laugh. She was the girl who'd loved him from afar, for years before he'd even noticed her, and now here she was again, going all gooey eyed over the memory that probably meant far less to him than it had to her, despite what he might have said. Either way, she wasn't here to amuse Lijah Byrne, she had a job to do, one she was very good at. Withdrawing her hand from his, Amy took a step back. He spent his whole life with people fawning over him, but she wasn't about to become one of them. He needed medical attention, not to have his ego inflated even further by the thought that she'd never got over him.

'It wouldn't have worked and thankfully I figured that out pretty quickly.' Her tone was cool and his mouth turned downwards in response, but he didn't have a chance to reply, as Nick yanked back the curtain of the cubicle and came in.

'Coffee's up.'

'Perfect timing, thanks Nick.' Amy arranged her face into what felt like a smile, but she couldn't be sure. She'd lowered her guard with Lijah by reminiscing about the night of his party, but she was already wishing she hadn't. Nothing about his lifestyle seemed genuine to her and it was almost impossible to believe that anyone who pursued that kind of life could be genuine either. Only a fool would think the last decade hadn't changed him beyond all recognition. 'I've cleaned Lijah's wound, but I want the surgeons to take a look at it to see if any of the tendons or ligaments need surgical intervention. Then we'll have to work out if he needs a tetanus shot, or if he's already up to date.'

'Where does that go, in his bum?' Nick laughed and Amy responded with a genuine smile this time.

'It can be arranged.' She tried to look more serious for a moment. 'For you too, if you don't behave yourself.'

'I'll be good I promise.' Nick grinned again, and inclined his head towards the coffees he was holding. 'I even tracked you down a mocha, I'm assuming you're still a chocaholic, Amy?'

'Guilty as charged. You must be used to Lijah's every wish being your command.' There was an edge to her voice that she couldn't stop from creeping in. She was on the defensive, but she didn't want Lijah to think he impressed her. He probably hadn't got a coffee for himself in years, but that didn't make him any more special than her other patients.

'He's pretty low maintenance actually, although he's still a teabag snob and it's always got to be Yorkshire.' If Nick was offended by her jibe about his job he didn't show it. 'You'd never believe he was born and bred around here the way he goes on about it.'

'It is pretty hard to believe.'

'Why do I get the feeling that isn't a compliment?' Lijah asked, but before she could respond Nick thrust a family sized packet of Maltesers in her direction.

'I'm glad you still like chocolate, because my decision to buy these for you must make me almost as big a hero as Lij. Although I just took a call from Dolly.' Nick turned towards Lijah and Amy caught her breath at the sound of the familiar name. 'And I don't think buying any amount of chocolate could compete with your heroics. The vet's confident the dog will make it, because of you.'

'Did you say Dolly?' Amy took a step closer to Nick, willing him to shake his head.

'Yes, do you know her?' Nick frowned and nausea swirled in her stomach. It couldn't be Monty. Dolly would have let her know. She asked the question all the same.

'The dog that got attacked... do you know what breed it was?'

'A little Jack Russell, wasn't it?' Nick turned towards Lijah again and he nodded.

'Yes, such a sweet little thing. His name's Monty.'

'Oh my God, are you sure?' Amy was desperate for Lijah to say something to convince her she'd got it wrong, but he was already nodding.

'Are you okay? Do you know whose dog it is?'

'Monty's mine.' Tears were brimming in her eyes as she looked at him again, and he took hold of her hand for a second time.

'I'm so sorry, but it sounds like the news from the vet is positive.'

'He doesn't deserve this.' Amy couldn't stop the tears sliding down her face, and she didn't even try. 'When his old owner was really sick, he lay on her bed for two weeks, only getting up when he absolutely had to. It was like he was making sure she wasn't on her own at the end. He's such a good boy.'

'He'll be okay, I promise. We'll do whatever we need to, and take him wherever he'll get the best treatment.' Lijah's eyes met hers and despite her doubts from just moments before, suddenly she knew she could trust him, just like she'd always been able to. Lijah had never once given her cause to doubt him, despite the numerous opportunities he'd had to go behind her back when they were together. She knew she'd been unfair to him by getting defensive after they'd reminisced about the party, but it came from the same sense of self-preservation that had made her push him away in the first place. Lijah was a good guy, he always had been, and if he said he'd get Monty whatever treatment he might need, she knew he'd keep his word.

'Thank you.' Amy wanted to lean on him for support, as she had so many times before. Lijah had been there through the toughest weeks of her life, after her father had suffered a heart attack, and he'd promised her that everything would be okay then too. He'd been right, and she just hoped to God he was right now, because she'd never forgive herself if anything happened to the little dog she'd promised Joan she'd look after.

9

Gwen leafed through her magazine as she sat in the waiting room of the GP surgery where she'd been a patient for more than forty years. She'd attempted to read the same article three times about how to 'eat clean for a glowing complexion', without taking a single word of it in, when her phone buzzed with a text. It was from Barry.

> Let me know what the doctor says and remember you promised to be honest. Don't just pretend everything is okay, when she asks. We need to get this sorted out and, whatever's wrong, I'll be there for you every step of the way. Love you so much Gee xxxxxxx

He always signed his messages off with seven kisses, one for every decade of Gwen's life. Usually it made her smile to see the string of kisses, but not today. Today all she could think about was what the doctor might say. Even her favourite pastime of people watching held no appeal. She just wanted the next half an hour or so to be over. If her GP suggested she had tests to find out whether or not the symptoms she was experiencing were the early stages of aphasia, she wasn't sure she could go ahead, despite promising Barry she'd do whatever it took to get to the bottom of the problem. He'd wanted to come with her to the appointment, and promising him that she'd be honest with the GP had been the only way to persuade him to stay at home. She didn't want to go back on a promise, because it was one of the foundations of their marriage that they didn't do that. But if it had been possible to cross her fingers at the same time as typing her response, she would have.

I'll tell her everything, I promise. Love you xxx

Gwen flicked over another page in the magazine, flinching as she read the headline of the next article.

Twenty ways to fight dementia before it's too late

What if it's already too late? The voice in her head was back again, outlining her deepest fears as if they hadn't been at the forefront of her mind for weeks. Aphasia was categorised as a form of dementia, but it had its own unique brand of cruelty. Gwen was her mother's daughter in so many ways. Despite living half a mile from her nearest neighbour, Alys Evans had loved people. There was nothing she liked better than a good chat, and would always have a cuppa ready for the postie, the milkman, or anyone else who might venture up to Dyffryn farm.

When aphasia had stolen Alys's words, Gwen had witnessed her mother's frustration, and the inability to communicate was what had made the light go out in Alys's eyes. She was cast adrift, a prisoner in her own body, the words she wanted to say trapped inside her, getting further and further out of reach as time went on.

Gwen's whole life had been built around her love of interacting with other people. The words of encouragement she'd spoken to women in labour, and the advice she dispensed with the sole desire of helping other people feel better about a difficult situation, had felt like her super power. She was self-aware enough to know that sometimes she put her foot in it, but even then she could always try to find a better way of saying what needed to be said. And sometimes things really did need to be said. When other people might shy away from difficult conversations, Gwen never did. It was who she was, except soon it might not be and the thought terrified her.

Gwen Jones to Room 3

The announcement flashed up on the digital screen in front of her and Gwen stuffed the magazine into her bag. It was silly, she knew she wasn't going to get any results today, even if she agreed to be tested, but that didn't stop her legs from trembling as she stood up. For a moment she even considered turning around and walking away. She could pretend to Barry that she'd seen the GP and that the tests had been ordered. What she'd do further down the line she didn't know, but that would be a problem for another day. Despite the urge to run almost taking over, something propelled her forward, and she knocked tentatively on the door to Room 3.

'Come in,' Dr Gustafsson called out, and she looked up and smiled as Gwen pushed open the door, her voice sounding far too upbeat as she continued. 'Hi Gwen, long time, no see. How's retirement suiting you?'

Gwen had got to know Vera Gustafsson quite well over the years, especially during her time at the Port Agnes midwifery unit. Vera was in her late fifties and exuded the sort of warmth that all GPs ought to possess. She cared about her patients, Gwen had experienced that on both a personal and professional basis, and she had a feeling it wouldn't be easy to fob Vera off even if she tried.

'I love it. Three or four shifts a week at the hospital and plenty of time for... other stuff.' Gwen forced a smile, she'd been intending to list some of the things keeping her busy, but the words had disappeared again, like water swirling down a plughole.

'Sounds like nothing's changed, Gwen. Still putting the rest of us to shame!' Vera gestured toward the chair next to her desk. 'Come and take a seat and tell me what I can do for you. I must admit I was surprised to see your name on the list of patients; it's been ages since you've had an appointment.'

'I know how busy you are and it's probably nothing.' Gwen was silently praying she was right, but she had too much medical knowledge to really believe that was true.

'I'm never too busy to see my patients, Gwen, especially one like you.' Vera's tone was gentle but insistent. 'What seems to be the problem?'

'I feel a lot like I did during the menopause.' It wasn't a lie. The confusion that had fogged her brain back then had felt as though it was never going to lift, but it had. There'd been a cure, or at least a solution, that had eventually made her feel more like the old Gwen. She was pinning all her hopes on a similar outcome this time around.

'What kind of symptoms are you having?'

'I just feel...' She hesitated again, knowing that if she crossed the line there would be no going back. Once she knew if she was in the early stages of PPA, she'd never be able to 'un-know' it. She'd have a ticking time bomb in her brain, and there'd be nothing she could do to stop the clock from counting down.

'You can tell me, whatever it is, I guarantee I'll have heard it before.' Vera gave her a sympathetic smile and Gwen took a deep breath.

'I just don't feel like me.'

'Do you mean physically or emotionally?'

'Both, I suppose.' Gwen sighed. 'I've lost all my oomph and I've been struggling to think straight.'

'How long has that been going on?' Vera pushed her glasses up her nose and Gwen swallowed hard. She didn't want to admit just how long she'd been feeling this way.

'Not long.'

'Confusion can often be the result of a UTI. Have you had any physical symptoms of one?'

'I have been needing to go for a wee more often, but at my age...' Gwen rolled her eyes and a thought popped in to her head that made her next smile a genuine one. 'An old school friend of mine from back in Wales called me a few months ago, to say things had got so bad with her bladder weakness that she was going into hospital to have a cafetiere fitted!'

'No, she didn't say that!' Vera's laughter filled the space between them.

'She did, and I told her to remind me never to have a coffee at her house.' Gwen laughed too, and for a moment she felt as though she was back, and that maybe she'd been making far too much of the symptoms she'd been experiencing.

'That's so funny, but all joking aside, I do think there's a good chance you've got a UTI and I'd like to rule that out before we look at any other possibilities.' Vera's glasses had slid down her nose again, and she pushed them back into position for a second time. 'Do you think you might be able to squeeze out a sample for me, so that we can test it now?'

'I can give it a go.' Less than five minutes later the results were in. Vera had performed a dipstick test and, to Gwen's surprise and relief, she did have a UTI.

'That could explain a lot, especially if you've had an untreated infection for a while.' Vera gave her a reassuring smile. 'But I'd like to run some blood tests too, to make sure there's nothing else going on.'

'Okay.' Gwen nodded. Blood tests she could cope with; they wouldn't show up anything she didn't want to know about and Barry would be satisfied by the news that the doctor had ordered further tests. For now she was choosing to believe that the antibiotics Vera prescribed her for the UTI would resolve all the issues. She wasn't going to think about the whole list of symptoms she hadn't mentioned, which deep down she knew weren't the result of a UTI. Ignorance was a form of bliss and she wasn't ready to give that up just yet.

10

Zahir Chatterjee was acting clinical lead in A&E, covering during Danni Carter's maternity leave. Danni was a friend of Amy's and if she'd still been at work, Amy wouldn't have hesitated to ask if it was okay for her to leave her shift early. Danni loved dogs every bit as much as Amy did, and understood that they could come to mean as much as family members to many people. She could have asked Esther, who was the most senior nurse in the team, but she was busy with a patient in resus. She felt far less comfortable asking Zahir. She had a good working relationship with him, but she wouldn't call him a friend. Added to which, staffing in the emergency department was always tight and they could ill afford to lose a staff member, but all she wanted was to get to Monty and see for herself that he was okay.

Amy had called Dolly, who'd put her on to speak to the vet, and they'd both reassured her that Monty was going to be all right. He had a nasty injury to his leg, which the vet had needed to operate on to clean and stitch the deep lacerations as a result of the attack. Somehow there were no broken bones, but there was nerve damage and risk of infection, and the little dog was going to need rest and rehabilitation. Amy was already panicking about how she'd manage his care while she was working, especially as he was likely to be far more nervous than before around dogs he didn't know well, and he might not be able to return to Dolly's care, even when he was better. Despite all of that, the most important thing was that Monty had made it through surgery and that was the toughest part for a small dog, apparently. That didn't stop her mind from whirring, thinking about what could have happened to the sweet little dog who just wanted to be everyone's friend; what almost certainly would have happened if Lijah hadn't been there to intervene and take some of the brunt of the attack himself.

'Are you okay?' Aidan asked as Amy came out of the cubicle where she'd left Lijah. It wasn't just her concern for Monty that was weighing heavily on her, she was worried about Lijah too. The years felt like they'd peeled away when she'd first seen him, as if Lijah had been a town or two away all this time, living an ordinary life that mirrored her own. But as much as she wanted to believe that fame hadn't changed him, she knew there was no way he could be the same old Lijah. The reactions of other patients, and even some of the staff, had been enough to tell her that. His fame set him apart, he wasn't the same as everyone else, and it had taken her less than an hour in his company to see that there were serious downsides to that.

When Nick had started talking about how they could smuggle Lijah out of the hospital without him being papped or mobbed by fans, Lijah had pulled a face, and it was obvious he found the mention of fans and press uncomfortable. She'd read the stories online about his so-called breakdown, and having witnessed his relationship with Maria first hand, she knew how much her death would have affected him, but he seemed incredibly tense in a way that went beyond his grief. She'd seen the same thing before with patients in recovery from some kind of trauma, as if they were in permanent fight or flight mode, because they didn't feel comfortable anywhere.

Lijah might be back in his home town, but he didn't fit in like the old Lijah any more. Amy was certain Maria would have provided him with a sense of home, even as his fame increased, but now she was gone and that had to make him feel rootless. It was hard for Amy to imagine when her whole life was so firmly embedded here. She couldn't walk down the street without bumping into someone she knew, and if she needed a friend there was always someone she could drop in on. Living her whole life in the area had made her part of a community she couldn't imagine finding anywhere else, and it felt like her safe place whatever troubles she might be facing. Lijah couldn't walk down the street either, but for entirely different reasons, and not even Port Kara could be his safe place any more. He probably had more money than he could ever spend, but Amy wouldn't want to trade places with him. Looking at the concern on Aidan's face as he waited for her to respond, she knew she had something money couldn't buy, and she was so grateful to have the support of her friend in the midst of her worries about Monty.

'I don't think I'm going to be any good to the patients, I just can't think straight.' Despite all the assurances, Amy couldn't get the image of the little dog, lying bloodied and broken, out of her head. She needed to see Monty for herself before she could really believe he'd be okay. Working in A&E wasn't the kind of job anyone should do when they were distracted, there was no room for error.

'You need to go home.' Aidan's tone was insistent, but she shook her head.

'I can't, we're short staffed already.'

'We'll manage. It's only an hour until the late shift starts. I can always give Eden a ring and see if she's able to come in early. She's only across the road and there's got to be a downside to being able to roll out of bed and straight into work.'

Eden Grainger was one of the newer members of staff. She lived across the road from the hospital with her parents, who took care of her little boy whenever she was working. She'd been really flexible about taking on extra shifts and she seemed keen to pick up whatever overtime she could, but they couldn't expect her to just drop everything and come in at such short notice.

'I can't ask her to do that.'

'You don't have to.' Aidan cut her off. 'I'll do it.'

Within five minutes he'd sorted everything out. Eden was coming in early, and Aidan had told Zahir, who hadn't raised any objection. There was just one more thing she needed to do before she left.

'I just wanted to say thanks again before I go.' Amy looked towards Lijah as she went into his cubicle. Some of her old insecurities had risen to the surface when she'd been talking to him, but she didn't want to leave things between them on a bad note, not after everything he'd done for Monty. He was wearing a woolly hat pulled down so low that it was half covering his eyes, and a long scarf that was wrapped around his neck several times. He looked like someone about to head out across the frozen plains of Antarctica. 'Is that your disguise? Given that the weather is starting to warm up, it might get you more attention rather than less.'

'This is the closest thing to a disguise we could lay our hands on.' Nick laughed. 'It was either that or one of those backless gowns and unfortunately his arse is even more famous than he is. A *Rear of the Year* award will do that; it looks like it's been sculpted out of marble, but then I guess you know that.'

Heat flushed Amy's face. Nick had always been good at

embarrassing her, and she wished she had a quick response that would turn things around on him, but all she could think of was just how nice Lijah's bum had always been. That was one thing the press hadn't got wrong. Thankfully Lijah was far more ready with a rebuff.

'The only famous arse here is you, Nick. See what I have to contend with? He's supposed to be helping me.' Lijah shook his head and looked at Amy. 'Are you going to the vets?'

'Yes.' Amy nodded. 'But I walked to work this morning, so I'm going home to grab my car, because the vet is in Port Tremellien.'

'I can take you.' Lijah's offer was tempting and not just because it meant Amy could get to Monty sooner, but she shook her head.

'You can't drive with your hand like that.'

'Maybe not, but Nick can.'

'I'm sure you've both got better things to do than—'

'We really haven't.' Lijah cut her off and shrugged. 'I'm supposed to be writing songs, but I think I'm going to have to get a job with Hallmark cards at this rate, because all I can come up with is cheesy lines that have been written a hundred times before, but in a far better way.'

'I highly doubt that.' Amy didn't believe it for a minute. Lijah had even more awards for songwriting than singing. She'd seen the pride in Maria's face every time it happened, and the awards had usually ended up in her cottage, as Lijah never seemed to settle in one place for long.

'Oh it's true. This is what I came up with yesterday, after spending the whole day trying to write. Brace yourself, because it's terrible.' Lijah let go of a long breath, before singing the lines he'd written, in a low voice, with a melody Amy knew was going to be impossible to get out of her head. He tapped the beat by drumming his fingers of his good hand on the cubicle trolley, and Amy was taken back to another time and place again, when she'd first witnessed the way music just seemed to flow through him. 'I'm surrounded by a crowd, but I'm drowning in the absence of you. The loneliness you left me is a raging storm that I can't get through.'

'It's sounds pretty good to me.' Maybe the lyrics weren't the best, but the rawness of his tone made her skin tingle, the way it always had done whenever she heard him sing live. When the words came out of his mouth, it was like he was laying all his emotions bare. It was what had made him stand out from the crowd amongst thousands of other aspiring singers.

'It's awful and you've got to let me come and see Monty, so I've got an excuse not to get back to the writing, because who knows what rubbish I'll come up with next?' Lijah pushed his hat up so that she could see his eyes. They were the colour of conkers and she'd never seen anyone else with quite the same shade. 'My whole career could be hanging on this, so you've got to agree to us driving you to the vets.'

'Well when you put it like that.' Part of Amy knew it was dangerous to spend even a moment more with Lijah Byrne. Losing him had smashed her heart to smithereens once, and it had taken her years to stop missing him. Their worlds were a million miles apart now, and he'd be gone again soon. It was obvious he didn't belong here any more and he'd probably leave as soon as he'd come up with a new song he was happy with. She'd already found herself hoping that would take far longer than planned. It was stupid, even if Lijah was in Port Kara, their paths probably wouldn't cross again. She was hardly likely to bump into him in the queue to buy a lottery ticket in the Co-op. She had to remember this was just a fleeting reconnection with her past. Nothing more.

'That's settled then. Let's go and see Monty.' Lijah placed his good hand gently on her back as they headed out of the cubicle and she tried to put the jolt of electricity that passed through her body down to the memory of her first ever love. She couldn't let herself acknowledge that no one since had ever come close, not even Zach. Lijah might think his lyrics were terrible, but Amy really had felt as though she was drowning in loneliness when he'd left Port Kara. So there was no way she was going to allow herself to indulge in the stupid fantasy of having Lijah back in her life, especially when everything that had happened since had proved that ending things on her terms was the right decision. Once they'd seen Monty, they'd go back to their vastly different lives and all she had to do in the meantime was stop her stupid heart from attaching itself to him for a second time. Otherwise, it would only have itself to blame when it got broken all over again.

Monty was truly amazing. With everything he'd been through he should have been feeling extremely sorry for himself, but as soon as he spotted Amy and Lijah his tail started thudding against the bottom of the crate where he'd been put to keep him safe during his recovery. Nick had stayed out in reception, where Dolly had been waiting ever since she and Monty had been dropped off, so it was just Lijah with Amy in the recovery area. The size of the wound on Monty's back leg made Amy gasp in shock, and when Lijah reached out to take her hand another jolt of electricity went through her. This was not a good idea, and she withdrew her hand like she'd been burnt.

'My poor little boy.' Amy pushed a finger through the bars of the crate, gently stroking the fur on this front paw, well away from his injury, and she earnt herself a lick with his sandpaper rough tongue, his tail thudding away again.

'He's such a great dog. He reminds me of Buster.' There was a pang in Lijah's voice and it was Amy's turn to squeeze his hand. Buster had been Lijah's dog when he was a teenager and although bigger than Monty, he'd had the same black and white colouring. Buster's tail had always been thudding against the furniture in delight at being surrounded by his favourite humans, too, and he used to wedge himself between Lijah and Amy, or between them and Maria, making sure he was in the heart of the action.

'Me too, but just look at the poor little thing. I'm going to be paranoid about him knocking the wound when I'm not around. I'm sure Mum will come to my place to keep an eye on him until she starts her new job, but I don't think it would be a good idea for him to stay with her once she starts work. I'll just have to see if I can get a bit of time off.'

'I could look after him when you're working.' Lijah might as well have told her he was going to paint himself purple, the idea was just as ridiculous.

'That's a really kind offer, but you're busy writing and, once I get Monty home, I can't keep moving him around. He's going to need peace and quiet, and the comforts of home.'

'We all need that.' The note of sadness was back in Lijah's voice again and it made something tighten in Amy's chest. She'd been right about how he was feeling, she was sure of it. 'I can write terrible lyrics anywhere. So I can easily come and dog sit at your place.'

'Don't be silly, I couldn't ask you to do that.' The thought of Lijah in the close confines of her flat made the pace of Amy's pulse pick up.

'You didn't ask me to do it, I offered.' Lijah's voice was soft and low. 'And you'd be doing me a favour, I need something other than writing to think about. A bit of dog sitting would be the perfect distraction. An excuse for why I'm not writing and who knows, maybe this handsome little boy will inspire me.'

'Is that still where you get your inspiration from? Stuff in your everyday life?' Amy's eyes met his and a smile spread across his face, making her pulse break into a gallop.

'You must have recognised yourself in some of my songs. That's assuming you don't switch them off the moment they come on.' He looked straight at her, and she flushed bright red.

'I did wonder, but I can't believe your songs are about me. Those days seem so... I don't know, so far away.' She was tripping over the words, but he was still smiling.

'It was perfect though, wasn't it? Those three summers when all we had to worry about was ourselves and each other.'

'Life was certainly simpler then.' Amy sighed. Lijah was right, it was as if they'd existed in a world of their own creation, one that didn't last, but she could see how he might be inspired by it, because it had felt pretty perfect back then.

'Coming back here was an attempt to recapture that feeling of home, but being in the beach house is like being in a gilded cage. I'm away from everything and everyone, apart from Nick, and the two of us see far too much of one another as it is. So, I'd love the chance to help out with Monty.'

'Okay.' Even as she found herself agreeing, Amy wanted to clamp her hand over her mouth for continuing this dangerous game. She was letting Lijah infiltrate her life, and it was clear he was bored and restless and filled with nostalgia for a time that would be impossible to recapture. She needed to try and keep things as business like as possible between them. 'If you're sure, it would really help, because we're already short staffed at work.'

'I'm positive and, like I said, you'll be doing me a favour.

Maybe I can take you out to dinner, to thank you for giving me a reason to get away from the blank page that's staring back at me every time I sit down to write.'

'I don't think that's a good idea.' He looked genuinely disappointed at her response. She didn't want to hurt his feelings, but she had to protect herself. Shrugging, she kept her tone deliberately light. 'We can't both go out at the same time and leave Monty, but I can't thank you enough for offering to help out and most of all for stopping that dog from hurting Monty even more than it did.'

'Anyone would have done it.' Lijah was smiling again, but the sadness in his eyes made Amy's throat burn. She'd always hated it when he was sad, but she was certain he'd get over her turning down his offer of dinner almost immediately. She had no such confidence in her ability to get over him for a second time, and if it came down to a choice about whose heart to protect, she had to choose her own.

* * *

Nick had been talking non-stop all the way back from the veterinary surgery and, until they'd dropped Dolly and Amy off, it was easy for Lijah to hide the fact that he was finding it hard to respond. He felt like an idiot for asking Amy out and expecting her to say yes. He was an arrogant fool, too used to being surrounded by people whose job it was to keep him happy to realise that some people had no interest in getting involved in the circus that was his life. Amy had always been her own person, that was one of things he'd loved about her. And he had loved her, more than he'd ever realised. Who the hell did he think he was, thinking she'd have any interest in going out with him again, after he'd chosen his career over their relationship, like it was nothing. It hadn't been nothing; it had been such a huge part of his life, and something he'd never been able to replicate. Amy had been so easy to be around, such good company, and he'd taken that for granted, because she'd never asked much of him. But they'd both changed; he'd seen her professionalism today and just how good she was at the job she'd always dreamed of doing. He couldn't expect her to just step in and be there for this latest crisis, not after a decade with almost no contact.

'Are you okay? You're very quiet.' When they were back at the beach house, Nick finally seemed to realise that Lijah had barely uttered more than a few words since they'd left the veterinary surgery.

'Just conserving my energy for my new job as a dog sitter.' Lijah ran a hand through his hair, wondering if he'd been mad to make the offer and Nick's response seemed to give him his answer.

'Lij, what the hell is all of that about mate? Please tell me you haven't convinced yourself that you've still got feelings for Amy.'

'No, of course I haven't.' His response sounded unconvincing, even to his own ears.

'Good, because getting involved with someone from here would be a crazy idea.'

'Funny that, because I could have sworn I heard you arranging a time to meet up with Dolly for a drink.'

'It's different for me.' Nick's expression was open. 'No one knows who I am, and no one is going to be following me, looking to take photos, or splashing pictures of the girl I'm with all over the internet. People can end up getting hurt when they're caught up in all of that, you know that as well as anyone. I know you think too much of Amy to put her through that, for the sake of something you know won't last. We'll be gone in a couple of months. Don't leave a trail of destruction in your wake mate, that's all I'm saying. Amy's great, and she definitely doesn't deserve that.'

'You're right and don't worry, I've got no intention of seeing Amy anywhere but inside the four walls of her flat, when I'm looking after Monty. I just want a bit of normality, that's all, to remember who I am, and I think it'll give me that. But we're just friends, there'll be nothing to feed the internet, I promise.' He held up a hand, as if he was about to swear on the bible. He knew Nick was right and the very last thing he wanted was to hurt Amy. He just wished he could find a way of numbing the pain inside himself that never seemed to go away. He wouldn't go back to self-medicating, but he had to find something that gave him a sense of contentment. He'd spent years thinking that the next thing he achieved would be the thing that would alleviate the constant nagging anxiety that had never truly let him find peace. Except it didn't matter how many records he sold, how many number ones he had, or how many concert venues he sold out, it never filled up the emptiness inside him. And he was an even bigger idiot to have thought, even for a split second, that Amy could be the one to fill that space. It wasn't fair on her; she was one of the best people he'd ever known and he'd do whatever it took to keep the promise he'd just made to Nick to ensure she didn't get hurt.

11

Lijah couldn't put off the trip to his mother's house any more. She no longer lived there, she no longer lived anywhere, but the whitewashed cottage, halfway up Smuggler's Pass, a narrow lane barely wide enough for one vehicle, would always be his mother's home. She'd fallen in love with Mor Brys years before Lijah had been in a position to buy it for her. When she'd first pointed the house out, promising him that one day they'd live somewhere as beautiful as that, he'd been about seven or eight, and they'd been living in a flat above the fish and chip shop on the outskirts of the village, the smell of which had clung to every item of clothing they owned and had driven their first dog, Colin, half-mad with longing. Mor Brys wasn't a particularly grand house, but it was perfect in its own way. The cottage was double fronted with a heavy wooden door and perfectly spaced windows, that somehow made it look as if the building was smiling. It was like a child's drawing of a house, and his mother had waxed lyrical about it every time they passed by. It wasn't until years later that they saw the inside of Mor Brys.

When Lijah was ten, his mother's dream house had come up

for rent. Maria was working more by then, but she still couldn't afford the place on her own and his father had just walked out of their lives for the final time, after years of coming and going. When his mother had asked Lijah how he'd feel about Claire moving in with them, he'd been delighted. She'd been like a second mother to him all his life and they'd spent as much time in her tiny little end of terrace house as in their own flat, although it would never have been big enough for them all to live in. Instead, Claire had rented out her house and the income she got from that had helped them afford the rent on Mor Brys. The new situation had worked out perfectly and for the first time Lijah understood what it felt like to have more than one parent on hand. Whenever Maria wasn't going to be home, his aunt would cook Lijah's favourite dinner of homemade pizza. Later on, she'd toast bread in front of the huge inglenook fire for supper, and ply him with plenty of snacks in between.

Claire had never married or had children of her own, and his mother had never had another partner after she'd split up from his father, at least as far as Lijah knew. He'd asked them once why they didn't go on dates, or try to meet someone else, like some of his friends' parents did, and his aunt's response had been short and sweet.

'Because we're happy as we are.'

He'd never doubted it was true. They weren't just siblings, they were best friends. They spent weekends together and went on holiday together, choosing one another over the chance to spend time with other people. The three of them were a tight knit little group, which became a group of four when Amy had become a part of their lives.

When Lijah had wanted to move to London to pursue a career in music, he'd been desperate for Amy to go with him. Leaving his mother and aunt behind had been tough, but they had each other, and he knew they'd be okay, but he hadn't dreamed he'd have to leave Amy behind too. He'd been sure she'd go with him. At first she'd promised she would, and had secured a place during her gap year to study for her nursing degree at South Bank University, instead of Plymouth as she'd originally planned. Then she'd started having doubts, telling him she wanted to study somewhere closer to home and that they needed time apart to see if they were meant to be together. For a long while he'd tried to persuade her that she was wrong, but she wouldn't listen, and in the end he'd done what he'd had a habit of doing his whole life and had pressed the self-destruct button.

When he'd realised Amy wasn't going to change her mind, Lijah had told his mother and aunt to stop passing on news about her, and had deleted all the photographs he had of her on his laptop. He wasn't leaving the door open for their relationship in case they were meant to be together, the way Amy had suggested, he was stamping out the last ashes of it instead. It wasn't because he didn't still love her, or wish they could make things work. It was because he needed to protect himself. She'd already made the decision not to come with him and he couldn't keep hanging on hoping for something to change. Making the decision to cut her off completely might have hurt like hell, but sometimes a clean break was the only way to prevent further pain. It was a habit he'd developed as a result of his relationship with his father, at least that's what a therapist had told him once, before he'd decided that therapy raked up more trauma than it was worth.

The legacy of his father's disinterest had caused Lijah more issues than anyone apart from Nick and Claire knew. Amy had known how much it affected him, back when they were together, but in some ways it had worsened over the years. It was behind the crippling anxiety that would often take hold of him just before he was about to go on stage, the imposter syndrome and fear of failure a consequence of rejection by a parental figure according to another therapist. It made sense he supposed; after all, if one of your parents considered you to be of no value in their life, what kind of value could you possibly have? It didn't matter how many people were screaming his name, or buying his records, none of that could fill the gap.

Lijah had quickly worked out that seeking validation through a string of meaningless liaisons wouldn't work either. That wasn't to say there hadn't been relationships, but the one-night stands had always left him feeling worse about himself instead of better, because in a weird kind of way they felt like another form of rejection, even if the decision to keep things casual was often down to him. He'd promised his mum that he wouldn't be another fatality of fame and, after she'd died, it was probably that promise that had saved him. His aunt had reminded him of it the day after they'd lost her, when he'd been so desperate to numb the pain he would have taken anything. But because of her words, he'd stuck to the medication the doctors had prescribed, and when that started getting out of hand, it had been the promise to his mother that had made him get help. Throwing himself into work hadn't seemed like an issue, and he'd kept going and going until the burnout had knocked him off his feet. Now he was back outside the cottage on Smuggler's Pass, about to see his aunt face to face for the first time since his mother's funeral.

The landlord had put Mor Brys up for sale just after Lijah's first album had hit the number one spot on both sides of the Atlantic – the album he'd penned in the wake of his breakup with Amy – and he'd been desperate to buy it so that his mum and aunt could stay in the home they loved. It had been a shock to discover that, unlike in the movies, he didn't suddenly get mountains of money the moment he had a hit record, and they'd almost missed out on the house, after someone put in an offer for the asking price. Fate was on their side, though, and by the time the sale fell through, Lijah finally had scraped together the money to buy it. Later on, when the money did start rolling in much faster, he'd offered to buy Maria and Claire something bigger and better, but his mum had turned him down flat.

'There is nowhere better.' And that had been that. Mor Brys was their dream home, and they'd insisted they wanted to stay there forever. Only none of them had realised that Maria didn't have forever, or anything like it, and within four years she was dead.

'Oh my love, am I dreaming, or is it really you!' Claire threw back the door before he even had the chance to knock. Her cheeks were flushed with colour and her eyes shining, as she reached up and took his face between her hands. 'I can't believe you're here, I've missed you so much.'

'I've missed you too.' There was a lump in his throat as he spoke, because there was someone missing, someone who should have been standing in the doorway beside Claire. It was what had made it too hard to face coming home before now. There were memories of his mother in every corner of the house, and he knew her absence would be gut-wrenching once he stepped inside. But the longer he stood on the doorstep, the more chance there was of someone spotting him. That would create another set of problems he wasn't sure he could cope with right now. The last thing either he or Claire needed was the press hammering on the door.

'Come in, come in. Where are your bags? You are staying, aren't you? Please say you're staying.' Her words came out in a rush, but there was a pang of desperation which proved how much she wanted him there. Guilt prickled at Lijah's scalp again. His aunt was the only person who'd felt the pain of his mother's death to the same extent he had, maybe even more so in some ways, because she'd been left behind in the house they'd shared, confronted by Maria's absence every day. Yet Lijah had let her face it alone. After the funeral, he'd left straight away, burying himself in work like never before. He could pretend to himself that his mother was back home in Cornwall, bustling around the house, listening to *Absolute 80s* on the radio and cooking up a storm. Except now he was about to go into the kitchen and the space she'd always occupied would be empty. He wouldn't be able to pretend any longer, and suddenly he wasn't sure he could do it. It was as if Lijah was frozen to the spot and, as he looked at his aunt, he couldn't even respond to her questions, let alone step across the threshold.

'Oh love, I know this is hard.' Claire wrapped an arm around his waist. He hadn't needed to explain it to her, she understood because she'd lived with the loss of her beloved sister every single day for the last six months. 'But you can't stand out there on the street forever. Sometimes, even when you know it's going to hurt, you have to do it anyway. If you don't, you're never going to be able to move past what you're feeling now.'

Lijah nodded and allowed his aunt to sweep him into the hallway, with her arm still around him, almost as if he was a young boy again. The breath caught in his throat at the familiar scent of vanilla – his mother's favourite smell. She'd always had wax melts on the go, filling the air with the aroma that reminded him of her baking, even when she wasn't busy whipping up a batch of cupcakes or her famous Victoria sponge. Baking was just what she always did, and then suddenly she was gone.

'Come on my love, I think we need a cup of tea.' Claire led the way down the hallway and for a moment he wanted to laugh.

That had been the solution to everything when he was growing up. He'd drunk champagne in some of the most exclusive clubs and best hotels in the world, but none of that came close to matching how it felt to sit across the table from his mum and aunt, just chatting about nothing much at all. It was just one more thing he hadn't realised meant as much as it did, until the chance to ever do it again had been taken away. Now he would give anything – *anything* – to be able to sit down with them both, for a cup of tea and some cake, and to put the world to rights. Being in his mother's kitchen without her was every bit as painful as he'd expected it to be.

'I can't believe she's gone.' They were the same words he'd said to his aunt when he'd come home for the funeral, and they'd cried together. He'd told himself at the time that he was already through the worst of it, but deep down he'd known he was lying to himself. He'd only glimpsed the pain, before stuffing it back down inside. Eventually it had come bursting out, like a broken jack-in-the-box that refused to go back in, no matter how hard he tried to force it.

'I couldn't either for a long time.' Claire flicked the switch to boil the kettle, and Lijah took a seat at the kitchen table. 'At first, I'd wake up every morning and it would hit me all over again.'

'I'm so sorry I didn't come home sooner. I let you down, but I just wasn't ready to face it.' Lijah could see the pain etched on his aunt's face, but she was already shaking her head.

'Don't be daft, if I could have got away from Port Kara, I'd have gone in a heartbeat. I kept seeing people out and about who looked like Maria from behind, because they had the same hair, or they walked the way she did. I'd convince myself it was her and that it had all been some horrible mistake, I even called out her name once or twice, and I honestly thought I might be going mad.'

The two of them had done everything together, and it used to be a running joke that you never saw one without the other. As teenagers, they'd been convinced they were going to be a singing duo, taking the eighties music scene by storm. The closest they'd ever got was belting out eighties hits at the regular Thursday karaoke night at the Lord Nelson in Port Tremellien, the same pub where he'd performed some of his earliest gigs.

Lijah knew that both his mother and aunt were incredibly proud of him for living the dream they'd once had, but they'd never treated him any differently. It had grounded him, making him feel normal. It was the same trick Nick had managed and he was so grateful to have people in his life who loved and valued him for who he really was. That circle had diminished when his mum had died, and he'd reduced contact with his aunt to text exchanges, so he wouldn't feel the absence of his mother quite so keenly.

'I'm so sorry.' He repeated his apology and she shook her head again. 'I ran away, and I knew I was leaving you to deal with all of this alone, but I just wanted to pretend it hadn't happened. When I'm on tour it feels like another world, and that's where I wanted to be, in a world where I hadn't lost Mum.'

'Of course you did. So did I, and I really do understand.' She wrapped her arms around him from a standing position, as he sat in the chair, squeezing so tightly that he had to turn his head to the side to stop it feeling as though he was suffocating. That was when he spotted what looked like holiday brochures spread out across the table. He'd seen the word Tenerife and a photograph of whitewashed villas below an azure sky. If his aunt wanted a holiday, he was determined to pay for the best hotel, wherever she wanted to go, and however long for. It was the least he could do and, if she even tried to decline his offer, which he knew she would, he'd tell her she had to accept. It was the only way to alleviate some of the guilt she was insisting he didn't need to feel.

'Thank you for not being angry with me, you're the best.' Gesturing towards the brochures as she finally released him, he fully expected her to dismiss the idea of a holiday, before he even had the chance to offer to pay for it. His aunt and his mother had always been careful not to hint at wanting anything, to ensure he didn't offer to pay for it for them. But he needed this chance to make things up to her, at least in some tiny way. 'Are you planning a holiday?'

'A holiday?' Claire looked towards the brochures and colour seemed to flood her face. 'Oh, they're not holiday brochures. They're details of properties.'

'Properties?' Lijah reached over and pulled one of the glossy brochures towards him, reading the text printed at the top of the cover page.

Vista Paraiso, Los Cristianos, Tenerife.

Just below the photograph of the whitewashed villas was another line of text.

Exclusive development of three and four-bedroomed luxury villas.

'Are you buying a holiday home?' Lijah looked at his aunt again and tried to remember if she'd ever mentioned wanting to visit Tenerife, let alone live there. But maybe she had visions of spending the winters somewhere warm. She was due to retire soon, after forty years working as a teacher at the local primary school. She'd always joked that her job was why she'd never wanted children – that and having a nephew like Lijah, as she'd often teased him – but it had been obvious she adored kids, and she'd been the best aunt he could ever have asked for. He suspected her decision not to have a family had more to do with the difficult divorce she'd been through before Lijah was even born, and the pact that she and his mother had made not to get involved with anyone after the breakdown of his parents' relationship. The sisters had each other and Lijah, so why would they want the hassle of anything else?

'Not a holiday home. Just a home. I'm moving out there Lij, to Tenerife.' If his aunt had said she was moving to a colony on Mars, he wasn't sure he'd have been any more surprised.

'What do you mean you're moving out there? Have you even been before?'

'Twice in the last six months.' Claire made it sound so normal, as if she'd just popped down to the Co-op in the village. 'In fact, if you'd come to visit last week, I wouldn't have been here, I'd have been out there.'

Lijah couldn't respond for a moment. The idea of his aunt moving away was a lot to process. He knew he should have come back sooner, but he'd never dreamed she'd come up with a plan to change her life this drastically, let alone so soon after his mother's death. It didn't seem right and he had to make sure this wasn't just a reaction to everything that had happened. He hated the thought of Claire living with regret, as well as the grief she was already feeling. 'Visiting a place twice doesn't seem like enough of a basis to move countries. What about all your friends here? And your job?'

'I'm retiring at the end of term and I'm studying to be a counsellor, so hopefully I'll be able to start a little practice once I'm settled. I'm after a four-bed villa and that way, even if I set aside a room for counselling appointments, I'll still have a couple of lovely spare rooms for friends to come and stay, and hopefully my nephew too.' She shot him a smile. 'I'm sure I'll see plenty of everyone, especially in January and February when the weather here is about as appealing as a week-old dishcloth.'

'What are you going to do without Thursday night karaoke, and your art classes, or yoga on the beach, or...' He was clutching at straws now, trying to list all the things that should tie Claire to Port Kara and he wasn't even sure why. He hadn't been home since the funeral, and before that his visits hadn't been anywhere near as frequent as he wished they'd been. She was right, too, he was in a position to be able to visit her wherever she was living. So why did he hate the thought of her not being at Mor Brys quite so much? He might have no idea, but his aunt was one step ahead of him again.

'Thursday night karaoke isn't the same without your mum. I tried it a couple of times, but it just hurt so much that she wasn't by my side, and when I sobbed my way through "Girls Just Wanna Have Fun", the landlord said he was thinking about barring me for making his customers so depressed they wanted to leave. I'm not even sure he was joking.' Claire's smile wobbled, her eyes shining with unshed tears. 'As for the art classes, they have those in Tenerife, and I can do yoga on the beach all year round there if I want to. I know it will feel strange, not living here, but I think it's time. I can't bear being on my own, and it isn't a home for either of us without your mum here, is it? Much as I love you Lij, and by God I do, I know coming back to see me isn't the same. I can't even begin to fill the gap your mum left behind, and the truth is I don't want to try. I want to be somewhere new, where every little thing doesn't remind me of her.'

'I get that.' Lijah nodded, because everything his aunt had said was true, but he was still worried she might be rushing into things and choosing to move thousands of miles away, to a place she barely knew, on a whim. He might not have been around much lately, but that hadn't stopped him worrying about his aunt and checking in on her by text. She'd never once mentioned a plan to move abroad, and she hadn't even told him about her trips to Tenerife. It all just seemed so sudden, and so random, almost as if she'd stuck a pin in a map and chosen to go on holiday there, to see if it was somewhere she could live. 'But why Tenerife? Do you know anyone there?'

'I've got a good friend who lives there, her name's Dee.' As Claire said the other woman's name, her eyes seemed to change, and the haunted expression turned into something completely different. 'We used to work together at the school, but then, about ten years ago, she went out to Tenerife and started working as a singer. We kept in touch via email, and she invited me and your mum out there to visit, but we never made it. When Dee heard about Maria, we started to email more often, and she invited me to stay again. I went over and ended up staying for three weeks. Then Dee said she'd come over here to visit me and, for the first time since we lost your mum, I remembered what it felt like to look forward to something.'

Claire's gaze met his and he didn't need to ask the question that had been forming in his mind. The way his aunt was talking about Dee wasn't the way anyone spoke about a casual friendship. She was talking like someone who'd fallen in love. He wanted to be thrilled for her, but the idea of her being in a relationship was so unexpected. The last few years had made him jaded too, realising just how many people who'd come into his life had done so with an ulterior motive. The thought that Dee might not be all she seemed, and that she might be taking advantage of his aunt in some way, made the hairs on the back of his neck stand on end. 'Are you and Dee going to live together out there?'

'I hope so, eventually, but she's got her own place, and I don't want to rush things. I've had an offer on my house in Port Tremellien, and I'm going to buy a place in Tenerife, so I can spend more time with Dee first. If it works out the way we're hoping it will, I'll probably rent out my place in Tenerife as an Airbnb, like I did with the house in Port Tremellien. It gives me the security of knowing I've got my own place to go back to if I ever need to.' Claire reached out and squeezed his hand. When he'd bought Mor Brys, she'd insisted on holding on to the little terraced house she'd bought when she split up with her ex-husband. It was her bit of security and the money she'd got from renting it out had been used to fund the trips she and Maria had gone on, giving them a reason to turn down Lijah's offer to pay for their holidays, no matter how hard he'd tried. Mor Brys had been bought in his mother's name, even though as far as Maria and Lijah were concerned it had belonged to both of them equally, and Claire wouldn't hear of it when Lijah had told her he was signing it over to her after Maria's death. She outright refused to sign the paperwork because, in her words, she already had her own house in the neighbouring village. It had always been important to Claire to hold on to something that was hers and hers alone, right from the start 'just in case Maria gets fed up and kicks me out one day!' It had been a joke, of course, but Claire had been sensible then and, deep down, Lijah knew he could trust her to be sensible now. He was still reeling from the news, all the same.

'Why don't you keep the house in Port Tremellien and let me give you the money for the villa? You might miss the cold, grey winters after all and want to come home.'

'Oh love, you know I'm never going to accept an offer like that, don't you?' She took hold of his face in her hands again. 'And anyway, I can't give myself an easy route back here. I've got to give making a new life for myself without Maria my best shot, somewhere completely different. And I can't do that if it's too easy for me to come back.'

'Do I get to meet this Dee and decide if she's good enough for my aunt?'

'She's more than good enough and your mum liked her; they met a few times back when Dee and I worked together. I just never dreamed things would develop like this, I didn't even know...' Claire trailed off for a moment. 'I've never felt this way about anyone before, let alone another woman. I thought I loved Richard, before he cheated on me, but it was never like this. It sounds ridiculous, but I feel as if I'm glowing from the inside out when I'm with her. You know, like those old Ready Brek porridge adverts on telly.'

'You've lost me there, Auntie C, but then you are bloody ancient.' They both laughed, as she pretended to try and slap him, but then her expression changed to something far more serious. 'You don't mind then, the fact that it's a woman?'

'Oh my God, of course I don't. Why the hell would I?' He shook his head, incredulous that she could even think that. It was a huge shock to hear that his aunt was leaving Cornwall and he had no idea how to feel about that, but he did know what he wanted for her. 'I've got to admit that you leaving Port Kara is the last thing I expected, but you deserve to be happy more than anyone I know and I'm so glad you've found someone who's brought that back into your life. I've been dreading coming here and feeling the loss of mum all the harder. But this is what she would have wanted, to know that you're finding things to look forward to again, and that's what I want too, more than anything.'

'For me, or for you?' She was one step ahead of him yet again, and he nodded slowly.

'For both of us, and I've got a feeling I'm going to need your help to make sure I find a way to do it. Even if you are shacked up with the love of your life in Tenerife, and you can't think of anything worse than having your annoying nephew hanging around, or ringing up asking for advice.'

'I'll always make time for my annoying nephew, I've been doing it for the last thirty years after all!' It was her turn to duck out of the way, as he pretended to make a grab for her. Then she put her arms around him again, pulling him into another tight hug that was so much like the ones his mother used to give him. His aunt was planning a whole new life, one neither of them could have envisaged a year ago, and he was thrilled for her. It gave him hope that he could find a way forward too, even if that was impossible to picture right now. He really hoped so, because his decision to come back to Port Kara had felt like the only way to stop himself from drowning in the grief he'd tried so hard to suppress. Now, with his aunt moving to Tenerife, he wasn't sure he could even call Port Kara home any more, and once she left he might have nothing at all to come back for.

* * *

Amy had given internet dating a good go after splitting up with Zach for the final time, before she'd decided never again. Her last experience had happened in the run up to Christmas, when her latest match, Aaron, had told her he wouldn't be asking her out on a second date as he didn't want to get into anything 'serious' when there were so many parties and opportunities to potentially hook up with other people. Yet now here she was, against all her better judgement, diving back into the shark-infested waters of dating again, all because of Lijah. He'd come back into her life and made it feel as if her whole world was spinning on its axis.

Reuniting with someone you'd spent so much time with in your teens, who was now a global phenomenon, had a way of throwing your own life into sharp focus, but there was more to it than that. Reminiscing with Lijah about the night they'd got together, had reminded her what it felt like to be in love and she couldn't pretend, even to herself, that she didn't care if she never felt that way again.

Amy had seen what a difference it made to her friends when they found someone they could share the good times with, and lean on when the going got tough. She'd thought she'd come to terms with waiting and hoping that one day it would just happen, without the aid of an algorithm, or swiping on so many profiles that she was in danger of getting RSI. Then Lijah had turned up at the hospital, and she'd remembered what it felt like to look into the eyes of someone who made it feel like butterflies were looping the loop in your stomach. She remembered, too, what it felt like to have someone you could confide in, just as the two of them had done when they were teenagers. He'd been the one person who'd been there for the good times, but every bit as ready to be leaned on when she needed him, like when her father had been ill.

It was Lijah who'd given her a taste of what it felt like to be in that kind of relationship and, deep down, she'd never stopped wanting to experience it again, no matter how grateful she was for all the good things she already had in life. Now here he was, even more beautiful than he'd been at school, when she and everyone else had been utterly convinced he was out of her league. Not only that, he'd strolled back into her life and heroically saved Monty, offering to help look after him while he recovered. No one had a right to be that amazing, especially not someone in Lijah's position. He was supposed to be arrogant, with a massive ego, because fame had gone straight to his head.

And yet as hard as she'd tried to spot those things, or tell herself they must be there somewhere, that wasn't who he was. He was different in a far more subtle way. Fame *had* changed Lijah, but she couldn't put her finger on how. Whatever it was, it didn't come with the arrogance she'd expected and that made if far more difficult to remember that he wasn't still the same old Lijah she'd fallen in love with.

It wasn't fair; he couldn't just turn up for a summer and ask to see her, acting like they were teenagers again, before disappearing back into a world she would never be part of. It would hurt way too much. Just the memories that seeing him again had evoked had made the longing to go back to those days almost unbearable. That was why she'd had to reactivate her dating profile, and swipe right on James, a physiotherapist from Truro with a nice smile and dreams of 'finding someone to grow old with just like his grandparents had'.

When she'd told her mother, Kerry, that James had asked to meet her for a drink, Kerry had offered to come and dog sit Monty. She'd left her watching re-runs of the *Great British Bake Off* on one of the satellite channels, and shouting at the screen that no one had the time or energy to make chocolate eclairs from scratch, when you could buy a four pack from the Co-op for less than three pounds.

Opening the door to her flat, after a somewhat underwhelming date with James, the smell hit her. It was undoubtedly the aroma of a kebab and she knew what that meant, even before she heard her brother's raucous laugh echoing down the hallway to the front door. She could just go out and turn around again, but she was tired, and she had work tomorrow. Nathan was probably cadging a lift home with their mum, so he'd just hang around until she came home anyway, which meant she might as well get it over and done with.

'You're early sweetheart.' Her mother smiled as she came into the room, and Nathan cut in before she could even respond.

'All right fat arse, I bet you got a whiff of this kebab, didn't you, and it sent you racing back like a homing pigeon.'

'Nathan! For God's sake, I've told you before about engaging your brain before you open your mouth.'

'Amy knows I'm only joking.' Nathan pretended to be outraged by the suggestion that he'd spoken out of turn. 'It's just how we banter, isn't it, fat arse?'

'Yep.' She gave him a tight smile. Years of experience had taught her that arguing with him, or showing any sign that his insults bothered her just added fuel to the fire. She sometimes wondered what would happen if she replied in kind, honing in on his insecurities, if he had any, and said, 'Yes, that's right, it's just banter, you socially inept moron.' But she didn't, because she knew it would probably hurt her mum far more than it would hurt Nathan.

'So how was the date?' Kerry patted the spot on the sofa beside her, and Nathan cut in again.

'Bet he's halfway to Land's End by now, ready to jump off a cliff if he thinks Amy is chasing after him.'

'He's already texted to ask for a second date, actually.' As soon as the words were out of her mouth, Amy regretted them. She hated herself for trying to prove Nathan wrong. She didn't need the validation of her date to prove she was worthy of more respect than her brother gave her, she already knew that. She knew too that Nathan was jealous of her, in a way that ate him up and made him lash out, especially when he'd been drinking, as he clearly had been tonight.

'Did his guide dog like you, too?' It was a joke he'd made at Amy's expense many times before and it really didn't bother her any more, but her mother wasn't nearly so hardened to it.

'Nathan, if you don't stop this, you'll be walking home.' Amy's family home, where her brother still lived, was over three miles from Port Kara and there was no way Nathan would want to walk it. He stuck out his bottom lip like the petulant child he so often appeared to be, and Amy squeezed her mum's shoulder. She'd seen how difficult it had been for her parents over the years, with Nathan. No one had ever quite been able to determine the cause of his challenging behaviour. A personality disorder of some kind was the closest they'd had to any kind of diagnosis, but Nathan had refused to see any more specialists as soon as he was old enough to have a say. He'd struggled at school, academically and socially, and he'd resented how well Amy had done, describing nursing as 'glorified arse wiping' in the wake of her parents' obvious pride when she'd completed her nursing degree. Most of the time Amy felt sorry for Nathan, but that didn't make him any easier to be around. She felt sorrier still for her parents, especially as Nathan didn't want to engage with the doctors who might be able to help him find a way of moderating his behaviour and mood swings.

'They just want to give me drugs that will dull my personality.' It had been his argument every time one of the family had suggested he seek help. Amy had been forced to clamp her mouth shut on more than one occasion, to stop herself from asking why anyone would want to persist with a personality like Nathan's. Instead, she kept quiet, fulfilling the role of the good, reliable, kind daughter she knew her parents desperately needed, and it had become a habit.

'Talking of dogs.' Amy said without missing a beat. 'How's Monty been?'

'Good as gold. Bernie was so gentle too, he must have sensed that his best friend was poorly.' Kerry gave a small smile. 'He lay down next to the crate where Monty was sleeping, poor little lamb. At least he's getting plenty of rest.'

'Yeah, except when I was dangling the kebab meat through the bars, that got him going.' Nathan grinned and Amy felt her fingers twitch. She knew he was lying; Monty was in a crate for his own protection, so that he didn't move around too much. There was no way Kerry would let Nathan dangle kebab meat through the bars, but the thought that it had even crossed his mind made Amy's hackles rise. She couldn't react, though, because Nathan would love it, and the only people it would upset would be Amy and her mother. She didn't want Monty to get aggravated either, if anyone started shouting, so she took a deep breath.

'Thanks so much for coming and sitting with him, Mum. I'll take you out to lunch as a thank you, as soon as Monty is okay to be left alone.'

'You don't need to do that sweetheart, but thank you.' Her mother leaned forward to give her a hug.

'You know Amy, she never needs an excuse for eating.' Nathan's verbal barbs didn't hurt any more because she'd heard them all so often over the years, but that hadn't stopped them doing damage in the past. It didn't matter how many times her parents had told her to ignore him, that it was his personality disorder talking and that nothing he said was true. She'd known the comments only hurt because they were true, at least in part. She wasn't slim, or beautiful, she was ordinary looking and at least a clothes' size or two bigger than most of her friends. As a teenager that had mattered a hell of a lot more than it did now, and Nathan had managed to home in on every single one of her insecurities, his words reinforcing how she already felt about herself. But she knew she was a nice person, she was kind and funny, and lots of people liked her. She had a good job too and had bought her own flat, all things Nathan would probably never achieve.

It didn't bother Amy so much now that she was never going to be beautiful or slim, she knew she was so much more than the sum of her parts, but those old insecurities had made her who she was, and she'd worked hard to achieve everything she'd got, to prove her worth to herself as much as to anyone else. It had also made her more willing to try and see past shortcomings in others. That was why she was considering agreeing to a second date with James, despite not feeling any physical attraction towards him, and the fact he'd talked about himself for the entire date, mostly with his mouth full. There were far more important things than just the way someone looked, and maybe the other things had been down to nerves, and a desperate attempt to avoid an awkward silence. No one was perfect after all, but even as the thought popped into her head, she couldn't help picturing Lijah. She just had to keep reminding herself that her version of Lijah didn't exist any more, if he ever really had. The whole point of returning to dating was to provide a new focus, and to help her keep any feelings for Lijah that had resurfaced entirely to herself. Like most things in life, that was far easier in theory than it was in practice, but she had to keep trying.

By the time she'd said goodbye to her mother, and Nathan had fired off a couple more insults before disappearing in the direction of Kerry's car, she'd decided she would give James a second chance. He might never be in Lijah's league, but then neither was she, and she'd paid a heavy price for giving him her heart first time around. There was no way in the world she was making the same mistake twice.

12

'In twenty-four hours, I'll be sipping champagne in the shadow of the Eiffel Tower with my handsome husband, and I won't even be thinking about emptying another one of these.' Aidan gestured towards the cardboard kidney bowl that contained things Amy didn't want to think about too much. They'd just dressed the wound of a twelve-year-old boy, who'd gashed his leg on barbed wire after taking a shortcut home across a farmer's field. It had been a two-person job, largely because the boy was thrashing around so much and then he'd vomited at the sight of the needle Aidan had produced to give him a tetanus injection. There was never a dull day in A&E.

'Some of us will still be here, and if you insist on being smug, you'll be going on my hit list with Isla. Did you see her latest Insta post? That waterfall is too beautiful to be real and she looks far too happy.' Amy wrinkled her nose, but then she smiled. 'I'm so glad she's having an amazing time and that her latest test results were so great.'

'Me too. Reuben FaceTimed us, and he was almost crying

with relief. She's not the only one who deserves a holiday though, Ames. When was the last time you had one?'

'Zach and I went to Majorca for a week just before we split for the final time.' Amy rolled her eyes. 'He spent the whole week drinking so much that he couldn't be bothered to get up in time for any of the trips I wanted to do. He just lay there on the sun lounger, slowly cooking under the heat of the sun, like a jumbo sausage, and it was all I could do not to stick a fork in him. Then there was the secrecy with his phone; he snatched it off me like his life depended on it when I tried to borrow it to take a photo. So I knew he was cheating again.'

'The man's a complete eejit, Amy. Can't say I've ever had a holiday from hell quite like that, but they can be intense because of how much time you spend together. If things are already rocky, they can definitely help kill a relationship off.' Aidan put both hands over his heart in an overly theatrical way. 'Luckily I'm going with Jase, who is the best company and we can't wait for our babymoon.'

'I've warned you about being smug and I might not be able to lay my hands on a fork right now, but I bet I can find a scalpel.' She grinned. 'Although seeing as you deserve it too, I'll let it slide one more time. I can't believe you and Jase are going to be parents in six weeks. How's Ellen doing?'

'She's absolutely huge, bless her, but apparently she's carrying a lot of water. Typical of my kid to have a taste for the high life already and demand a built-in pool.' Aidan laughed. 'Me and Jase thought we ought to make it up to her and her family, so we've rented Shell Cottage for them for the long weekend; they arrived this morning. She's meeting me after I finish work, just for a catch up before Jase and I head off to the airport. I offered to meet her down at the cottage, but she said she wants an hour's break from the kids after the journey. It sounds like even an hour in a car with two under-sevens is pretty stressful.'

'I can imagine.' Amy raised her eyebrows.

'What about you, what are your plans for the weekend? Any chance you might be meeting up with a certain someone?' Aidan linked his arm through hers. 'Imagine all the amazing holidays you'd go on if you were with Lijah Byrne.'

'There's more chance of me winning the lottery than that. I saw photographs of him watching his last girlfriend modelling at New York fashion week. So I don't think an A&E nurse is quite his type, although he is going to help me out with Monty. Mum's looking after him today, but she's starting her new job soon and Lijah has said he'll come down and dog sit. I still can't believe he's actually going to turn up when the time comes, but I really hope he does.'

'So you can lock eyes over a bowl of Winalot?'

Amy couldn't help laughing, which was just as well because she didn't want Aidan to know just how strong her feelings for Lijah still were. It was just nostalgia, that was all, and once his mask slipped, she'd see first hand that he was no longer that boy. As far as she was concerned, that moment couldn't come fast enough. 'No, I want him to turn up so I don't have to work out what the hell to do instead. I can't leave Monty on his own, and because everyone else keeps insisting on going on all these amazing holidays, I can't take any time off either.'

'But he did ask you out, didn't he?'

'Only because he's here for the summer supposedly to write his next album, and bored enough to offer to dog sit. I get the feeling he's got writer's block and is willing to do anything to avoid confronting it. I'm sure being back here is hard for him, since he lost his mum, and he's trying to take his mind off that too. His aunt told me that Lijah threw himself into work after

Maria died, in an attempt not to think about it, but I'm not about to be his new distraction.' Amy wasn't sure whether she was trying to convince herself or Aidan, but every time she thought about Lijah the temptation to call him and say she'd changed her mind about going out was almost overwhelming. She had to stay strong and remember why that would be a very bad idea. 'Anyway, I've met someone.'

'You have?' Aidan's eyes widened in surprise. 'Are you back online again?'

'Uh-huh. He's a physiotherapist.'

'And very good with his hands I bet.' Aidan winked.

'We haven't got that far yet.' Amy pulled a face, not wanting to admit even to herself how unappealing she found the idea. 'But he's doing things with his life. He's got his own place in Port Tremellien, and he's planning to open his own practice eventually. He's sensible, professional and he seems to want a long-term relationship, which makes him unlike most of the men I've dated.'

'What about funny, sexy, kind? You haven't mentioned any of the qualities you're going to need in a partner, so that they stand a chance of matching up to you.'

'Saying things like that is why I love you and forgive you for jetting off to Paris, despite the fact you're leaving me to deal with all the overflowing kidney bowls.' Amy planted a kiss on his cheek, before pulling away again. 'But for now we better get on with some work, or Zahir and Esther will be on the war path.'

Lijah wasn't the only one capable of burying himself in work to provide a distraction from the problems in his life. When Amy was busy, she could go a whole ten minutes without thinking about him, and right now she'd be willing to empty every kidney bowl in the building if it meant she could keep his return in perspective. Their worlds were a million miles apart, and this was just a flying visit. She just had to get through the next few weeks without making a total idiot of herself by falling for him all over again, and emptying a thousand kidney bowls was more appealing than that.

Lijah had taken to going on very long walks since being back in Port Kara. The crowds hadn't yet descended in the numbers they did during the summer and, if he stuck to the clifftops and coastal paths, he could often walk for an hour or more without coming face to face with another human. After the dog attack, Nick had suggested that Lijah take it easy for a while but, despite the size of the beach house, it made him feel hemmed in. Walking had always helped him to think and, when he'd been trying to decide whether or not to move to London he'd walked miles every day. His best melodies had often come to him when he was outside, and exercise had helped him untwist the knots in lyrics when they just wouldn't flow properly. His reason for walking so much these last few days was only partly due to the writing of his next album stalling completely. He was spending far more time thinking about life in general than he was about lyrics, and desperately trying to work out what it was he wanted to do with his life. He'd promised his aunt that he'd find a way to move forward and yet, since being here, he'd harked after the past more than ever. Suddenly he wanted to be that nineteen-year-old again, trying to make the decision about whether to leave Port Kara for London, and wanting with all his heart to choose the other path.

Maybe if he'd stayed, he'd have spotted the signs of his mother's undiagnosed heart condition and he'd have got her the help she needed before it was too late. Maybe if he'd stayed, he and Amy would still be together and, even if he hadn't been able to save his mother, she could have had the joy of seeing him settled, possibly even starting a family of his own. It was what she'd always wanted. 'Don't let what happened between me and your father put you off finding someone to share your life with. When it works, it's amazing, just remember what your nan and granddad were like.'

A wistful smile had appeared on her face whenever she'd spoken about her parents. They'd died within about a year of each other, when Lijah was fifteen, but they'd been childhood sweethearts, together for over sixty years by the time they died, married for fifty, and still devoted to one another.

He couldn't get Amy out of his mind and had this crazy feeling that she was the one who could fill the gap in his life that had widened even further since his mum's passing. Deep down he knew it was because she was a link to the past and that secure foundation that had meant so much to him. Amy had been close to his mother and his aunt, and he didn't have to worry about whether his family dynamics made sense to her, she understood them, and being around her felt so easy as a result. It might explain why all of his walks lately seemed to end up passing by St Piran's hospital. He couldn't try to pretend, even to himself, that it was the most picturesque part of Port Kara.

He wasn't even sure what he was hoping to achieve by being there. Would he call out if he suddenly saw her? And, if he did, what would he say? It wasn't like he needed an excuse to talk to her, he'd be looking after Monty soon, helping Amy's mother to take care of the little dog while she was at work. He just wanted to talk to Amy, and tell her about his aunt's plans to start a new life and how, as much as he was thrilled for Claire, it had left him feeling more rootless than ever.

The jokes he'd made to Nick about starting a gardening business and staying in Port Kara hadn't been completely in jest. Maybe the gardening idea was far-fetched, he hardly knew the difference between a tulip and a daffodil after all, but he had seriously considered the idea of staying in Port Kara, and of rediscovering the happiest version of himself, the person he'd been just before he left. He'd achieved more in his career than he'd dared to dream, but it hadn't made him happier. He'd made some friends since becoming famous, people who understood what that felt like, but he'd never been sure how genuine these friendships were, and how much of it was because his career was in the ascendence. He'd lost two of those friends in the past year due to addiction, and drug taking was a backdrop of so many of the parties he was invited to. He wasn't an angel, but the promise he'd made his mother was always on his mind.

The trouble was, with Maria gone and his aunt about to leave, Nick and Amy were the only ones who made Port Kara feel like home. He couldn't hold Nick's career back, just because he'd decided to jeopardise his own, and Amy had only agreed to see him again because he was looking after Monty. If Port Kara was no longer his home, he had no idea where that left him, but for some reason he felt as though Amy held the key. She'd been the one he'd spoken to about some of the biggest decisions of his life, and she had this uncanny knack of taking her own feelings out of the equation. She must have wanted him to stay in Port Kara, but she'd urged him to leave, because she knew that was best for his career. She'd given him the proverbial kick up the arse he'd needed back then to follow his dream, instead of waiting for it to happen. Maybe that's what he needed now, a kick from Amy to push him down the right path. Whatever the reason, the urge to see her again had brought him back to the hospital every single day.

When Lijah had pulled out of the tour, he'd cut off his trademark dark wavy hair, that had fallen almost to his shoulders. When Lijah had said he wanted to cut off all his hair, Nick had been the one to wield the clippers, despite the fact that they both knew when the press got hold of it, they'd compare it to when Britney Spears shaved off all her hair, just another symptom of what they'd already described as Lijah's spiralling mental health crisis. Lijah didn't care what they wrote, for him the decision to cut his hair was all about anonymity and being able to blend into the background. And it had worked to an extent.

Combining a short crop with sunglasses that covered his distinctive eyes meant he hadn't been recognised nearly as often, except now the driver of the blue car heading towards where he stood, outside the hospital, slowed down as she drew level with him, staring in his direction. He dropped his gaze, turning to hurry along the pavement in the opposite direction. Lijah had always tried to interact with fans when they approached him, but he just wasn't feeling up to it. So when the blue car passed him again, slowing down for a second time, he sighed and raised the collar of his jacket in an attempt to obscure his face. He'd gone about another twenty or thirty metres, when he drew level with a heavily pregnant woman, stepping to the left to make sure he was on the roadside as the car passed by.

'Thank you.' She had a cheerful sing-song voice, but Lijah didn't respond as he spotted the blue car coming towards him again. It was going fast, clearly trying to catch another glimpse of him before he had the chance to disappear down a side road. He heard the rumble of a lorry coming from behind him, and turned to look. It was a wide-load and it had moved out past a row of parked cars. There was no way the blue car was going to fit through the gap that remained, but when he turned back again, expecting to see the driver slowing down to a stop, he realised the woman was still staring at him, not looking at the road. Everything seemed to be happening in slow motion as he waved his hands and screamed out the word, 'Stop!'

The young female driver was so close now that he could see the look of terror on her face when she realised what was happening. There was an elderly man just in front of Lijah, walking with the aid of a stick, and he lurched forward, pushing the man and himself towards the fence, just as the blue car mounted the pavement. The wing mirror of the car clipped him hard, like a punch in his side, pushing him even further forward.

'Jesus Christ.' He turned his head to look at the car, but his words were drowned out by the squeal of the brakes and then the most blood-curdling scream he'd ever heard in his life. The car had come to a halt, but the screaming hadn't stopped.

'Are you okay?' He drew back from the elderly man, helping to steady him.

'Yes, I'm all right, thanks to you.' The man looked shocked, but Lijah was already moving in the direction of the car. They were less than a hundred metres from the hospital, and up ahead he could see a couple of people running in their direction, but he was by far the closest to the car, and the lorry that was now blocking the road.

It was only when he reached the side of the car that he saw the pregnant woman lying on the pavement. She'd obviously been hit, but it wasn't her who was screaming, it was the driver. Lijah had never felt so inadequate in his life; he didn't have any medical knowledge, not even basic first aid. It would have been far easier to try and comfort the driver of the car, whose face seemed to be frozen into a scream, the sound she was making still unearthly, but something told him the woman on the pavement needed him more, even if he couldn't do anything to help in a practical sense. No one deserved to be alone in a moment like this.

'Can you hear me?' Lijah crouched down next to her, and she gave a little whimper. 'Okay, don't try to talk if it's too hard.'

'The baby.' Her voice was strangled, and one of her legs was at a weird angle. Lijah had to look away as a lump lodged in his throat, even before she grabbed for his hand, clinging to it like she was never going to let go. At least she still had some strength left, surely that had to be a good sign.

'It's okay, we're going to get help. You're going to be okay.' He had no idea if that was true, but he hoped to God he was right, as footsteps came thundering down the pavement towards him.

'Oh my God.' The young man who'd run up to them looked ashen. 'My girlfriend's gone into the hospital to tell them what's happened.'

'That's good.' Lijah nodded as another woman joined them, the lorry driver just behind her.

'Whatever you do, don't move her.' The lorry driver's tone was forceful, and Lijah nodded.

'Can someone please check on the driver?' The screaming had finally stopped, but she still hadn't got out of the car.

'I'll do it.' The woman moved towards the door of the car and, as the elderly man suddenly appeared in the road too, visibly shaking, the lorry driver helped him towards a bench by a bus stop, twenty feet further down the pavement.

'I'm scared.' The pregnant woman was still gripping Lijah's hand, but her voice was even weaker than before.

'I know, but I'm going to stay here with you until help arrives and I promise you and the baby will both be okay.' He was taking even more of a risk now, not just giving the woman an assurance but making her a promise that might well turn out to be a lie. It didn't matter for now, though, and Lijah knew it was what he'd have wanted to hear if it were him. It was clearly a struggle for her to speak, but something told him it was a good idea to keep her talking. 'The doctors are going to be here really soon, but I'll be here until they do. I'm Lijah, what's your name?'

'Ellen, and...' Her eyes flickered for a moment as if she was trying to focus on him, but instead a single tear rolled down her face, swiftly followed another. 'The baby isn't mine.'

13

The woman who'd come into the reception of the emergency department had been shouting so loudly that Amy had been able to hear her from the cubicles. She'd described a car mounting the pavement just outside the hospital and at least one pedestrian having been hit.

Meg, the newest doctor in the team, had headed outside with Esther and Eden, along with a couple of the paramedics who'd just dropped off another patient. Within minutes the patients started to arrive in the department, the team having split up to deal with individual casualties. The first was a young woman who was sobbing hysterically, who Eden quickly moved into a cubicle, followed by an elderly man who seemed more shocked than hurt. Esther was reassuring him as she wheeled him through to a second cubicle. It took far longer for the final patient to arrive, and to Amy's utter surprise Lijah was by the woman's side, as Meg and the paramedics wheeled her in.

'Amy, can you come through to resus, please?' Meg asked before she had the chance to ask Lijah what on earth was going on. 'We've stabilised the patient's neck and spine until we can be certain of her injuries, and we had to use sedation to perform a manual reduction to a displaced fracture in her lower left leg, to restore the radial pulse. So we'll need orthopaedics down here. We're also going to need obstetrics to check how the baby is doing, and make a decision about whether she needs to deliver, and we'll need to continue monitoring her vitals in the meantime.'

'Of course.' Any questions could wait, the fact that the patient who'd been hit by a car was pregnant made her blood run cold. It was almost unheard of for someone to be hit by a car and come off unscathed, but for a pregnant woman the chance of serious injury was even higher. She could be under sedation for as little as fifteen minutes, depending on the dose she'd been given, but at least for now she wasn't in any distress.

'I think it's best if you wait outside now.' Meg's tone as she turned towards Lijah was gentle but firm.

'Yeah.' He looked hollowed out with shock and Amy reached out to squeeze his hand.

'Do you know her?'

'I was just there when the accident happened.' He gave a visible shudder at the memory. 'Before she was sedated, I promised not to leave her until her husband got here. Will you let me know how she is?'

'When I can.' Amy squeezed his hand again, before following her colleagues through to resus. She'd talk to Meg or Esther later about how much she could share with Lijah. She tried not to think about how badly she'd wanted to wrap her arms around him and tell him he was amazing for stepping in to help a stranger in a situation that must have been terrifying. But in the meantime, all that mattered was making sure the patient got the best possible treatment, even if her chest ached at the thought of leaving Lijah, wondering and worrying about what was going on.

'Okay, this is Ellen. Her vitals are stable, but her injuries suggest—' Geoff, one of the paramedics began speaking once they were through to resus, and Amy's heart lurched at the sound of the woman's name.

'Oh God no, please.' Amy hadn't been able to stop herself from cutting Geoff off. A pregnant woman called Ellen outside the hospital, that was far too much of a coincidence. Amy had only met Ellen once, but as she stepped forward to look more closely at the patient's face, bile rose in her throat.

'She's Aidan's surrogate.' Meg's hand flew to her mouth in response to Amy's words, but she regained her composure quickly.

'Do you know where he is?'

'He was in paediatrics with a patient.' Amy was shaking now, even before Meg uttered the words she knew were coming.

'I think you should go and get him. I'll get someone else to contact his husband.'

'Okay.' Amy was nodding, but her feet wouldn't seem to move.

'Would you rather I did it?' Meg stepped forward and touched Amy's arm, but she shook her head. Aidan was her friend and as much as she hated the idea of giving him the news, he should hear it from her. Shaking her head again, Amy blew out a long breath and finally took a step towards the door, knowing she was about to have one of the most difficult conversations of her life.

* * *

Amy needed to tell Aidan what was going on, but Lijah was out there, in reception, just a few feet away, and she knew he'd be there for her if she asked him to be. Suddenly she realised she *did* want him to be there for her. She'd been so used to not leaning on anyone for so long, that she fought the urge for a moment. She always had to be the strong self-reliant one in the family, and Zach hadn't been the sort of person she could ever have relied upon. Since Lijah, there hadn't been anyone who'd she'd been able to be totally honest with about how she felt, but they'd been together as teenagers, with big emotions that had spilled out whether she wanted them to or not. It would have been impossible not to be honest with him – they used to share everything. She'd known how he felt about his dad leaving and how much he worried about wanting to make sure his mother and aunt were okay. He'd seen how difficult her home life could be because of her brother, and his house had become a place to escape to when Nathan's behaviour was at its worst. He'd been her rock before, and she needed that today, because she was terrified she was about to break Aidan's heart.

'Lij.' Amy's chin wobbled as she stood in front of him. His head was bowed and the collars of his jacket were pulled high up around his face, sunglasses obscuring the eyes that would have given him away otherwise, despite the closely cropped hair. If she didn't know that about him, she might have thought he was playing up to a celebrity stereotype, wearing dark glasses indoors, but even the little she'd seen of him had made her strongly suspect that nothing he did was because he enjoyed being recognised.

'Hey.' He got to his feet, removing the sunglasses, his voice filled with concern, and she leaned into him, breathing in the citrussy scent of his aftershave. 'Is it Ellen?'

'Yes, no...' Her voice trailed away and she couldn't seem to catch her breath.

'It's okay, just breathe for a moment.' He stepped back, and she took a couple of slow breaths until she was finally ready to speak.

'Ellen is a surrogate and she's carrying a baby for my friends. It's been such a long road for Aidan and Jase to get to this stage, and all they've ever wanted is a baby of their own. They're supposed to be going to Paris tonight, for a babymoon, and now I don't even know if there's going to be a baby. They're bringing the obstetric team down, but with an impact like that...' Amy couldn't finish the sentence. 'I need to find him and tell him what's going on, but I don't think I can do it by myself. You were with Ellen, so I wondered if—'

'I'll come with you.' She hadn't even finished the sentence before Lijah made the offer.

'Thank you.' She moved towards the door that led the cubicles, her heart thudding so loudly in her ears that it seemed to beat out the rhythm of her feet. There was a section of the emergency department dedicated specifically to paediatrics, which was where Aidan had taken his six-year-old patient and her mother, after the little girl had fallen off the arm of the sofa when she and her sister were pretending to be unicorns. Unfortunately, Eliza had been wearing a plastic tiara at the time, and some of the shards of plastic had become embedded in her forehead when both Eliza and the tiara had hit the wooden floor. Amy knew he had been waiting for the play therapist to arrive, so that she could distract the little girl, while Aidan removed the splinters of plastic, and glued the wound where some of the skin had split on impact. He'd be checking her over for any signs of concussion in the meantime and would order a scan if he felt she needed one. Amy was almost certain he'd still be with the patient as a result, and her shoulders sagged when she heard his voice, partly in relief and partly because the moment when she had to break the news was getting closer.

'You're doing brilliantly Eliza, one more piece and we'll be ready to get my magic glue out. Then you can pick not one, not two, but three stickers. There are lots to choose from, but maybe not the unicorn ones, because they're far too naughty aren't they? Just look what they made you do!' Aidan's laugh was echoed by giggling from the little girl and Amy felt her heart contract all over again. He was going to be an amazing dad and all she could do was pray he got the chance.

'Right, that's it, that's the last piece out.' Amy hesitated, exchanging a glance with Lijah and wondering whether she should wait until he'd glued the wound on Eliza's head, but she had no idea whether the obstetric team had already made a decision about the baby. What if hesitating cost Aidan the chance, to be there when the baby was born, or worse still cost him the chance to say goodbye. Amy drew back the curtain.

'I'm so sorry to interrupt. I need to have a very quick word with Aidan.' Amy gave Eliza's mother a tight smile and she wondered if the other woman could see how fake it was. The little girl was being kept occupied by the play therapist, and she barely even glanced in Amy's direction.

'I'll be right back, don't go galloping off anywhere!' Aidan winked at Eliza, who giggled again and followed Amy away from the cubicle.

'Hey what's up?' For a moment he didn't seem to notice that Lijah was standing a few feet away and then he grinned, before lowering his voice into the kind of theatrical whisper Eliza's mother could probably have heard. 'Ooh very nice too; didn't I tell you he'd be back?'

'We need to have a chat, in the relatives' room if it's free.'

Amy tried to keep her tone light, but she'd clearly failed as Aidan's smile slid off his face.

'What's the matter, is it Jase?'

Amy shook her head. 'I really think it would be better if we—'

Aidan cut her off. 'Just tell me.' His voice had risen and there was naked fear in his eyes. He knew something awful had happened and there was no good way of telling him.

'It's Ellen; there's been an accident, she's been hit by a car and—' Amy had barely begun before Aidan smacked his fists against his forehead.

'No, no, no. She's supposed to be here in ten minutes. It must be someone else. It's not Ellen, it can't be.' Aidan's eyes were wild with terror by now, and he grasped Amy by the shoulders, clearly desperate for her to reassure him that he was right about it being someone else, but she seemed to have lost the power of speech again and she was terrified she was going to burst into tears if she tried to carry on. Lijah stepped forward instead.

'It's definitely Ellen. I was there when it happened. A car mounted the pavement just outside the hospital, but they've stabilised her and—'

'What about the baby?' This time Aidan's question cut Lijah off and Amy swallowed hard, desperately trying to rein in her emotions to allow her to speak.

'We don't know yet, they've called the obstetrics team down and both Ellen and the baby are in the best possible hands. But you need to get to resus to be with her, I can take over here.'

'I can't go to resus, I can't be with her if they say the baby's gone.' Aidan shook his head again. 'I can't do it. I just can't.'

'You can. Esther's there, she'll support you and someone was going to call Jase to come in too. I know this must be incredibly hard, but Ellen needs you, Aidan.'

'I can't. If we lose the baby... I just...' Aidan dropped his head into his hands. 'I can't.'

'What if I came with you?' Amy reached out, but he flinched away from her.

'I've got to get some air, I can't do this now.' Before she could reach for him again, Aidan turned away from her, breaking into a run.

'Oh God, we need to go after him, I'm scared of what he might do, but I can't just leave the patient either.' Amy felt as if she was being torn in two. She desperately wanted to run after Aidan, but a big part of her was terrified of making things worse. She'd already made a hash of breaking the news to him.

'I'll go.' Before she could even protest, Lijah had set off in the same direction as Aidan. She had no idea what he'd say if he found him, or whether he'd be any more successful than she was at persuading Aidan that he needed to be with Ellen right now, but she didn't have much choice other than to let him try. All she could do was pray that Lijah's gift with words extended beyond the lyrics of his songs, and that he could find a way to get through to Aidan before it was too late.

* * *

Amy could barely breathe as she headed back to the emergency department. Aidan had been every bit as devastated as she'd feared he'd be, and her stomach felt as though it was made of lead. Aidan and Jase were made to be parents. There had been so many obstacles in the way, and some of Aidan's family had been resistant to the idea at first. Even after Isla had offered to become their egg donor, there'd been another bump in the road, when she was diagnosed with a chronic illness. None of them had been sure at first if the egg donation could go ahead, or whether there was any risk of passing on the condition, but thankfully they'd eventually been given the go ahead.

Finding a surrogate had been another huge step, and Amy had witnessed Aidan's joy when he'd shared the news that Ellen had agreed to help them, but even then it didn't go smoothly. Although Ellen had fallen pregnant, she'd had a miscarriage before they reached the twelve-week scan, and Amy's heart had broken for Aidan and Jase. It had come at a time when their friend Danni's pregnancy was becoming more obvious, and a talking point in the department. Aidan had never shown a shred of bitterness, and had fussed around Danni more than almost anyone else. He'd been so happy for her, despite his own pain, and the whole team had been thrilled when he'd finally announced Ellen's second pregnancy to everyone, after the twelve-week scan had confirmed everything was looking good. Amy might have teased him about leaving her in the lurch when he went on paternity leave, but she'd been thrilled for him, her eyes filling with tears the day he'd shown her the first scan photos, unable to hold back his own tears every time he got them out.

'We're actually getting our dream, Ames. I can't believe it. I would ask you to pinch me, but I know you'll enjoy it far too much, especially after you got the short straw with Stella Steve yesterday.'

'It's your turn next time, no rock, paper, scissors contests to decide who gets to tell him that the cause for his headache is the amount of lager he's consumed.' Amy had sighed then. Steve was one of their regulars, turning up in A&E at least once a week, reeking of alcohol and sometimes worse. They'd referred him to various services to try and support him with his addiction and other problems, but he never went to any of the appointments. All they could do was check him over, and try to clean him up a bit, making another referral for help each time, before discharging him. The last time he'd been in, Amy had gone to the hospital shop to buy Steve a sandwich and a few other basics before sending him off, and when she'd got there Aidan was already queuing to do the same thing. They might joke about whose turn it was to see Steve, but it was really just a coping mechanism for dealing with the frustration they felt at not being able to help him. It was always sad when a patient didn't seem to have anyone who cared about them enough to feel like it was worth caring about themselves, and Steve was one of those people.

'I promise I'll see him next time he's in. Now look at this scan picture again and pinch me, just a little bit, so I know this is real and that me and Jase really are going to get our baby.' He'd leaned his head on top of hers then, but she hadn't pinched him.

'It's real. And that little baby is so lucky to have you and Jase.' Just for a moment she'd felt a stab of something that felt a lot like fear, scared that she might never experience that kind of joy first hand, but then she'd shaken it off. Aidan's joy was infectious and it hadn't waned once, but now that dream might be slipping through his fingers and Amy's throat was choked with a very different set of emotions.

For as long as she could remember, she'd tried to fix things for other people and to make them feel better. But there was nothing she could do to fix this for Aidan. She felt as if she'd failed him, not handling it well enough when she'd broken the news, and standing there, as if she was frozen to the spot, when he'd taken off. She should have gone after him straight away. She'd let him down and if it cost Aidan his one chance to be there when the baby arrived, whatever the outcome, she'd never forgive herself.

When she reached the door to resus, she hesitated for a

moment. Taking a deep breath, she pushed it open, offering up another silent prayer that miraculously everything would somehow be okay. Her biggest fear was that Ellen wouldn't be there, because things had taken a terrible turn, and Amy's whole body flooded with relief to see her hooked up to a series of monitors, her eyes open now that the sedation was wearing off. Jess, who was one of the senior midwives from the maternity department, was by her side, along with Ameera Shah, a consultant obstetrician, who was scanning Ellen's abdomen. Meg was still there too, and Amy held her breath as her colleague walked towards her.

She tried to read Meg's expression. There was a pinched look of concern about her, but she'd noticed that look before. Amy didn't know that much about Meg yet, because she hadn't taken up any of the team's offers to meet up outside of work, but she had the look of someone who'd seen far too much trauma. It was etched on her face somehow, which made it impossible to read how she was feeling.

'How is she?' Amy whispered the question, not wanting to cause Ellen any further distress, and Meg bit her lip for a moment before answering.

'We sent her straight in for a CT while we were waiting for the obstetrician. The good news is there's no indication of any other internal bleeding, but the placenta...' She glanced over her shoulder towards Ellen, and then back to Amy again. 'There's an obvious break to her left leg, but the rest of her reflexes are normal, which is a really good sign. She might need an operation to stabilise the fracture, but I've got a feeling the baby is going to need to take priority.'

'Thanks for letting me know. Aidan freaked out a bit, but Lijah has gone after him, so I'm sure he'll be here soon.' Amy really hoped she was right, but before Meg could even respond, the situation escalated.

'There's evidence of placental abruption, on the boundary of stage two and three.' Ameera exchanged a glance with Jess. This didn't sound like the good news Amy had been praying for.

Ameera turned towards Ellen. 'The baby's heartbeat is strong and stable, but there's evidence of damage to the placenta, which is causing some bleeding. Given that you're thirty-four weeks pregnant, I think the best course of action would be to perform a C-section as soon as a theatre is available. We can administer corticosteroids to help the baby's lung development, but I think given the severity of the damage to the placenta, the bleeding is likely to worsen if we don't take action.'

'The baby's parents...' Ellen's words were barely audible and, as she tried to sit up, Meg put a hand on her shoulder. The blocks around her neck had been removed, but even if she had escaped with just a badly broken leg, getting up was out of the question for now.

'I don't want you to worry about any of that.' Meg looked away from Ellen, towards Amy, and she nodded in response to the unspoken question. 'Aidan and Jase are both on their way. Right now, we need to focus on you and the baby.'

'I can't lose their baby.' Ellen's tone was pleading and Ameera shook her head.

'We're not going to let that happen.'

'Is there anyone else you want me to call for you, Ellen?' Amy moved closer to the bed as she spoke.

'My husband. Aidan's got the number.' The effects of Ellen's sedation had mostly worn off, but she'd been given strong painkilling medication as well, and she was slurring her words slightly, as if she'd had too much to drink.

'I'll make sure we get hold of him, try not to worry, everything's going to be okay.' Amy's words didn't sound convincing, even to her own ears. She just hoped Ellen hadn't noticed the wobble in her voice, and that Jase would be here soon. At least then he could get hold of Ellen's husband, and be there if they decided to deliver the baby early, because there was no guarantee that Lijah would be able to find Aidan, let alone persuade him to be with Ellen in time for the arrival of the baby.

14

Lijah had taken off in pursuit of Aidan almost straight away, but he hadn't been able to catch him. He'd headed down the corridor that led outside to the hospital's main car park, but there'd been no sign of him and peering into cars had only earnt him funny looks, a few of the occupants doing a double take when they clearly realised they recognised him from somewhere. He didn't need to get into one of those all-too-familiar conversations right now.

'Has anyone ever told you that you look just like Lijah Byrne?' Or, 'I'm sure I recognise you from somewhere, do you work in the Co-op on the high street?'

He needed to find Aidan and persuade him that no matter how difficult it might be to face the prospect of losing someone, not being there if the worst happened would be infinitely worse. Lijah knew that better than anyone.

Heading back to the hospital, he stopped at a sign pointing the way to various wards and departments. He barely knew Aidan, so how the hell was he supposed to work out which way he'd gone? Suddenly his gaze landed on two words: *Hospital*

Chapel. That had to be worth a shot. It was where Lijah had gone when he'd got the news that his mum had collapsed. Well not exactly a hospital chapel, but the multi-faith prayer room at LAX, the airport he'd headed straight to when he'd got the call and had discovered the next plane he could get on wouldn't leave for three hours. He'd prayed then, for the first time in as long as he could remember. He'd done it again when he'd got to Scotland, in the chapel at Broadford Hospital, but he hadn't even known what he was praying for. His beloved mum was already gone by then and nothing could bring her back. Lijah had been desperate for something, anything, to alleviate the crushing pain of knowing he'd never hear her voice again, never be able to ask her advice, or get folded into one of her hugs that had the power to make everything feel right.

There'd been no divine intervention, but he'd been able to breathe at least and that was enough. Just breathing in and out was all he could hope for without his mother. If he could just keep going, keep working, he thought he might find a way through it. It was the moment he'd decided to press ahead with his ill-fated tour in the wake of her death, as a way of trying to avoid his grief.

Lijah's pace quickened as he headed towards the chapel, moving too fast for anyone to speak to him, even if they did recognise him. Amy had looked devastated when Aidan had disappeared, and he'd been torn between wanting to comfort her and going after him. For once he wanted to be the one who found a way to make things better for her, rather than the other way around. Lijah had leaned on Amy often during the three years they'd been together. The only time she'd needed him in the same way had been when her father had been taken seriously ill, ironically with a heart problem, like the one that had killed his mother. The rest of the time, he'd been the one who'd always seemed to need her more.

Reaching the door of the chapel, it suddenly dawned on Lijah that he had no idea what he was going to say to Aidan, even if he was inside. How was he supposed to persuade this stranger to come with him? He had to try, for Amy's sake as well as Aidan's.

Going inside, he spotted Aidan straight away. He was sitting on the front pew, his head buried in his hands. Aidan was clearly desperate to be a father, and to give his child everything he could, most of all love, and now that might be denied to him. Sometimes life was so unfair.

'Hi.' Lijah's voice was low as he drew level with where Aidan was sitting, but his head still jolted back in shock, his face deathly pale and his eyes red rimmed.

'I don't know what I'm doing here.' Aidan's words mirrored the thoughts that had been going through Lijah's mind when he'd sought solace in the chapel on the day of his mother's death. 'I don't even think I believe in all of this. All the church has been to me, is an axe for my father to grind, but I don't know what else to do.'

'Sometimes there's nothing you can do but hope and pray, even if you're not sure there's anyone listening to your prayers.' Lijah was trying desperately to find the right words to offer some comfort, and to avoid saying anything that might cause Aidan even more pain. 'But there is something you can do this time. You can be there for Ellen, and for Jase. Whatever happens they both need you, and I think you need them too. If you're sitting here, and the worst does happen, it won't make it any less painful, it'll just layer guilt on top of everything else. And if the baby comes without you being there, you'll never get a second chance to witness those first moments, and you'll be filled with regret, even if everything's okay. I know it's scary having to face what might be happening with Ellen and the baby, but there's no upside to staying here.'

'I can't let Ellen see me like this. I don't want her to think that all I'm worried about is the baby, because that's not true, but I can't hide the fact that the thought of losing the baby is killing me. Jase has had to be strong for me so many times in the past, but he's going to need me now and I'm just going to let him down.'

'Just being there is enough. I promise you the only way you'll let him down is if you aren't there.'

'Do you think...?' Aidan swallowed hard. 'From what you saw, do you think Ellen and the baby will be okay?'

'Her leg seemed to have taken the brunt of the impact, but she was stable by the time they brought her in. So yeah, I think they're both going to be okay.' He was still offering assurances he had no qualifications to make, but he knew it was what Aidan needed to hear and if it persuaded him to get back to the emergency department right now, that was all that mattered. Lijah might not be certain that Ellen and the baby would be okay, but he didn't have a shred of doubt that Aidan needed to be there, whatever the outcome, and that he'd regret it to his dying day if he wasn't.

'Will you walk back with me?' Aidan looked at him. 'I'm not sure I trust myself to make it there otherwise.'

'Of course I will.' Lijah held out a hand to the man sitting in front of him, a virtual stranger he somehow felt an instant connection with, and pulled him to his feet. Aidan might be about to go through the toughest moment of his life, or he might be about to experience the greatest joy he'd ever known and finally fulfil his wish of becoming a father. Either way he wouldn't be facing it alone, and Lijah was more certain than ever that all that really mattered in life was having someone to share the highest of highs, and the lowest of lows with. And he wanted that for himself.

* * *

'Where's Aidan?' It was the first thing Jase asked when he got to the hospital. Amy's shift had officially ended about twenty minutes after Ellen was admitted, so she was waiting for him when he arrived.

'He freaked out when I told him about Ellen's accident.' Amy repeated what she'd told Meg, and Jase gave a shuddering sigh.

'He's not the only one.' He clawed at the collar of his jumper, and Amy could see how terrified he was. He and Aidan were so close to fulfilling their dream, and now there was a chance it would all be snatched away. 'I don't know what we'll do if we lose the baby, she's already our whole life. I'm not sure we'll be able to carry on.'

'Oh Jase, it's going to be okay.' Amy put her arms around him. 'They're preparing Ellen for theatre now.'

'I need Aidan, whatever happens.' His eyes filled with tears as he pulled away again. 'He doesn't even know we're having a girl. He wanted a surprise, but I just had to know. I couldn't wait and I didn't understand how Aidan could, but he said he wanted to make it even more special. The sonographer gave me an envelope and I was terrified I was going to let it slip. That's been my main worry for months; I never dreamed that something like this would happen.' Jase's voice caught on the words. 'It's so stupid, because it doesn't matter, all that matters is that I've got Aidan and our baby girl. They're everything to me.'

'We're having a girl?' Aidan's voice behind them made Amy jump, and she sprang away from Jase, as though they'd been caught doing something underhand. Her breath quickened when she realised Lijah was with him.

'Yes, we're having a girl.' Jase nodded, a sob escaping from his throat. 'Oh God, please let her be okay, I couldn't bear it if anything happened to her, or to you. You can't freak out on me now, I need you.'

'I know.' Aidan held his arms out to his husband and the two of them clung together. They were in the eye of the storm, but they had something to cling to, and that's what would get them through whatever happened with Ellen and the baby. It would break their hearts if they lost their daughter, but they would find a way to carry on because they had a reason to, and that reason was each other. Amy turned to look at Lijah and, as their eyes locked, her stomach somersaulted. Oh no. This was not happening. She was not letting Lijah back into the place in her heart that had never belonged to anyone else. Except it seemed she didn't really have a choice and, when he stepped forward and reached for her hand, the somersault went into freefall. This wasn't good, this wasn't good at all, not if she wanted to stand a chance of protecting herself from getting hurt again. Amy just hoped it was the emotion of the moment, because she couldn't allow this to happen. Either way now wasn't the time to worry about it, because she needed to make sure Aidan and Jase were with Ellen.

'You guys should get up to theatre; they're about to take Ellen in for her C-section.'

'Are they going to let us both in?' Aidan gave Amy a look of pure desperation. He was always kidding around and making jokes, but he looked like a different man, his mouth turned down at the corners. All she could do was hope that within the next hour he'd have a reason to smile like he'd never smiled before.

'Ameera said as far as anyone is concerned, you're staff, you're in there as a theatre assistant, which means Jase gets to be Ellen's birthing partner, but you're both going to miss it if you don't get up there right now.' Her tone was firm. She knew the urgency in her voice was probably the best way to try and counter their fear. Whatever the outcome, they both needed to be with Ellen.

'Will you come and wait outside?' Aidan's face searched hers. 'I don't want to call anyone until we know what's happening, but I might need you to phone around for me if—'

It was another sentence Aidan couldn't finish, but he didn't have to, and Amy nodded, her hand still in Lijah's. She knew she should have let it go, but she couldn't, because she needed someone in that moment too. If Aidan and Jase got bad news, they'd need her, but suddenly she wasn't sure she was strong enough unless she had Lijah's support.

'Can you come too?' She kept her voice low and Lijah squeezed her hand as he nodded. She was going to have to release his hand eventually, but she couldn't have let go in that moment if her life had depended on it.

Aidan and Jase had been rushed through to get changed into scrubs for theatre and the corridor outside the theatre was quiet. There was a row of four seats halfway down, about twenty metres away from the double doors that Aidan and Jase had disappeared through. Amy had explained to Lijah that only emergency surgery would take place at this time in the evening, and it felt eerily silent, almost deserted, as the two of them sat and waited for news.

'How did you persuade Aidan to come back?'

'He was worried that he wouldn't be able to give Ellen or Jase the support they needed and that him being there might somehow make things worse. I said sometimes all people need is for you to be there, and that's enough.'

'Sometimes it really is enough.' She was looking at him like she wanted to say something else, and he had an almost overwhelming desire to reach out and touch her face. They'd held hands all the way from the main entrance to the hospital, but they'd broken off to hug Aidan and Jase and wish them luck, and it was like the spell had been broken too. His fingers had twitched with the desire to reach for her hand again. Instead, he'd rested his hands on his legs.

'Claire's moving to Tenerife, she's met someone.' He needed to talk to someone about his aunt leaving, someone who understood why that had left him feeling as though the last of the roots he had in Port Kara had been wrenched from the ground.

'I know.' She smiled. 'We still chat and meet up for coffee every once in a while too. She told me all about Dee, and it's so nice to see her smile again after losing your mum.'

'I should have known you wouldn't stop visiting, just because Mum was gone.' Lijah sighed, wishing he could say the same about himself.

'In a way it was always easier spending time with Claire than with your mum.' She shook her head when he widened his eyes in surprise. 'I really loved Maria, but sometimes seeing her made me miss you more, especially when she seemed determined to try and convince me that you'd be back eventually and that we'd pick up where we left off. When I said we needed to split up, to give you a chance to make a go of things, I held on to that hope too, for far longer than I should have done. Then when your career started to go crazy, I had to accept that our moment had passed. But your mum still kept insisting that you'd come home eventually because of me, and that was hard to hear when...' Her words drifted away to nothing.

'When what?' He couldn't stop himself from asking the question. He didn't know what she was going to say, but he knew what he wanted it to be.

'When that's what I still wanted too, deep down: for you to come home.' She looked at him and he couldn't hold back the smile that was tugging at the corners of his mouth. This had been exactly what he'd wanted to hear, but she shook her head again. 'I knew it could never work. You lived in a whole different world, surrounded by people as famous and successful as you. Mine was the ordinary, mundane life you'd wanted to escape from, and I know the only way you'd come back here was if something went horribly wrong with your new life. So I stopped wishing for that, because you were living the life you'd always wanted.'

'I never thought of your life as ordinary or mundane. I missed everything about Port Kara, especially—' He'd been about to tell Amy that she'd been what he'd missed the most, but she didn't let him finish, cutting him off by standing up.

'I'm going to get a drink; do you want one?' It was clear by her tone and her decision to remove herself from the situation that this conversation was over. The last thing he wanted was to put any pressure on her, especially when she was already so worried about the baby.

'I'll go.' He moved to stand up, but she put a hand on his shoulder.

'No, I need a minute. I've got to call Mum and let her know I'll be back late for Monty.'

'Tea would be great then, thank you.' Maybe it was for the best that she hadn't let him finish. He needed to process his own thoughts. Losing his mother and then hearing that his aunt was moving away had done something strange to him. It was as if he was desperate to cling to the last vestiges of his past, and all of that now suddenly seemed to be wrapped up in Amy. That was a lot to put on her, he was a mess right now, and she deserved so much better than that. He didn't want to cause her any pain, even accidentally. He had to be certain of his plans before he told her just how much seeing her again had affected him.

'Still one and a half spoons of sugar?' She smiled, lifting some of the tension between them, and he couldn't believe she remembered, even as she teased him about the reason. 'One isn't sweet enough, but two is far too sweet. That was always your justification for being so awkward, wasn't it? Still Goldilocks then! It's good to know some things never change.'

'No, some things never do.' He returned her smile, but she had no idea he wasn't just talking about the way he took his tea, and he wasn't going to tell her, at least not until he'd got everything straight in his head. But as he watched her walk away to get the drinks, he felt more confused than ever.

Amy was back within a few minutes, clutching two cardboard takeaway cups and as she came back down the corridor towards him, suddenly there was no doubt left in his mind. He still had really strong feelings for Amy, and he was almost sure it wasn't just because he felt rootless. The trouble was, he had no idea whether acting on those feelings would be the right thing for her, or whether she'd even be interested.

'Here you go, Goldilocks.' She laughed as she passed him the drink and the urge to kiss her was so powerful he had to grip the edge of his seat with his other hand, to stop himself from acting on it.

'She's here! She's okay and she's here!' Aidan's shout reached all the way down the corridor and Lijah looked up to see him thundering towards them, just before he scooped Amy into his arms and spun her around, coffee cup and all.

'Oh my God that's brilliant, I'm so happy for you both.' She was already crying as Aidan finally set her down, and tears were pricking Lijah's eyes too. He barely knew this man, but there was a wave of emotion welling up inside him all the same.

'She's beautiful Ames, you should see her. She's got loads of hair and the most amazing eyes. She's tiny, only four and a half pounds, but she's absolutely perfect. Thank you so much for making sure I didn't miss it.' He planted a kiss on her cheek and then reached down towards Lijah, doing the same to him. 'You too Lijah. I mean any other time I'd have been totally star struck, but what you did today... making me see how stupid I was being. I can never thank you enough.'

'I didn't do anything special, I'm just so glad things worked out.' Lijah shrugged. 'I feel really lucky I got to be part of something so amazing.'

'I want you both to meet her as soon as you're allowed, but right now I've got to get back to my husband and my baby girl, because I miss them already.' Aidan wasn't even trying to hold back the tears any more, but he was smiling too.

'Get yourself back in there. The introductions to your beautiful daughter can wait. Just not too long, okay?' Amy hugged him again, and then he turned and ran back down the corridor in the opposite direction, as Lijah got to his feet.

'How amazing is that?' He looked at Amy and she nodded, her eyes glassy.

'It wasn't nothing, you know, what you did for Aidan. You don't even know him, but you still managed to make him see sense. I'm not sure many people could have done that, and I'm so glad you did.' She leaned towards him as if she was about to follow Aidan's lead and plant a kiss on his cheek, but then she moved her head slightly so that their lips met. All the feelings he'd been trying not to act upon came rushing to the fore again, and suddenly he was holding her and kissing her as if he'd been waiting a decade to do it again, and it turned out he had. It felt so right and all of the doubts and questions seemed to fade away in that moment, because he was incapable of thinking about anything else when he was kissing Amy. Just like he always had been.

15

When Gwen had got up for work, she'd felt as though she was wearing one of those old-fashioned diver's suits that helped the wearer to sink to the bottom of the ocean. Her limbs were heavy and her movements slow, like she was struggling to recover from a bad bout of flu. The spring dance show with the Port Agnes Quicksteppers was usually one of the highlights of her year, but she had to drag herself on to stage for the two numbers she was involved in, half-heartedly swaying her hips and hiding at the back, hoping no one would notice how much she was slowing down. When she'd performed a foxtrot with Barry, she'd been like a ragdoll.

'Is everything okay?' Nicky Kirby, who ran the dance group, was one of the loveliest women Gwen had ever met, so she'd never have come out and asked directly what the hell was wrong with her, but it had been clear something was.

'Just a few aches and pains that's all.' Gwen had seen the look on Nicky's face, and the faces of two of her friends from the dance group, Isobel and Maureen, who she'd persuaded to attend, promising them that you were never too old to follow a passion, even if you thought your dancing days were over. Everyone relied on Gwen to be the cheerleader for older women, and to dismiss age as a just a number. She couldn't admit she felt every single second of her seventy-two years and that a rocking chair and slippers suddenly held far more appeal than a sequinned dress. She'd be letting the side down if she told anyone that, and it might make her friends doubt their own abilities, so she'd painted on a smile instead, dropped a wink and made the sort of comment she was famous for. 'I'll have to start making Barry do more of the work in the bedroom!'

The only activity of any kind she wanted to do in the bedroom these days was to sleep. The irony was that despite her exhaustion she was having trouble sleeping, but when Barry reached out to her and brushed a hand against her thigh, she did something she'd never had to do with her husband and had faked it. It wasn't the kind of faking that involved over-exaggerated moans of pleasure, but a pretence of snoring that was so convincing it would have given Meryl Streep a run for her money.

The antibiotics for her water infection hadn't been the miracle cure she'd hoped for. There was still a fogginess that hadn't lifted, the like of which she hadn't experienced since the menopause, but if she was honest with herself it was even worse this time. There were a host of other symptoms too, a general loss of interest in everything from food to life in general. It was as though the sunshine had gone behind the clouds forever, and the woman who stared back at her in the mirror as she got ready for work looked so much like her mother had in the early stages of her illness.

Gwen had watched Alys slip slowly away into the same kind of fog she was experiencing now, never to return, and she felt as though she was clinging on by her fingertips or she'd follow her mother into that abyss. For now, she was faking other things too, trying to pretend to everyone, even Barry, that she was the same old Gwen, cracking jokes and weighing in with advice whenever she felt it was needed. But it was if she was putting on a show, an actor in her own life story. She was terrified that if she stopped acting, the tenuous grip she had on her old self would slip completely. She couldn't let that happen.

Heading into the hospital and opening the shop, she greeted everyone she encountered with her usual enthusiasm. No one would have guessed she was nursing a secret fear. Over her years she'd got used to hiding her own emotions in order to still be able to do her job. She'd had to do it all the time when her mother was entering the latter stages of aphasia, and again when her daughter had been left devastated by her fiancé cheating with one of her closest friends, just three months before their wedding. Her heart had broken for her daughter, who'd been so distraught she'd just wanted to curl up and hide from the world. Gwen had given the advice she always did in those kinds of situations and told Sally that the best thing she could do was go out and grab life by the short and curlies, and show her arsehole of an ex-fiancé just what he was missing.

'I don't want to meet someone new. I just want my old life back,' Sally had sobbed in response to her mother's suggestion.

'I'm not talking about finding a new partner, at least not a permanent one. You need to road test a few this time around. You wouldn't buy the first pair of shoes you saw, just because they fit would you? It's the same with men, especially when your last pair of shoes ended up leaving your feet covered in blisters. You need to make sure the next ones are a perfect fit, not an okay fit. I never thought Dean was anywhere near good enough for you anyway.' Gwen had laughed when her daughter had widened her eyes in response. 'But that's not why I want you to get out there. You wanted to travel before you met Dean, but you didn't do it because he liked his job and the fact that all his drinking buddies lived nearby. You've got nothing holding you back now sweetheart, go out and do what you want to do.'

It had taken another two weeks of sobbing before Sally had started to take on board any of her mother's advice, and during that time Gwen had felt almost as miserable as her daughter, hating to see how the light had gone out inside the girl who'd always been so full of life. But Gwen had continued to go to work every day, smiling at her colleagues and the women she was supporting through pregnancy and labour. They didn't want to hear about Gwen's worries, or feel that her focus was on anything but them and their babies at such a special time. No one would have guessed how worried Gwen was that her daughter might allow an idiot like Dean to ruin her life.

In the end, she needn't have worried. By the time the date of the wedding came around, Sally had applied to spend the summer as a guidance counsellor for a children's holiday camp in one of the American national parks. It had been just the start of what had turned in to almost three years of globetrotting and adventure, during which time Sally had met a lovely new partner, with whom she now had three children. She'd told Gwen later that her mother's positivity had helped convince her that things really would be okay in the end. If Gwen had shown Sally just how hurt she was for her, she might have wallowed in her grief for far longer. It had been proof, if she ever needed it, that a brave face was sometimes all that was needed to carry someone through to better days. And it was the same now. She'd rather maintain the façade that life was all sunshine until she was forced to accept that it wasn't, and she hoped to God that there really would be better days ahead.

'Hi Drew.' Gwen held her hand up in greeting to the man

with sandy blond hair, who gave her a shy smile in response. Drew was a pathologist, working in a part of the hospital most people didn't know anything about, and which they wanted to pretend didn't exist. No one wanted to think about the morgue, or the people who worked there, but Drew was a lovely man. He was quiet and shy, and he bought the same thing every day, two newspapers – one broadsheet and one tabloid – a packet of wine gums, and a bottle of sparking water. She'd tried tempting him when they'd had special offers on Fruitellas or Chewits, but he never wavered.

'Just the usual thanks, Gwen.' He set his purchases down on the counter, and something about the dependability of his routine lifted her heart. Surely she couldn't be about to face a terrifying diagnosis when life was ticking by the way it always did, with Drew turning up to make his daily purchases. It felt reassuring and safe, even though there was absolutely nothing logical about her thought process.

'How are you?' She asked him the same question every time she saw him, and he always give the same answer.

'Nothing to complain about, how about you?'

She'd been about to respond and tell him she was doing great, the same lie she trotted out to everyone who asked, but her response was cut off by the arrival of Esther and her husband Joe, a consultant psychiatrist.

'Have you heard the news?' Esther was beaming, not seeming to realise that she'd cut into Gwen and Drew's conversation, and Drew was far too polite to say anything. Esther didn't wait for Gwen to respond either. 'Aidan and Jase's baby girl was born last night, in St Piran's.'

'How wonderful, but that's early, isn't it?' Gwen was trying to do the calculations in her head, but she just couldn't shift the fuzziness.

'Yes, Ellen was hit by a car. It must have been terrifying and it could have been so much worse! She had a badly broken leg and the impact damaged her placenta, so they had to deliver the baby early. They're both okay, but Ellen's had surgery and the baby's in special care. We're all desperate to meet her, but she can't have visitors yet, apart from Aidan and Jase. He's coming down at ten to show us some photos and tell us the baby's name. Can you get someone to cover the shop, so you can come down?'

'I'm so glad they're both okay, although it sounds as if it was really scary for all of them. I wouldn't miss seeing Aidan's photos for the world and I'm doing rounds this morning, once Caroline gets in. I'll make sure I time it so I'm in the emergency department at ten.' Just the thought of seeing Aidan and witnessing his joy at the arrival of his daughter, lifted Gwen's mood a bit more. It was a reminder that anything was possible. There was a time when Aidan and Jase had doubted they'd ever be parents, and Ellen's accident must have been terrifying. She knew Aidan wouldn't have been able to stop himself from imagining the worst, and she was thrilled it had all worked out okay. She desperately wanted to believe that everything might still be okay for her too.

'Brilliant, we'll see you at ten then.' Esther turned towards Drew, suddenly seeming to notice him for the first time. 'Sorry for interrupting, I'm just so excited!'

'No problem. It's always good to hear happy news.' Drew smiled and not for the first time Gwen found herself wondering about his life, but he was already halfway out of the shop. 'See you tomorrow, Gwen.'

'See you tomorrow.' She raised her hand in response, wishing everything was as predictable as Drew and the purchases he made at the shop. She wasn't asking for much, just to be allowed to live her life the way she always had, and she couldn't bear the thought of letting any aspect of it go.

Amy hadn't come down from the high she'd been on since the delivery of Aidan's daughter, but as overjoyed as she was for her friend, it wasn't the only reason she had to smile. The kiss she'd had with Lijah had been even better than she'd remembered. He'd been the first person she'd ever kissed. When she'd first started thinking about who her first kiss might be with she'd always pictured it being Justin Timberlake, and she'd practised quite a lot on his poster, but once her friendship with Lijah had deepened, she'd only ever imagined kissing him. Darcy, her best friend at school, had warned Amy that her first kiss – when it eventually happened – probably wouldn't be up to much.

'When I kissed Jake Stanford in Year 8, it was like he was trying to take my tonsils out with his tongue.' Darcy had pulled a face. 'And there was spit. *So much spit.*'

Amy had shuddered in response, suddenly wondering if she really wanted to kiss anyone at all, but when she and Lijah had finally moved beyond friendship, she'd realised she was willing to risk a DIY tonsillectomy, as long as he was the one performing it. As it turned out, the kiss had been good, really good, probably made even more so by her low expectations. She tried not to think about just how much experience he might have had to perfect his technique. It probably hadn't meant anywhere near as much to him, but that first kiss was a pivotal moment for her, a rite of passage she'd known even then would reserve a place in her heart for Lijah Byrne. She hadn't anticipated just how big a space in her heart he'd end up occupying.

By the time they'd been dating for a few months, she'd allowed herself to hope that although she'd never be his first kiss, she could be his last first kiss. It had been stupid to think that a couple of teenagers could make it, and she'd grieved for the loss of that dream for a long time after they'd split up.

When they'd kissed the night before, she'd realised that a part of her had never stopped grieving for it, because she'd never felt that way about anyone else. She had no idea where this was going, or if the kiss was a one-off, but she was determined not to turn herself inside out trying to work out what it meant. Even if it did turn out to be just one perfect kiss, she was glad it had happened. It had reminded her what it felt like to be with someone she was hugely attracted to. And she knew for certain it was something she hadn't experienced since Lijah. She also knew she didn't want to settle for anything less.

Amy wasn't sure she believed in soul mates, the world was just too big for that. But what she did believe in was the potential to find 'her person'. She wanted the kind of relationship Gwen and Barry had, still sharing adventures in their seventies. Even though she knew for sure now that Lijah leaving would break her heart again, she was grateful, because it had reminded her that some things were worth risking that kind of pain for.

* * *

'Here she is, Ellis Ciana Kennedy-Taylor. I know it's a bit of a mouthful, but it's a name that means a lot to us.' Aidan held up the photo of his daughter on his phone, looking every inch the doting father he was, a whole crowd gathering round to look. 'I'll be bombarding you with photos on our WhatsApp group all the time, but I wanted this to be the first time you all saw just how beautiful she is, because let's face it, she's the most amazing baby ever born.'

Aidan laughed as if acknowledging how biased he was, but Amy nodded. 'She's absolutely gorgeous and I love her already, because she's bringing Isla and Reuben home early.'

'Some might call that selfish.' Aidan laughed again, as he wrapped an arm around her waist and pulled her closer towards him. 'But I completely agree with you.'

Isla and Amy had quickly become close after they'd started working together, and she missed her friend. She'd been so glad to see Isla set off on an adventure after her diagnosis, but St Piran's just wasn't the same without her. The fact that Amy wanted to speak to Isla about Lijah, was just one of the many reasons she couldn't wait for her friend to come home.

'I love her name and I'm sure Cian would have been really touched.' Amy laid her head against Aidan's shoulder for a moment. He'd told her before about losing his childhood friend and it was obvious his daughter's middle name was a tribute to him. She'd been about to ask him about the baby's first name, when Gwen took the words out of her mouth.

'Did you choose Ellis for a special reason too?'

'About as special as it gets.' Aidan let out a long breath. 'She's only here because of the generosity of two amazing woman Ellen and Isla, so what better name could we have given her, than a combination of the two. We could never thank them for what they've done, but this feels so right.'

'It's beautiful!' It was Esther who'd taken the words out of Amy's mouth this time. 'And I know Danni is already lining up play dates with baby Caleb soon as Ellis is out of hospital.'

'I can't wait.' Aidan couldn't seem to stop smiling, and Amy was thrilled to see her friend so happy. It was almost impossible to believe how distraught he'd been the day before and it was amazing how quickly things could change. He squeezed her waist again. 'In the meantime, while she's here and Jase and I still have a bit of free time to call our own, I want to say thanks in a bigger way. I haven't worked out how I'm going to do it yet, but I feel like the luckiest person in the world right now. I've got everything I ever wanted, and it only feels right to give something back. We see so many people who are struggling; families who can barely afford to feed their children, and people who should have decades left, but who suddenly find themselves facing a life-changing diagnosis. Not to mention the loneliness of some of the elderly people we treat. That hits me right here every time.'

Aidan slapped his hand against his chest, shaking his head. 'I know I'm probably not making any sense, but it's like I've had... what's the word?'

'An epiphany?' Amy tilted her head to one side.

'I wouldn't go that far, I don't want to be struck by lightning.' He grinned. 'It's more of a re-evaluation of what really matters. You know, like Scrooge on Christmas Eve. I woke up this morning with the knowledge that my daughter is going to be okay, and I just want to give something back.'

'Maybe you're on to something with that Scrooge reference.' Gwen laughed at the look of mock outrage on Aidan's face. 'Not because you're a skinflint, you're always the first to buy the coffees, and once or twice I've even known you to share a Twix.'

'To be fair he only said he wanted to give back, not share his chocolate.' Meg grinned.

'Why do I suddenly feel picked on?' Despite his question, Aidan still couldn't wipe the smile off his face.

'You didn't let me finish.' Gwen furrowed her brow for a

moment, as if she was struggling to remember what she'd been about to say, but then it seemed to come back to her. 'I just meant we could do something that focuses on the past, the present and the future. You know, like the ghosts in Scrooge. We need some kind of project that would help out the very young, the elderly and a group in the middle.'

'*We*?' Aidan sounded surprised. 'It's a brilliant idea, but I don't want to railroad anyone into something they might regret.'

'And I don't want to muscle in, but I've felt a bit…' Gwen paused again. 'I don't know, a bit flat lately. I'd love to get involved in a new project, something to give me back my get up and go. So, if you want any help, you can count me in.'

'Me too.' Eden sounded almost nervous as she made the offer. 'All I've done since I moved back home is work and look after my little boy. It would be great to get involved with the community somehow.'

'You can count me in as well.' Amy looked up at Aidan. 'It sounds like we might have a St Piran's charity project in baby Ellis's honour.'

'Fabulous, so what now?' Aidan scanned his friends' faces for a second time.

'Whatever it is I'm in too, and I hate to be a party pooper.' Esther sighed. 'But some of us really ought to get back to work. Maybe we can meet up later in the week and bounce around some ideas. I know Danni will want to be involved too.'

'Getting together sounds like a great idea. I'll put something in the WhatsApp group.' Aidan's face must have been hurting from so much smiling.

'Brilliant.' Amy really wanted to get involved with the project, whatever it turned out to be. It might mean asking Lijah if he could look after Monty a bit more often, but that was no bad thing either. Even if their kiss had been a one-off, she couldn't deny how much she liked having him around; it was too late to protect her heart, it was already Lijah's and it always had been. She just had to remember it would never be the same for him, and try her best to play it cool, even if that felt next to impossible.

16

'Everything okay?' Wendy blurted out the question as soon as Gwen picked up her phone, the urgency in her voice obvious.

'Yes, I'm fine, why?'

'Because you were going to pick me up for the dance class.' Her friend sounded confused. 'You did say you would, didn't you?'

'Oh God, Wendy, I'm so sorry. It's just that there's been...' She blinked frantically, trying to think up a possible reason why she'd forgotten the arrangement. But she'd already told Wendy everything was okay, so she could hardly invent some kind of domestic crisis. There had to be a rational explanation for why she'd not only forgotten to pick up her friend, but had forgotten the dance class altogether. The trouble was, there was no explanation that would cut it, and it scared the life out of her. 'I'm sorry, I got distracted doing something else, but I'm on my way now and I'll give Nicky a ring on the way over to let her know we're running late. We'll only miss the warmup, so it should be fine.'

'Maybe for you,' Wendy laughed, 'but I'm like the tin man

until my joints warm up. So, if I can't work tomorrow, I might need to rope you in for a shift!' Wendy was the head of housekeeping at St Piran's and had recently joined one of the dance classes Gwen attended, in preparation for her upcoming wedding. She and her fiancé Gary, who was a nurse in the emergency department, were also having private lessons with Nicky to prepare for their first dance.

'I'll take you for a medicinal drink afterwards, you'll be fine.' Gwen attempted an upbeat tone, even though she felt anything but, and all she could do was hope that somehow she'd be fine too, despite the fact that the evidence suggesting otherwise was stacking up all too quickly.

* * *

One of the reasons Gwen enjoyed dancing so much was the endorphins it released. It didn't matter whether it was belly dancing or ballroom, she always felt good once she started to move and, about twenty minutes into the class, her worries finally started to recede a little bit. Another thing she liked about the class was the inclusivity, and Nicky always found ways of making sure that everyone who wanted to come along could do so. A couple of the very elderly group members mostly enjoyed just watching, but they'd join in with a few parts of the class. Brenda was the oldest member of the group at eighty-six and she used either a walker or a wheelchair to get around, depending on how much her arthritis was flaring up on any given day. She always came to class wearing one of her many sparkly sequinned tops and she was a huge fan of *Strictly Come Dancing,* knowing the name of every dancer and all the celebrity winners. Brenda told Gwen that coming to Nicky's classes was the highlight of her week, but she had no idea how much she raised everyone else's spirits by joining in so enthusiastically when she could, and applauding everyone else wildly when she couldn't. She'd just taken part in a Charleston-style dance, with lots of upper body movement, and she'd had a huge smile on her face the entire time.

'That was so much fun, but I really need a wee now!' Brenda's cheeks flushed red as she spoke, and Gwen wasn't sure whether it was from exertion or because she was having to ask for some help. Brenda's daughter, Amanda, was her carer, and she'd dropped her off to the class, but she wouldn't be back to pick her up for another thirty minutes.

'I'll take you.' Even as Gwen made the offer, she could see the reluctance on Brenda's face.

'I couldn't ask you to do that. I can't always' – Brenda lowered her tone and leaned in closer – 'pull my own knickers back up.'

'You can ask me and there's nothing I haven't seen in all my years as a midwife. All I want to know is whether your knickers are as sparkly as the rest of your outfit!' Gwen gave Brenda a wink to put her at ease.

'Sadly not, but as my daughter says, if there's ever any danger of me falling off the toilet, I'll be okay, because my knickers will act as a parachute!' Brenda laughed and Gwen couldn't help joining in. This dance class was turning out to be good for the soul for all kinds of reasons.

In the end, the trip to the bathroom passed without incident and there was no need to deploy Brenda's parachute pants. It was a few minutes later when all the drama started. One of the other dancers, Julie, moved a bit too close to where Brenda was sitting watching, and caught the heel of her shoe on Brenda's leg. Most people would have escaped with a simple scratch, but Brenda's skin was paper thin and the heel of Julie's shoe caught the surface of a varicose vein on the side of Brenda's shin.

'On my God, I'm so sorry.' Julie blanched as she looked; there was blood everywhere and it was like the scene of a murder within a couple of seconds. 'Someone help her, please, quickly!'

'It's okay.' Brenda clamped a hand over the wound as Gwen reached them, sounding very matter of fact, despite the growing puddle of blood pooling around her wheelchair. 'I always bleed like a stuck pig.'

'Can I have a look?' Gwen waited until Brenda nodded, before crouching down to look at the wound, but there was too much blood for her to see how serious it was.

'I'll get the first aid kit, do you think I should call an ambulance?' Nicky widened her eyes as she took in the amount of blood.

'It might be quicker for one of us to drive her in, depending on how bad the injury is. If you can grab me some paper towels, I might be able to stem the flow of blood for long enough to see how big the wound is.'

'I'll be right back.' Nicky was true to her word and within a few moments she was back with the paper towels and a first aid kit that included several different sizes of dressings.

'How are you doing Brenda? Does it hurt?' Gwen looked at the older woman as she spoke, but Brenda shook her head.

'A slight sting, but it's nothing. I had four children, back in the day when painkillers were considered unnecessary!'

'You're made of tough stuff.' Gwen smiled and then turned her attention back to Brenda's leg. As she suspected, the wound was tiny, but because of the varicose vein it was mimicking an arterial bleed. As soon as the pressure on it was relieved the blood started spurting everywhere. It looked like the work of a serial killer.

'It might stop bleeding eventually, but I think this is going to need cauterisation or maybe stitches.' Gwen looked up at

Brenda. 'But if I dress the wound fairly tightly, we should be able to contain the bleeding for long enough to get you to the hospital. Otherwise we might end up on an episode of *Crimewatch*, because it's going to look like I've tried to finish you off.'

'Nothing will finish me off. All the illnesses I've had in the last ten years, I think I must be part cockroach!' Brenda was still laughing, but poor Nicky looked white as a sheet as she leaned down to talk to Gwen again.

'Are you sure we shouldn't call an ambulance?'

'It could be hours if we do that.' Gwen turned towards Wendy, who was already busy mopping up the blood, as if she was at work. 'Would you be okay to come with me and sit with Brenda in the back until we get to the hospital?'

'Of course. We might just need to swap if the bleeding starts again. I'm okay with the clean-up, but I won't be much use with anything medical.'

'Worst case scenario, you'll have to be like the little Dutch boy who plugs the dam with his finger.' Gwen couldn't help laughing again at the expression on Wendy's face, reassured at how funny Brenda seemed to be finding the whole thing too, when a lot of people would probably be panicking. Brenda had clearly been through a lot in life, but it seemed laughter really might be the best medicine and it was something Gwen hadn't done nearly enough of just lately. Helping people had always been like another form of medicine for Gwen and had allowed her to put her own problems into perspective. It was something she was determined to carry on doing for as long as she possibly could, and she just hoped nothing would come along and force her to stop.

17

Lijah hadn't stopped thinking about the kiss he'd shared with Amy. It had brought back memories of falling in love for the first time, and it seemed to have reignited his desire to write music again, something that had all but deserted him since his mother's death. He'd been trying to force it since returning to Port Kara, but all the lyrics had been downbeat, with a hidden undercurrent of loss, even when his grief wasn't spelled out in the song itself.

He was meeting Amy today so that they could go through Monty's routine, before he began helping out properly. After they'd kissed, Lijah had wanted them to go out on a proper date, and at first she'd seemed keen. But within two days she'd backed out, blaming work and acting as if the kiss hadn't even happened, despite him being sure it had broken down the barrier between them. She'd finally agreed to meet him in her lunch break and, when she'd said there wouldn't be time to get to a restaurant, he'd told her that he'd bring in some lunch for them.

'I won't have long, maybe enough for a quick sandwich from

the hospital shop at best.' She's sounded so reluctant, he'd almost told her not to worry, and that she could just write down everything he needed to know about Monty. Except the thought of not seeing her had made his chest ache, so he'd decided to try and do something to remind her of just how good things used to be. He'd made her the same lunch he'd made on a day he'd never be able to forget, and he just hoped the memories it triggered would be just as special to her. Either way it had to be worth a shot.

Lijah was already waiting on the bench, fifteen minutes before Amy was due to have her lunch break. She'd warned him she might be late, but he'd wanted to make sure he was there when she came out. He was wearing a baseball cap, pulled low down over his eyes, which made it a lot easier for him to keep a low profile. Normally Nick would accompany him, or there'd be a bodyguard with him, which he hated. But now that Nick was spending every spare moment he could with Dolly, Lijah had put his foot down and said he didn't want a bodyguard while he was back home. Port Kara was the one place he wanted to be able to feel like the old Lijah, and he was prepared to take the risk that presented. He felt safe here, and blending in the way he was right now allowed him to pretend that nothing had ever really changed. But, when he glanced up he realised there was a car hurtling towards him, and the feeling of safety shifted instantly, adrenaline making his scalp prickle.

As he jumped to his feet, unable to believe that this could be happening again, relief flooded his body as the car skidded to a halt in front of him.

'I'll get Brenda out, if you can go and let them know we're coming in please, Wendy.' Lijah watched as a woman with ash-blonde hair stepped out of the car, and shouted the instruction to another woman who had just got out of the back seat.

'Okay.' Wendy disappeared through the doors into the emergency department, and Lijah walked towards the car as the other woman wrestled with a fold up wheelchair that looked too big for the boot of her car.

'Can I do anything to help?' He made the offer and she looked up at him, nodding.

'Yes please. I managed to wedge this thing in here, but I'm not sure how and I can't seem to get it out. I could do with a bit of muscle.'

'Sorry, you've just got me then. I'm more brain than brawn, trouble is I'm not that clever either.' Lijah grinned and her shoulders seemed to relax in response, as she looked at him properly for the first time.

'But you've got a sense of humour about yourself, which is worth far more. Are you Lijah Byrne, or do you just really look like him?'

Lijah considered picking the second option for a moment, but then he nodded. 'That's me.'

'I'm Gwen, a friend of Amy's. She's told me all about you.' There was a twinkle in Gwen's eyes as she looked at him, and he really wanted to ask her what Amy had said. But before he could, she turned back towards the rear passenger door of the car, leaving him to wrestle with the wheelchair.

'Come on then Brenda let's get your seatbelt off and get you inside so they can take a look at you.' Gwen's tone was gentle but firm, and Lijah had a horrible feeling she'd get Brenda out of the car before he could free the wheelchair. It really was wedged into the boot, forcing him to try and reposition it several times to get the angle right to free it.

'That's it, got it.' Lijah finally managed to get the wheelchair out and set it down, unfolding the seat and clicking the handles into place.

'Chauffeur service, and they say the NHS is on its knees.' Brenda smiled at him from her position in the back of the car. 'The question is, does that service extend to helping one old girl get another even older girl out of the car, because if Gwen tries to lift me she might become a patient too. I usually have to rope my son-in-law in to get me into the wheelchair.'

'Hey, less of the old girl, Brenda. You speak for yourself!' Despite her words, Gwen didn't seem remotely offended. 'You're only as old as you feel.'

'That may be, but eighty-six years of chip butties went into making this body, so I still wouldn't recommend you try lifting me, even if you feel thirty years younger than you actually are.'

'I think I've met my match in this one.' Gwen was smiling again as she turned to Lijah. 'But I don't want you hurting your back either, so would you mind just making sure Brenda doesn't try anything silly please, like getting herself out of the car, and I'll see if I can find a porter to give us a hand.'

'I thought we'd already established that I'm the muscle around here.' Lijah took off his hat, putting it on the roof of the car, and mimed rolling up his sleeves. 'Right then Brenda, let's do this.'

'I think I might burst a varicose vein more often, I haven't had this much attention from a handsome young man since I was in my twenties.' Brenda looked as though she was really enjoying herself. 'The only trouble is you really remind me of someone, and I think it's my grandson. So sadly I don't think this is going to be the start of something wonderful.'

'Don't rule it out before you've even given me a chance.' Lijah grinned before gently helping Brenda to swing her body round, so that her feet lifted over the lip of the car door and she was sitting on the edge of the seat facing outwards. 'Right, are you ready to stand up? I'll be there to steady you if you need me.'

'I'm ready. Ooh it's almost like we're dancing.' Lijah had hooked his arms under hers and she was right, it could have been a slow dance shuffle as he helped her into the wheelchair.

'Thank you, and if you ever give up the day job, you've got a future in portering.' Gwen gave him a nudge. 'Although I doubt it pays as well as what you do now.'

'Please don't tell me you're a lawyer, it was going so well between us.' Brenda wrinkled her nose.

'No, nothing like that, but I quite fancy the idea of portering, so how about I escort you inside to see if I've got what it takes?' Retrieving his hat, Lijah put it back on his head and pushed the wheelchair towards the entrance of the emergency department, reaching the doors just as Wendy and Amy appeared.

'Lijah?' Amy's face registered her surprise.

'He's been such a help.' Gwen looked from her to Lijah and back again, the look of mischievousness returning to her eyes. 'I couldn't get the wheelchair out of the boot and Brenda was struggling to get out of the car too. If it hadn't been for Lijah, we'd still be out there.'

'He's been wonderful.' Brenda looked at Amy too. 'And if I was fifty or sixty years younger, I'd definitely ask him for his number.'

'Looks like you're the hero of the hour.' Amy's expression was hard to read. 'But I think I can take over from here.'

'Sounds like a good plan.' Lijah let go of the handles of the wheelchair and walked around to the front, leaning down to say goodbye to Brenda. 'You take care of yourself Brenda and make sure those doctors get you sorted.'

'I think it's all a lot of fuss over nothing, I bet it's stopped bleeding now.' Before anyone could stop her, Brenda gave the bandage on her leg a surprisingly vigorous yank, pulling it downwards and sending a fountain of blood shooting up, making Lijah take the kind of leap to safety that an Olympic long jumper would be proud of.

'Brenda, I think there might be some people who would have appreciated a warning that they were in danger of being in the splash zone before you took the bandage off.' Amy didn't seem remotely fazed, and Lijah watched in amazement as she stopped the bleeding within seconds by temporarily re-dressing the wound. This was what real heroics looked like and it was the kind of thing Amy did every day, with probably far more challenging injuries. Something shifted in his chest as he watched her work, all the feelings he had for her deepening. He opened his mouth to tell her that he thought she was amazing, but she didn't give him a chance.

'Let's get you through to a cubicle then Brenda, I think we've established that the bleeding hasn't stopped.'

'I hope you get everything sorted.' Lijah briefly rested a hand on Brenda's shoulder.

'Thank you my love and I still think you're a hero, even if the sight of blood did make you jump like a jack-in-the-box!' Brenda gave a hearty laugh and when Lijah looked at Amy, he could see the amusement in her eyes too.

'I'll come and find you when I can. I don't think the emergency department is your natural home.' Amy's mouth was twitching, as if she was fighting the urge to laugh.

'Bang goes my idea of becoming a porter then.' Lijah gave a theatrical sigh. 'I'll see you outside when you're ready. I'll be on the bench, and I've made us lunch.'

'Perfect.' Her mouth curved upwards this time and all he could think about was kissing her again.

* * *

Amy was twenty minutes late to meet Lijah and she wasn't sure whether he'd still be waiting, but he was sitting on the bench where he said he'd be, writing into an A5 hardback notebook. It was like stepping back in time. When they'd first got together, he'd spent lots of time scribbling in notebooks, writing lyrics and making notes of ideas. She'd been fascinated by the way his mind worked and the fact he could create amazing things out of nothing. He'd always had a beautiful face, but he had an even more beautiful mind. She knew that creativity came with a price though, and that he thought more deeply and felt more deeply than most people. There were times when it could torture him, and she could see what his mother's death had done to him, even from a distance.

Lijah had never spent a lot of time on social media, and he hadn't posted anything publicly in the time since his mother's death, but that didn't stop the press intrusion. She'd seen the photographs of him looking distraught outside his mother's funeral, when the gutter press had used long range lenses to catch him at his most vulnerable. Then there'd been reports of his performances on the tour he'd embarked on in the wake of her death, his voice breaking in certain songs, and the haunted look that some reports suggested was down to addiction. Amy would have bet all she owned that the haunted look had come from heartbreak, and there'd been so many times she'd thought about reaching out to him. Instead, she'd checked in on him via Claire and had hoped he'd find a way to process his grief, instead of burying it.

'How's Brenda?' When Lijah looked up at Amy, her heart seemed to speed up. After the kiss she'd questioned whether they really could pick up where they'd left off, and a big part of her had really wanted to try. The trouble with Lijah was there was just too much at stake. She couldn't enjoy a fling with him for whatever it turned out to be, because there were always going to be deep feelings involved when it came to him. If things went any further between them and she let even more of those feelings reignite, it was going to hurt so much when it ended, as it almost certainly would. She just couldn't risk it, no matter how many memories the kiss had brought back and how attracted she was to Lijah. Within two days of the kiss, she'd decided that going back to keeping him at arms' length was a far safer bet, but that was much harder to do in person. The draw she felt towards him was almost overpowering, and she sat as far away from him on the bench as it was possible to do.

'Brenda's fine. The vein was stitched, it was never going to stop bleeding on its own.'

'Oh.' Lijah blanched. 'I wish visualising that didn't turn my stomach, but what can I say, I'm a wuss.'

'Your leap out of the way when the bleeding started did suggest that.' She grinned, his comment breaking some of the tension that was building up inside her, but when he mirrored her expression her pulse started racing again. This wasn't good, this wasn't good at all.

'I know. I'm pathetic.' He shrugged, still grinning, and she had to clamp her hand to her side to stop herself from reaching out and touching the dimple that appeared in his left cheek. She'd traced that dimple with her fingertips so many times, when they'd been lying side by side.

Lijah gave a mock sigh. 'Sadly my complete inability to deal with blood has scuppered my plan to go into portering, so I think it's going to have to be gardening.'

'As I recall, you regularly severed the heads of all your mum's flowers when you mowed the lawn for her. So, I'm not sure that's for you either.' Amy lifted her bag on to the bench in the space between them, as if that provided a barrier she wouldn't be able to cross, no matter how loudly her body screamed at her to do so. She had to listen to her brain and stay where she was.

'No gardening then either, jeez. Looks like I'm doomed to be a songwriter then.' He passed her one of the sandwiches, and she took a bite, a memory of one of the most amazing days of her life immediately flooding through her.

'Is this what I think it is?'

'What else?' He smiled that slow smile of his and suddenly she was seventeen again, in the run up to their end of year exams in the first year of sixth form, when the two of them had been at Lijah's place revising together.

'As I recall, the first time you made me this sandwich, it was because you had almost no food in the house.'

'That's right. Mum and Claire were in Italy, and they'd left me plenty of money to go food shopping, but I'd forgotten to get anything in. It was only after I'd already offered you something to eat that I realised how dire the situation was.' Lijah shrugged. 'There I was, desperate to impress you with my culinary skills, and all I had was some bread, half a jar of peanut butter, an apple, and a little bit of cheese. Peanut butter sandwiches seemed far too basic and there wasn't enough cheese to just use that, so I had to improvise.'

'Peanut butter, apple and cheese toasties. Who'd have thought that would work, especially cold.' Heat rose up Amy's neck at the memory of why they hadn't eaten the sandwiches when they were hot. She'd been dubious when he'd presented her with his creation all those years ago, but after she'd taken the first bite she'd leaned towards him.

'It might sound disgusting, but it tastes amazing,' Their faces had been just inches apart as she spoke. 'In fact, I'd say it deserves a chef's kiss.'

'I'd rather have one of yours.' Lijah's voice had been low, and he'd held her gaze. They'd been going out for almost a year by then, and even though they'd kissed hundreds of times, they'd never had sex. Lijah had gone out with other girls before Amy, but when they eventually slept together, it would be the first time for both of them. The fact that they were home alone with no chance of disturbance seemed to heighten the intimacy and suddenly it felt as if the moment might be right. They'd taken their relationship quite slowly and Lijah had never pushed her to take things further, but it was Amy who made the first move in the end, sliding her hand to the button of his jeans.

'Are you sure?' He'd checked and double checked as they'd fumbled awkwardly to undress each other, and she'd nodded every time, still leading the way.

'Are you?' She'd laughed at the expression on his face when she'd asked him that, and the look in his eyes had told her all she needed to know, even before he'd nodded.

It hadn't been perfect that first time, there were awkward moments, neither of them having enough expertise to make it seamless, and both nervous that they were doing it right. Yet somehow it had still been amazing. Now sitting here, it was if it had happened only yesterday, instead of what sometimes felt to Amy like another lifetime altogether.

'I'll always be glad that I got the chance to let that sandwich get cold.' Lijah was holding her gaze again, just like he had that day.

'Me too.' The urge to kiss him again almost took over, but somehow she stayed rooted to the spot, at her end of the bench.

'I probably shouldn't admit this, but these cold toasties are still my go to when I need something to cheer me up, and I've been eating a lot of them lately.'

Lijah's words were a timely reminder of why Amy shouldn't give in to her feelings. She couldn't be the human version of his favourite sandwich, there just to cheer him up during a tough time, until he was ready to move on. Getting tangled up in Lijah's life would be messy. Amy had been the subject of press scrutiny before, when one of their old school friends had sold a story to a journalist about Amy and Lijah's teenage romance. The article had made much of the fact that some of Lijah's songs had almost certainly been written about Amy, whose picture had been positioned side by side with Lijah's latest girlfriend. It was a comparison Amy didn't want or need, and she'd hated every moment of the attention it had generated. She wasn't going to go through all of that again for something that had even less chance of working now than it had before. But every time she looked at Lijah, all of the sensible advice she'd been giving herself seemed to fall out of her head. The best thing she could do was help him realise that Port Kara didn't hold the answers, in the hope he'd leave before she did something really stupid. She had to remind him where he really belonged.

'Now that your plans to become a porter have been derailed, maybe you should consider getting a food truck selling these toasties, although we both know you were born to be a musician. I remember your mum telling me that when she was pregnant, you used to kick like mad as soon as she put some music on.'

'I love that you know those stories.' He sounded genuinely touched and as she finally raised her gaze to meet his, her stupid, rebellious body reacted again. 'No one else I meet from now on is ever going to hear those stories from Mum, or know her like you do. I don't want to lose touch with you again, Ames. Promise me we won't do that.'

'I could make that promise, but once you're back out on the road…' It was her turn to shrug, even if the gesture felt anything but casual. 'You'll forget all about me.'

'I could never do that.' His voice was low, and she had to

press her body into the bench, to stop herself edging closer to him.

'How long are you planning on staying anyway?' Her words sounded sharp, as if she couldn't wait to see the back of him and in a way that was true, but not for the reasons he might think.

'Are you trying to get rid of me?' Amy had expected a smile to accompany his words, but she realised he was frowning. She might be desperate to protect herself, but that didn't mean she wanted to hurt Lijah in the process.

'Of course not.' She bit her lip. She couldn't tell him the reason she wanted him to leave, not without giving herself away.

'I know you probably think Port Kara will be a worse place with me here. The press have a way of turning everything into a circus.' Lijah sounded exhausted and her heart seemed to constrict, as if she could feel his pain in a physical way.

Suddenly she wanted him to know that what he'd done today had made a difference to people. 'Port Kara isn't worse for having you around. You might not be cut out for a career in medicine, but it was so lovely that you helped Brenda and Gwen.'

'Anyone would have done that.'

'No, they wouldn't.' This time she couldn't stop herself from lifting off her bag and sliding down the bench towards him. 'I only met Brenda today, but she's a real character and she's got a very soft spot for you now. I've known Gwen a long time, she volunteers at the hospital and is normally a firecracker too, but there's something going on that she clearly isn't ready to tell me about. Today, when she and Brenda were talking about you was the first time I've seen her looking anything like her old self in a while. I think the sight of you leaping six feet into the air gave them both a reason to smile.'

'I'm glad to be of service.' Lijah laughed, the melancholy that had seemed to cloak him disappearing. 'To be honest it felt good, helping someone out. I wish I could do more stuff like that. Not just donating money, or promoting a charity, but helping in a practical way.'

'Why don't you then?' Amy was almost certain she knew the answer to her question, but she couldn't help hoping there was a solution that would allow Lijah to lead some kind of normal life. Then maybe, just maybe, he might be able to stay after all.

'Without wanting to sound like a total dick, it's hard when people just see a celebrity and not a person. They're not interested in the real me.' Lijah pulled a face. 'God, that really does make me sound like a dick, doesn't it? But I just want to get stuck in and do something that really helps, like everyone else.'

'Brenda didn't recognise you and I suspect a lot of people of her generation wouldn't know who you are.' Amy took a deep breath, wondering if what she was about to suggest was ridiculous, but if Lijah meant what he'd said, maybe it wasn't so crazy after all. 'Aidan has decided he wants to do something as a way of saying thank you for the baby's safe arrival. We came up with this idea of a kind of all-year-round version of *A Christmas Carol*. But our version of focusing on the past, the present and the future is to create projects to help those in need across at least three generations. There are so many elderly people who need support, anything from practical help in their homes, to combating loneliness. So if you really want to, you could get involved with that. But I know you're busy with the album, not to mention helping out with Monty so...'

She'd given him a get-out-of-jail-free card, but he was already nodding. 'I'm not too busy and I'd love to help, if I can.'

'That's great.' She couldn't stop herself from reaching out and taking his hand, squeezing it hard to try and counter what felt like the jolt of electricity passing through her body.

'It would be nice to meet some new people who I know for certain like me for me. I haven't had that in a long time.' Lijah grinned suddenly. 'Or maybe they'll hate my guts, but at least I'll know it's real.'

'It must be hard having to question people's motivations all the time.' Even as Amy thought how much safer it would be if she let go of his hand, she found herself stroking her thumb across his palm instead. It was hardly fifty shades of grey, barely even one shade of vanilla, but there was something so intimate about it and, when their eyes met again, she knew she'd lost the battle.

'I hate that I have to doubt everyone I meet and I've missed this, *us*, more than I could ever explain.' Lijah was still looking at her, but Amy couldn't trust herself to answer. If she did, she was going to blurt out that she'd missed this more than she'd ever have believed possible. She needed to act as if she'd accepted that this thing between them would eventually end, that it was just a fling to be enjoyed while it lasted, to prove to themselves they'd never have gone the distance. That way she might stand a tiny chance of believing her own act and, when whatever this was ended – which it undoubtedly would – it might not completely destroy her. Leaning forward, she kissed Lijah hard, letting her actions do the talking. Suddenly she knew she was willing to pay the price she'd inevitably have to pay, because doing anything else would have meant walking away from Lijah for good, right now, and that was the one thing she just couldn't do.

18

Lijah had spent three days at Amy's place, supposedly keeping an eye on Monty, even though the little dog was already zooming around as if nothing had happened. Amy lived in a lovely sunny garden flat in a converted Georgian house. She had a walled garden and the interior of the flat was exactly as Lijah would have imagined it. There was a big squashy sofa, with brightly patterned cushions, and a huge colourful painting that dominated one wall, facing a set of oak shelves with collections of books, plants and quirky ornaments arranged haphazardly. It felt warm and welcoming, and a little bit chaotic, but in the most charming way. It was so like Amy herself, but Lijah suspected she had no idea just what a beautiful space she'd created, just like she had no idea how beautiful she was, but then she'd never been able to see herself the way he could. His breakout hit had been written about her inability to recognise how wonderful she was, and nothing had changed in the past decade.

The attraction between them was as strong as ever, but when he'd tried to talk to her about where they went from here, she'd shut down the promises he'd wanted to make about doing whatever it took to give them a proper chance this time around.

'Let's not talk about the future. We just need to enjoy the moment. You don't know what you'll be doing in three months' time, let alone a year from now. Coming back to Port Kara must make it easy to remember all the good times, but it was never enough for you.' She'd fixed him with a serious look when he'd tried to protest. 'My life is here and I love it, but you've always needed more than that and I doubt very much that's changed. So let's just take it a day at a time, and not promise each other anything we might have to go back on.'

In the end he'd found himself agreeing, because he needed to be sure the things he was feeling for Amy were as real as they seemed. Nick had warned him that trying to go back would never work and he desperately wanted to believe that his best friend was wrong, because right now he couldn't imagine wanting to go anywhere Amy wasn't. But the truth was he'd left Port Kara and Amy behind once before, despite how much he'd loved her then, and he needed to be sure he wasn't going to let her down again. He hadn't felt as if he belonged in Port Kara back then, but the truth was he hadn't found anywhere since where he'd felt he belonged either. He could just imagine what a therapist would make of that, but he wasn't going to give them another chance to go poking around inside his head. He'd drawn a veil over that when one of them had advised him to write a letter to his inner child about how his relationship with his father made him feel. If he was going to put pen to paper, he'd rather just channel all of that into writing a song. Lijah had done everything he could to leave that hurt little boy he'd been behind, the one who'd sobbed his heart out on his tenth birthday when his father had decided that his latest girlfriend was worth more than his son. He had absolutely no desire to reignite those feelings again.

It was different for Amy. He could see how much she loved the life she'd built for herself in the time they'd been apart. In so many ways she was the same girl he'd fallen in love with, but different too, stronger and more self-assured. She'd always had this crazy idea that he was out of her league, which he'd never understood. But even if she still didn't realise how beautiful she was, she seemed to have much more of an idea of her true worth these days. It was easy to see how good Amy was at her job and how much a part of the community she was too. He couldn't drag her into the life he'd been so desperate to escape, even if she'd been willing to leave; it was too toxic. But as much as he'd loved being back in Port Kara since reconnecting with Amy, he couldn't pretend the years in between hadn't happened and so much had changed in the place he'd once called home. All of that meant he still had no idea where he really belonged, and Amy was right, they couldn't promise each other anything until he worked that out.

Resisting the urge to go snooping while he was at her flat had taken all of Lijah's self-control. There didn't seem to be any evidence of Amy having had someone special in her life, not if the photographs that lined the hallway were anything to go by. There were photos of visits to some romantic destinations, including Paris and Vienna, but they featured landmarks, not the kind of selfies couples took to mark a memorable trip together. So, if she'd been with someone on those trips, she clearly didn't want to remember them. There were lots of photographs of her with friends, some of whom Lijah recognised from the hospital. There were family photographs too, including some of her brother, Nathan, and Lijah couldn't help the involuntary curl of his lip. He'd witnessed how often Nathan had put Amy down, feeding into the mass of insecurities she'd already had back then. He knew Nathan had issues, and that Amy and the rest of the family had always excused his behaviour as a result, but he had a feeling Nathan used that to get away with being deliberately cruel. Lijah had been forced to walk away on several occasions to stop himself from giving Nathan a few home truths of his own.

He'd just caught sight of a couple of pictures in the hallway that made him catch his breath, when the front door suddenly opened. If Amy was annoyed to find him looking at her photographs, she didn't show it.

'That was a good night.' She gestured towards a picture of the two of them, alongside his mum and Claire, all dressed up for an eighties-themed night that Maria had got them tickets for. They were wearing bright neon outfits with back-combed hair and all four of them were laughing, capturing the kind of genuine joy that photographs often missed.

'It was brilliant.' He couldn't help smiling as he looked at it again. His mum had often joked that she might have ended up marrying Andrew Ridgely, one half of her favourite band when she was growing up, but she'd never even managed to see Wham! in concert, let alone meet her teenage pin-up. She'd always added the caveat that she wouldn't have swapped any of that for the chance of being Lijah's mum, but she'd sacrificed so much to bring him up with almost no support from his father. Having the chance to relive the carefree days of her youth always made Maria so happy, and sharing in that had resulted in some of the best memories of Lijah's life too. Knowing that Amy had been a part of that made him feel even closer to her, and whatever happened between them this time around, it was something they'd always have.

'Your mum and Claire didn't sit down once all night. Every

time I tried to catch my breath, they'd drag me up to dance again. I remember how much my feet hurt the next day, but my face ached from smiling too. It's still one of the best nights I've ever had.'

'Me too.' He smiled again at the memory of his mum singing at the top of her voice all the way home, until the rest of them had finally joined in. She hadn't wanted the night to end and her joy had been infectious.

'Do you remember that weekend?' Amy pointed out a second photograph. It was one he'd already spotted, but he couldn't reveal how much seeing that photograph again had affected him, so he just nodded in response.

'It was taken during that trip to London you blew all your birthday money on. Even though I tried to persuade you not to,' Amy turned to look at him and he nodded again, as if she was telling him something he didn't remember every detail of. They'd spent a weekend in London, during the year between them leaving school and Amy heading to university. Most of the trips they'd taken in that 'gap year' had been on a shoestring, staying in hostels as close to home as Dublin and as far flung as Marrakesh. They'd both worked at the local Co-op in between, picking up shifts to save money for their trips, coming home after each mini adventure to top up their travel fund. It wasn't the kind of gap year some of their friends had experienced, spending six months in Asia, or teaching English in South America, but it had been perfect because they'd been together. He'd written songs while she slept with her head in his lap, waiting for flights in the early hours of the morning, just because they were the cheapest. He hadn't realised it back then, but that year had been the best of his life.

Splashing everything he could spare on a decent hotel had made that weekend in London different. They'd felt like proper grown-ups, checking in and examining the contents of the mini bar, before deciding not to indulge because they could probably get a night in one of their usual hostels for the price of one drink. It had been a wonderful couple of days, and they'd talked about all the things they wanted to achieve once their gap year ended. They'd planned how they'd move to London together, so that Amy could study and Lijah could take steps towards making his dream a reality. He'd really thought it was going to happen back then; it wasn't until six months later that Amy had dropped the bombshell and said she wouldn't be going to London to study for her degree after all. If he'd known it when they'd taken that photograph on Westminster Bridge, with the London Eye in the background, he wouldn't have been smiling. But in that moment he'd really believed that weekend was the precursor to the rest of their lives together. He had friends who couldn't think of anything worse than getting into a serious relationship at nineteen, and had talked about what a waste it would be to get tied down to someone during 'the best years' of his life, but Lijah didn't feel that way, and he'd never have broken things off with Amy if she hadn't ended things first. That didn't mean he hadn't taken advantage of his freedom since, but no one had ever been able to fill her shoes and he'd never felt the same way about anyone since.

'I spent every penny I had on that hotel.' His voice was low when he finally spoke.

'And do you still think it was worth it?' Amy curled her fingers around his, and he didn't even need to think about his response this time.

'It was worth far more than that.' It might not have been the start of the life he'd envisaged for them, but those two days had remained every bit as special to him as they'd been at that time. It had been a taste of the life he was so desperate to create for them: where he'd be able to take Amy to a fancy hotel any time she liked, once he'd made a go of his career. Losing her had been a casualty of his success, but it didn't take away from how perfect that weekend had been and he wouldn't have changed a single thing about it. He wouldn't have changed anything about the three years he'd spent with Amy, except for the fact they'd ended.

'I've sometimes thought about going back to that hotel, but I knew it would just have made me miss you more.' Amy looked down at the floor as she spoke. Every so often she let her mask slip, revealing a hint of the vulnerability she seemed determined to hide. In those moments, Lijah couldn't help wondering if she was finding it every bit as hard as he was to take things day by day, and go with the flow, as if they were starting out on something untested, with someone they barely knew. No matter how hard they pretended, they both knew that was not what they were doing. Whatever was happening between them was based on years of friendship that had grown into first love, and it made it very hard to act as though this was something new. Either way, whenever Amy showed even a glimpse of that vulnerability, she'd cover it up again, going straight back to the rules she'd set out for how this needed to be played. They were keeping things low-key and not telling anyone they were more than friends. It would add way too much pressure according to Amy, and keeping it casual was best for both of them when Lijah had no idea how long he'd be around. The trouble was, every time he saw her, it got harder and harder for him to stick to those rules. 'We could go back the hotel together. You've got no idea how close I came on that trip to—'

'Yoohoo!' a shrill voice suddenly called out, cutting him off, as the front door swung open for a second time. Amy and Lijah sprung apart in the instant before her mother, Kerry, came into the hallway. They'd agreed that other people's expectations would just make it even harder to take it day by day. It hadn't been difficult for Lijah to see the logic of that particular rule, when Amy had suggested they keep the fact they were dating again to themselves. Although he wasn't even sure dating was the right word for it, not when it all had to be done so covertly.

'Oh God, I'm not late, am I?' Kerry widened her eyes.

'No, why?' Amy's attempt to sound nonchalant was accompanied by an exaggerated shrug.

'Because you're both waiting in the hallway ready to shoot straight out of the door.' Kerry suddenly beamed as she turned to look at Lijah. 'Anyway never mind that, it's just so lovely to have you back! It's been far too long.'

Amy's mother threw her arms around him and he didn't even try to resist her embrace.

'It's really good to see you too, Kerry.' His smile was genuine. He'd always liked her, even if he thought she did go too easy on Nathan. Unfortunately, they weren't going to have long to catch up, but in a way he was glad, at least there was less chance of him making his feelings for her daughter obvious. Amy had been on an early shift, and had arranged for her mother to come over after work to keep an eye on Monty, so that she could take Lijah to meet Albert, as part of the befriending service he'd agreed to volunteer for. It wasn't unheard of for celebrities to do that kind of thing, but it usually happened in a blaze of publicity, and all Lijah wanted to do was blend in.

'I hate to cut the reunion short.' Amy leaned down to make a fuss of Monty, who'd wandered out from the lounge and into the hallway, his tail thudding against the wooden floor. 'But we're supposed to be at Albert's in ten minutes, so we're going to have to make a move.'

'You'll just have to come to dinner while you're here, so we can catch up properly. Promise.' Kerry waggled a finger at Lijah and he nodded, earning him another hug. It might make it difficult to hide his feelings for Amy, but any excuse to spend time with her felt like a good one. If he was honest with himself, it had been a factor in his desire to volunteer, even if it was far from being his only motivation. Amy could set as many rules as she wanted and he'd try his best to follow them, but that didn't mean he wasn't going to take every opportunity he could to be with her.

* * *

'Do I need to know anything about Albert?' Lijah asked as Amy drove them towards his house.

'He's a widower, with no children and he doesn't seem to have much of a support network. He's lonely and I think that's affected how well he's taking care of himself, as if he can't really see the point. It's sad, because he's a lovely man.'

'It must be hard when you don't think anyone really cares whether you're there or not.' Lijah tried to keep the wistfulness out of his voice, but he didn't quite pull it off, and he quickly changed the subject, asking about Amy's day. Anything to stop things from getting too personal.

'Here we are.' Amy pulled up outside a farmhouse, which also looked as if it had been neglected for a while, but it was in a beautiful spot, high up on the cliffs surrounded by paddocks, with far-reaching sea views. It hadn't been what Lijah had expected at all.

'Hi Amy. I've made some tea and opened the biscuits, so I'm all ready for you.' Albert made the pronouncement as soon as he opened the door, and it immediately took twenty years off his age when he smiled and held out his hand to Lijah. 'I'm Albert, but my closest friends always called me Albie, and I gather that friendship is the point of this whole exercise. Unless there's something they haven't told me, and you're doing community service and didn't fancy litter picking.'

There was a gleam in Albert's eye and Lijah couldn't help laughing. 'Damn, you found me out! I'm Lijah, nice to meet you Albie.'

They followed him inside and Lijah could see straight away what Amy had meant. The house wasn't dirty, but maintenance seemed to be a thing of the past. The leather sofa had worn away in parts, causing rips and tears, and the rug was threadbare too.

'Sorry, it's not a palace, but since Lizzie died, I can't seem to find the will to replace anything. She was always the one who made a house feel like a home.' Albert gestured towards a photograph on the mantlepiece of a couple in their middle age, standing outside a church in a haze of confetti.

'We were married for twenty years, but she's been gone for more than ten now and the whole house is missing her touch.'

'I'm sorry, you must really miss her.' Lijah couldn't stop himself from glancing in Amy's direction. All those years alone; it was a long time to be without the person you loved.

'I do, but it gives me comfort to think she's with Brian now, her first husband. It might all be mumbo-jumbo that heaven stuff, but I hope she's there with him, because she was a really good woman who went through a lot and she deserves to be reunited with the person she loved the most.' Albert sat on an armchair that was covered by a crocheted throw, and gestured towards the sofa. 'Don't stand on ceremony you two, sit down.'

'Thank you.' Lijah was trying not to let his face register shock at the way Albert was talking. He couldn't imagine loving someone, marrying them and not feeling hurt that his wife would always love someone else more. But maybe he hadn't lived a long enough life to put himself in Albert's shoes, and he had a feeling there was more to the story than they'd been told so far.

'Oh I forgot to bring the biscuits in, I'll go and get them.' Albert moved to stand up, grimacing suddenly and putting a hand on his back, where the pain clearly was.

'Are you okay?' Amy was up on her feet immediately and Albert nodded.

'Just the blasted sciatica. All those years as a farrier was bound to take a toll in the end.'

'Let me put some of this ibuprofen gel on for you.' Amy was already opening the tube that had been left on the side table by his chair, not giving him the chance to protest.

'And I'll grab the biscuits.' Lijah got to his feet too, not wanting to cause Albert any embarrassment by sitting opposite and watching him having the gel applied.

'They're on the kitchen table.'

The biscuit tin was hand decorated with tiny painted flowers and, like the rest of the house, it was clearly well used, but still beautiful. Lijah took his time before going back into the living room, only returning when he heard Amy say that she was going to the bathroom to wash her hands, which he knew meant she had finished.

'This is beautiful Albie, did you paint it?' Lijah handed the tin to the older man, but Albert shook his head.

'No, Millie did.' He must have noticed the questioning look on Lijah's face. He knew Albert didn't have any children, and he'd already said his late wife's name was Lizzie.

'She's the one that got away, isn't that what you youngsters say?' Albert had a wistful look on his face, and he didn't wait for Lijah to answer. 'I did some work on her father's estate and we fell in love, but she was from a wealthy family and I was a farm hand. Her parents had arranged for her to get engaged to another landowner's son. She said she'd run away with me, but I was scared she'd regret it. So I left before I had to witness her getting engaged, even though it nearly killed me to go. I trained to be a farrier as far away as I could get, up in Yorkshire. I only came back to Cornwall after I married Lizzie and we bought this place. Millie made the tin for me when I still worked for her father, bringing it down each day to the fields where I was working, with some cake or biscuits in it. That's how I knew she liked me. I took it with me when I decided to stop working for her father, and I've kept it ever since.'

'Have you ever tried to find her?' Lijah couldn't stop himself from asking, and Albert laughed.

'Life isn't one those romance novels, at least that's what I told Millie.' The mirth slid off Albert's face and he suddenly looked bereft. 'There's a chance Lizzie will get a reunion with her Brian, but it's not going to happen for me and Millie. Not here and not up there, because I let her go. I should have taken the chance to be with her when she gave it to me, because one thing I've learnt in life is that failing is better than giving up before you even start. Don't let any opportunities that come your way pass you by, lad, that'd be my advice.'

'What are you two gossiping about?' Amy smiled as she came back into the room.

'Life, love and missed opportunities.' Lijah looked directly as her as he spoke, but she quickly turned towards Albert.

'Sounds like you two are bonding already. Have you thought any more about rehoming a cat or dog, Albie? Caroline said you've been considering it?' Her change of subject was as swift as it was complete, and she clearly had no intention of talking about missed opportunities. That would have gone against the rules. Despite avoiding some subjects, the conversation flowed easily and the three of them talked about pretty much everything else, the next hour flying by.

'So what's the verdict then, lad? Will you be coming back to see me again, or was once enough for you?' Albert asked the question as he saw them to the door.

'Oh, I'll be back, if you'll have me?' Lijah smiled. 'I've had a great time.'

'Of course I'll have you.' Albert looked genuinely delighted. 'I've not got many friends left these days.'

'Me neither. So, it sounds like we're a match made in heaven.' Lijah hadn't meant to admit that out loud, and he'd seen the look that had crossed Amy's face in response. He knew what was coming, as soon as they were back in the car together.

'What did you mean about not having many friends? Whenever I see pictures of you, you're surrounded by people.' She kept her eyes fixed on the road and he was thankful for that, but there was no point in lying to Amy, she'd always been able to see right through him.

'I'm talking about proper friends. Most of the people who call themselves my friends have no clue who the real me is. I'm grateful to have Nick.' It would have been so easy for him to tell Amy how grateful he was to have her too, but that would have crossed another line she'd written in the sand. Amy wasn't his any more, not in the way he wanted her to be. She was looking at him intently now, though, her eyes locking with his as she spoke.

'Is that why you came back to Port Kara?'

'Partly. I just wanted to be somewhere that didn't feel fake and now I don't know if I can face going back to living how I was before. But everything changes and when Claire moves away, a huge part of what made Port Kara home will go with her. I suppose I should have realised you can't recapture the past, no matter how much you might want to.'

'I suppose not.' He'd only repeated the same thing she'd said to him, when she'd told him why they needed to take it a day at a time, but her voice was small as she continued. 'So you're definitely not staying?'

'I still don't know, I don't know what I'm going to do, but I need to decide, because it's not fair on Nick. I can't end his career by letting him hang around waiting for me, just because I'm not sure if I want to carry on with mine.' Lijah sighed. 'Although I've barely seen him since he started seeing Dolly. So, who knows, maybe his heart will end up in Port Kara even if mine doesn't. Although I'm hoping it will.'

'Lijah.' There was a warning note in her voice that told him he was pushing it too far. He almost told her he couldn't do this; he couldn't keep his emotions in check the way she wanted him to, because it felt like the last ten years hadn't happened when he was around her. But there was a good chance she might push him away altogether if he did that, and what Albie had said had really hit home; he didn't want to let any opportunities pass him by. Suddenly he was certain, whatever else he decided about his future, he wanted Amy to be a part of it. Except he'd told her that before, and he'd still chosen his career over her, instead of staying in Port Kara and fighting for what they had.

Lijah knew why she'd ended things back then, because she thought it was best for his career, and he suspected she'd do it again for the same reasons, unless he proved to her, beyond all doubt, that it wasn't what he wanted. He couldn't just come out and say it. He had to prove it to her and that was going to take time. For the first time since she'd set the rules, he could see the value of taking things day by day. He wasn't going to ignore Albie's advice and let this second chance pass him by, but he couldn't risk trying to rush things with Amy either. Instead he held up his hands, acknowledging that what he'd said could be construed as breaking her rules and offered up an apology.

'Sorry, it's just that days like today make me realise what really matters. I don't think I could have had an afternoon like we've had with Albie anywhere but here.'

'I'm so glad it worked out between the two of you and if it gives you another reason to stay in Port Kara, I'm not going to complain.' She touched his hand, her mask slipping again for a moment, before she took her hand away again, changing the radio station to *Absolute 80s*. The sound of Spandau Ballet's 'True' instantly filled the air.

'This was another song your mum loved, wasn't it?'

'It was.' Lijah somehow resisted the urge to tell Amy that Maria had loved her too, and that so did he; that would definitely have been breaking the rules. Instead he joined in, as she started to sing along with Tony Hadley. Wherever his mum was, he hoped she could see them, because he knew it would have made her incredibly happy that Amy had given him a second chance, and he was going to do his very best not to blow it this time.

* * *

Gwen might have got away with no one noticing her funny turn while she was working at the hospital shop, if Caroline hadn't been on shift too. Her friend knew her too well and had immediately realised that her behaviour was off.

'I'll just get your...' Gwen could picture the word she wanted, piles of coins stacked on top of one another, but she couldn't find the word itself, and her movements seemed to become faltering, as if she was in slow motion.

'It's okay.' The customer smiled. 'Just put the change in the collection box.'

'Thank you.' Gwen's head felt as though it was full of cotton wool and her fingers fumbled as she tried to select the right coins to put in the collection box beside the till, but every movement was like wading through concrete.

'Are you okay?' Caroline spotted the sign that something was wrong instantly, but Gwen still wasn't ready to face up to it.

'I'm fine, my head's just a bit... It's just a bit achy.' She was really having to concentrate to explain something that should have been so simple.

'Are you sure? You don't seem your normal self lately and you've mentioned having a bad head a few times.' Caroline's eyes searched her face.

'I'm just...' It was as if she was incapable of completing a sentence, and she had to force the rest of it out; even her words seemed to have slowed down. 'Feeling my age.'

'You're probably doing too much.' Caroline looked up as Meg, Esther and Eden all came into the shop, speaking with a new urgency as they approached the counter. 'It would be worth asking someone with a bit more medical expertise for some advice, though. I'm worried about you.'

'Hey Mum.' Esther greeted her mother and Caroline went around the counter to give her a hug.

'Hello darling. This is good timing, I was just suggesting that Gwen speak to someone about her headaches. She's been getting them a lot lately.'

Gwen wanted to protest, but she still couldn't shake off the feeling of wading through concrete, and suddenly everyone was talking about her like she wasn't even there.

'Any other symptoms?' Meg asked, and when Gwen shook her head, the young doctor narrowed her eyes. 'You should always get persistent headaches checked out. It would be a good idea to go and see your GP as soon as possible, or I could run some basic checks.'

One of the benefits of working at the hospital, and of knowing so many of the staff, was that if Gwen had wanted to queue jump and get some advice from a specialist, it would have been easy. But as kind as Meg's offer was, she wasn't about to take up a doctor's time when other patients were waiting. At least that's what she told herself. The truth was she wasn't ready for what Meg might discover, so she shook her head again.

'Promise me you'll at least go and see your GP?' Meg urged and Gwen managed a nod, swiftly moving the conversation on to talking about Aidan's baby, and asking if anyone had been to see little Ellis. After that, Caroline had insisted that Gwen go home early and Eden, who'd just finished an early shift, offered her a lift, despite the fact she lived opposite the hospital. Gwen had wanted to refuse, but she'd felt unsafe to drive and she'd been forced to accept Eden's kind offer as a result. Barry was out weeding the front garden when she arrived and the absence of her car meant he knew something was wrong. When Eden pulled away and Gwen turned to go in to the house, Barry stood facing her, his arms folded, clearly determined not to let her fob him off this time.

'You've got to see someone about what's going on, Gee. You can't keep pretending this is normal. You're not well. You might not want to admit it, but it's obvious.' There was a new steeliness in his tone now.

'I just need to cut down a bit.' Her head wasn't quite so fuzzy, but she still felt exhausted. She didn't want to use what little energy she had fighting, but she couldn't agree to go and see the doctor, because she knew what they were going to find and when they did there'd be no going back. She'd be on the same path that had robbed her mother of who she was, bit by bit, until there was almost none of her left. The idea terrified Gwen, and she'd do anything not to have to face it, even if it meant digging her heels in and arguing with Barry about the same thing over and over again.

'You need to see someone, Gee, I mean it. And the kids think so too. Sally said she'll go with you and—'

'You've been talking to the kids about it?' She cut him off, her voice sharp as anger and fear flared up inside her like a flame igniting. They were talking about her behind her back, like she was incapable of being part of the conversation, or of making her own decisions. It was happening already, she was losing control of who she was and what she wanted. She couldn't let it get any worse. 'You had no right to talk to them about me.'

'We all love you and we're just worried about you. That's all.' He moved towards her and reached out, but she flinched as if he was going to hit her.

'I'm fine. Stop interfering and treating me like a child. I'm not a bloody child!' Her voice was shrill, almost a shriek by the last few words and she moved away from him towards the door.

'Where are you going?' Barry's voice was full of concern, but she didn't stop.

'I'm going out, and I don't need your permission believe it or not.' She slammed the door behind her, tears stinging her eyes. All she wanted was for Barry to hold her and tell her it would all be okay, as he had so many times before when they'd had a crisis in their lives. But he couldn't do that, because Gwen had a terrible feeling it wasn't going to be okay, and that things were never going to be the same again.

19

Aidan and Jase had gone all out for the party to mark baby Ellis's discharge from hospital. And, as Aidan had announced, it was only the start.

'Thank you all for coming today. We thought this would be a great way for everyone to meet our beautiful girl, and we didn't want to wait until the christening, so there'll be another party for that, and one for her first birthday, and for every other milestone we're going to be lucky enough to share because of Isla and Ellen and their incredible generosity. So clear your diaries for the next eighteen years!'

Aidan and Jase had hired Bocca Felice, a beautiful Italian restaurant that overlooked the sea, and Aidan had confided in Amy why they'd decided against having the event at home.

'The place is in chaos, Ames. Parenthood is...' He shook his head. 'Amazing, exhausting and extremely messy. The thought of hosting this many people and having everyone at our place, with the baby just out of the hospital, was too much. We thought this was a great way to contain it all, give everyone a chance to see her in a time slot we can control, so that we didn't keep having to put everyone off. Now that the doctors have said she's as healthy as a horse, this seemed perfect.'

'It is perfect and she's so beautiful.' Amy lightly touched the blanket that was tightly wrapped around the baby, as she lay peacefully in her father's arms.

'She is, isn't she?' Aidan sighed, and then glanced across the room. 'I'm really glad Lijah could make it, he was so kind the day she arrived, but I didn't think for a moment he'd want to come to something like this. He must get invitations to some amazing events.'

'I can't think of an event more amazing than this.' Amy's eyes glistened as she spoke, and she meant every word.

'You're right of course.' Aidan planted a kiss on her cheek, the baby nestling between them for a moment, before he moved back again. 'But I think the reason Lijah is here is you. And the volunteering, it's all an excuse to spend time with you. The question is, what are you going to do about it?'

Amy had to swallow hard for a moment to stop herself from telling Aidan everything. She was desperate to have someone to confide in because her feelings for Lijah were getting out of hand, despite the rules she'd set for them. If she confessed to Aidan that they were seeing each other, and that it felt like they'd plunged straight into a full-blown relationship, he'd get excited and start talking about how many celebrities there'd be at the wedding. Aidan wouldn't be able to keep it to himself either, it's just the way he was, but it would make it even harder when Lijah left if everyone found out. She'd have to deal with her friends' disappointment as well as her own heartbreak. So she shook her head instead. 'He's having a tough time, that's all, and it made him want to come home, but this isn't his home any more and he'll realise that sooner or later. So what I'm going to do, is precisely nothing.'

'Because you don't want to risk getting your heart broken?'

'He's not interested in me like that.'

'Oh come on, Ames, you're not that dim.' Aidan gave her a nudge, grinning, but before she could respond someone grabbed her from behind and spun her in a circle.

'I've missed you so much!' Isla looked incredible. Her sun-kissed skin was part of it, but there was a glow about her that was more than skin deep.

'I've missed you too. Never go away for that long again!' Amy hugged her friend hard. It was wonderful to have her home, and even better to see her looking so happy.

'Nice of you to show up.' Aidan was still smiling, his tone jokey, and Amy knew Isla's flight home had only arrived back the evening before. She'd texted Amy to tell her she was spending the night with Aidan and Jase, and that she couldn't wait to see her at the party, but jet lag must be hitting hard.

'Sorry, we set an alarm, but we slept right through it.' Isla looked over her shoulder to where her boyfriend was chatting to Jase. 'I think Reuben would still be asleep if I hadn't physically rolled him out of bed. Why didn't you wake us?'

'I remember me and Jase trying to wake Rube up when he was a teenager, and it wasn't a pleasant experience. We love our nephew to pieces, but a morning person he is not.'

'Hmm, I found that out on our trip, and a whole lot more, too. Thankfully most of it was good.' Isla's eyes sparkled.

'Do I need to buy a hat for the wedding?' Aidan raised his eyebrows.

'Not yet, well not for me and Reuben, but there's always Lijah Byrne and his muse, our very own Amy Spencer.'

Amy had been about to protest, but Aidan got in first. 'We were just talking about that, weren't we Ames?'

'Yes and I was just saying there's nothing to talk about.' Amy kept her tone light, part of her still wanting to confide in her friends, despite knowing what the consequences would be, but the desire to try and keep things low-key was even stronger. 'He just needed a break from work and the chance to be normal for a bit, that's all. And he thought coming back home would give him the opportunity to do that.'

'Hmm, I'm not sure about that.' Isla turned her head towards where Lijah was standing, and Amy followed her gaze. There was a large group of people circling him and, Isla was right, Lijah couldn't just walk into a room and blend in seamlessly, no matter how much he might want to. The realisation was like a stab in the gut, and she knew what it meant. It meant he'd be leaving Port Kara all the sooner. He'd come home to get away from the circus that his life in the spotlight had become, but Port Kara wasn't another world, people still knew who Lijah was. Once he realised that his hometown wasn't the solution, it would have far less to offer. It hadn't been able to hold him a decade ago, and she couldn't imagine it would now.

'Well, seeing as you two have let me down. I guess my next hat will just have to be worn in honour of Wendy and Gary's wedding.' Aidan shook his head. 'But I still think you're wrong about Lijah. I've seen the way he looks at you, Amy.'

'We're old friends and there's a bond between us because I was close to his mum. If you read any more into it, I'm afraid you're wrong, but I'll let you off seeing as you've got baby brain. After all, who can blame you for not being able to think straight when you've got this gorgeous girl in your life?' Amy had been certain that bringing the conversation back round to Ellis would be the best way of changing the subject, and she'd been right.

'I fell in love the moment I met her yesterday.' Isla stroked the baby's cheek. 'She's absolutely perfect.'

Amy murmured in agreement as Aidan and Isla cooed over the baby, stealing another glance at Lijah. He chatted to everyone who approached him, a smile on his face, even though she knew he'd rather be left alone. He'd always tried to make people feel like he was interested in them, it was one of things she loved about him. There was no denying she did still love him, but some people were better loved from afar and Lijah was one of them. The trouble was, the longer he stayed, the harder it was to remind herself of that. The rules she'd set down for them had been as good as useless in stopping her feelings for Lijah deepening and, no matter how many times she gave herself a good talking to, it was impossible to keep an emotional distance between them when he was around. If Amy wanted to protect her heart, she had to help Lijah realise that he needed to leave Port Kara, even though she knew how much it would hurt when he did. If he stayed much longer, her feelings for him were going to get even stronger and there was a chance she might never get over him.

* * *

Lijah had felt touched to be invited to the party that Aidan and Jase had thrown to welcome their daughter to the world. It had been wonderful to feel like part of a proper community for a little while, and most people had treated him like any other guest. There'd been a handful who'd cornered him for about fifteen minutes, paying him far more attention than they would have done if he'd had some other job, but he'd managed to extricate himself without doing or saying anything that someone might be able to make a headline out of. *Lijah Byrne displays his arrogance by telling party guests to leave him the hell alone.* The press would have a field day with that, and he hated always having to keep his guard up against that kind of thing, but he'd been burnt in the past.

Lijah had spent the rest of the time watching Amy and wishing he could be a part of the life she'd made for herself in Port Kara, surrounded by friends who loved her for the wonderful person she was. He envied the authenticity of her life; it was something he was never going to have. He'd wanted to walk over to her and slip his arm around her waist, so that everyone would know how he felt about her, but she'd made him promise not to do anything that gave them away. Lijah had done his best to respect Amy's wishes, but he had a feeling anyone watching him would have been able to tell how he felt. His eyes kept sliding towards her, even when he was talking to someone else and, as much as he'd enjoyed chatting to some of her friends, he'd rather have spent every moment with her.

He'd had to leave the party before the food was served, having already arranged to have dinner with his aunt. He didn't want to miss out on that, because she was flying out to Tenerife to spend some time with Dee, and there were decisions Lijah needed to make about where his own future lay. Claire had also promised to make her famous homemade pizza. He'd never been able to find another pizza to match it, not even in Italy, and his stomach was already growling when he reached Mor Brys.

'Hello sweetheart.' Claire enveloped him in a warm hug, as she greeted him at the door. 'The pizzas are in, so it won't be long. And you don't need to knock, this is your home and it always will be.'

'Not when someone else is living in it.' He couldn't keep the note of sadness out of his voice, as he stepped inside, but guilt twisted in his gut as Claire's face fell. The last thing he wanted was to make her feel bad. She deserved to be happy, and he was so glad she'd found someone who made her smile the way Dee did, just by talking about her. 'Ignore me, I'm being stupid.'

'No, you're not.' Claire reached up and touched his face. 'Your mum is in every corner of this house and it's going to be such a wrench for me to leave. But I need to if I'm ever going to find a way to live without her. That doesn't mean we have to sell the place, though, does it?'

'It seems a crime to let it sit empty.' The cottage had the most amazing views of the harbour from almost every window at the back. It was why his mum hadn't wanted to move somewhere bigger, or further out. She'd loved Mor Brys, it was her home and Claire was right, she was still here in every corner. But the thought of it sitting empty and quiet, without all the life his mum had brought to the place was unbearable. It wasn't fair of him to put that on his aunt, though, and he didn't want to do anything that might make her doubt whether she was doing the right thing. 'We don't have to make any decisions yet.'

'Oh yes we do!' Nick's voice carried down the hallway and Lijah shook his head as he followed Claire into the kitchen. His best friend was already sitting at the table tucking in to garlic ciabatta, before the pizza had even made it to the table.

'I might have known you'd be first in line for food.' Lijah grinned and turned to his aunt. 'I barely see Nick these days, because he's in love.'

Pulling a silly face, Lijah fluttered his eyelids, earning him an eye roll from Nick. 'I could say the same thing. Your nephew has rented a huge mansion on the cliffs, but where does he spend most of his time? Dog sitting in a tiny flat, where a certain Miss Amy Spencer lives. So if anyone is in love, I think it's Lijah.'

'You're right.' Lijah shrugged, trying to play it cool. 'I do love Monty.'

'Hmmm. You keep telling yourself that's why you go and dog

sit.' Nick shook his head. 'Tell me Claire, have you got any idea why he seems incapable of admitting his feelings?'

'Unresolved issues with his dad?' It was her turn to shrug and Nick laughed.

'Your aunt is a very wise woman!'

'We've been studying attachment theory on my counselling course, and what Lijah's father did would affect anyone.'

'You can stop talking about me like I'm not here, and hand me some of the ciabatta instead.' It was bad enough trying not to give the game away about him and Amy, but a conversation about his father was one Lijah definitely didn't want to get into. Not today. Not ever.

'You can have some garlic bread in exchange for the answer to a question.' Nick whipped the ciabatta out of Lijah's reach as he spoke.

'If it's another attempt to psycho-analyse me, you can forget it.'

'It's not. It's about when you're going to be ready to restart the tour. I'm getting pressure to give the promoters an answer. Don't get me wrong, I'm enjoying the break, and I won't lie and say that spending time with Dolly hasn't been great, but we can't hide out here forever.'

'The choice is yours, I can either stay here and get the next album written, or I can go on tour. I can't do both.' Lijah caught his old friend's eye, and he couldn't have lied to Nick again even if he'd wanted to; they'd known each other for far too long. It was just lucky the question Nick asked next wasn't the one Lijah had been anticipating.

'And tell me, how is the writing going?' Nick didn't break eye contact as he waited for an answer.

'Better than it was. I've got about ten potential songs so far, but I can't seem to finish any of them.'

'Sounds like something is blocking you and I don't think it's losing your mum, because writing was always your solace when things were tough.' Claire frowned, and Nick finally dropped his gaze, turning towards her and nodding.

'I think you're right Claire. He just needs to work out what it is that's blocking him and do something about it.'

'You're doing it again, talking about me like I'm not here.' Lijah's tone was tight. 'Even if I never finish the album, or go back on tour, the world's not going to end, is it?'

'A lot of people will be very disappointed.' Nick sighed.

'Everyone who earns a living out of me you mean, including you.' Lijah regretted the words as soon as he'd said them, but before he could apologise his aunt interjected.

'Lijah!' Claire so rarely raised her voice, it forced him to look at her. 'You know that's not true, and I understand you're having a tough time, but lashing out at the people who love you isn't going to solve anything.'

'It's all right Lij, I know you don't mean it, but whatever it is you're struggling with, Claire's right, you need to face up to it. Burying your head in the sand isn't going to help, you know that as well as I do, because we were both there on the tour.'

'I know and I'm sorry.' Lijah leaned down and hugged his oldest friend for a moment, before turning back to his aunt and doing the same, shaking his head when he finally pulled away. 'I just... I thought coming back here would solve everything, that I'd be able to write again and work through all the stuff I was feeling, like I have before. The tour was suffocating me, and it's been better here, but I still can't clear my head enough to be able to let the words flow the way they need to.'

'I know you're not going to want to hear this, but maybe it's time to think about having some counselling again, sweetheart.' Claire squeezed Lijah's arm, and he sighed.

He hated the thought of opening up all those old wounds again, but it wasn't just the issues with his career he needed to sort out. If he didn't work out what he wanted to do with his life, he was going to lose Amy all over again and that was one thing he was certain he didn't want to do. Turning to his aunt, he nodded. 'Music has always been my therapy, but you're right, it's not working the way it has in the past. So maybe it is time to try something else.'

'I think a breakthrough like that deserves a bit of garlic ciabatta.' Nick held out the plate, whipping it away again, just as Lijah reached out for it.

'God I hate you sometimes.' This time when Lijah laughed it felt completely genuine, and Nick grinned in response.

'It's just lucky you love me the rest of the time, and deep down you know I love you too, even if you are a pain in the arse sometimes.' Nick finally let Lijah take a piece of garlic bread and they exchanged a look that needed no words. The love between him and his old friend went way beyond music and it was a bond that meant the world to Lijah. Nick had given him the closest thing to a feeling of home in all the years he'd been away. With his mum gone and Claire leaving, he still didn't know if Port Kara could ever truly feel like home again, but he still believed Amy held the key to that, wherever he might be. The trouble was, she seemed certain that what they had couldn't last. If it didn't and Nick decided to leave Port Kara too, Lijah couldn't imagine not going with him. He'd tried so hard to play by Amy's rules, but he hadn't been able to stop himself from falling in love with her again, probably because he'd never really stopped. It was time to quit pretending and lay his cards on the table; he couldn't be half in and half out of Amy's life. It was everything or nothing, and he just hoped to God she'd choose the first option.

20

Barry had suggested pulling out of the charity dance display several times, but Gwen had flatly refused to accept she wasn't up to it. She had struggled at the spring dance show and things had got even worse since then, but she still couldn't admit it. She was supposed to be dancing a waltz with Barry, and leading the belly dancers in their display, and she secretly doubted she could do it, but agreeing with Barry that they should pull out would have confirmed something was really wrong and she was still desperate to deny that. Somehow she got through the waltz, but it felt as though Barry was pushing her around the dance floor like she was an old fridge that needed shifting, ready to be taken to the dump.

'Are you feeling okay?' Nicky came over to Gwen, just before the belly dance display was due to start. Gwen had always been the epitome of confidence, never worrying that the belly dancing outfit exposed flesh that some people would suggest was better covered up 'at her age'. She didn't buy into any of that. There'd been a rough patch during menopause when she'd wanted to hide away all together, but she'd done what she'd always done and thrown herself wholeheartedly into solving the problem.

One of the first steps had been to volunteer as a life model for an art class and it had allowed her to see herself from other people's point of view. Not as a past-her-best has-been, as she'd been feeling, but as someone who'd earnt every scar and wrinkle, and who had far more character and strength because of them.

This was different though. This time if she was in the early stages of aphasia no amount of positive thinking, medical intervention or pushing herself out of her comfort zone would help. She just wanted to hide away and pretend it wasn't happening, but Nicky was standing in front of her, waiting for an answer, so she forced a smile.

'I'm fine. Ready to shake what my mama gave me.' Gwen gave Nicky a demo, the coins on her outfit rattling and her brain feeling like it was following suit. She could get through this, though, all she had to do was fake it and shake it, and no one would know there was anything wrong.

'Barry's a bit worried about you, so if you want to give this a miss, I'm sure Janet could go up front.' Nicky's tone was gentle, but Gwen shook her head hard, making it hurt even more.

'He's just fussing.' She moved towards the side of the stage, not giving Nicky the chance to try and dissuade her from going on again, and moments later the music started up.

At first Gwen's movements felt reasonably fluid, but then it was almost as if her batteries had died, and she couldn't seem to follow the beat of the music. Exchanging a desperate look with Janet, who'd mouthed the words, 'You okay?', Gwen shook her head and dropped to the back of the group, allowing Janet to take over up front. Suddenly Gwen couldn't seem to remember any of the movements, and she stood there, shaking her body aimlessly from side to side.

'What's wrong darling?' Barry was there as soon as she came off stage. 'And don't say nothing, because I know there is.'

'I...' The words refused to form and she widened her eyes in terror, her legs suddenly feeling as if they'd given way beneath her, and he had to catch her in his arms.

'Shall I call an ambulance?' Nicky was right there too, but Barry shook his head.

'I'll take her in, if you can just give me a hand to get her to the car. It'll be quicker and I'm not taking no for an answer this time. Whatever is going on, it's been happening for far too long already.' Barry stroked Gwen's hair away from her face, as she managed to steady herself. 'I know you're scared about what this might be Gee, but it's going to be okay. I promise. We can't keep pretending you don't need to see a doctor.'

'I know.' She managed the words at last, silently praying that Barry would be able to keep his promise that everything would be okay, and wishing she wasn't so certain that a life changing diagnosis was only hours away.

'Well hello there Mrs Jones, you're always full of surprises, but that must be the best outfit you've worn to work yet!' The smile on Amy's face died as she looked at Gwen's expression. She was sitting on a chair in the waiting area of the emergency department, where she often stopped to chat to patients when she was doing her rounds with the hospital shop trolley. Gwen was wearing a green belly dancing costume and Amy would have assumed it was fancy dress, except Gwen had a black tailcoat draped over her shoulders and there were tears glistening in her eyes.

'Hey, what's wrong?'

'I think I'm... my head is going.' Gwen blinked hard, speaking slowly. 'My mother had it and...'

'She's terrified she's got aphasia.' Barry, who Amy had met several times, suddenly appeared besides them. 'But I don't think it's that. Her symptoms are different and sometimes she seems almost fine. She had a water infection, and we hoped that might be it, but sometimes she can't seem to find her words, although there are other things too. I don't know, but she needs to see someone, don't you sweetheart?'

'It's going to be okay. Have you checked Gwen in?' Amy had to force the words past the lump in her throat, as Barry sat down taking his wife's hand and nodded in response. Amy hated the fact that they were talking about Gwen rather than to her, but it was clear she was struggling to find the words she needed. 'Right, I'm going to go and speak to someone to see if I can do anything to hurry things along a bit.'

'Thank you.' Gwen's words were barely more than a whisper, and Amy couldn't bear seeing her friend looking like a shadow of her former self. Gwen was everyone else's cheerleader, her sense of humour unfailingly brightening up a tough day. It didn't seem possible that something could come along to dim that light, and she hoped with all her heart that Barry was right about something else causing his wife's symptoms.

* * *

By the time Amy left the hospital, Gwen had already been given a series of blood tests and was booked in for both a CT scan and an MRI. Amy had been there when Barry began listing the symptoms, which had been reassuring and terrifying at the same time. Amy had googled aphasia at the first opportunity, and while Gwen seemed to be having some trouble focusing on getting her words out the way she wanted to, the other symptoms she had didn't seem to fit at all. Amy felt a wave of relief as Barry reeled off the things that had been happening, until she realised just how many symptoms Gwen had been experiencing. It might not be aphasia, but it could be something just as terrifying.

There'd been the problems with Gwen's memory and concentration, slurred words and slowed movements, all of which they'd thought initially might be caused by the UTI, but which hadn't cleared up when Gwen's water infection had. There'd also been dizziness, headaches, muscle weakness and nausea, which had left Amy wondering if it was something neurological. She'd had a patient come in before with similar symptoms, who'd been diagnosed with a brain tumour, and Amy had been desperate for the doctors to find something that would prove Gwen didn't have anything like that. Even with the barrage of tests that had been ordered, it would probably be a while before they knew what was wrong. She'd eventually had to leave the hospital with a heavy heart, having made Meg promise to call her if there was any news, so that she could come back and offer Gwen whatever support might be needed.

Before she'd left work, she'd gone in to check on her friend one last time and had found Gwen all on her own.

'Where's Barry?'

'Gone outside to cry.' Gwen had still sounded exhausted, but there was far more clarity in her speech.

'Oh Gwen.' Amy had wanted to cry too, but she'd dug her fingernails into her palms instead.

'I've always dreaded losing him, but it's going to kill him if

I'm really ill.' Gwen had sighed heavily, leaning back against the pillow. 'But that's what comes of going all in, isn't it? Love should be all or nothing, otherwise it's a waste of the life you could have had.'

Amy had wanted to promise Gwen that she'd be okay, but that wasn't a promise she could make. Instead, she said one thing she knew for certain to be true. 'Not many people get to have a love like you two, and it's pretty obvious you haven't wasted a moment of the time you've spent together.'

Gwen had squeezed her hand after that, too tired to continue the conversation and Amy had waited until Barry returned, his eyes red rimmed just as Gwen had predicted. There was no way Amy would have left before Barry came back, and she'd texted Lijah to let him know she was running late. He'd replied straight away, telling her not to rush and asking if it would be okay for him to take Monty around to visit Albert, so that he didn't have to cancel the scheduled visit. The vet had said Monty could go for short walks now and that he could be taken out in the car, so she'd been happy to agree. The truth was Monty would probably be okay to be left alone now, but then she'd have no reason to see Lijah as often as she did, especially when Amy had been the one to insist they kept things casual. She knew that seeing him as little as possible was the safest thing to do, but Monty had given her an excuse not to listen to that logic. Soon that excuse would be gone, and as much as she was delighted that Monty was nearly better, not seeing Lijah almost every day was a prospect she didn't want to think about too much.

The longer he stayed around, the harder it was to imagine life when he finally left again, but that was exactly why she had to do something to persuade him to leave Port Kara sooner rather than later. Whether that was by reminding him that he belonged on the stage, performing the music he loved, or some other way, it didn't matter. She told herself that if she didn't do it soon, it was going to be too late, but deep down she knew it probably already was. The fact he was willing to do whatever it took not to let Albert down said so much about the man he was.

When Amy eventually arrived at Albert's farm to pick Monty up, Lijah answered the door and her breath caught in her throat, just like it had the first time she'd ever seen him.

'Hi.' It was all she could manage.

'Hello.' He smiled and the lines she'd been rehearsing about this never working between them, and him needing to stop hiding out in Port Kara and get back to his own life, felt like the last thing she wanted to say. She didn't want to get dragged into the drama that surrounded Lijah, any more than she wanted to risk letting him break her heart again. She'd built a great life for herself and had known exactly what it was she wanted, before Lijah had turned up again. It should have been so easy to tell him all the reasons why trying again would be a mistake, but it turned out that logic didn't stand a chance when feelings got in the way. It was Lijah who broke the silence between them.

'Are you coming in? I've just made some tea for Albie and we're about to start on the chocolate biscuits. Monty's been drooling ever since he heard the rustle of the packet.'

She returned his smile; talking about the dog was safe ground and something she could manage. 'That sounds like Monty, they say dogs copy their owners and I can sniff out a biscuit from a hundred metres. As you can probably tell.'

He shook his head. 'Why do you always put yourself down Ames? You did when we were teenagers and you're still doing it now. I wish you could see yourself the way others do.'

'Some old habits die hard; you must know that.' Her laugh sounded hollow, as she moved past him down the hallway, wanting to get to Albert and Monty so they could change the subject and talk about something – anything – other than the two of them. She wasn't ready to have the conversation she'd planned, she wasn't sure she ever would be, but either way now definitely wasn't the time. Reaching the door to the living room quickly, she pushed it open to see the little dog curled up next to Albert on the sofa. 'How are you, Albie? Monty certainly looks at home.'

'I'm all the better for Monty and Lijah visiting and seeing you is just the cherry on the cake. Having a beautiful woman come to see me is always a treat.'

'Thanks, but I think beautiful might be stretching it a bit!' Amy saw the look that crossed Lijah's face, but before he could say anything, Albert launched his own protest.

'Don't talk nonsense. You remind me of Elizabeth Taylor in *Raintree County*. I was only ten years old, but it was the first time I remember seeing a girl and thinking how beautiful she was. I watched as many of her films as I could after that, until I met Millie and I forgot about everyone else, even Elizabeth Taylor. I probably shouldn't tell you that you remind me of my pin-up, should I? It's not the done thing these days.'

'I'll let you off.' She smiled, the only film Amy had ever seen Elizabeth Taylor in was *The Flintstones* and from what she remembered she'd played a very glamorous grandmother, but Amy decided to take it as compliment all the same.

'Good, because you need to start realising how beautiful you are.' Albert wagged a finger at her, sounding just like Lijah, who immediately echoed the sentiment.

'I keep saying the same thing.' She couldn't look at him, otherwise he'd realise that she'd long since lost the battle to play this cool. Thankfully Albert saved her from having to respond at all.

'Trust me, you'll wish you realised how beautiful you are

now when you get to my age!' He laughed. 'There are lots of things I wish I'd made the most of, going out dancing on a Saturday night with Millie for one. She'd sneak out of the big house and meet me at the village hall, and I'd whirl her around the dancefloor all evening. When you're young you think you'll be able to do those things forever and I wish I'd appreciated it a bit more.'

'You could still go dancing. My friend goes to a great dance class where everyone's included.' Amy tried not to think about whether the days of Gwen dominating the dancefloor would soon be over. 'I can give you the details if you like.'

'I don't think that's for me, but if you could transport me back to the late 1950s or even the early 1960s just for one night, I might be persuaded.' Albert sighed and then Monty started howling for no reason at all, making sure the attention was back on him, and the conversation quickly moved on to the subject of dogs and Lijah's plan to get one as soon as he worked out where he wanted to settle permanently. Amy tried not to be too disappointed that he was still so uncertain. Less than an hour ago she'd been intending to try and persuade him to leave Port Kara. Now here she was, feeling gutted that he hadn't come to the conclusion he needed to stay. Heading out to the kitchen she started washing up the mugs, so her face couldn't give her away.

'Do you think we could organise it?' Lijah's question as he followed her into the kitchen a few moments later, made her head shoot up.

'Organise what?'

'A dance in the village hall with some of Albie's favourite music from the fifties and sixties. We could invite other people from the befriending service.'

'You'd want to do that?' Amy already knew what his response would be, so it was no surprise when Lijah nodded.

'You know how much Mum loved music from the eighties. She always said there was something about music from her youth that seemed to recharge her. We spent so much of our time listening to it in our teens, and it's those eighties songs that can take me back to being a carefree kid too, even though we weren't born when they came out. There's nothing better than seeing people getting lost in the music they love, and it would be so brilliant to see Albie doing that.'

'It might take a while. Will you be around long enough?' She held her breath, waiting for him to answer, and he nodded.

'I've got nowhere I need to rush off to and I can stay as long as it takes to...' He hesitated for a moment as if he was going to say something else, but then seemed to think better of it. 'I can cover any costs, but I'm just not sure where to start with organising it.'

'I'll talk to Aidan and see what he thinks.' Usually the first person Amy would have spoken to would be Gwen, but her friend had far more important things to focus on right now. 'It's a lovely idea, though, and I'm sure Albie would be really touched that you've thought of it.'

'Do you ever wish you could go back to a time when things were simpler?' His voice was soft and her fingers twitched with the longing to reach out and touch him, but she gave an almost imperceptible nod of her head instead. She couldn't risk Albert walking in and seeing them together. The fact this relationship was just between the two of them was the last one of the rules she was managing to cling to. If that went, she'd be in even deeper than she already was.

'Me too.' There was a sigh in his voice, and then Albert called out his name, interrupting whatever Lijah might have said next.

'You'd better go and check he's okay and tell him about your idea. I won't be a minute.' Staring into the washing up bowl,

Amy held her breath again until he disappeared. If she could go back to when they were teenagers, she'd do it in a heartbeat despite all the angst and heartbreak when it had ended between them. It would be worth it to have those years with Lijah again, because there was no doubt in her mind they'd been the happiest of her life.

21

After Lijah's sixteenth birthday, Maria had continued to make up for lost time and birthdays had become a big deal at Mor Brys. It always began with the 'birthday balloon'. It was a tradition Lijah's mother had started, where she'd plan something exciting for his birthday, from a day at the theme park, to tickets to see his favourite band. Maria wouldn't just announce it, though, or hand over the gift, she'd reveal the secret by putting a tiny slip of paper inside an inflated balloon. It would be hidden amongst lots of other balloons, the number matching the number of years the birthday was marking. The three of them would then chase around trying to find the balloon with the message inside, popping it to discover the secret, but woe betide anyone who popped the wrong balloon, because that would result in a forfeit. After that, there'd be a birthday breakfast, and it was just the start of a day made special by all the things Maria did to make it so. She'd done the same for Claire every year too.

When Lijah had left home, he'd ended up spending his birthday elsewhere most of the time, but his mother would postpone the celebration until the next time he got home and go all out then. He'd never forget what she'd said to him on his last birthday.

'You're still my little boy, and that won't ever change, not until the day I die.' Neither of them had any idea just how soon that day would come, and he was so glad now that he'd always come back to celebrate his mother's birthday, knowing that was the only gift she really wanted. Now they were working through a series of firsts, without Maria, and today was his Aunt Claire's first birthday since his mother's death, which meant it was down to him to somehow make it special.

'You look worn out.' Claire smiled at Lijah as he flopped into a chair after the birthday breakfast had been served, eaten and cleared away, but it wasn't any of those things that had sapped his energy. It was impossible to fill the gap his mum had left behind, but he'd been determined to find joy in the day. And the truth was, even though things would never be the same, for the first time in a long time he could envisage a way of being truly happy again. When he thought what his own birthday might be like in years to come, he didn't want to try and replicate the things his mum had done for him, because it would never be the same without her. He wanted to share the day, and every other special occasion, with someone he loved, someone he could start his own traditions with. That someone was Amy, but every time he tried to get past the wall she'd built up, she changed the subject. She seemed determined to stick to the rules she'd set out and at first he'd thought it was to make sure they were both certain this time around. Only now he was beginning to wonder if she'd been certain all along, certain that she didn't want to be with him long term. He couldn't blame her. His life was crazy and she'd only seen tiny hints of just how insane it could be. If she was exposed to the full extent of it, he could guarantee Amy wouldn't want to be a part of it. Maybe this was just a way to get him out of her system once and for all, to finish off the unfinished business they'd had. It was trying to second guess Amy's motivations that was wearing him down, but her rules meant he couldn't even ask Claire's advice. And he wasn't going to be responsible for spoiling his aunt's birthday, so he shot a grin in her direction.

'Blowing up sixty-one balloons will wear a person out. We might just have to go for one giant hot air balloon next time.'

'Cheeky sod.' Claire laughed, hurling a cushion at him. 'Although I'm not sure I want to start the tradition with Dee for her birthday; my lungs are a lot older than yours.'

'I'll buy you a balloon inflater for Christmas.' Lijah tried not to feel the sharp stab of regret that his aunt's plans for the future revolved around moving away. He'd have to go to Tenerife if he wanted to see Claire at Christmas, or on her next birthday, and they'd probably never celebrate at Mor Brys again.

'Are you okay, Lij?' His aunt moved to sit beside him. 'I'm sorry the breakfast got interrupted by that call, but the estate agent was really keen to let me know my offer on the villa had been accepted.'

'Don't be silly, it's great news.' Lijah had seen the look of happiness on his aunt's face when she'd got the call, and how excited she was to start this next phase of her life.

'You will come and see me once I'm out there, won't you? I'm going to miss you so much. Even though you were away a lot, your mum and I always knew you'd be home sooner or later. But without Mor Brys...'

'Home isn't a house, it's the people.' Lijah picked up one of the many scatter cushions on the sofa, some of which were emblazoned with affirmations about life and love. 'You've probably got that embroidered on one of these.'

'It's a good job I love you.' She threw another cushion at him, narrowly missing a vase filled with stargazer lilies, which were giving off the most amazing scent. 'Look what you nearly made me do!'

She was smiling despite her words, and he pulled a face. 'I'm not taking the blame for you hurling your positive affirmation cushions all over the room. They're beautiful flowers, though.'

'They are, but then Amy always sends something lovely. I'm so touched she still remembers my birthday, and she never missed your mum's birthday either.'

'Really?' His eyebrows shot up as she nodded and he wondered not for the first time how different things might have been if he and Amy had never split up. He had to accept that he'd never know, and one thing this visit home had taught him, was that you couldn't go back and expect everything to be exactly like it was when you left, because things never stayed the same.

'Right then, Lij, I'd better go and get in the shower, because Dee's going to FaceTime me and I don't want her to see my hair looking like a bird's nest.'

'She'll have to get used to that sooner or later.' Lijah grinned again, as she whacked him with a cushion for a third time.

'You do know you're supposed to be nicer to your favourite aunt on her birthday, don't you?'

'I'm taking you on a boat trip, aren't I? You can't have it all.' Lijah smiled, thinking about how excited his aunt had been when she'd discovered the surprise. He'd chartered a boat to take them down the coast, because spending time on the water had always been one of Claire's favourite things to do.

'I know and I'm very lucky to have a nephew like you.' She hugged him, and he felt another twist of guilt in his gut at how long he'd gone without seeing her after his mother's death. It was no wonder Claire had gone searching for a new life, and he only had himself to blame if there was very little room in that new life for him. Nick had been right, he'd needed to work out what he wanted. The trouble was, now that he'd worked out what he wanted, he had no idea if it was even possible to make it happen.

* * *

'Well, my first night shift back has been very interesting, but I didn't expect to end it wearing your spare shoes.' Isla waggled her feet.

'They're so big you look like a little kid playing dress up in your mum's high heels. Although I don't think many kids would want to dress up in those. They might be the sort of thing a nun would wear, but my God are they comfortable, at least when they fit.' Amy looked down at the very sensible, black slip-on shoes Isla was wearing, which were at least two sizes too big.

'When someone is sick on your trainers, any alternative is good.' Isla shuddered at the memory.

'I think we should start introducing a fine system for drunks who clog up A&E, whose reward for checking them over is either abusing us or throwing up, sometimes both.' Esther grimaced. It had been a long night for all of them, and Meg had ordered in some proper coffee and doughnuts, which had been delivered just in time for the end of their shift.

'That's an idea, although I'm not sure we could enforce it.' A slow smile crept across Meg's face. 'Perhaps we could introduce a policy of taking the temperature of drunks with a rectal thermometer instead. That should sober them up.'

'I think I'd rather keep coming in to work with spare shoes.' Amy grimaced. 'Do you think Danni and Aidan are missing all of this?'

'From what I remember of having young babies, they'll be dealing with plenty of projectile vomiting.' Gary picked up one of the sticky doughnuts, all this talk of sickness clearly not putting him off. 'Oh my God, these look delicious, where are they from?'

'That new shop in Port Tremellien, *Americana*. It opens at 6 a.m., which makes it perfect for an end-of-night-shift order.' Meg picked up a doughnut, topped with what looked like maple syrup and pecans.

'I think I'm going to have to persuade Wendy to have a doughnut stand instead of a wedding cake.' Gary said. 'This beats fruit cake hands down.'

'I'm going to try one of the raspberry ones. That way I can tell myself its healthy.' Zahir reached for a doughnut, and Amy had been about to follow suit when her mobile started to ring. It was twenty past seven in the morning and no one ever rang her that early, unless it was with news that couldn't wait. She didn't want that, because in Amy's experience, news that couldn't wait was never good. The last time she'd had a call that early it had been about her grandfather dying, and she shivered as she reached for the phone, her heart lurching when she saw the call was from Lijah.

'Hello.' She moved away from her friends to the far side of the staffroom as she spoke, to make sure she'd be able to hear him. But when the caller responded, it wasn't Lijah.

'Hi Amy, it's Nick.' His tone was serious and her heart had already started to race, as she tried to think what possible reason there could be for Nick using Lijah's phone that wouldn't bring bad news. What he said next did nothing to reassure her. 'Is Lijah with you?'

'No, I'm still at work. I've just finished a night shift and Monty is with Mum.'

'Shit.'

'What's up?' Her heart was galloping by now, and the depth of Nick's sigh did nothing to reassure her.

'I stayed at Dolly's last night, but I came home early because we're supposed to be having a call with the promoters of the Asian leg of the tour at 8 a.m. They're based in Tokyo and it was the only time that really worked for everyone. Except Lij isn't here, and his bed doesn't look like it's been slept in. He left his phone here too and he never does that.'

'He must have forgotten it when he went over for Claire's birthday celebrations. Maybe they went on longer than expected, and he stayed over?' She held her breath, willing Nick to thank her and say he hadn't thought of that, but instead he sighed again.

'I tried there. He left about ten o'clock last night, after they'd been on a boat trip and then out for dinner. Claire said he seemed fine, but I know how good Lij is at faking that he's okay, and never more so than when he's really struggling.'

'Oh God, you don't think...' Amy clutched the phone so tightly it made her fingers hurt. Lijah had tried so hard to suppress his grief, but now he'd lifted the lid on it there was a chance it might have become overwhelming, especially with his aunt about to leave too.

'No, I don't think he'd do anything like that, but I'm still really worried about him. He doesn't seem ready to go back on tour and that's fine, we can delay as long as he likes, but I don't think coming back here has given him the answers he thought it would. He seems a bit lost, and I don't know how to reach him. Maria was his sounding board for so much and, without her, he doesn't know which way to go. I think he'd give anything to be able to ask her advice one more time.' Something clicked in Amy's brain, in response to what Nick had said.

'I think I might know where he is.' She was already moving towards her locker to gather up her stuff. 'He always used to go up to the cliffs at Dagger's Head to watch the sunrise when he was on the cusp of a big decision. I remember going up there with him just before he decided to move to London.'

'That's where Maria's ashes were scattered too, so he probably feels closest to her there.' Nick paused and, when he spoke again, he sounded hesitant. 'Shall I meet you at Dagger's Head?'

'Do you want to?' Amy knew from experience that some people found the grief of others hard to handle, but she couldn't imagine Nick feeling that way about Lijah.

'I think it might be better if it was just you. He's got it into his head that I want to push him to restart the tour, when all I really want is to know he's okay. He's my best friend, but we can never completely separate that from our working relationship. Whereas you and he...' Nick hesitated again. 'What you have is something he's never had with anyone else, and I don't think those feelings have changed.'

Amy might not allow herself to believe Lijah loved her, because of what it would do to her if she was wrong, but she could accept he needed her, and being needed was a role she was comfortable with. 'I'll go to Dagger's Head now and I'll let you know as soon as I find him.'

'What if he isn't there?'

'He will be.' Amy was more certain of that than she had been of anything in a long time, she just wished she was half as confident about what to say when she found him.

* * *

Amy spotted Lijah from about fifty metres away, sitting on a rock above the cliffs at Dagger's Head and staring out to sea. She thought about calling out to him, but she wanted to just watch him for a moment. He looked like the version of Lijah she'd fallen in love with first time around, just an ordinary boy, not a household name everyone thought they knew. Except Lijah had never really been ordinary, there'd always been a magic about him and the fact he was so blissfully unaware of it had made it all the more magnetic. She was only a few feet away from him by the time she eventually spoke.

'What are you doing up here?' His head shot up in response to her question.

'Thinking.'

'What about?'

'What to do next.'

'What do you want to do?' She looked at him and he held her gaze so intently for a moment that it was almost painful, but she couldn't look away.

'I want to sit on the sofa with you, Mum, and Claire, listening to cheesy eighties songs and the two of them arguing about whether Duran Duran or Wham! are the best.' Lijah gave her a half smile. 'Then I want us to sneak up to my room like we used to. I wish I'd never let what we had slip through my hands.'

'But we did let that happen.'

'No, I did. I shouldn't have just accepted it when you said we should break up.'

'You had dreams you needed to follow. You couldn't do that in Port Kara.' It had all made so much sense to Amy then and she'd been certain she was doing the right thing, the way she always tried so hard to do, but Lijah was shaking his head.

'I should have told you that I couldn't follow my dreams without you, because you were in all of them.' Lijah's eyes didn't leave her face. 'I don't care if that's the cheesiest line you've ever heard, because it's true.'

Amy wanted to laugh and tell him it was cheesy and that all of this was just nostalgia, but she couldn't trust herself to talk about their relationship, because she'd never be able to stick to the rules if she did. It was easier to change the subject, just like she'd done every time Lijah had tried to get her to talk about where this might be going. 'I need to let Nick know I've found you and that you're okay. You missed a call with Tokyo.'

He didn't say anything and he was still watching her when she'd finished sending the text.

'Why are you staring at me?' There was an edge to her tone, the fear of him realising how she felt making her harsh.

'Don't you ever wonder what would have happened if I hadn't gone to London?' His eyes were still on hers and her mouth wouldn't seem to form the answer she wanted to give. So she found herself blurting out the truth.

'All the time.' His eyes widened in surprise, and she managed to recover herself a little. 'But only since you've been home.'

'Home. That's a funny word, isn't it?' Lijah stood up and took a step towards her so that they were almost touching. 'I had such an overwhelming urge to come home, but when I got here it didn't feel like home any more. Mor Brys isn't home without Mum, and Claire is moving away soon. Renting the cliff house didn't help either. Nick is with me all the time, so sharing a place with him here is no different to us living anywhere else. The only time I've had any sense of really coming home is when I've been with you.'

'I can't be your sticking plaster, it's not fair on me, because, because...'

'Because what?'

'Because I still love you.' Amy shook her head, wishing she could stuff the words back down her throat. She wasn't supposed to admit that, not even to herself.

'You make that sound like the worst thing in the world.' Lijah's whole face seemed to change as he smiled. 'But it's the best thing I've heard, because I feel exactly the same way. I never stopped loving you either, so you'll have to tell me again why there's a problem.'

Amy's breath caught in her throat and all the things she'd told herself about why this could never work seemed to desert her again, but somehow she plucked the most important reason out of the air.

'Because you're famous and everything has changed for you. This isn't your life any more, but it's still mine, it always has been. I'm not looking back at it with rose-tinted glasses, because I'm still living it and I don't want to give it up. When this doesn't solve all your problems, or it turns out not to be enough for you, it'll still be my life.' She clamped her arms to her side, desperately trying not to reach for him.

'I'm not asking you to solve my problems or to give up the life you've built for yourself, all I'm asking for is a chance to prove I mean what I'm saying. What harm could it possibly do to give this another chance? A proper chance, not one that feels like we've both decided it's over before it's even begun.' He was so close to her now that she could see the sincerity in his eyes, but somehow she still couldn't trust he meant it.

'You could date anyone you like, so why the hell would you choose me?'

'I could ask you the same question.' Lijah narrowed his eyes and she pulled a face.

'It's not the same for me and you know it. If you want to prove this isn't just some trip down memory lane for you then I need to hear it.'

'Because I love you and I've never felt that way about anyone else. You're the best person I know, and I can be completely myself with you, but for some reason you still seem to like me.' He took hold of her hand and she couldn't remember what she'd been about to say, instead she found herself closing the gap between them and the next moment they were kissing. Anyone could have seen them, but suddenly she didn't care. The rules had been a stupid idea that could never have protected her from getting hurt, because she'd had no chance of sticking to them. She loved Lijah and it was going to break her heart if he walked out of her life again, whether they snatched bits of time together secretly, or the whole world found out that they were seeing each other again. When she eventually stepped back from him, her cheeks were flushed, and the decision was made. Her heart had been all in from the moment Lijah had come back into her life, and now the rest of her had followed suit.

'Do you want to come back to my place?' It was a straightforward question, because there was no point playing games any more, and he smiled in response.

'That's the easiest decision I've had to make for a long time.' Lijah put an arm around Amy's waist, pulling her into his side, and she let go of a long breath as they started to walk. It might have been an easy decision for him, but she still wasn't sure whether putting her heart on the line like this was the stupidest decision she could possibly make. She had no choice, though. Gwen had talked about not wasting the time you were given, and that the only way to live life was to give it all or nothing. So, if having nothing was the alternative, Amy might as well at least try to have it all, whatever that might end up costing her.

22

Gwen had been put through more tests than she could have listed, even if her brain hadn't felt like it was made of marshmallow, and some of the results had already come back. When she and Barry had described her symptoms to Meg, she'd hit upon the mention of increased thirst and the resulting need to go to the loo more often.

'It could be diabetes. If that's gone undiagnosed, it could also explain some of the confusion.' Gwen had wanted to latch on to Meg's words and will them to be true. No one wanted diabetes, but there was treatment she could have to stabilise her insulin. To her disappointment the tests for diabetes had come back negative, and her confusion couldn't be blamed on another UTI either. Her blood pressure was low, which could explain the dizziness, the headaches, and possibly even some of the confusion. But she couldn't pin her hopes on it being that simple, not with the other symptoms she'd had: the desperate low mood, the loss of interest in eating and a lethargy that felt all consuming at times, like life was just too much. She'd watched her mother experience those same feelings when her illness had started to progress. It didn't matter how often Meg or any of the other medical staff tried to reassure her that her symptoms didn't fit a diagnosis of aphasia, she could feel it in her gut. In meant that despite her exhaustion she couldn't sleep, because the results of the tests could come at any time.

'Come back to bed.' Barry's voice was gentle but firm as he came into the living room, where she lay on the sofa, staring into the darkness, as she had been for the past couple of hours.

'There's no point, I'll just end up lying there awake and that will disturb you.' Gwen hated nighttime lately, the endless hours of darkness when the fear crept in, and nothing could shake it. There'd been a time not so long ago when she'd have happily gone back to bed just to be with Barry, even if she was struggling to sleep, but now the night felt like her enemy.

'You could just come up and have a cuddle. Sitting here on your own worrying won't solve anything.' When she didn't move, Barry crossed the room and joined her on the sofa, taking hold of her hand. 'Whatever happens, whatever all of this is, you don't have to face any of it on your own. We've always been side by side, and that's not going to change.'

Gwen didn't answer for a moment. The clarity of her thinking seemed to come and go, which was part of the torture. She could convince herself for a little while that she was okay, but then there'd be another incident where she couldn't coordinate her thoughts with her speech. Right now, Gwen knew exactly what she wanted to say and when she finally started to speak, her mouth seemed willing to comply for once. 'I don't want you to have to be there when I stop being me. I don't want to put you through that.'

'You'll never stop being you, not to me. And there's nothing you can say that will make me change my mind about staying by your side until one of us shuffles off this mortal coil. I'm not going anywhere and, if you're not coming back to bed, I'm staying here with you.'

Gwen's response was so quiet that if Barry hadn't sat down beside her, he might not have heard it. 'I've been so lucky with the life we've had, and I can't complain if that luck runs out, but I really don't want it to.'

'Neither do I, but I wouldn't trade a day of the life we've had for anything. No matter what.' Barry pulled her towards him and Gwen rested her head on his shoulder. She didn't want to be facing any of this, and she was still terrified, but if she had to go through it she was so grateful it was with Barry. He'd always loved her unconditionally and she knew he meant what he said, because if the situation had been reversed she'd have felt exactly the same.

* * *

Amy and Lijah had been openly 'back together' for a grand total of thirty-six hours before the first photographs of them holding hands had appeared online. Lijah had tried to keep things low key and to protect his identity since he came home, but someone who'd witnessed the accident had leaked the fact that he'd been involved in helping Ellen, and there'd been even more press sniffing around after that. It meant a photographer was there when Amy and Lijah had gone out walking with Monty, on one of his first short walks. The vet had suggested getting a pet pushchair, so that the little dog didn't overdo it, and they'd pushed Monty down to the beach and then let him out for a little while when they got there. Neither of them had noticed the photographer lurking in the distance, snapping shots of them.

The weather was getting warmer, and Lijah hadn't been wearing a hat, his joy at Amy finally being willing to give things a proper go making him drop his guard more than he should have done. He hadn't wanted to play into the fears she'd expressed by acting like a paranoid celebrity, but he should have known the risk he was taking. His reticence had given the press the perfect opportunity to capture candid moments between the two of them, the headlines that accompanied the pictures as salacious as possible, to guarantee the maximum number of clicks on the article.

> Troubled singer, Lijah Byrne and his childhood sweetheart enjoy time on the beach with their baby

It was only later in the article that the journalist admitted the 'baby' in question was in fact a dog. The majority of the story was just as full of half-truths and fabrication as the headline, but worse than that it had stirred up a hornets' nest of interest from other journalists and, by the third day, it was obvious it was really getting to Amy.

'They were outside the hospital again today.' There was a sigh in her voice when she got back to the flat, where he'd been waiting with Monty. Lijah had wanted to pick her up from work, but she'd told him it was a bad idea, because it would just encourage the journalists. 'I thought they were going to follow me all the way home.'

'It'll calm down, I promise.' He swept the hair away from her face as he spoke, hoping he was right, but she looked close to tears.

'Have you read what they wrote?'

'Don't take any notice of that, they just make up whatever they want.' He was doing his best to make it sound easy, when he knew from bitter experience it wasn't.

'The comments from people online are worse than the article itself. I can live with being described as curvy, when I know they mean fat, and having a girl-next-door charm, when I know they mean plain, but the comments...' Tears welled up in Amy's eye, and she furiously wiped them away. 'I hate myself for caring so much, but my God some of the comments are horrible.'

'You're beautiful, inside and out.' He wished she could see it, but he knew she probably never would. 'The people who post horrible comments are saying far more about themselves than anything else. It's got nothing to do with you, there's something wrong with them and people like that just need an outlet for their hate. You get used to it after a while and it gets easier to ignore.'

'I don't want to get used to it. One of them said I should have been drowned at birth and another said that if we did have a real baby, it wouldn't look like a dog, it would look like a pig, because it would take after its mother.' She tried to laugh, but she didn't quite pull it off, and he felt capable of violence towards the people who were deliberately setting out to hurt Amy.

'There are some awful people out there, but I promise you that—'

She cut him off before he could finish, pulling away. 'I knew this would happen and that people would say I wasn't good enough for you.'

'It's the other way around, you're far too good for me.' He pulled her closer again, relieved when she didn't resist. 'Don't let anyone take this second chance away from us. Please, Ames.'

'I won't.' She nodded, but he could see the doubt those comments had put in her eyes. She'd admitted it was other people who'd made her question whether things could work out between them the first time around, so-called friends who'd suggested that when his career took off he'd inevitably outgrow her. It meant they'd never had the chance to find out for themselves. Amy had seemed far more assured when they'd reconnected, and he'd assumed it was the desire to protect the life she'd built for herself that had made her set parameters on their relationship. But he'd seen the signs that her self-doubt was still there and he knew from experience just how damaging online comments could be to someone's self-worth. He couldn't bear the thought of this coming between them.

Kissing her gently, Lijah wished she didn't have to try and grow a skin thick enough to deal with all the hatred out here. He'd had years of that, and it still had the power to drive him to the edge at times. Whatever Amy might believe, he wanted to protect her from every kind of hurt. Yet, because of him, she was being exposed to a vicious onslaught. Part of him knew it would be kinder to walk away, but he couldn't do that, because he was already struggling to imagine his life without her and he didn't even want to try.

* * *

'Can you tell me again exactly where the pain is?' Amy was spending the shift triaging patients and she was almost certain the man in front of her was trying to pull a fast one. She had enough experience to recognise the signs when she saw them. The man didn't wince, until she directly questioned him about the source of his pain, and when he did react it was with clinical regularity. *One, two, three, wince. One, two, three, wince.* His description of his pain had been textbook too, almost as if he was reading it out, which was why she'd asked him to repeat it.

'It started just below my belly button and then radiated out until it was concentrated on the right-hand side of my abdomen.'

'It sounds like it could be appendicitis.' Amy made some notes on the computer, turning back in time to see the man, whose name was Tom, trying to take a surreptitious photograph with his phone. 'What are you doing?'

'Just a hospital selfie, you know, for Instagram.'

Amy's scalp prickled. It was on the tip of her tongue to tell him to get out and stop wasting hospital resources, but she could just imagine how that would be reported. So, she breathed out slowly instead. 'I'll go and speak to one of the doctors. They'll need to do some test to establish whether it's appendicitis.'

'What kind of tests?' For the first time, Tom's over-confidence seemed to desert him, and the corners of Amy's mouth twitched, something Meg had said recently inspiring her.

'A rectal examination is the best way, but you'll probably need an enema first.' It was an outright lie, one she could get into serious trouble for, but it was worth it for the look of sheer horror on his face. 'I won't be long.'

Amy almost laughed as she left the room and she had a funny feeling that, by the time she came back, Tom would have made a miraculous recovery. As it turned out, he'd disappeared altogether, and she was more certain than ever that he'd either been a journalist, or a member of the public hoping to make a bit of money by selling a story. The thought of being photographed at work made her feel sick. She was just trying to do her job in a service that could ill afford time wasters, and the idea of having her face splashed all over the papers horrified her. She didn't want to believe anyone could sink low enough to make up an illness, but she knew they could and she hated the fact it might make her doubt a genuine patient, in future.

'Tough shift?' Isla asked when they had the chance to catch up properly in the staff room, just before Amy was about to head home.

'I had a journalist in, pretending to have appendicitis and trying to take photos of me.' Amy frowned. 'I don't know if I can do this.'

'Don't let them take this away from you Ames.' Isla lowered her voice to almost a whisper as Eden came into the staff room. 'It's obvious how you feel about Lijah.'

'You don't have to whisper. Eden knows about me and Lijah. Everyone does.'

'I think it's great.' Eden smiled. 'But then I always was a sucker for a good love story, and you can't beat one about childhood sweethearts who get back together.'

'It's probably the reason why the press are so interested. It's a really nice feel-good story and we all need more of those these days.' Isla was beaming and Amy envied her naivety, but then her friend probably hadn't looked at the comments on the articles about her and Lijah. There was nothing feel-good about those.

'They're interested because no one can believe someone like him would go for someone like me.'

'Why do you keep saying things like that?' Isla's tone was sharp. 'If you ask me, he's the lucky one.'

'You have to say that because you're my friend and I love you for it.' Amy blew her a kiss. It was the same thing Lijah had said, but she still didn't believe it. 'He could date one of the world's most successful models if he wanted to. I know because he has in the past.'

'He's dated you in the past too, it's not like his feelings have come out of nowhere.'

'That's different, he wasn't famous then.'

'Is that why things finished first time around, because Lijah met other people and thought he could do better?' Isla was giving her an appraising stare, and Amy suspected her friend already knew the answer to her question.

'I ended it.'

'Why?' Isla was still looking at her.

'Because I thought that's what would happen, and other people told me that's what would happen. So I wanted to end things before it did.'

'Do you think that saved you any pain, or just made you wonder whether you'd ended something that could have worked?' Isla didn't even seem to need to blink, and Amy gave an exaggerated shrug, wishing her friend hadn't read the situation quite so accurately.

'Probably the second thing, but I didn't know what was going to happen with Lijah's career then. Now I do, and he's got the whole world at his feet. How am I supposed to believe a life here, with me, could ever really be enough?'

'What about if it had been the other way around?' Eden gave her a questioning look. 'If you'd been the one who became famous, don't you think you'd still want to choose Lijah?'

'Would I have had a choice between him and Ryan Gosling?' Amy laughed, but Isla wasn't letting her off the hook.

'All the things you've been through in the past ten years, and all the people you've met, haven't altered your ability to fall in love with Lijah again have they? So why should it be any different for him?'

'I never said anything about being in love with him.'

'You didn't have to.' Isla shook her head. 'Stop overthinking it. Nobody knows for sure whether they'll last forever, even if they are in love. Sometimes you've just got to enjoy life as it comes and accept you can't control all the outcomes.'

'Oh, and if Lijah can introduce you to Ryan Gosling, feel free to send him my way, seeing as you're already in a relationship.'

When Eden laughed, they all joined in, but there was still an uncomfortable feeling niggling in Amy's gut. She didn't want other people's opinions to drive a wedge between her and Lijah again, and she knew Isla was right about learning to enjoy the moment. But that was a lot harder to do when it felt as if half the world's press was desperate for her life to fall apart, and that every internet troll would be waiting to celebrate when it did.

23

Gwen's hands were shaking. It wasn't a new symptom, at least she didn't think it was, but it had felt lately as if there was something new every day. There were good days and bad days too, and that wasn't something Gwen's mother had experienced with the aphasia she'd been diagnosed with. Gwen had been determined not to look online, but she hadn't been able to resist, and Doctor Google had subsequently informed her that she could have anything from vascular dementia to Parkinson's disease, which having the shakes could be a symptom of. But she knew, deep down, that her hands were shaking due to fear. She needed to know what the doctors had discovered on her scans, but at the same time a big part of her wanted to beg Barry to take her back out to the car and just drive, anywhere she wouldn't have to face the possibility of news that would change everything, forever.

The thought of being trapped in her body with no way to communicate with the people around her felt like the worst form of torture. Talking and laughing, supporting people and offering advice, was the biggest part of who Gwen was. She was known for being a straight shooter, and for her near-the-knuckle sense of humour that usually worked its magic to lift the spirits of her colleagues and patients when they needed it most. Not being able to do that would be hell, and she'd miss the interaction more than she could explain. But even worse than that, was the thought of not being able to talk to her family, and most of all to her husband.

Barry had been her other half, her partner in crime, and her best friend for over fifty years. They'd had a physical relationship for all of that time too, and she knew it sometimes made her younger friends slightly uncomfortable when she was open about the fact. She didn't care if anyone else thought that older people should lock that side of themselves away, the connection she had with Barry went beyond worrying about wrinkles or any of that other stuff. They'd known real love, and her seven decades had taught her that wasn't nearly as common as it should be, and that it was something to be celebrated.

The reason Gwen handed out advice so freely, and was so open about her own relationship, was because she wanted her friends to know that real love did exist, and that when you got the opportunity to experience it you shouldn't let it pass you by. Love didn't look the same for everyone, and she didn't pretend that she and Barry hadn't had moments of frustration, or the ups and downs that everyone experienced. But Gwen firmly believed no one should settle for second best, and she'd be the first to say that no one should rely on someone else for their happiness either. That was the thing about love, though: when you found the real thing, it added so much more to life, and it was an incredible bonus she wished everyone could experience. The downside of finding that kind of love, was that the most precious of gifts were always the hardest to part with, and the thought of losing that connection to Barry, of laughing with him and talking to him, was truly unbearable. Gwen looked at him now, sadness etched on his face, and she was desperate to lift his spirits, the only way she knew how.

'I want you to promise me something.' Her tone was insistent, and he turned towards her, already nodding his head.

'Anything.'

'I want you to promise me that even if I stop being able to communicate altogether, and tell you what I want, that you'll never, ever put me in a pair of those Velcro sandals that Elena used to put Mum in, with fluffy red bed socks. Just know that if you do, I might not be able to protest, but I'll be screaming inside.'

'I promise.' For a moment, a smile played around his mouth and then the sadness descended again. He was every bit as scared as she was of what the results might bring, and somehow that made it even more terrifying.

Over the years, especially at big milestone moments, like when they'd lost their parents, Gwen had occasionally thought about the fact that one day one of them would be left alone. Every time it happened, she'd quickly shut the thought down, because there was nothing she could do to control it and she hadn't wanted to waste one moment of their life together thinking about what came afterwards. It would be like spending the whole of Christmas thinking about bleak January days, when the mountain of Christmas cards was replaced by ugly brown envelopes demanding payment for bills. No. She'd been determined to enjoy the good times, and leave the worrying until she had no choice but to face it. Only now that day had come, and they were sitting outside a consultant's office waiting to hear how this amazing love story was going to end. There was only one way she could get through it, the same way she'd got through all the tough times over the past fifty years, and just as her name was finally called, she grasped Barry's hand, wishing she never had to let it go.

'Whatever they say we'll be okay.' His tone was suddenly certain, and he squeezed her hand even more tightly as they walked into the consultant's office together.

Gwen had resisted the urge to look up Dr Grainger's speciality when she'd been given the appointment over the phone. It hadn't been a name she was familiar with, but she did recognise the doctor's face once they were sitting opposite one another. Dr Grainger came into the hospital shop once a week or so, and she always bought a Crunchie bar and a mocha, but that was all Gwen knew about her. They were in the outpatients' clinic, which ran appointments for everything from urology to audiology, so that hadn't given her any clues about Dr Grainger's area of expertise. Her title gave away the fact that she wasn't a surgeon, but second guessing wouldn't change anything, and Gwen was finally ready to hear what she had to say. Thankfully, once Dr Grainger had made the introductions, she cut straight to the chase. Looking at her computer screen briefly, she turned back towards Gwen and Barry, who were still clutching one another's hands.

'We've had the results of your scans and some of the blood tests that haven't already been shared with you. One of the tests takes five days to process and we wanted to review the results of that, alongside the scan imaging. I know it's probably seemed like a very long wait to get the news, but we've been able to make a definite diagnosis.'

Dr Grainger's pause made Gwen's stomach drop and she didn't know whether the younger woman was waiting for her permission to deliver the killer blow. She'd have been convinced beforehand that there'd be no way of ramping up the tension even further, but she'd have been wrong. She needed an end to this one way or another, because ignorance had stopped being bliss a long time ago, but it took all her strength to utter one word in response.

'And?'

'You have Addison's disease.' For a moment Gwen wasn't sure she'd heard correctly. She'd been so certain that Dr Grainger was going to say aphasia, and when she'd heard the 'a' sound, adrenaline had flooded her body, making the roots of her hair feel like they were on fire.

'What's Addison's disease?' It was left to Barry to ask the question, because Gwen was still too shocked to speak. She'd never heard of it, all she knew was that it wasn't any of the things she'd feared the most. She didn't have aphasia, or dementia, or motor neurone disease. So whatever Dr Grainger was about to say, she couldn't imagine it being any worse than what she'd expected.

'Addison's disease is caused by a disorder of the adrenal glands, which sit on top of the kidneys. It results in damage to those glands, meaning you don't produce enough of the cortisol or aldosterone hormones. This can result in a number of symptoms, including the low blood pressure, dizziness, loss of appetite, increased thirst and difficulty in concentrating that you presented with. It also causes low mood, which might account for some of the other symptoms you described.'

'Is it serious?' Barry was still asking all of the questions, instinctively understanding that Gwen was struggling to process what the doctor was saying.

'If left untreated it can be very serious, even fatal, but with the right treatment patients can have a normal life span. Gwen will have to stay on medication for the rest of her life, and if she experiences an adrenal crisis at any stage, it will be treated as a medical emergency and you'll both need to know how to administer a hydrocortisone injection. I know it's a lot to take in, but it really is a manageable condition, and my team will be here to support you. So I don't want you to worry too much.'

'It's about the best news you could have given me.' Gwen finally found her voice. 'I was struggling so much to concentrate on anything, and I'd convinced myself I had aphasia, like my mother, but now I wonder if the fear was making everything worse. I tried to talk some sense into myself about how different some of this was from what Mum went through, but I was worried I was losing my mind because the symptoms kept coming and going, and it felt like I didn't know myself at all any more.'

'The symptoms of Addison's disease can be very debilitating and can mimic a number of other conditions. They can also come and go in the earlier stages of the disease, but I promise it will all get much better once you start treatment.'

'Thank you.' Gwen could happily have hugged the woman sitting opposite, who was now giving her a reassuring smile. One thing she knew for certain was that Dr Grainger would never be paying for another Crunchie bar herself, but there was still one question she needed to ask. 'What causes Addison's disease?'

'It's usually a problem with the autoimmune system, which makes the body attack itself. When that happens to the adrenal glands, it disrupts the production of the hormones. We'll be carrying out some more tests to make sure we don't need to treat another underlying condition, but there's nothing in the tests we've conducted so far to raise any concerns, and we've been able to rule out it having been caused by cancer cells in the adrenal glands. Hopefully we'll be able to get you back on track and feeling much more like your old self really soon.'

'There's nothing I want more than to feel like my old self. Thank you.' Gwen felt the pressure of Barry's hand again as she spoke, knowing there was nothing more he wanted either. They continued holding hands through the rest of the appointment, as Dr Grainger, a consultant endocrinologist, outlined the next steps in Gwen's treatment.

'I don't know about you, Gee, but I feel like I've won the lottery three times over.' Barry was grinning from ear to ear as they walked down the corridor towards the pharmacy, where they'd be picking up Gwen's first prescription.

'Me too and I love you so much.' She tugged on his hand to stop him and he turned to face her.

'Not as much as I love you Mrs Jones, and that wouldn't have changed whatever your diagnosis had been. But now we can plan for lots more adventures, I know we've never held back on those, but if there's something we want to do, I'm not going to let anything stop us.'

'Me neither and while we're on the subject, there are a couple of things I want to do straight away. The first one is this.' Letting go of his hand, she reached up to touch his face, pulling it close to hers and kissing him like her life depended on it. Someone walking past gave a wolf whistle, but Gwen had never been shy about showing how much she loved her husband and right now he might as well have been the only other person on earth.

'Well, that was great.' He grinned when she finally let him go. 'Dare I ask what the other thing is?'

'I want to go and buy a pair of killer heels that cost far more than they should, and that are far too fancy for someone like me. Then I want to wear them to go dancing as soon as I feel up to it. No Velcro sandals for me, not now, not ever.'

'You were made for killer heels, my darling girl, and nothing is too fancy, because you deserve the best.' Barry took hold of her hand again, and they continued down the corridor together, into a future they were determined to treasure every second of, no matter what it threw at them.

* * *

When it was just Amy and Lijah together, it was easy to believe he was the same person he'd been back when they'd first met, an irresistible juxtaposition of confidence and insecurity that had allowed him to perform in front of crowds of people – albeit fairly modest crowds, back then – but at the same time had left him stuttering slightly when he'd first admitted how he felt about her. Their go-to date in those days had been the cinema. They'd gone by bus most weeks to the one in Port Tremellien, which had two screens. The main screen seated up a hundred and fifty people, and the smaller screen less than thirty. Screen two had always been their favourite. There was something about the cosiness of it and Lijah had said when he made it with his music, he'd buy them a house with their very own cinema room, which would be a replica of screen two.

It had been a fun game of make believe, one they'd indulged in more and more as their relationship progressed, talking about how many children they'd have, where they'd live, and how they'd balance Amy's nursing career with Lijah's dream. Amy had never doubted that Lijah had the talent, but people from fishing villages on the west coast of Cornwall didn't become famous. She hadn't realised until later how much a part of her had hoped it wouldn't happen. It wasn't that she didn't want Lijah to get his dream, she just didn't want anything to change or come between them. She'd have been happy to continue getting the bus to Port Tremellien and playing make believe, because screen two was enough for her as long as she had Lijah. She didn't need a cinema room of her own.

It was when she realised what Lijah was willing to sacrifice to follow his dream that she'd known they wouldn't last. He wanted a life so different from the one she loved, and she couldn't hold him back from that. She knew she couldn't follow him either, desperately clinging on to his coat tails and hoping there was enough of the old Lijah left to still want her around, even if he wanted everything else to change.

Even now, she had no idea how she was supposed to be certain of that. When they shut out the rest of the world, it was much easier to believe that he was still the same Lijah, whose dreams had always included building a future with her. But the trouble was, the rest of the world didn't seem to believe that could possibly be true, and as much as Amy didn't want to listen, the things people were saying online tapped into every insecurity she'd ever had. She was trying not to look, just as Lijah had advised, but it was much harder than she would ever have thought possible. If she let it, the vitriol some people spouted could reach her even when she was within the sanctuary of her own home, and she was trying to devise strategies to counter that.

Closing the door behind her when she came in from her shift, Amy hung up her coat in the hallway, leaving her phone in the pocket, determined not to let the rest of the world creep in for a while.

'How was your day?' Lijah was in the kitchen when she walked through. He was still keeping an eye on Monty, even though the little dog didn't need constant watching any more. Amy suspected he wanted an excuse to be at her house all the time, as much as she wanted an excuse for him to be there. Lijah looked remarkably at home in her place, cooking the same pasta bake that had been his speciality at eighteen, and acting as though there was nowhere else in the world he'd rather be, and no one he'd rather be with. She had to remind herself they were just playing make believe again, because this wasn't his world any more and, regardless of what happened between them, they wouldn't be able to spend their whole lives hanging out in her little flat.

'Work was busy, not helped by the fact that at least some of the patients were journalists faking an illness to try and get a photo of the woman who's stolen Lijah Byrne from his public.' Amy wrinkled her nose.

'Stolen my heart maybe.' He laughed at the expression on her face.

'Are you going to have enough cheese left for the pasta with lines like that?' It was something she said to him a lot, any time he tried to talk too much about feelings, but they both knew it was a defence mechanism, because it was the same line she'd used when they were teenagers, for the exact same reason. She couldn't help joining in when he laughed in response, and he clearly wasn't put off by her accusations of cheesiness.

'I was going to write a song for you too, about how I've only ever made pasta bake, for the one girl who made my heart ache. You can forget that now, and it had an Ivor Novello award written all over it too!' He was laughing even more now, the warmth in his conker-coloured eyes making something inside her ache with longing, despite the ridiculousness of the fake lyrics.

'I'll suppose I'll just have to accept that I'll never be your muse again.' She gave a mock sigh.

'Too late for that.' His expression was serious for a moment, but then he smiled again. 'So tell me Miss Spencer, how many rectal exams did you offer to the gutter press today?'

'Just the one.' She shrugged, returning his smile, not wanting to talk about the journalists any more. They were supposed to be trying to keep the rest of the world out. 'Can I do anything to help you with dinner?'

'No, I'm just about to put it in and I've sorted out a couple of films for tonight too, if you're up for it?'

'Sounds perfect. What are we watching?' It was hard to take her eyes off his face and she saw the upturn of his mouth, as he fought to keep a straight face.

'*World War Z*, followed by *Monsters University*, just like the good old days. We don't want you getting too scared!'

'You're never going to let me forget that, are you?' She pretended to punch him on the arm, and he pulled her towards him.

'You don't forget taking your girlfriend to see the latest Brad Pitt movie and finding yourself going straight from that into the other screen, with mostly six-year-olds in the audience.' They were face to face as he spoke and it was hard not to lose her train of thought, but she'd never forget that day either.

'Something about the zombies in that film really freaked me out, especially when that guy a few rows behind started making weird noises, like he was turning into one. I had to watch *Monsters University* to make it feel like everything was right with the world again. And don't pretend you didn't jump like mad when Brad Pitt was stuck in that lab with the zombies. I reckon you were every bit as keen to watch *Monsters University* afterwards to make everything right in your world again too.'

'Everything was always right in my world as long as I was with you.'

'You really aren't saving any of that cheese for the pasta, are you?' Her tone was teasing, but it had to be. As much as she wanted things to work out between them, she couldn't forget that Isla had been right about something else too and sometimes even love wasn't enough.

24

Lijah had pulled out all the stops to organise the kind of dance Albert had longed to recreate. It had been easy to understand why his new friend wanted to relive those special times from his youth, nights that seemed golden and perfect in a way he might never have appreciated at the time. It was the same way Lijah felt about the years he'd spent with Amy. He'd always known how special she was, but it had taken him seeing a whole other side of life to truly appreciate how genuine, extraordinary and authentically herself Amy truly was. She didn't spend all her time trying to fit an arbitrary mould of 'perfection' like so many people he met. They ended up looking like carbon copies of one another, their personalities seeming to disappear with the last vestiges of originality. Amy wasn't like that, she never had been, and she'd never expected him to change either. She hadn't tried to talk him out of going to London, or attempted to curtail his plans in anyway. She loved him for who he was, even when that had torn them apart, and it had taken him a long time to realise just how amazing that made her. People said first love had a power unlike any other, so it was easy for him to understand why Albert wanted to be back in that moment too, even if it was just for one night.

Lijah's pursuit of his dreams might always have been about the music rather than the money, but that didn't mean he hadn't thought about what success might bring him in that respect. It turned out the old cliché about it not buying you happiness was true, but it did make life easier, and it could do a lot of good if you let it. Not having to worry about money certainly made things easier when it came to planning events like this. He'd hired the hall, caterers and a band to recreate as closely as possible the dances of Albert's youth. Amy had spoken to Aidan and Caroline about inviting other users of the befriending service, as well as some other older residents in the Three Ports area who might enjoy the dance. There was no cost, but any donations they chose to make would be ploughed back into future events. Whatever the dance raised, Lijah planned to make a very big donation, to ensure that this wouldn't end up being a one-off event. He didn't know whether he'd still be around for the next one, because the tour promoters and the fans who'd bought tickets couldn't be held off forever, not if he wanted a career to go back to. All he knew for certain was that he didn't want to leave Amy behind this time. But any fool could see she was becoming even more reluctant to enter his world, and he understood that too, because a big piece of him didn't want to be a part of it either. That was a problem he hadn't found a solution to yet, but he wasn't going to give up until he got there. In the meantime, being able to do something like this for Albert made it feel like all of the downsides of that life were almost worthwhile.

'Looks like our boy's having fun.' Lijah gestured towards where Albert was dancing with a lady called Glenda, who Caroline had introduced him to.

'I know, I almost feel like I'm Albie's mum at the school disco, spying on him through the window.' Amy grinned. 'I think I'll start flagging before he does though, I swear when the band started playing it was like fifty years had been taken off him.'

'Music can do amazing things.' Lijah was counting on it. The songs for his next album were finally starting to take shape and almost all of them had been inspired by his return to Port Kara, especially the rekindling of his relationship with Amy. He just hoped that when she eventually heard them, any doubts she might still have would finally disappear and she'd believe how much she meant to him, because words alone didn't seem to be enough.

'Oh my goodness it's Gwen, I'm so pleased she's made it.' Amy's smile lit up her whole face, and Lijah knew just how worried she'd been about her friend. Gwen was one of those people who got under your skin and, even though Lijah hadn't known her long, he'd been delighted to hear that her health scare hadn't been as serious as everyone had feared. She looked on good form today and she was accompanied by an elegant-looking woman with ice-blonde hair piled on top of her head, and a regal air that commanded attention. She must have been ten years older than Gwen, but she strode into the room as if she owned it.

'This is quite the event you two have organised.' Gwen kissed them both on the cheek when she reached them.

'It's more down to Lijah than me.' Amy's tone was insistent, but before he could protest, Gwen introduced her friend.

'This is Camilla, we met when she was a patient at the hospital, but she's more than ready to go dancing again now.' Gwen smiled. 'And this is Amy, one of the nurses in A&E, and Lijah, who volunteers with the befriending service and who organised the dance.'

'Your outfit is amazing.' Amy smiled at Camilla, who seemed to stand even taller in response to the praise.

'Thank you. It's really nice to have an excuse to dress up. The only one who takes me out these days is my horse.' Camilla had a cut-glass accent and a surprisingly throaty laugh that hinted at a mischievous nature not far below the surface.

'Great to meet you, Camilla.' Lijah loved the fact that Gwen's introduction had been so simple. He was just Lijah, who volunteered with the befriending service and organised events like this.

'You too and, please, my friends call me Cami. I keep telling Gwen that, but she insists on introducing me as Camilla, like I'm the queen herself!'

'Cami it is then.' Lijah smiled and then suddenly a voice cut through the air.

'Millie?' Albert said her name like a question as he crossed the room towards them, but his face displayed certainty as she whirled around to look at him.

'Albie, is that really you?' Her expression softened when he nodded and Lijah's fingers curled around Amy's as she reached for his hand. Camilla and Albert must have changed so much over the years, but they'd recognised each other instantly.

'I thought all your friends called you Cami?' Gwen gave her a questioning look.

'They do now, but it used to be Millie when I was younger...' She exchanged a glance with Albert. 'Someone I loved disappeared and hearing the name Millie made me sad, because he was the one who first shortened my name that way. So, I became Cami instead.'

'I'm sorry.' Albert's apology was so simple and so brief, but it seemed to be enough. Within moments he and Cami were back on the dance floor together, just like they'd been more than six decades earlier. For all Lijah knew, Cami might be married with a hoard of children and grandchildren, but in that moment it didn't matter, because when she was with Albert, it was clear they were the same young couple who'd been completely besotted with one another all those years before. Lijah found himself hoping there wasn't anyone waiting for Cami back home, because even if that meant that she and Albert had missed out on something special, at least they might now have a second chance. He didn't even try to deny that part of the reason he wanted that for them so much, was because he desperately wanted it for him and Amy too. He needed to believe no matter how much time had passed, or how different people's lives had been in their time apart, none of that was important once they found each other again.

* * *

'I still can't get over Albie and Cami's reaction when they saw one another.' Amy's face glowed in the low light of the street-lamp as she turned to look at Lijah. They were walking back from the dance hand in hand through the deserted streets, both of them on a high after the event.

'It was amazing, like you could almost see the years falling away, and when he held her as they danced...' Lijah demonstrated, by placing his hands in the same position as Albert's had been and twirling Amy around. 'Do you ever think our generation missed out?'

'We had our moments.' She reached up, pressing her lips against his and making it clear their moment was far from over.

When they finally pulled apart, she took hold of his hand again, leaning her head on his shoulder. 'I love the idea that it's never too late for second chances.'

'I'm really glad they got their second chance, but I'm even more thankful that we got ours.' He paused as she looked up at him, waiting for her to tease him again about being sentimental, or sounding some kind of warning about most second chances ending the same way as the first, but for once she didn't.

'Me too. My biggest regret was not giving us the chance we deserved, but now we've got it.'

'We won't need another one.' He kissed her again, forgetting about Cami and Albert, or anyone else. All that mattered was that Amy was prepared to let her guard down enough to really give them a shot, and the rest of the world could have disappeared. That's why he didn't spot the photographer standing by a tree, less than twenty feet away, capturing a moment between him and Amy that should have been just for the two of them. But they were never going to get that kind of privacy, and when Amy discovered just what fame could cost them, her willingness to give them a second chance might well disappear forever.

25

Lijah hadn't seen his father in over twenty years. His mother had told him, when he was about eighteen, that it had been their shared love of music that had drawn his parents together initially. They'd met when Maria had gone to a gig at a music festival where Stewart was performing with his band, Surf and Turf. Lijah had almost choked on his dinner, laughing at the name of the band, and he still smiled when he thought about how hard his mother had been laughing that day too. Apparently, Stewart had named the band after his favourite meal, although Maria had said it could have been worse, they'd nearly been called Stewart and the Surfers. Despite her reaction to the band's name, Maria had accepted an invitation to go for a drink with Stewart, and the rest had been history.

From what Lijah could gather, the pregnancy had surprised both his parents, but Maria had never once used the word 'accident' or 'mistake' to describe it, despite how flaky his father had turned out to be. For Maria it had only ever been a blessing, and when it became clear that Stewart wasn't going to change anything about his life to accommodate a baby, it was Claire who'd stepped into the breach. Stewart had joined another band by the time Lijah arrived, and they'd got a job performing on a cruise ship. He hadn't even met Lijah until he was six months old, and after that the visits only seemed to come when he was down on his luck. Claire had told Lijah about his father knocking on the door of their flat and asking for a place to stay after he'd been sacked from the cruise ship for 'inappropriate behaviour'. Every time Stewart came back, he'd put on an act for a while that he wanted to make a go of things with his family, but it would only ever last until the next job offer, or the next woman came into his life. Lijah had never understood why his mother had given Stewart so many chances, until his aunt had tried to explain it after Maria's death.

'Your mum was always a soft touch.' Claire had given him a level look. 'And I think you take after her more than you know. She let him stay, because she couldn't bear the thought that if she didn't he might just disappear altogether, and that one day you'd ask why she didn't give him another chance. I think Maria felt sorry for him in a way too. She always wanted to help everyone, and I think she still hoped Stewart would surprise us all and step up to the plate. But a leopard doesn't really change its spots, does it?'

Lijah had understood what his aunt was trying to say. He had no memory of his father coming to stay that first time, but it had happened again several times, up until Lijah had turned ten years old. Even at that age, he'd realised his father only came back to them out of desperation not love. He didn't hear from his dad in between and there'd be months, sometimes years of nothing but silence. On Lijah's tenth birthday, his father had done another one of his disappearing acts, this time involving the woman who ran the chip shop underneath their flat with her husband. Stewart hadn't turned up or left a gift. Worse than that, the party Maria had organised for Lijah and a handful of his schoolfriends had descended into chaos after the woman's husband had stormed up to the flat and demanded to know where Stewart and his wife had gone.

The relationship hadn't lasted, of course, and the woman had returned to her husband within two weeks. When Lijah's mother had asked him how his father's reappearances in his life made him feel, he'd finally felt able to be honest.

'I don't like it when he's here. I prefer it when it's just us. If he wants to come and see me, that's okay, I just don't want him living here, because he always goes again.' Lijah could still remember how difficult those words had been to say. His aunt was right when she said he was like his mother in many ways, and it hadn't been easy to ask his mother not to let Stewart keep coming and going. Lijah hated the idea that it might hurt her when she realised that her attempts to keep his father in his life hadn't been a positive experience for him. But he'd been forced to take the chance of hurting her, to try and make sure Stewart couldn't keep disrupting the happy home they'd created.

Within a month his father had turned up again, expecting to pick up where he'd left off, the way he always had before, but this time Maria had turned him away. He'd begged and pleaded at first, but when that hadn't worked he'd stood outside the building shouting abuse and calling Maria and Claire 'stupid bitches' and far, far worse things, which had made Lijah boil with rage. His fists had curled into a ball, and he'd wanted to go out into the street and punch his father square in the face, but he'd known how much that would upset his mother. Instead, he'd buried his head in his pillow, so that he couldn't hear his father shouting, and had pledged never to allow Stewart to be a part of his life again.

His father had sold many stories to the press over the years, about Maria and Claire driving a wedge between him and Lijah, saying he didn't want anything other than a chance to know the son that he allegedly 'missed every single day of his life'. There'd no doubt been a pay day for Stewart, but his decision to go to the press had come back to bite him, when several women had come forward accusing Stewart of being abusive and using coercive control. No charges had ever been brought, and Stewart had kept quiet for the last few years, clearly not wanting to poke the hornets' nest. Despite the fact none of the accusations had led to a prosecution, it was one second chance Lijah wasn't prepared to give. Men who took advantage of someone else's vulnerability for their own ends were the lowest of the low. All of that meant it shouldn't have been a surprise when Nick rang Lijah up with some news.

'I've had a heads up from Pete Mcintyre that your father has been touting a new story to the press. It looks like he's had an idea to make some money from you and Amy getting back together.' Pete was one of the few tabloid journalists who seemed to have some integrity, and Lijah and Nick had built up a bit of a friendship with him over the years.

'How the hell can he do that? Stewart was out of my life long before I even met Amy.' Lijah had the same desire to punch his father that he'd had the last time he'd seen him. Amy already had enough to contend with, without Stewart getting in on the act.

'By making stuff up like he always does.' Nick sighed down the phone. 'Look, it's probably nothing, but I thought you should know, so you can prepare Amy to ignore anything she might read.'

'I've already been telling her to do that. But you're right, knowing that Stewart is about to spout more of his crap will give her a chance to steer clear of that too. Thanks mate.'

'No problem. That's what I'm here for, and I will be as long as you need me.' Nick sighed again. 'Although we have got to talk about how long that might be, and what we're doing about the last leg of the tour. The promoters won't wait forever.'

'I know, and we'll sort it out soon, I promise.' Lijah hated messing his friend around, and the fans who'd booked tickets, but still hadn't seen him perform. He really would deal with it soon, but for now his priority was supporting Amy through the frenzy their relationship seemed to have stirred up. He just hoped Nick was right and that Stewart's attempt to sell a story would come to nothing, because the last thing he needed right now was his excuse for a father turning up to make things even harder for Amy than they already were.

Amy had tried really hard not to look at the photographs of her and Lijah kissing when they'd been shared online, or at any of the comments that had been made about them. But she hadn't been able to avoid the magazines and tabloid newspapers in the hospital shop that had the image of her and Lijah kissing on their front covers. This was supposed to be her safe space, where she didn't have to wonder whether people were staring at her and analysing her every move, but the press had eroded that bit by bit. It had started when they'd come into the emergency department and pretended they were patients, and now they were splashing her picture all over magazines and newspapers anyone could pick up. And it wasn't just her photograph, it was the habit they'd developed of positioning her picture side by side with photographs of Lijah and some of his rumoured previous girlfriends, all of them beautiful and famous in their own right. These women were used to moving in Lijah's world and they looked like they belonged there. Amy didn't. They might as well have printed 'Lijah Byrne is obviously having some kind of breakdown', because that's what the pictures said without them actually having to write it.

'It'll calm down.' He'd given her the same assurances as before, but it was like being told to ignore a bully who was everywhere. It was just as impossible as it had been when her mother had told her to ignore the jibes her brother had made while they were still living under the same roof. When it was just Amy and Lijah, life felt pretty damn perfect, and she didn't want to keep ruining the time they spent together by asking him for reassurance. He had no way of knowing whether the press would eventually lose interest in their story, and he had bigger things to worry about. The promoters were still pushing for a date to reschedule the tour, he had his next album to deliver, and he'd been told to expect another made-up story from Stewart to appear in the press any day, but so far it had been unnervingly quiet.

Amy had been there when his father had dealt him another blow, and withheld the money that Lijah's paternal grandparents had set aside to help him learn to drive, and to buy him his first car. Maria had kept in contact with them and had made sure Lijah saw them, even after his father walked out for the last time. Sadly they'd both died before Lijah reached his teens, but they'd often told him about the money they'd put aside, which would be his when he turned seventeen. Except when his birthday came around, there'd been no money. His father had long since spent it, denying any knowledge of his parents' promise. Lijah had been distraught at another kick in the teeth from his father, further evidence that Stewart couldn't give a damn about him.

Thank God he'd had so much support from his aunt and his mother, but with Maria gone, and Claire's plans to move to

Tenerife gathering pace, Stewart's latest betrayal must have hit him all the harder. 'I don't want to go back on tour, not if it means leaving you,' Lijah had said, as he trailed a hand down her arm the night before. 'This is where I want to be.'

'You'll miss the thrill of it sooner or later, and I know you, you won't want to let down the people you've made a commitment to.' She'd smiled then at the look that had crossed his face, knowing she'd been spot on, but it was bittersweet. She didn't want him to leave either, it felt so much easier to imagine them having a future together when he was right there next to her. Even though she knew he'd have to leave Port Kara eventually, she couldn't stop herself from suggesting ways to put it off, at least for a little while. 'Just don't try to rush it, you've been through such a lot this last year.'

'I won't be rushing anything, especially not this.' He'd kissed her then and the rest of the world, and all the pressures it brought with it, had receded again. It would have been so easy to hide away in a little bubble together, but she loved her job, her friends, and her parents, so it was impossible to avoid the real world for long. Instead, she hurried past the hospital shop at the end of her shift, deliberately not popping in for the takeaway latte she'd normally have bought for the journey up to her Mum and Dad's house. Now that Lijah was staying at her place more or less full time, it had been more than a week since Amy had seen her mum and she'd promised to pop in on the way home, when Kerry would be back from her new part-time job as a school secretary.

Lijah had offered to cook again, ready for when she got back. A curry this time, and his culinary skills had definitely come on during their time apart. He'd made an amazing tagine a few days before, and when she'd asked him where he'd got the recipe, he'd casually mentioned that a friend called Azizza had taught him to make it. Even Amy knew who Azizza was, a beautiful Moroccan singer with the kind of success that meant she only went by her first name. It was another reminder of just how far apart their worlds had become in the ten years since they were last together, and the kind of company he'd kept. Everyone had a past, Amy knew that, but Lijah's life was like a peacock's feather, and hers was like a pigeon's. Why would anyone choose a pigeon over a peacock, when the world was overrun with pigeons?

Her mind was still racing by the time she reached her parents' place, but she was determined to push all the unwanted thoughts out of her head and enjoy some time with her mum. She'd picked up some chocolate and fresh cream eclairs from the Co-op just up the road from the hospital, and some dog chews for Bernie, to make it up to him for not bringing his best buddy, Monty, to see him. Amy was looking forward to a good catch-up, a cup of tea and a cream filled pastry. Seeing her mum might be one of life's simple pleasures, but she treasured the opportunity to do so even more these days, knowing it would have been all too easy to take Kerry for granted if she hadn't witnessed how much losing Maria had affected Lijah.

'Hello darling.' Her mother hugged Amy tight the moment she arrived. 'You look worn out. I'd say I hope they're not working you too hard at that hospital, but I already know they are.'

'It does seem busier than usual lately.' Amy didn't mention that part of that was down to journalists trying to get in to see her whenever she was on duty. Even when she wasn't, photographs of the hospital department where she worked still seemed worth the effort of the charade for them. She didn't tell her mother that another reason for her tiredness was because she wasn't sleeping. And that when she woke up in the early hours, she often disappeared down an internet rabbit hole, googling things about Lijah and desperately trying to convince herself that she wasn't setting herself up to get her heart broken all over again.

'Come on then, let's have a cuppa. It's just the two of us for now. Dad's still at work and Nathan's gone out on his bike, so it'll be lovely.' Her mum linked an arm through Amy's, giving her a conspiratorial smile. They both knew why it would be lovely without Nathan there. Sometimes Amy wanted to ask her mum how she lived with the constant spectre of her brother's mood swings, which could change the atmosphere at any moment, and whether it affected her parents' relationship, but she already knew it did. Nathan was like a real-life version of the people who commented on online articles, occasionally playing nicely, but more often using his words as weapons, with no concern for how that might make someone else feel. So she wasn't sorry not to be seeing him.

Just as Amy had hoped, the first half an hour at her parents' house had been just the tonic she needed. She'd chatted with her mum about lots of wonderfully mundane things. Kerry had told Amy all about her new job, and the school headmaster whose head moved back and forwards in a kind of pecking motion when he walked, which had earnt him the nickname Professor Chicken from some of the children.

'Kids can be horrible, but they don't mean any harm, at least not in this case.' Amy's mother poured them both another cup of tea.

'I still feel sorry for him. I remember how relentlessly I got teased when Nathan cut my fringe while I was asleep.' Amy gestured towards one of the framed photographs on the dresser. 'Look at me. I look like Jim Carrey in *Dumb and Dumber*.'

'It was just lucky you didn't get your eyes poked out, waking up screaming like you did when he was midway through scissoring off your fringe. I had no choice but to even it up.' Her mother sighed. There'd been so many instances like that, and there was no point Amy asking why her parents hadn't done more to rein in Nathan's behaviour. It was a conversation they'd had many times before and it only made her mum and dad feel guilty. Nothing they'd tried with Nathan had any long-lasting effect and in the end they all just seemed to accept that was who he was. Kerry turned away from the photograph to look back at Amy. 'Anyway, your hair grew back quite quickly, and he only did it because he was jealous. You were such a beautiful little girl.'

You're the ugly duckling in reverse. Nathan's favourite insult came back to her as it so often did, but she was saved from responding to her mother by the roar of a motorbike arriving on the driveway.

'That sounds like Nathan now.' Amy looked up, wondering if it would upset her mother if she made a dash for the back door before her brother walked in through the front. She just wasn't sure she could face him.

'I'll just put these away.' Amy's mother scooped up the plates, with the tell-tale smears of chocolate and cream, almost running into the kitchen, like a guilty dieter about to be caught out. Amy didn't have to ask what the hurry was, she knew it was because Kerry wanted Nathan to have as little ammunition as possible to comment on his sister's weight, as he had so often before.

'Oh, there she is, my celebrity sibling!' Nathan came into the room, still wearing his motorbike leathers, the smile on his face looking like it had been painted on. 'I was hoping you'd be here.'

'It's nice that Nathan came home early to see you, isn't it?' Kerry walked back into the room, the hopeful expression on her face making a lump form in Amy's throat. Her mum wanted nothing more than to see her two children getting along, but Amy could already tell Nathan was building up to something and, less than five seconds later, he'd pulled a newspaper out of his messenger bag and slammed it down on the table.

'Have you seen this?' The smile on his face was stretched even wider now, making him look like the Joker, and Amy was relieved to look away from him until she saw the headline.

Lijah Byrne's father grooming underage girls with a promise of meeting his son

Even as Amy read the words, she knew it had nothing to do with Lijah, but if she'd needed any indication that the rest of the world might not see it that way, Nathan gave it to her.

'Makes sense now why he's been hanging around you. You're the perfect cover story for a paedo. Who's going to suspect him of that if he's supposedly back with his old girlfriend. I knew there had to be some explanation for why he was with you, when he could be with anyone.' His laugh was high, in pitch and volume, but their mother's shout cut straight through it.

'Nathan, stop it!' Kerry's face was flushed bright scarlet, but her son was only just getting started.

'You didn't seriously think he was with Amy for any other reason do you? Christ, look at her, and look at the sort of women he's dated since he left this shithole. This explains it all.'

'I'm going now Mum.' Amy got to her feet, and when Kerry tried to stop her, she shook her mother off as gently as she could. 'I'm sorry, but I need to get out of here before I say something I can't take back.'

'Nathan, apologise now.' Her mum looked distraught, and Amy wished with all her heart that Kerry wasn't caught in the middle of this.

'She's just pissed off because she knows I'm right.'

'Bye Mum.' Amy planted a kiss on her mother's cheek, not

stopping to hear anything else her brother might have to say. She needed to get out of here, to find Lijah and to tell him that this latest headline proved what she'd suspected all along. It could never work between them. She knew the story wasn't true and, as much as Nathan's vicious words had touched a nerve he'd exposed far too many times in the past, that wasn't the reason she was going to have to end things with Lijah. She couldn't live like this, at the mercy of whatever lies the press wanted to print, in a goldfish bowl where the concept of privacy would be lost forever. Amy hated being the centre of attention. She'd worked so hard to create a life she was proud of and she couldn't give that up, not even for Lijah. But she had no idea how she was ever going to be happy again if she let him go a second time.

26

Lijah's face fell as soon as Amy walked through the door, and she knew why. The emotion was radiating out of her, like an effervescent tablet fizzing in a glass, but she had to get through this and say what needed to be said. Tears were stinging her eyes when he looked at her and she was almost gulping for air.

'What's wrong, have you seen the article?' Lijah's eyes were full of concern and all she could manage in response was a nod. 'It's got nothing to do with me, Ames, you have to know that.'

'Of course I do, but you're wrong when you say it's got nothing to do with you.' She'd held up a hand to silence his protests. If she let him stop her, she was going to weaken, and she couldn't afford to do that. 'I know you can't control your father's actions, that's not what I'm talking about.'

'What are you talking about then?' The note of desperation in his voice made something twist in her gut, but for both of their sakes she had to keep going.

'I'm talking about the fact that this is headline news because of who you are, and that the only reason those young girls were willing to talk to an old letch like Stewart is because he probably let them think it would get them access to you. The media are never going to stop writing articles about you and we're never going to escape from this. I can't even imagine what it'll be like going in to work tomorrow, but our worlds are just too different Lijah. I love you, I really do, but I'm not meant for your world, and you're not meant for mine either.'

His body seemed to sag and it wasn't until he answered that she realised he was relieved. 'You love me and I love you. That's all that matters Ames, don't you see that?'

'No it isn't. I wish it was, but it really isn't.' Tears streamed down her face at the unfairness of it all. She'd found someone she loved, who loved her, but it didn't matter how much, it was still going to be taken away from them by other people. As he reached out towards her, her body went rigid. If she let him make that connection she'd never be able to ask him to leave. 'Do you know what my brother said when he showed me the article? He said it explained everything, and that people would know you were using me to cover up your secret life, because no one could possibly believe you wanted me for me.'

'You know that's not true. Since I came back I've realised it's only ever been you. Nathan gets off on lashing out at you and saying the most awful things he can think of.' Lijah tried to reach out again, but it was like she was made of stone. Amy held her breath until she'd regained enough composure to answer him, forcing herself to be cold when he was the one person she wanted to comfort her.

'But this time he's right, isn't he?' She shook her head when he started to protest again. 'Not about you having some sordid secret life, but about the fact that no one can believe we're together. Aren't you embarrassed when you read what people say about me? And what choosing me says about you?'

'The only people I'm embarrassed for are the ones who go

online spouting hatred, and who can't see how incredibly lucky I am to have you in my life. I always knew it, I just wish to God you did too. If you could see yourself through my eyes for one moment, it would change everything. As for what people write, you wouldn't be seen dead with me if you saw some of the comments aimed in my direction. I've had them all: ugly, talentless, stupid, crazy, narcissistic, the worst singer alive, with music that's only fit to be played in public toilets, because it would be a cure for constipation.' He caught her eye and for a moment she wasn't able to stop herself from smiling. 'Oh, you can laugh, but that's what someone said, word for word. I stopped reading all that stuff years ago to protect my mental health, and so I could appreciate the here and now. I value that more than ever since we reconnected. I know I keep saying it, but please don't let other people come between us again. They don't have to, not unless you let them.'

'They already have, and I know even if we fight it they won't stop trying. People like the natural order of things, beautiful people with beautiful people, the rich and famous with rich and famous, or some kind of combination of that. They won't accept you settling for someone like me, and I'm done with not feeling good enough. I felt like it all the time when I was growing up because of Nathan, and even back when we were teenagers there were people who told me you'd never stay with me. That's partly why I told you to go to London without me, to put things to the test, and I proved them right. Since then I've worked hard to build up my self-esteem and create a life I'm proud of, to prove to myself that I'm worth something, and for the first time I genuinely believe it. Except now I can't move without someone telling me I was right all along, and that I'm not worthy, at least not when it comes to you. Your fame is too much for a place like Port Kara, but it's my home. Even if I followed you into your world, I'd just be wondering how long it would be before I got left behind again. And if things didn't work out between us, I'd have lost everything I've worked so hard to achieve. I can't live my life like that Lijah, I really can't. Not even for you. I want you to leave, for both of our sakes.' The words sounded so stark, and a huge part of her was desperate to take them back, but she knew she couldn't.

'No you don't. If I thought you did I'd walk out of the door right now, but we love each other and we can find a way to work the rest out.' It didn't matter what Lijah said, or how much she wanted to believe him, it wouldn't change anything. They carried on talking, going around in circles for what felt like forever, but somehow Amy held firm, in the end delivering the killer blow that if he really loved her he'd understand why she needed him to leave. That didn't stop her stomach clenching in pain when he finally agreed to pack up his stuff, which seemed to have found its way into her flat over the past few weeks.

'You don't know how much I wish things had turned out differently.' Lijah looked like a broken man when he turned to face her in the doorway one last time, and all she could manage in response was to nod, tears streaming down her face as the door closed behind him. She tried to steady herself against the wall, but it was no good and she slid down on to the floor, Monty coming to sit beside her, sensing something was wrong.

'It's just you and me again now, boy.' She pressed her face into his fur and let the tears keep coming. She'd lost Lijah for a second time, and it was even more painful than she'd feared.

* * *

After Lijah had left, the flat looked completely bare, like when Christmas decorations come down, and what's left behind feels greyer and duller, as if the light has been sucked out of the room. It was how Amy felt too, and it hadn't gone unnoticed. Her colleagues and friends kept asking what was wrong, and trying their best to persuade her to change her mind when they discovered what had happened.

'Every relationship is a risk, Amy. You can't go into one without knowing you're putting your heart on the line. If I hadn't taken a risk I'd never have said yes when Barry asked me out on a date, and my life would have been so much smaller if I hadn't shared it with him.' Gwen had been one of the first people Amy had spoken to about what had happened, and she clearly wanted to try and help, but she didn't understand. No one really did, even when Amy tried to explain it.

'What happened with you and Barry is different. You came from the same place, and you moved in the same circles. Yes, there was a risk for you and Barry, but I already knew what would drive me and Lijah apart in the end. Why put myself through all of that, when it was obvious from the start it was never going to work?'

Gwen had shaken her head in response, clearly still not convinced. 'Something outside of our control could have driven us apart too, one of us could have become ill and left the other one alone. I know that better than anyone, and it's something everyone in a relationship has to face eventually. But even if that had happened years before our time, I'd still have been glad we took the chance to be together. I'd rather have had three years with Barry, than a lifetime without him. I know more than ever how lucky I am, because we've had five decades and counting, but real love doesn't come along for everyone. So many people don't get to experience a single day of that, never mind three years, or five decades. I know you love Lijah, and that he loves you, it's written all over your faces every time you're together.

Don't miss out on having something lots of people never get, just because of the what ifs and maybes.'

'It isn't what ifs.' Screwing her face up, Amy had desperately tried not to cry. She'd done far too much of that already. 'The attention we've had is relentless, and it'll drive us apart eventually. You've been asking me what's wrong and why I'm so sad, because it's obvious that letting go of Lijah is breaking my heart. But if I try to hold on to him, and I let my feelings deepen even further, there's a chance I might not survive when he eventually realises this can't work. I need to get out now to stand a chance of getting over him.'

In the end, Gwen had stopped pushing and she'd taken instead to fussing around Amy, bringing her little treats from the shop, and passing on ridiculous knock knock jokes that one of her grandchildren had told her. Lijah kept calling and messaging her too, but she didn't reply, and eventually she'd blocked his number, and then deleted it, so she couldn't change her mind and reach out to him. She was staying in the spare room of the flat Isla and Reuben shared, above his delicatessen, because there was no chance of Lijah coming to find her there. She wasn't sure she'd be able to turn him away again if she saw him face to face, so hiding in her friends' flat felt far safer. Amy hadn't been able to face staying with her parents and having Nathan remind her at every opportunity that he'd seen this coming. Lijah had come to the hospital to try and speak to Amy, just once, but it had caused a furore when someone had recognised him, and all it had done was serve to illustrate that their worlds didn't mix. She hadn't seen him since, so when she walked outside the hospital to get some air during her break, and looked up to see a familiar face, it took her breath away.

'Nick, what are you doing here?' She couldn't dampen down the hope that Lijah had sent him, and told Nick not to leave until

Amy had agreed to thrash things out, so that they could pick up where they left off. She wanted to believe that Lijah was missing her as much as she missed him, even though she knew there was nothing Nick could say to change her mind.

'I came to say goodbye.'

'You're going?' It was such a stupid question, given what Nick had just said, but he nodded anyway.

'We're going back on the road, restarting the tour. Lijah's decided it's the right time, now that you and he...' Nick looked awkward for a moment. 'With Claire leaving soon, he just doesn't think there's anything left for him here now and our flights are booked for the day after tomorrow.'

'What about you and Dolly?' It was almost as if she was pleading with him to find a reason to stay. Amy had no idea what she was trying to achieve, but she suddenly felt desperate to stop Nick leaving Port Kara, knowing that Lijah wouldn't go on tour without him.

'We're going to see what happens. We both knew I wouldn't be here forever and that we were only having fun while it lasted, but we've become a lot closer than either of us expected. Dolly is going to arrange for another dog walker to cover her for a couple of weeks over the summer and fly out when we're on the Japanese leg of the tour. She won't be able to stay long because of her business, but she said even if we decide this was just a meaningless fling, she's always wanted to go to Japan, so she might as well come while she's got the offer of free accommodation.' Nick laughed. 'That's one of the things I like best about Dolly: her brutal honestly and the fact she's got her own stuff going on. I know that's one of the things Lij likes about you too, although we both know it goes a lot deeper than that.'

'Nick, don't please.' She'd thought this was what she wanted, but it was too hard. She couldn't listen to Nick telling her what a mistake she was making, and it was her eyes that pleaded with him this time. Eventually he nodded.

'Bye Ames. I hope everything works out for you.' He pulled her into a hug and then let go. 'He really does love you, you know and I don't think anything could happen to change that. Whatever you might think.'

'Bye Nick.' She turned then, going back inside the hospital and breaking into a run, not stopping until she reached an empty consulting room. Slamming the door behind her, she put her hand over her mouth, trying to stifle the sob that was so desperate to escape. Nick didn't have to try and convince her that Lijah loved her, she knew he did, and it was what made such a painful decision even harder.

* * *

'I'm not going to go to Tenerife.' Claire made the statement and folded her arms tightly across her chest, in a way that Lijah recognised. It signalled that his aunt meant business. It hadn't been a move she'd pulled very often when he was younger, but it had always made him stop and take notice when she did, because she so rarely got strict with him.

'Yes, you are, don't be ridiculous.' He mirrored her body language. This was one battle he wasn't going to back down on, no matter how much his aunt tried to dig in her heels. She was starting a new life with her girlfriend and he'd take her to Tenerife himself if he had to.

'How can I leave you when you're like this? It breaks my heart that things haven't worked out with Amy. Your mum and I both loved that girl, and she's so good for you. I can't believe that what the papers have been saying has cost you the best thing that ever happened to you.' His aunt must have seen how hard the words hit him, and she reached out to hug him. 'Oh Lij, I'm sorry, me and my big mouth. It just makes me so bloody angry.'

'Me too.' His voice was muffled. 'It makes me incredibly sad too, but I love Amy and the last thing I want is for her to be unhappy. I could see what this was doing to her, but all I could think about was how much I wanted her in my life. If I'm going to do what's best for her then I need to respect her wishes.'

'What about what's best for you?' Claire pulled away to look at him.

'I think I lost sight of that a long time ago. But I can't write anything right now, every time I try it's just so bitter. So, I figured I might as well go back on the road, see my commitments through and then take it from there.' Lijah had no idea what that meant, or how he'd even get through singing his old material, when he knew now that every song was about Amy. But that was a problem for another day. For now he just had to keep going somehow, say goodbye to the last people in Port Kara who meant something to him, and try to pretend he'd never been back.

'Whatever happens, I want you to promise me you'll try and rediscover what's best for you. *Promise*.' Her gaze didn't waver from his face, and eventually he nodded.

'I promise.' When she hugged him close again in the kitchen of Mor Brys, he held on to the moment, knowing it might be a long time before he felt a sense of home like this again. If it ever happened at all.

27

Amy had been avoiding going back to see her parents since Nathan had taken such great delight in the awful headlines. She couldn't face the thought of him tormenting her further. It didn't matter that the press had been forced to apologise for any indication that Lijah might be involved in the grooming of underage girls, or the suggestion that he was using his father as a 'pimp' to line up casual flings with women who were of legal age to consent.

The police had arrested Stewart and had themselves issued a statement that there was no evidence whatsoever of Lijah's involvement in anything that had happened, and that he hadn't seen his father in twenty years. Nathan wouldn't care about that, he'd find some way of using what had happened to continue to ridicule Amy. It had become a sport to him over the years, and even though she knew his behaviour was caused by a personality disorder, his refusal to get help made it far harder to excuse.

'Where's Nathan?' It was the first thing Amy said to her mother when she arrived at their house, having already made the decision to turn around and leave if he was there.

'He's fishing with David. He won't be back for hours.' David was her brother's only friend, although Nathan was lucky even to have held on to him, the way he treated him. 'Oh, sweetheart you look exhausted.'

Amy's mother hugged her, before ushering her through to the kitchen, where the table was already laden with lots of Amy's favourite foods, almost as if a party was being thrown in her honour.

'What are we celebrating?' She tried to smile, but she couldn't quite pull it off.

'I just thought it would cheer you up. I made you some Mars Bar cakes.' Her mother gestured towards a plate piled hight with slabs of chocolate crispy cakes. It was one of Kerry's specialities, made from melting Mars Bars and butter, and mixing in Cocoa Pops, before letting it set and spreading more chocolate on the top. It had about a million calories a slice, probably, and Amy would normally have dived straight in, but not today. She seemed to have lost interest in everything.

'Thank you. I might have some in a minute, but just a cup of tea would be lovely for now.'

Her mother gave her a level look. 'Why are you doing this Amy? Denying yourself what you really want.'

'I said I'll have some later and—' Amy could barely keep the note of exasperation out of her voice, but her mother cut her off mid-sentence.

'I'm not talking about the Mars Bar cake. I'm talking about ending things with Lijah. Claire rang me last night and said he's as miserable as you are. You've both looked so happy being back together and it's done my soul good to see it. I don't think I've seen you like that since he left. I know we're all supposed to make ourselves happy these days and not rely on anyone else, but I don't care how old fashioned it is, most people want to find someone to love, who loves them back. I know you want someone in your life, sweetheart, and no one is going to be able to match Lijah for you. Please don't throw that away.'

Everybody seemed to be giving her the same advice and a huge part of Amy wanted to take it, but it was nowhere near as simple as everyone seemed to think. She wouldn't just be having a relationship with Lijah, she'd be having one with every person who felt they had some stake in his life because of his fame.

Amy hated being the focus of attention, except on the odd occasion when she'd had a bit too much to drink and her inhibitions melted away, allowing her to get up and dance or belt out some karaoke. The rest of the time, she was much happier out of the limelight. If she continued seeing Lijah, the attention would be on her far more than she wanted, and she couldn't imagine any of it being positive. She knew her mum wanted the best for her, and that everyone could see how she felt about Lijah, but none of them really understood. All she could do was try to explain things to the people who cared about her, in the hope they might eventually get it.

'We come from such different worlds, Mum. It would never work, and I need to get out now before my feelings for him become even stronger.' Just then the front door slammed, and seconds later Nathan came into the room, his face like thunder, making her heart sink.

'David forgot the bait, so I told him he's a dickhead and he stormed off. Stupid wanker.'

'Nathan, there's no need for language like that, go upstairs and calm down.' Kerry's tone was even, but Amy could see the muscle pulsing in her mother's cheek.

'Oh, why because *she's* here?' He jabbed a finger towards Amy. 'You can't just send me to my room, I'm not a bloody kid. I'm not disappearing just so she can sit here shovelling food down her throat. That's not going to help, is it? Maybe if Amy ate a bit less, she'd be able to keep hold of a boyfriend.'

'Get out!' Suddenly Kerry was on her feet, her voice was shaking, and Amy could see in her eyes how furious she was.

'What do you mean, get out?' Nathan sneered in response, but their mother didn't waver and it was as if something inside her had finally snapped.

'Get out of this house and don't come back until you're ready to admit you've got a problem and that you need help for it. You can't do this any more Nathan, and I can't let you.'

'You can't just throw me out.' Nathan's tone was still cocky, but there was a flicker of something else in his eyes. Something that looked a lot like fear.

'Yes I can. Now get out, and I mean *now*!' Kerry walked towards her son, she was a good six inches shorter than him and far lighter, but suddenly she was a force to be reckoned with. For a moment it looked like Nathan might react, or refuse to leave, but then he turned on his heel, shouting a warning as he went.

'You'll all be sorry for doing this. I'll make sure of it.' The slamming of the door behind him seemed to shake the whole house, and for a few seconds Amy and her mother just looked at one another, before Kerry burst into tears.

* * *

Lijah had just one more goodbye to make before he left Port Kara. Being part of the befriending service had given him far more that he'd given in return. It had made him feel part of a community for the first time in a very long time, and meeting Albert had been the biggest part of that. He was a bit too old to be a father figure to Lijah, but he was the sort of father Lijah wished he'd had, although almost anyone would have been better than Stewart. But as much as Lijah detested the man, he couldn't blame Stewart for the end of his relationship with Amy. If she hadn't made the decision over that headline, she'd have made it over another, and he couldn't blame her either. Lijah would love to walk away from the relentless intrusion, but he knew he'd be willing to go through that kind of hounding for the rest of his life if it meant he still had Amy.

'Well, this is very good timing young man.' Albert greeted him with a hearty slap on the back, when he met Lijah at the door. 'You can help me pick out an outfit for a date with Cami this evening. I'm still getting used to calling her that instead of Millie, but whatever name she goes by, she's still the girl for me.'

'That's brilliant, Albie.' A genuine smile tugged at the corners of Lijah's mouth for the first time in what felt like forever. 'Where are you off to?'

'Out for dinner. It'll be our tenth date since we got back in touch.' Albert stood back and waved Lijah in. 'Come on through lad, there's a nasty storm brewing out there.'

'Ten dates, wow. You must have seen each other almost every day since the dance.'

'Almost, but it's still not enough for me.' Albert was beaming when they reached the living room, and then he turned slightly, picking up the photograph of his wife that he'd shown Lijah before. 'I must admit it makes me feel a bit guilty.'

'You shouldn't feel guilty. I'm sure Lizzie would have wanted you to be happy.'

'Oh, she would, I'm just not sure how she'd feel about me being this happy. I haven't felt like this since I was with Cami first time round.' Albert sighed again. 'Me and Lizzie were happy enough, but I always knew I wasn't the love of her life, and I know for certain now that she wasn't mine either. It's always been Cami. There are plenty of people you can muddle through life with and get by okay, but everyone deserves to be the love of someone's life. I'm glad Lizzie had that with Brian, but I'm even more grateful that I had it with Cami, and that now I've got to the chance to rediscover it. The thing that makes me feel guilty, is that I wouldn't be experiencing this if Lizzie was still around. If she hadn't died, I'd never have been in a position to meet Cami again. Over the years, I tried to convince myself that the strength of my feelings were the folly of youth and that they would have worn off eventually, even if we'd stayed together, but I know now that isn't true.'

'I'm sure Lizzie knew you loved her, even if it wasn't quite the same and it sounds like you were lucky to have that companionship together.' Lijah was saying what he thought Albert needed to hear, but what the older man had said had really got him thinking. No one wanted to spend their life feeling second best. 'Does Cami know how you feel?'

'I think so, I can't seem to hide it.' Albert smiled again. 'And she's been pretty up front too, telling me the reason she never married was because no one else measured up to what we had. That makes me feel guilty too. I left Cornwall, thinking I was doing it for her and that her life would be better if I disappeared. That way, she wouldn't have to give up the estate and she'd be able to marry someone who could give her the lifestyle she was used to. Except I didn't stop to ask her what she wanted. She says she'd have given all that up to be with me, and that she'd happily have traded it for the decades we missed out on. Still, you can't turn back the clock, can you?'

'No.' Lijah's mind was racing, as he looked at Albert again. 'If the roles had been reversed, would you have given everything up to be with Cami?'

'Like a shot. I built up my business and bought several houses in Yorkshire, I've still got some of them, as well as the farm, but none of that matters when you're lonely. Before you came to visit, I'd go days without speaking to anyone sometimes and I used to talk to myself just to make sure my voice hadn't disappeared altogether.' Albert looked so sad for a moment, and Lijah had to swallow hard against the lump forming in his throat. Then the older man seemed to shake himself. 'Still, that's all behind me now and I just feel so lucky that me and Cami have been given this second chance, even at our age, and second chances should never be wasted. But I'm sure you didn't come here to listen to me droning on about all of that.'

'Actually, I came to say goodbye, Albie.' Lijah didn't miss the look of sadness that crossed his friend's face, and he shook his head. 'Except the truth is I don't want to leave, and what you've said made me realise I need to tell Amy everything I want to say, before I even think about going. If I give you some advice on what to wear on your date with Cami, will you give me some advice on what to say, so I have the best chance of not blowing it?'

'You've got yourself a deal.' Albert winked. 'I'll put the kettle on first, though, lad. I think we're going to need a strong brew, and if all those years in Yorkshire taught me anything, it's how to make one of those.'

Lijah nodded, silently hoping that the years in Yorkshire had taught Albert far more than that, because he was going to need all the help he could get if he was going to persuade Amy not to waste the second chance they'd been given.

28

Just as Albert had predicted, the storm clouds had closed in and, as the heavens opened, day seemed to turn into night within a matter of seconds, despite being only mid-afternoon. Lijah had rung Aidan, the only one of Amy's close friends he had a number for, and had hastily explained why he wanted to see her and how urgent it was that they got the chance to speak before he caught his flight. She'd blocked his number, and he had no idea whether she was at work, home, or somewhere else. Aidan had promised to try and track Amy down, and Lijah had been staring at the phone, willing it to ring ever since. He just wanted a chance to explain how he felt before he went away. It would give her time to think, him being on tour, and the knowledge that if she wanted him to, he'd be coming back as soon as his commitments were seen through. They could go wherever she wanted after that, the Outer Hebrides, Timbuktu, or stay right here in Port Kara. It didn't matter to him as long as they had the chance to see if they could make it.

'Amy's brother's gone missing.' Aidan had called him back a few minutes later, sounding almost as breathless as Lijah felt.

'Apparently he threw one of his hissy fits at lunch time and said something about making them all sorry.'

'Sounds like Nathan.' Lijah clenched his jaw.

'Yes, it does. Except this time someone's found his rucksack and coat on the cliffs near Dagger's Head. He can't have had a lock code on his phone, because the person who found it managed to use it to call Kerry. Now Amy and her parents have gone out looking for him. The rescue team have been called out too, but there was an incident at one of the old copper mines, so a second team is coming from Port Tremellien. This weather isn't helping anything, it's so windy, the rain is coming down sideways.'

'I'm going to go and find her.' Lijah's chest tightened at the thought of Amy being out on the cliffs in weather like this and it was clear he wasn't the only one who was worried.

'I know I should probably try and talk you out of that, and tell you how dangerous it might be, but Ames is out there and...'

'I'm going straight there now.' He didn't need Aidan to finish, because all that mattered to Lijah was getting to Amy and making sure she was okay. The thought of anything happening to her was unbearable, and if he'd needed any more indication of how strong his feelings for her were, this was it.

* * *

There'd been times in Amy's life when she'd hated her brother. Not that kind of faux-hatred that siblings sometimes had for one another, but the deep-seated kind when the idea of a world without him had seemed far more appealing than one with him in it. That sensation never lasted long, and deep down Amy had known she didn't really hate him, she just hated the way he behaved, and what that did to the people around him, especially her parents. She didn't really want a world without Nathan, she just wanted a world where Nathan got the help he needed and he could interact with the people who loved him in a way that was enjoyable, rather than toxic. Even if she had genuinely wished him ill, her mind would have been changed when she saw the expression on her mother's face after the call came in to say his coat and rucksack had been found on the cliff.

'No, please, he can't have done anything stupid.' Kerry had broken down in tears in the middle of the conversation and Amy had been forced to take the phone from her and finish the call. She'd gone cold when the person had described finding Nathan's belongings on the cliff. Like her mother, Amy desperately wanted to believe he wouldn't do anything to put his life at risk, but Nathan's ability to think logically was severely impaired and he was capable of catastrophising and turning what his mother had said into a situation where he was prepared to do almost anything. Despite a GP suggesting that Nathan had a severe personality disorder, he'd refused to see the specialist because he didn't think anything was wrong with him. He claimed benefits and, when he was forced to go to job interviews, the way he presented himself was more than enough to put off any potential employers. His world had become smaller and smaller, and his behaviour more extreme, getting him into fights when he insulted the wrong people. He was a disaster waiting to happen and, when Amy reached the cliffs with her mother and got out of the car, a trickle of dread ran down her spine, along with the rivulets of rain that had quickly found their way in through the neck of the coat she'd grabbed off the hook in her parents' porch.

'We should split up, so we can cover ground in both directions.' Amy's father had come straight from work to meet them in the car park at Dagger's Head and Kerry had run into her husband's arms.

'You and Mum go together towards Port Agnes, and I'll go the other way.' Amy looked over her mother's head towards her father, silently mouthing the words, 'She needs you.'

'Okay, good idea, but keep in contact and be careful, Amy. The rescue team are on the way and the last thing they need are two casualties.' Her father's tone was firm, and he wagged a finger at her when she nodded. 'I mean it, sweetheart, promise me you'll be careful.'

'I promise.' The wind in Amy's back propelled her forward as soon as she stepped away from her father. She'd been sent an alert by a weather app on her phone with a red warning for high winds, which could reach sixty miles an hour. They weren't anything like as high as that yet, but being up on the cliffs still made it pretty hair raising and the sea was churning, grey and foreboding, crashing up against the cliff with enough violence to drown out the sound of anything else. It wasn't even 4 p.m. yet, but she was already using a flashlight. The visibility wasn't the only challenge. When she tried to call out Nathan's name, in between the sound of the waves crashing against the cliffs, her voice was lost on the wind, making it pointless to even try.

Amy had been up and down the coast on various boat trips enough times to know there were some ledges and hollows in the cliff face, and despite the promise she'd made her father, she moved closer to the edge of the cliff, forcing down the fear that made her breath catch in her throat and her scalp prickle. She was close now to where her brother's coat had been found. The person who'd called her mother had met them at the car park, to hand over Nathan's belongings, in case there was anything she'd missed which his family might pick up on. She'd described the exact spot where she'd found his things, at a point where the clifftop narrowed and two rocky outcrops jutted out towards the sea in a V-shape. There was a crevice where the V-shape began, and it was where Amy was heading. The coat she'd borrowed was already heavy with rain, and the wind was so strong now that she was fighting to keep moving, almost bent double with the effort.

'Nathan!' She screamed his name again, despite the futility of the effort, pushing forward once more, just as she spotted a flash of red about two metres below the top of one of the rocky outcrops. Edging close, she could see it was Nathan and he looked like he was clinging to the side of a narrow ledge.

'Oh God. I'm coming, Nathan, just hold on.' He wouldn't be able to hear her, but she hoped he would somehow sense she was there and keep holding on.

'Amy!' The sound of her name was almost a whisper on the wind She was imagining it, she had to be, because she was certain she wouldn't be able to hear anyone calling out. Yet when she turned to look over her shoulder, she realised she wasn't imagining it and that Lijah was running towards her. Relief flooded her body and not just because it meant they had more chance of finding Nathan. She hadn't realised just how much she'd wanted to see him again until that moment. She couldn't think about why for now, she just knew she wanted him there.

Amy raised a hand to greet him, but she couldn't wait, the wind was getting more and more vicious, making it almost impossible not to be propelled along and her chest ached when she tried to breathe. It was probably even worse for Nathan, it would be getting harder and harder to hold on, and if she waited for Lijah, and watched her brother slip away, she'd never forgive herself.

'Amy, wait!' This time she knew she wasn't imagining it, but she had to keep going, picking her way over the rocks as the cliff top jutted further out into the water and the surface became more treacherous. She half-expected Lijah to reach her before she got to where Nathan was, but he was still about thirty feet away when she reached the place above were her brother was clinging to the ledge.

'Nathan, don't move. We're going to help you get back up here, just hold on.' She almost screamed the words, but thankfully he heard her, his head jolting back in response.

'Chunks of the ground keep dropping off and I don't think I can climb up the way I came down, the rain is washing the hand holds away. You've got to get me up.' Nathan tried moving and another huge lump of mud, sand and rock broke away, dropping into the sea below. The water was now almost black, mirroring the sky above it.

'Amy stop!' Lijah repeated his plea, but she still couldn't wait; the next piece of ground that broke off could take Nathan with it. Instead, she lowered herself down on to another ledge, just a couple of feet above Nathan's head, and about four feet to the left of him. She could see the footholds and grooves in the cliff face that Nathan must have used to climb down, but the weather was changing everything. The ledge wasn't that far below the cliff top and it looked like plenty of people had used it for climbing practice. Getting back up to the top would probably have been easy in dry weather, but Nathan seemed to be paralysed with fear and for good reason. One false move could be disastrous now that the rain had made everything so much more treacherous.

'It's okay I'm here.' Amy flattened her back against the cliff, trying not to look down and gingerly removing the ruck sack she'd grabbed when she left her parents' house. She had no idea what she was going to do now, she'd just felt an instinctive need to get closer to Nathan. As she reached down to try and get her mobile phone out of the pocket of the borrowed coat, she realised one of Bernie's extendable dog leads was in the pocket on the right-hand side. Her parents always bought the strongest leads on the market for their English Bull Mastiff, and anyone who'd ever been on a walk with him when he spotted a squirrel, would know why. The webbing of the lead was about an inch wide and there was a quality sticker on the handle describing it as a twelve-metre lead that guaranteed to restrain a dog of up to seventy kilograms. Whether it was strong enough to hold Nathan's weight was doubtful, but if it gave him the reassurance to keep holding on until the rescue team got there, it had to be worth using. She just needed him not to panic and try anything stupid, that was all. Amy pulled out about four metres of the lead before locking it in place, so it wouldn't suddenly retract back into the handle.

'I'm going to throw you the end of this lead, try and grab it.' Amy was amazed when the clip end of the lead landed just inches from her brother's hand. It helped that she was above him, so gravity had more to do with where it landed than any skill on her part.

'Amy I'm coming down,' Lijah called out to her.

'No, I might need you up there, and we've got to let someone know where he is. Can you do that, please?'

'Okay, but if anything happens, I'm coming straight down.'

She didn't answer, looking towards her brother instead. 'Try to wrap the lead around your waist and clip it in place. I'll hook the other end over something stable.' Amy searched around her, looking for a tree stump or anything else that was secure enough to fix the other end of the lead to, but there was nothing. It seemed to take forever for Nathan to put the lead around his waist, but there still wasn't anything she could tie her end to.

'I'm coming down,' Lijah called out again, but Amy looked up and shook her head.

'I don't think the ledge will take it. I need to get the other end of this lead up to you and there's plenty of length if I extend it to the full range, but I don't think I'm good enough at throwing, and if it goes down instead of up...' She couldn't finish the sentence, closing her eyes for a moment to try and work out what on earth to do. When she looked up again, Lijah was lying on his stomach leaning down towards her. He couldn't reach her, though, even with both their arms fully extended, and she tried not to think about what that meant for her chances of getting up on the clifftop again.

'I'm going to see if I can find something up here to use.'

Lijah edged away again and it was a couple of minutes before he reappeared, dangling down a length of orange baling twine towards her. It was just about long enough for her to reach and tie around the handle of the lead, which she'd extended to its full length. Within seconds, Lijah had pulled the handle up and was holding on to it as another huge clod of earth broke away from underneath Nathan and hurtled into the sea, making both him and Amy scream. Time was definitely running out, the torrential rain fast eroding what was left of the ledge where Nathan was sitting. They couldn't hold on any longer, and Amy couldn't bear to think about what might happen if any more of the ledge where her brother was sitting fell away.

'We're going to have to get you up now, Nathan,' Lijah called down. 'We can't wait for the rescue team to get here.'

'It's not strong enough.' Nathan sounded terrified, and Amy could hear the blood whooshing in her ears, even above the sound of the storm.

'The webbing is really tough, it's as good as any rope,' Lijah called down again, his voice steady. 'Just make sure you've tied it around your waist as securely as possible, and then I want you to use the same footholds that you used to climb down to get back up. Don't worry about slipping, because I've got you if anything happens.'

'I've knotted it three times and put it through the clip. Do you think that's enough?' Nathan suddenly sounded like a little boy and tears stung Amy's eyes.

'You're going to be fine, I'll feed my end around a rock, so there's no risk of me letting you go. You'll be up here before you know it.' Lijah paused for a moment. 'Right, are you ready?'

'Okay.' Nathan nodded and very gingerly stood, getting to the first foothold, just before another piece of ground fell away, making him scream again. Lijah called out encouragement and instructions every step of the way. He was as good as his word, too, and within minutes he'd hauled Nathan up onto the cliff top beside him.

'I'm going to undo the lead from Nathan's waist and send it back out to you,' Lijah called down to Amy again, and then it was her turn.

'I'm scared!' She looked up at him and he nodded.

'I know you are, but I won't let anything happen to you. You can trust me.'

'*I can trust you.*' She whispered the words to herself over and over as she secured the lead around her waist, repeating them on a loop until she'd climbed back up to the top of the cliff, finding each foothold slowly and carefully, moving at a pace that had felt agonisingly slow, when all she'd wanted to do was get back up as quickly as she could. She'd only slipped once, and Lijah held fast to the rope until she righted herself again, with Amy silently repeating the mantra that she could trust him until she finally got up to where he was.

'Thank God.' Lijah held on to her like he never wanted to let go, and for a moment she let herself be held. There was so much she wanted to say, all the stuff that had gone through her head as she'd been on that cliff face, despite trying to block it out by repeating those same four words over and over: *I can trust you.* But, before anything else she needed to make sure Nathan was okay, so she pulled away from Lijah, stepping backwards without looking. All she heard was a terrible crack, before a searing pain ripped through her, and the darkness of the storm closed in completely.

29

Amy had come round to find Lijah kneeling beside her, promising her it would be okay. The pain in her ankle had been so bad it had made her sick and Lijah had held her hair back, not baulking at the sight of her at her very worst, sobbing and vomiting. He'd taken care of her and made her believe his assurances that she'd be okay. She could tell her ankle was badly broken just by looking at it. She'd stepped back into a narrow crevice between the rocks, her ankle wedging and twisting in the opposite direction to the rest of her body as she fell. The sound of her bone cracking was something that would haunt her for a long time.

Once the rescue team and paramedics arrived, they'd taken over, but Lijah came in the ambulance with her. Amy had managed to phone her parents to let them know that she and Nathan were both okay, and that they were being taken to St Piran's in separate ambulances. Her mother had cried with relief and had said they'd head straight to the hospital. When she'd asked if either of them were injured, Amy had played it down and said she'd done something to her ankle and that it looked as if Nathan was just in shock. In truth, she'd known she'd almost certainly need surgery and she'd wanted to hug the paramedic when he'd administered some strong pain relief, although not as much as she'd wanted to hug Lijah. She'd been forced to let go of his hand, when she was being treated by the paramedics, and she'd felt the absence of it immediately. Her hand had felt cold and out of place when it wasn't in his.

Once they reached the hospital, her suspicions had been confirmed and she'd been taken into surgery to have the bone in her ankle pinned. Her parents had arrived before she'd gone to theatre, and they were waiting by her bed when she was brought up from post-op in the private room she'd been given while she fully recovered from the effects of the anaesthesia.

'Where's Lijah?' Amy asked as soon as her eyes allowed her to focus and realise he wasn't there.

'He's waiting outside. I told him he should go home, but he said he needed to know you were okay.' Her mother smiled. 'He thinks the world of you, you know.'

Amy didn't respond to her mother's words, she knew they were true, but she also knew things were more complicated than how they felt about one another. 'He's supposed to be getting on a plane in a few hours, but I really want to see him before he goes.'

'Okay sweetheart, I'll get him to come in soon, but Nathan wants to see you too.' Her mum's voice quivered. 'I know you might not feel up to that yet, but I think this has shocked him and he seemed so worried about you. I think he does love you, in his own way.'

'Is he okay?'

'A few cuts and bruises, but he'll be fine thanks to you and Lijah.' Amy's father planted a kiss on her forehead, before standing up straight again. 'You make quite the pair.'

'You really do.' Her mother's tone was gentle. 'Do you want me to ask Lijah to come in now?'

'Yes please.'

'We'll leave you to it, sweetheart.' Kerry kissed her cheek. 'But we'll be right outside if you need us.'

'Thank you. I love you both.'

'We love you too, darling, so much.' Her father gently squeezed her shoulder, before they both left the room.

Amy tried to run her hand through her hair, but it got stuck in the tangles. She must look a wreck, but suddenly the realisation hit her that it didn't matter. Lijah loved her, he'd made that so clear over the last few weeks, but it had taken a near disaster for her to really believe it and to realise how precious it was. Walking away from that for a second time would be something she'd regret for the rest of her life.

Lijah had been recognised by both of the paramedics and most of the rescue team who'd turned up too late to really be of any help. Some of them had given him sideways glances, but he'd acted like the Lijah she knew and had loved since she was just a kid. He didn't change in the wake of other people's attention and all he'd cared about was making sure she was okay. The sideways glances had stopped quite quickly as a result, and the paramedics had dropped their slightly awed tone, speaking to him like they would to anyone else. If Amy gave up her chance of being with Lijah, she'd be robbing herself of something she knew she'd never find again, she'd be punishing both of them for something neither of them had done. Lijah hadn't let his fame affect who he was, and she didn't treat him any differently than she had before he found success. Other people were the problem, and she'd let other people take far too much from her already. She just hoped she hadn't left it too late.

'Hello you.' Lijah's voice was warm as he came into her room.

'Hello.' Amy suddenly felt shy, she was about to make herself incredibly vulnerable by admitting how she felt and that wasn't something she usually did. Humour had got her through the bullying at school, enabling her to make jokes about herself, in order to get ahead of anyone else who might have been intending to make her the punchline. When her relationships after Lijah hadn't worked out, laughing at herself and the situation had been her salvation yet again. She didn't let anyone know how she was really feeling, in an attempt to move past difficult emotions as quickly as possible. It was a protective strategy, but now she was about to lay herself bare.

'You scared the hell out of me, you know.' Lijah's tone was still soft, but there was a flicker of something far more fierce in his eyes. 'Please promise me you won't ever do anything like that again.'

'I'll try not to.' She smiled. 'I'm so glad you were there, but I still don't understand why you were?'

Amy had a vague recollection of asking him about that after the accident, but in the blur of pain and medication it all felt jumbled.

'I went to see Albie and he made me realise I hadn't told you everything I needed to say. Being back here has shown me what's important, and what makes me happy, and that's not fame. I still love writing songs, but the thought of performing again doesn't excite me like it used to.' He looked directly at her. 'If it costs me the chance to be with you, I don't want any of it. I love you Amy and what makes me happy is you. It's always been you.'

Warmth spread through her body and this time it had nothing to do with the painkillers. Lijah was willing to sacrifice everything to be with her, and she didn't doubt for a moment he meant it. Now it was time for her to be honest, and she took a deep breath to steady herself. 'It's always been you for me too. But I don't want you to give anything up for me.'

'I won't be giving anything up. I've built the first genuine connections I've had in years since coming back home. When I told Albie I was leaving, he wasn't sad because he wanted me around for who I was, he was sad because he wanted me to stay for what I was: his friend. I don't need fame to make me happy, and I realise now it's never really made me happy. Being back here and spending time with you has made me realise where I really belong. But if I haven't got you, I haven't got anything, and I—' Amy held up her hand, cutting him off. She had to get this out before she lost her nerve.

'I want to be with you, Lijah, whatever that might look like. I thought I had to sacrifice us to hold onto my career, because without that I'd go back to being just Amy. Except now I've realised that my job isn't what makes me worthy of love, because just being Amy is more than enough. I can get used to the stuff that comes with being a part of your world, even if that means moving away and leaving my job, but I could never get used to not having you as a part of mine. I love you so much.'

'I think I might have to get you to start co-writing my songs.' He grinned, taking hold of her hand and entwining their fingers. 'You've got no idea how much I love you, but I'm planning to spend the rest of my life showing you.'

'*The rest of your life*? Are you sure it's not too early to be making that kind of promise?' Her tone was teasing, but the look in his eyes couldn't have been more certain.

'I wasted ten years looking for someone like you, but no one even came close. I'm never making the same mistake again, Amy, and I don't want to waste any more time.'

'Me neither, but you're restarting the tour, and I'm not even going to be able to fly out to see you until I'm over this.' Amy gestured down towards her leg.

'Nick didn't rearrange the tour, even though I asked him to. He just pretended he had, in an attempt to make us both realise what we were giving up.' Lijah grinned. 'Luckily for him it paid off.'

'I think I might love Nick a little bit too.' Amy laughed at the look that crossed Lijah's face.

'As long as it's not as much as you love me.'

'Nowhere near.' She caught her breath as he kissed her, love and desire pulsing through her in a way that not even the after-effects of an anaesthetic could dampen. This was the real thing, and it wasn't always going to be easy, but no relationship ever was. All she knew for certain, was that if she focused on how she felt about Lijah, she'd be able to get through whatever else came her way. Amy didn't care whether other people believed that soul mates existed, because until recently she hadn't either. Now she knew without any doubt that Lijah was hers and he was her best friend too. As Gwen had reminded her, most people never found a relationship like that and she wasn't giving up her chance of happiness for anyone.

* * *

Nathan came in to see Amy the day after her operation. He'd been discharged from hospital on the day of the accident and when he'd come to visit her, Amy had been waiting to hear whether she could go home too. Lijah had joked that she and Monty would now be a matching pair, but he'd also made it clear that he'd be there for whatever Amy needed. Lijah had told her that the final leg of the tour would have to be rescheduled eventually, to fulfil the commitment he'd made, but that he wouldn't be going until she was recovered enough to fly out and join him for at least part of it. After that, he wanted to concentrate on writing, but he wasn't sure yet whether that would be for himself or other artists.

Amy wasn't worried about the details. They could take it a stage at a time and work it out together. She wasn't ready to give up nursing, she loved her job and her friends at St Piran's, but her career would probably look a bit different in the future too. There was a chance she might switch to agency nursing for a while, rather than having a fixed contract. It would give her more flexibility to go out and join Lijah while he was on tour, but all of those decisions could wait for another day. For now, they'd be going back to Mor Brys. Claire was flying out to Tenerife at the weekend, and the lease on the rental of the house on the cliff had almost expired, Nick having arranged to stay at Dolly's place until he worked out what he wanted to do next. It felt like going full circle, returning to the house where they'd spent so much time when they'd first dated.

When Amy's mother had asked her if she'd be willing to see Nathan, she'd said yes, but she wanted it to be at the hospital. She didn't want him coming to Mor Brys and trying to spoil what she and Lijah had. The first few days back there were just for them. She wanted to close the door on the rest of the world, at least for a little while, and just hang out with Lijah and Monty.

'You okay?' Nathan looked sheepish, his usual arrogance decidedly absent.

'I'm getting there. How about you?'

'I need to sort myself out, and accept that there's something weird going on up here.' Nathan gestured towards his head. 'One of us could've died.'

'I'm glad you're going to get some help, I know it's a big step to take, but I really think you'll feel better for it.'

'Yeah, that's all I wanted to say really.' He shrugged and she nodded in response. It was probably too much to hope that he'd apologise for what happened, but she'd much rather hear that he was finally going to get some help. Nathan suddenly whipped the baseball cap he was wearing off his head. 'Here, you might want to wear this when they let you out, in case there are any press around. Your hair looks bloody awful.'

She laughed then, not doubting for a moment that her brother was telling the truth. It might have been delivered in his usual brutal style, but she had a feeling that somewhere deep down inside of Nathan, his latest dig at her appearance had come from a place of love. Maybe, just maybe, there was a chance they could build on that in the future.

30

By the time Gary and Wendy's wedding came around, Amy was a lot more mobile, but she was still wearing a boot-style cast to support the bones in her ankle. It was hidden under a flowy summer dress and Lijah looked amazing in a royal blue linen suit, as her plus one.

The wedding service had been beautiful, and Gary hadn't been able to hold back the tears when he saw Wendy walking down the aisle towards him. His speech had referenced the fact that he and Wendy had first dated at school, and Lijah had squeezed Amy's hand, whispering close to her ear.

'This could be us next.'

She'd raised her eyebrows, answering him in a whisper. 'It could if you get really lucky.'

'I already am.'

'So cheesy.' She'd grinned then, the familiar warmth that came from being near Lijah spreading right through her. Amy knew what he'd said wasn't just a cheesy line, and that he'd meant it when he said he felt lucky, because she did too.

The reception was proving to be every bit as special as the

service, and Amy and Lijah were sitting side by side, watching her friends from St Piran's having fun on the dance floor. He'd met them all now, and every single one of them treated him like a normal person. He was Amy's boyfriend first and foremost, and Gwen had summed it up: *It doesn't matter what you do for a living, all that matters is that you treat Amy well.*

It was great to see Gwen looking and acting so much more like her old self, and her treatment for Addison's disease was managing the condition effectively. Gwen was in front of them now, twirling around the dance floor with Barry, giving Isla and Reuben a run for their money. Aidan and Jase were dancing too, with baby Ellis held in a papoose between them, and Danni and Charlie's baby boy was safe in the arms of his Uncle Joe, who was cooing over the baby with his wife, Esther, while his parents made the most of the chance to slow dance alone. Amy had seen Eden and Meg at the bar earlier toasting the happy couple, and she loved the fact that Gary and Wendy had included the newest staff members too, like they were already old friends. That's how life was in St Piran's, and it was why she couldn't ever imagine herself leaving it behind completely.

'Do you want to try and dance?' Lijah stroked the back of Amy's hand, but she shook her head.

'I'm happy sitting here just watching everyone.'

'Me too. It's been brilliant today, hasn't it? Like being part of a big family. I've never had that before.' Lijah gave her a slow smile. 'Although we've got plenty of time to work on creating one of our own.'

'I'd love that, but even if it doesn't happen, the family I've got will still be enough, as long as you're a part of it.'

'You're stuck with me now. You had two chances to get away and you blew them both.' He was still smiling, the look in his eyes making her desperate to kiss him.

'Well thank God for that.' Amy leaned forward in her seat, pressing her lips against his. She and Lijah were together again, and she didn't care any more if there was someone at the wedding waiting to snap a photo and send it to the press. Let the media do their worst, and the commenters say whatever they wanted to say. None of it mattered, because she had something wonderful, something that no one could spoil unless she let them. Amy was never making that mistake again, or changing the way she lived her life to suit anyone else. This was her time, and she was finally learning to shine.

* * *

MORE FROM JO BARTLETT

In case you missed it, the previous book in The Cornish Country Hospital series from Jo Bartlett, *Lessons in Love at the Cornish Country Hospital*, is available to order now here:

www.mybook.to/LessonsinLoveBackAd

ACKNOWLEDGEMENTS

As always, I want to start by thanking my wonderful readers. I'm so grateful to you for choosing my books and I will never take that for granted. It means so much to receive your messages of support and they really help keep me going when I'm struggling with a plot line, or another deadline is looming. Thank you all so much.

I really hope you've enjoyed the fifth instalment in *The Cornish Country Hospital* series. It's always a joy to return to the setting and the characters who have begun to feel like friends after all this time. The caveat I give for each new book is that I'm not a medical professional, but I've done my best to ensure that the details are as accurate as possible. If you're one of the UK's wonderful medical professionals, I hope you'll forgive any details which draw on poetic licence to fit the plot. I've been very lucky to be able to call on the advice of a good friend, Steve Dunn, who was a paramedic for twenty-five years and to whom I can go to for advice on medical matters when I need to and, as ever, I continue to seek support and advice in relation to maternity services from my brilliant friend and midwife, Beverley Hills.

This book features both Amy and Gwen's stories, and the latter has a personal connection for Beverley, whose own mother, Pamela, suffered from primary progressive aphasia. As such, this book is dedicated to Pamela, by both Beverley and her stepfather, Jeremy, who miss her every day.

This is the point where I begin to thank all the other people who have helped get this book to publication. At the end of *Together Again at the Cornish Country Hospital*, I wrote a long list of book reviewers and social media superheroes, who have played such a big part in bringing this new series to readers and spreading the word to others, including by regularly commenting on and sharing my posts. I wanted to take this chance to thank as many people as possible again and, as such, my thanks go to Rachel Gilbey, Meena Kumari, Wendy Neels, Grace Power, Avril McCauley, Kay Love, Trish Ashe, Jean Norris, Bex Hiley, Shreena Morjaria, Pamela Spearing, Lorraine Joad, Joanne Edwards, Karen Callis, Tea Books, Jo Bowman, Jane Ward, Elizabeth Marhsall, Laura McKay, Michelle Marriott, Katerine Jane, Barbara Myers, Dawn Warren, Ann Vernon, Ann Stewart, Nicola Thorp, Karen Jean Wright, Lesley Brett, Adrienne Allan, Sarah Lizziebeth, Margaret Hardman, Vikki Thompson, Mark Brock, Suzanne Cowen, Debbie Marie, Sleigh, Melissa Khajehgeer, Sarah Steel, Laura Snaith, Sally Starley, Lizzie Philpot, Kerry Coltham, May Miller, Gillian Ives, Carrie Cox, Elspeth Pyper, Tracey Joyce, Lauren Hewitt, Julie Foster, Sharon Booth, Ros Carling, Deirdre Palmer, Maureen Bell, Caroline Day, Karen Miller, Tanya Godsell, Kate O'Neill, Janet Wolstenholme, Lin West, Audrey Galloway, Helen Phifer, Johanne Thompson, Beverley Hopper, Tegan Martyn, Anne Williams, Karen from My Reading Corner, Jane Hunt, Karen Hollis, @thishannahreads, Isabella Tartaruga, @Ginger_bookgeek, Scott aka Book Convos, Pamela from @bookslifeandeverything, Mandy Eatwell, Jo from @jaffareadstoo, Elaine from Splashes into Books, Connie Hill, @karen_loves_reading, @wendyreadsbooks, @bookishlaurenh, Jenn from @thecomfychair2, @jen_loves_reading, Ian Wilfred, @Annarella, @BookishJottings, @Jo_bee, Kirsty Oughton, @kelmason,

@TheWollyGeek, Barbara Wilkie, @bookslifethings, @Tiziana_L, @mum_and_me_reads, Just Katherine, @bookworm86, Sarah Miles aka Beauty Addict, Captured on Film, Leanne Bookstagram, @subtlebookish, Laura Marie Prince, @RayoReads, @sarah.k.reads, @twoladiesandabook, Vegan Book Blogger, @readwithjackalope, @mysanctuary and @staceywh_17. Huge apologies if I've left anyone off the list, but I'm so thankful to everyone who takes the time to review or share my books and I promise to continue adding names to the list as the series progresses.

My thanks as ever go to the team at Boldwood Books, especially my amazing editor, Emily Ruston, and my brilliant copy editor and proofreader, Candida Bradford, who both shaped this story into something I can be proud of. I also want to thank my good friend Jennie Dunn, and Meena Kumari (for a second time!) both of whom provide great support with final checks on the novel.

I'm also hugely grateful to the rest of the team at Boldwood Books, who are now too numerous to list, but special mention must go to my marketing lead, Marcela Torres, and the Directors of Sales and Marketing, Nia Beynon and Wendy Neale, as well as to the inimitable Amanda Ridout, for having the foresight to create such an amazing company to be published by.

As ever, I can't sign off without thanking my writing tribe, The Write Romantics, including my fellow Boldies Helen Rolfe, Jessica Redland, and Alex Weston, and to all the other authors I am lucky enough to call friends, especially Gemma Rogers, who is another fellow Boldie.

Finally, as it forever will, my most heartfelt thank you goes to my husband, children and grandchildren. I am never happier than when we are 'together again', and every story I write is for you.

ABOUT THE AUTHOR

Jo Bartlett is the bestselling author of over nineteen women's fiction titles. She fits her writing in between her two day jobs as an educational consultant and university lecturer and lives with her family and three dogs on the Kent coast.

Sign up to Jo Bartlett's mailing list for a free short story.

Follow Jo on social media here:

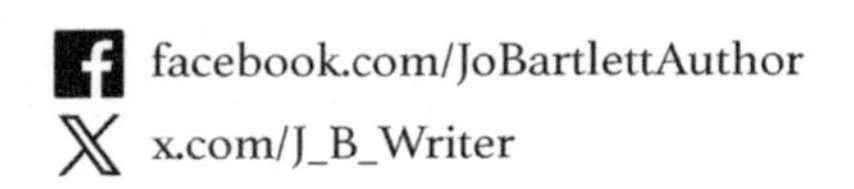

ALSO BY JO BARTLETT

The Cornish Midwife Series

The Cornish Midwife

A Summer Wedding For The Cornish Midwife

A Winter's Wish For The Cornish Midwife

A Spring Surprise For The Cornish Midwife

A Leap of Faith For The Cornish Midwife

Mistletoe and Magic for the Cornish Midwife

A Change of Heart for the Cornish Midwife

Happy Ever After for the Cornish Midwife

Seabreeze Farm

Welcome to Seabreeze Farm

Finding Family at Seabreeze Farm

One Last Summer at Seabreeze Farm

Cornish Country Hospital Series

Welcome to the Cornish Country Hospital

Finding Friends at the Cornish Country Hospital

A Found Family at the Cornish Country Hospital

Lessons in Love at the Cornish Country Hospital

Together Again at the Cornish Country Hospital

Standalone Novels

Second Changes at Cherry Tree Cottage

A Cornish Summer's Kiss

Meet Me in Central Park

The Girl She Left Behind

A Mother's Last Wish

Printed in Great Britain
by Amazon